NINE LIVES

A TED CHESTER NOVEL
NEAL R. SUTTON

For The Cats Of Thissio.

Chapter 1
Athens

THE ABANDONED WAREHOUSE WAS once vibrant and full of life. The building was a shadow of its former self, now run down and neglected as it stood under the moonlight. It used to be fully operational, with three hundred workers producing clothes and leather sandals, but now it was disused during daylight hours. Although its structural premises still represented the foundations of what it once was in the height of its former use, it was now crowded with individuals of different classes and cultures. Previous gatherings would have been solely for business purposes—fully operational mass production of garments.

Nowadays, it was solely for pleasure that a number of people were assembled under the warehouse roof. It was in the winter months in early January, shortly after New Year, but the accumulated bodies warmed the venue. Its event was a house music concert with a line-up that included English DJ star, Duke Dumont. The DJ was already a few songs into his set when he transitioned to his next song.

A ringing noise cascaded through the open air, and a female voice began to add melody to the music. She was singing passionately, and her vocals blasted through the surrounding speakers. The beat was low so as not to overshadow the dulcet lyrics. The vocals started to rise in volume, reaching a peak then stopping. The beat dropped and made a repetitive bassline, with the drum running at 120 beats per minute, containing syntheses and rifts. The bass and rhythm of the music reverberated through the warehouse structure. Its sound echoed off the brick walls and was met with enthusiasm by everyone dancing. The light show from the main stage came from behind the DJ, expelling strobe and laser lights of multiple colours and illuminating the mass crowd.

A man and woman twisted their bodies to the music among the crowd. They were both in their late twenties; she had long blonde hair and stood tall. He had a dark, short-back-and-side-style haircut with a stubble beard to match. They were catching glances at each other's moves and exchanging smiles, closing their eyes to become absorbed into the rhythm. They weren't strangers to one another; they were lovers, and shared their passion for music together as they absorbed it into their veins. The beat became more intense, with the bass increasing its BPM as the singer reached a passionate climax to her vocal pitch.

Another man navigated through the crowd, reaching into his jacket pocket and picking out a balaclava face-covering. He had a southern European look about him, with jet-black hair to go with his beard of the same colour. He was fighting his way through the packed crowd, fixated on the two people dancing and embracing each other's company. The beat reached its accelerated peak, and the vocals performed a ratcheting to match.

The man reached into his inside pocket and grabbed a firearm. Raising it in one motion, he aimed it towards the couple. Without hesitation, he pulled the trigger as the music reached its pinnacle. The summit of bass continued to keep its intensity for a while, masking the sound of the gunshot. The light from the gunpowder was lost in the renewal of the laser show shining upon the ravers. The man who'd fired the weapon removed his mask and turned back into the horde of oblivious dancers he was engulfed by.

The man who'd been dancing so joyfully and energetically fell lifelessly to his side. The lean mass of his body knocked into the next dancer, who moved backwards. The man bounced off him and fell to the floor on his back. Another person nearby noticed the fall, and, upon looking down, realised their T-shirt was covered with blood from the bullet as it had entered the man's skull and squirted on impact.

The blonde woman began to realise the harsh nature of what had just happened and now stood in shock and confusion. Once she saw the red substance glisten on the floor, she looked around for the culprit, but everyone in her vicinity was either dancing or staring at the body on the floor in horror. The person who had fired the shot was nowhere to be seen. She began shouting at the onlookers, but her cries for help were overwhelmed by the music volume and weren't understood or heard. She was frantically pointing at them and the body on the floor. She knelt next to her partner's body and started to push hard against his chest with both hands locked together on his chest bone. She began to perform mouth-to-mouth, her hair brushing against the floor and smearing the blood.

Meanwhile, the armed man made his way through the crowd. He bumped into nearly everyone he reached, receiving glares and snarls from some goers because of his aggressive nature. He continued towards an opening in the crowd, not looking back or acknowledging the people he shoved. He reached a walkway separating the huge number of dancers and the refreshment and restroom area, including an exit door. Two other men met him, and the armed man immediately transferred the gun to another figure who walked towards the door, keeping it concealed in his jacket. The two men exchanged glances and made their way towards the exit, disappearing into the night.

The climax of the music chimed in the air as it reached the crescendo. The sounds were particularly like those of a church organ chiming. On-goers recognised the situation, which had just occurred as the music volume decreased. In their horror, they observed the man's body on the floor. The beautiful young woman beside the man's body was on her knees, pleading and begging for a response by tapping his face and shaking his shoulders. She continued to push repetitively on his chest, but there was no response. His open, dead eyes stared up towards the warehouse ceiling.

The music's rhythm faded into the air as those beyond the initial layer of onlookers heard the woman's shrieking. Unlike the powerful vocals of the women singing, this time it was powerful screams of panic filling the venue. The man's eyes were fixed on the ceiling above, with blood pooling on the floor around his skull. Through the ever-so-slight fracture in the warehouse roof, the moon shone through, looking down upon him. The song reached its endpoint, and the high-energy vibe of the ravers descended into a sad and depressing moment as the piercing screams filled the warehouse's interior.

Chapter 2
Amsterdam

THE FEW TREES ALONG the canal edge were now bare of their foliage deep into the winter months. The water trickled below the rising sun as it perched over the uniquely shaped surrounding building towering over the canal. International Liasion Officer Ted Chester was charging between the pedestrians on the canal side path. His tall frame saw him tower over the people causally moving through the pathway. His short jet-black hair remained in place, alongside his beard, with a dusting of grey spots in both. Sweat was forming around his forehead, face and chin, forming droplets. He was approaching Torsensluis Brig Bridge in the city's Grachtengordel-west area, the oldest and most expansive bridge. Once he approached the junction bridge, the walking path finished, and a significant walking and cycling route met overhead. He stopped to allow the traffic to pass before crossing the road to continue his path along the river. He pulled out his phone from his shorts pocket to check the song, which was beginning.

Mac Miller – Self Care.

Ted wasn't a follower of heavy rap, but Malcom's music hit differently from others, with its chilled vibe and good ambient beats offering energy for his exercise excursion. Ted crossed the busy walkway and accelerated as the path declined towards the river. The music cut out, and a noise deafened his ears because his headphones were attached to the phone's sound system. It was his phone ringing. He slowed down and stopped on the side of the canal. He reached for his phone, which was in his pocket. The screen revealed the caller. It was Simon Taylor, his senior back in Britain. Simon oversaw the International Liaison Officers, or ILOs, across Europe. He liaised with Ted throughout his posting in Amsterdam, which was shortly expiring after its two-year contract, anticipating his new posting in only a few months in the Greek capital of Athens. He pressed the green button to accept the call and spoke through his headphones and speaker.

"Hi, Simon," Ted said, breathing heavily.

"Hi, Ted. You okay?"

"Just getting in my exercise for the day."

"Ah, sorry to disturb you."

"Go ahead," he said, catching his breath.

"Okay. We've got a bit of a situation that we need you to help us with. I've already cleared it with Sander at the National Korps."

Ted looked at an empty bench beside him between a large selection of chained bicycles and took a seat.

"What's wrong?"

"It's about your posting to Athens. I know your official date is next month, the end of February. But we need you to go there tonight."

"Tonight? Why? What's wrong?"

"There's no easier way to put it, so... the current ILO there, Daniel Belfield, has been murdered."

Ted was leaning forward on the bench, catching his breath, but when Simon said those words, he leaned back more to take in the announcement, looking up at the overcast clouds in the sky.

"Murdered?" Ted asked.

"They think so. He was shot dead at a music venue last night—a bullet to the head. The place was full of thousands of people."

"Sounds professional."

"I agree. His girlfriend was with him, trying to revive him. Still, he was gone as soon as the bullet entered him."

"Any witnesses?"

"We have three who witnessed the gunshot. Still, the person disappeared as soon as the flash happened. Most were unaware it had happened until they saw him fall to the ground. The team searched the CCTV there through the night, but the initial report was that the shooter was wearing a mask, so we don't have a description of the suspect or any links."

Ted rubbed his head as he pondered on the scenario.

"The CCTV does not show the shot?"

"That's our problem. They don't have CCTV inside the warehouse. Only on the exit and entry points of the venue, so I don't think that's going to be much use with that."

"Any other victims?"

"No. This isn't deemed terror-related. It was a targeted attack, with only Daniel as the victim."

Ted hadn't encountered an ILO murder investigation or heard about one in the organisation's past. Although it wasn't linked to the National Crime Agency, the only prior similarity he knew was in the mid-1970s, an MI6 officer was murdered in Dublin by the Provisional Irish Republican Army.

"Have you come across this before, Simon?"

"I've known about assassination attempts. But never had one be performed."

Ted reflected for a moment, offering a moment of silence before continuing.

"So what're the plans?"

"I've made plans to get you a flight to Athens tonight, giving you enough time to say your goodbyes with the Korps and pack. I appreciate that it's not enough time, but we need you to support the Hellenic Police. I'll make all the arrangements to sort out temporary housing for you and your family before you find somewhere you can settle."

"It's not enough time," Ted said as he stood up, his legs having started to seize up in the rested position.

"I know, Ted, I'm sorry. We have a replacement for you in Amsterdam, so you don't need to worry about that. The officer's post ends in Madrid next week. It fits perfectly."

"But I've not finished here yet, Simon, you know this."

An outlay of breath came from Simon down the phone.

"I know, Ted. I get that; Operation Hawk, and you want to see it out. But Ted... you have done more than enough on that case. It's in the hands of the justice system now. You no longer need to run through the streets to get them; that's Interpol's job now."

Ted knew Simon was right. In the summer of last year, Ted was a lead officer on Operation Hawk, an investigation into a group of Eastern European organised crime members who were sex trafficking young women across Europe. The investigation crossed Europe—and some of its capital cities—before the OCG's senior members were killed or captured, with most of the victims saved from the depths of its underworld. Some members were on trial in The Hague for sex trafficking crimes, and a verdict would come later in the year. Despite the success of its operation, some officers and victims didn't make it to see justice served. Ted felt guilt and pain for those that didn't make it. Although one set of victims came to his mind daily, even at night. He felt culpability; he couldn't save two girls in Timişoara, where the operation terminated. Ted's investigative group were too late for them both before they were transferred and lost from their reach. Several leads suggested the United Arab Emirates as the destination, but the case had gone cold since that proposal.

"You still there, Ted?"

Ted broke away from his thoughts.

"Sorry, yeah. I understand."

"Listen, I will meet you there when you arrive, as I need to help investigate this, too. This won't just be you—I want justice for Daniel, as does everyone else here. It's one of our officers. We need to find out why this happened."

"Yeah, I'm in. Have you contacted the team there?"

"I have. The Headquarters for the Hellenic Police is in Athens. The Ministry of Citizen Protection oversees them. They are responsible for Greece's public security services and treat this seriously. I've spoken to some senior officers who are open to us assisting them and working together."

"Do they know why this happened to Daniel?"

"They're not completely sure. However, they did say he was investigating something, and they're not sure if it's related."

"Do you know what Daniel was investigating?"

"That's something I've asked. They seemed to know something but didn't want to communicate it over the phone."

"Right, send me the details, and I'll meet you there."

"Thanks, Ted. Remember to say goodbye to Sander before you go."

"Yes, I will do."

"See you tonight, Ted."

The phone disconnected, and the song restarted from the point it was interrupted. Ted was about to restart his running but turned to look at the canal. The murky waters were somewhat beautiful in their frozen state. Surrounded by the tall individualised town houses that made up the landscape of most of the city. Ted thought of his current situation and how it would play out. His family's position was a tentative one at best. His wife and two daughters were still struggling with moving from England, which strained his relationship with his wife during his two-year tender. She and their two daughters were homesick, and the thought of moving from one unsettled location to the next would be uncomfortable for all. They knew of the impending move to Athens, but the sudden change due to the circumstances could cause a disturbance within the mindset. The original plan would be for his wife and children to continue living in Amsterdam longer until they transition to Athens in the late spring. Shortly before Ted's last major operation in the summer, they had moved to one of the town houses from an outer suburb near Vondelpark. After Timişoara, they were moved into another residence in the city, and Ted was given a leave of absence. His children were home-schooled to limit contact outside as the investigation faded and any threats of revenge diminished.

Ted picked out his phone again from his pocket and unlocked it. He searched the contacts, selected Sander, and clicked dial.

"Hey, Sander, you in your office?"

"Yes, I'm in. Are you coming to visit me? I thought you were on annual leave until next week, Ted?"

"We went home for Christmas, but we came back a few days earlier before New Year to try and get the girls settled into the house and school again."

"Yeah, come by. Why don't you meet me in the café on the third floor? I'll get you one of those coffees you like."

"That will be nice. See you there in twenty."

The phone disconnected again, and the track replayed through his headphones. The lyrics *Let's go and travel through the unknown* flowed through his ears as the song mellowed into a psychedelic mood. The next few hours would require him to prepare for his travels, investigating the cold-blooded death of the ILO he would be replacing. As the song suggested, Ted would be travelling through the unknown.

Chapter 3

S ANDER MEYER HELD A cup in each hand and raised the one in her right as a welcoming gesture as Ted entered the police station café. Ted was still wearing his running hoody and running pants, complete with running shoes.

"Morning, Ted," Sander said.

"Morning."

She placed the coffee cups on the table nearest to her as Ted approached, exchanging a spaced hug once Sander noticed the sweat from him. Sander was in her Korps uniform, with her blonde hair in a ponytail. She was forty-five years old, but looked not a day over thirty. Sander was the chief of police for the Dutch Korps, and Ted had worked under her for nearly two years during his ILO posting in Amsterdam. They had worked together on significant drug operations from organised crime groups out of Amsterdam. Supporting a more comprehensive network of authorities from South America, from connecting flights to and from Europe that passed through the city's airport. Sander also worked with Ted on the sex trafficking operation in Amsterdam and Berlin.

Ted had the most tremendous respect for Sander, not just professionally but as a person and for her family of two sons and husband. Regularly, her family would join Ted's to eat and spend time together, with Sander trying to help Ted's wife, Rose, connect with the city, help her integrate more, and feel more relaxed and at home.

The café was full of uniformed and plainclothed officers taking a break from their desk duties or outdoor pursuits.

"How was Christmas?" Sander said as they both sat down.

"It was good. Good to see everyone, have a bit of normal living for a little while back in the UK. Yours?"

"Yes, excellent. Venison and plenty of vegetables and kerstbrood. What's not to love!"

A traditional Christmas dinner in the Netherlands includes venison, goose, hare, or turkey with kerstbrood eaten as a traditional Dutch oval-shaped fruited Christmas bread.

"Ah, nice. Do they have any here? I'm a little peckish."

"It's only seasonal in this café, unfortunately. However, I'll petition to have it annually. I must have some pull with being senior around here," she said, laughing.

"Flat white?" Ted said when he finished laughing with her, pointing at one of the cups.

"Sorry, yes, this one. I've got the latte," she said, lifting his coffee cup and passing it across the table.

"Did you read De Telegraaf?" Sander said.

"I try not to read the papers," he said, sipping his hot coffee.

Sander called the capital-based newspaper company the largest Dutch daily morning newspaper. Specifically, she referred to the upcoming criminal justice trials in The Hague surrounding the arrested and deceased OCG group suspects involved in Ted's previous investigation.

"It's a good piece. Normally hate reporters, but they did a good job, and the story reflects what we accomplished. When they came to us about the story, we didn't give any details on the identities of key suspects, as we need to keep everything close to our chest before we go to trial."

"I'll try and get a copy at some point."

Sander gave a slight smile. At the same time, she took a sip of her latte. She stopped and blew on the coffee to cool it down before taking another mouthful of the cup's contents.

"So, is this it, Ted? The end," she said with a smile.

Ted looked up at Sander after taking a sip from his coffee cup. He took another one to waste time before responding.

"Simon told me he told you. Which helped, I must admit, because I don't think I could have come here and told you myself."

Sander blew on her coffee one more time before taking another sip. Once she finished, she started to nod.

"Yes, I would have shouted at you in front of all of these people," she said, pointing around the room.

"That wouldn't have been good."

"I'm only messing," she said with a smirk. She continued, "Simon told me you were leaving, but he didn't tell me why. You finish in a month; couldn't it have waited?"

"You could call it an early assignment. The ILO has been murdered there, and I need to go and investigate," he said, whispering as the statement went on.

"Dear God," she whispered back, not to draw attention from other officers in the café. "How?" she continued.

"Shot at a music venue. Bullet to the head. Sounds like a professional hit."

She leaned back in the seat, twisting the coffee cup on the table and looking at it before looking back at Ted to respond.

"Wow. Seems targeted. Going after an officer like that, he must have been up to something, or maybe just wrong place, wrong time."

"The Greek authorities believed what he was investigating, something that got him killed. But they won't tell us what he was investigating until we arrive. Still, something caught up with him—I don't know what."

Sander continued to twist her coffee cup around in a circle on the table sombrely before changing the conversation.

"Who are they sending to replace you?" she said, smiling at Ted.

"Don't know. They're coming from Madrid shortly after I leave; I don't have a name."

"I was going to get you a leaving present and organise something, but now..."

"It's okay. It is what it is. I'll try and come back and visit when I'm done there. Besides, if Interpol brings anything up, I'm back to see it."

"Good, I hope you will be, Ted."

"They will owe me a few day's holiday with this, so I could use them to visit."

"That would be nice. Let me know when," she said with a smile. "You spoke to your wife about this move?"

Ted pulled a face. He started to look down and twirl his coffee cup before picking it up and drinking its remains.

Taking his reaction as a no, she spoke, "Good luck when you do."

"Thanks."

"Listen, Ted, it's hard for her and the kids. Just think about it from her perspective. You two will work it out; I know you will. You are a great family together. You two and the kids. You're both special people, you know."

Ted smiled.

"Thank you for everything, Sander. I really mean it. As a work colleague, but more importantly, as a friend."

Ted took in a deep breath as he sat, then exhaled. He stood up and offered a hand out to her. Ted could see her emotions changing on her face, and it was time he looked into her eyes—that hurt the most. She stood up, too, and accepted the hand from across the table.

"Thank you for everything again," Ted spoke.

"Don't worry about it. It's been an honour, Ted. This isn't the end. I'm sure we will keep in touch."

"I will do. By the way, I don't think Rose and the kids are coming with me yet; it's too soon. We didn't even plan for this, so I suspect Rose will be around if you wish to visit them."

"Of course!" She smiled.

"Look after them for me."

"I will; I'll visit her and the kids this week!"

"Thanks, Sander. The kids are like nieces to you. They see you as Auntie Sander."

Sander laughed, and so did Ted. It was a good distraction from the emotional feelings deep-rooted with the goodbye. The laughing stopped, and so did the smiles as Sander spoke, bringing back reality.

"Are you going to say goodbye to the officers upstairs?"

"Yeah, I will head up now and say goodbye. Thanks for the coffee."

"Don't mention it; I will stay here and take my break. I don't get to take much of those these days."

"Don't blame you; keep safe, Sander. I'll be in touch."

"Likewise," Sander said with a nod.

Ted picked up the near-empty coffee cup and left Sander alone at the table. He approached the café's exit door to a hallway and threw the empty cup into the trash. Navigating his way through the hallway, Ted reached the steps which led to the ascending floors. He was heading to the central police office, where he had worked alongside Officers on the previous sex trafficking case.

As he reached the level, a door led through to the workspaces. Adjacent to the door was a memorial plaque for fallen officers who had died on duty. Ted had walked past it numerous times over his career but hadn't visited in over a month. He noticed new names had been engraved on the plaque. Officer Mees Zenden died in an apartment complex raid in Amsterdam on the first night of Operation Hawk. There were two new names underneath. The first was Officer Myles Gerwin, who was hit by an oncoming vehicle that failed to slow down near a road traffic accident he had attended to before Christmas. Underneath was another name, which made Ted uneasy on his feet.

He grabbed onto the rail, a barrier to the drop below. The plaque listed Officer Finn Bakker, the last name at the bottom of the ladder of fallen officers. Finn was the officer who leaked information to the organised crime group on Operation Hawk. After discovering his allegiance, he allowed Ted and the operational officers to shoot him in self-defence in a police car park in Berlin rather than face criminal charges. He could picture the last sight of Finn's body looking up at him with wild, dead eyes. The media were unaware of the revelation, which would be how it was left. The family he left behind included two sons under four years old and a partner of five years. Sander concluded that he died in the line of duty so the family could receive a one-off payment for his death insurance via the Dutch Korps. The other officers agreed, and a pact was formed, with death in the line of duty signed and sealed.

Ted placed his hands on the doorframe for the last time. In a normal situation, the transition to his new post would have been easy and simple. However, this wasn't the case; after the police station, he would head back to his home to tell his family, too, which would be harder to announce than the officers in the control room beyond the stairwell door. He knew Rose would be disappointed and unable to drop her life and climb aboard a plane with their family in three hours. Secretly, he would be glad; he believed the new assignment wouldn't have been the safest environment for his family. On the other hand, how many more new officers' names would he have to read on various plaques in the future? He didn't want to answer that.

Chapter 4

T ED PLACED AN OVERNIGHT bag on the suitcase's standing ledge. He had no case files to pack; he just needed his clothing for the foreseeable future and his service weapon. He could hear his daughters laughing and playing together in their bedroom, which gave him warm and cold feelings. He warned his wife, Rose, before heading back to their city house from the police station to defuse the initial confrontation.

Over the phone, she was upset and frustrated with the news but couldn't show her true feelings, as their kids were in her company. She was coming to terms with the impending move in the next few months but still had feelings of hesitation, but with the snap decision, it was something they weren't ready for anytime soon. They discussed options over the phone, including her moving back with the children to England with her parents. They also discussed them staying in Amsterdam for the children's sake, but the mental health effects would be too much with loneliness and no support networks for her now that Ted would be away. Sander could have offered some support to Ted's family, but they would have needed attention, which wouldn't have been possible due to Sander's busy job.

The guilt consumed him as she poured her heart out to him on his arrival home, but in a much lighter fashion as the children were in earshot. To Ted, this job was his life and all he ever wanted to do, even growing up. Ted had the best upbringing he could have had, with loving parents, and he showered his children with affection and love even more. However, growing up, school life was hard for him, and being unable to fit in left him lonely and sometimes in despair. Ted could see the similarities with his twin daughters Ivy and Florence, who were eight and a half years old. When he was younger, he channelled his emotions to help others rather than fighting the class bully he faced. He knew he wanted to be a police officer from a young age, helping people and fighting crime; if he lost that, he feared what would happen to him.

After finishing his education, and through his tough skin and motivation, he began his career by joining the Cheshire Police Force in England as an officer, then joining the National Crime Agency as a criminal support officer, and from there to his promotion role as an International Liaison Officer. Through the daily battles from growing up and the effects in adulthood, the job gave him stability, balance, and a purpose in life, and he carefully balanced the things in life that meant the most to him as well.

Ted hadn't discussed the situation with his two daughters yet. He felt anxiety build in his chest over the thought of bringing the news to them. They were both young girls with big hearts of love and personalities eager to learn and investigate things. He headed downstairs to help with the housework before agreeing it was probably right to tell Ivy and Florence now rather than later before he would have to leave. Once he discussed his leave, they were upset that they were losing their dad so soon after returning from England.

The plan was to take them out for one last meal, an early dinner in the city, before returning to the house to collect his suitcase and bag for the airport. His wife agreed she would drop him off at the departure gate with the kids to say goodbye, but not see him at the departure gate. They went to Pizza Beppe Centrum, which served authentic Neapolitan-style pizza from one of their favourite restaurants in the city. Once they finished and returned home, they went to the airport around twenty minutes southwest of the city. They'd reminisced about previous adventures as a four, and the girls asked questions about Athens and what it was like.

Rose and Ted had both visited the Greek capital on a stop back from the island of Kos one holiday before having children. Although it was a brief one-day stop, he wasn't an expert, but he knew about the history and monuments it held and all of its meaning. Although, all he could picture of the city was the dark reality of the investigation he was facing. A saying came to mind as they rode along, one that he made up and thought loomed well with previous cases and presently. *In beauty, there is always darkness.* He envisioned the beautiful Greek architecture that flowed through the city, and the underworld of crime, which brought darkness to any place on earth, not just that city.

They reached the drop-off point of Schipol Airport, moving into a space from which a car had just vacated.

Ted looked at Rose. "I know you said you don't know, but have you thought about what you will do?"

Rose kept her head forward, watching cars drive in and out of the drop-off point outside the terminal doors.

"I think we will go back to England. With you not around, we need support; having family around will help us. I'll contact the British school here about virtual teaching or online work so they can complete the academic year here at least."

Ted swallowed the lump in his throat and started to nod while looking down towards the footwell of the passenger side seat.

"Sorry," he said.

"It's okay, Ted. Do what you need to do. We will be fine back in England." She smiled.

Ted wasn't sure if the smile was genuine or faked, but he returned the gesture.

"Thank you," Ted said as he leaned over for a hug.

"Let's do this outside—let's get your bags," Rose said.

Rose waited for the traffic to pass before exiting, and Ted exited the car onto the pavement near the terminal. Ted opened the back passenger door, and his two daughters jumped out and hugged him. He knelt, embraced them for the final time, and kissed their foreheads, instructing them to behave at their best for Mum. Rose came around the back of the car, opening the car's boot. Ted reached in to get his belongings, placing them on the pavement beside him. They exchanged a hug and kiss as they said goodbye, and he received one last hug from Ivy and Florence before they reentered the vehicle.

"Shall I message you when I land?" Ted said.

"Yeah, don't worry about it waking me up—just message. See you soon, Ted; love you," Rose said as she disappeared beneath the vehicle's roof into the driver's seat.

"Love you, too," he seemed to say to himself as she disappeared.

The vehicle pulled out onto the one-way system and soon became lost in the trail of cars. He was left alone in the early dark evening under the spotlight of a street lamp. He decided to temporarily erase the guilt from his mind, as Ted knew he had a three-and-a-half-hour flight to ponder it all if he didn't get any sleep.

Ted had two last people to call about his departure. It would only be a phone call because he wouldn't have been able to see them in so little time. Both were situated south of the city near Rotterdam, in the coastal town of The Hague. Ted pulled out his phone to make a call as he wheeled his case towards the terminal's check-in desk.

"Ted! How are you?"

"Not bad, yourself, Luuk?"

Luuk Visser worked for Europol and on Operation Hawk with Ted. They had become friends more than colleagues over recent months, watching Dutch football together at the home of Ajax Football Club, Luuk's favourite team. Ted saw him as a hard-shelled personality, with his tattoos and big muscular body, but Ted learned he had a soft centre, which he liked.

"Good man. I'm looking forward to the football restarting."

"Ah, yeah, you have those weird Christmas breaks, don't you?" Ted replied.

"Yeah, yeah. So why the call? I'm just finishing up here to head home."

"I'm going to Athens earlier than expected," Ted said.

A verbal pause embraced the conversation.

"How come?" Luuk finally responded.

Ted explained the situation about the murder he was now about to investigate. Luuk said he had heard about the shooting on the news, gathering traction around Greece, Europe, and possibly the wider reaches this morning on the media channels.

"Is Fenna with you?" Ted asked.

"Day off today. You want me to pass on the message?"

"It's okay. I'll give her a call later. Listen, I'm at the airport; I know it's only brief, but I've had to tell Rose about this, and I've been spending time with them all day, so I didn't have time to call earlier—sorry."

"No worries at all. I understand; I hope the family are okay. Well, best of luck, Ted."

"Thank you. Keep safe, too, and keep me posted on the trial. I know I can catch it on the media, but let me know if you hear anything first-hand; I want to be a part of it still."

"Will do. Have you read the news article before you go?"

"I've not, but Sander told me to, so I will see if they have a copy here at the airport."

"Catch up with you when I have an update Ted."

"Thanks, Luuk. Take care."

Ted disconnected the call. He continued to work his phone and call Fenna Berg, who also worked for Europol and was present on the sex trafficking case. Fenna answered the phone after a few rings.

"Hello, Ted."

"Hey. You okay? Day off today?"

"Yeah, I've been dress shopping today. I managed to find one I liked."

"Great news; when is the big day?"

"June 16th. You have the invite!"

"Yes, yes. Summer wedding, I remember."

"Yes, could you imagine doing it in this cold we've had?"

"Not at all," he said, laughing.

Ted changed the conversation to the topic of leaving for Athens. She was upset that she didn't get to say goodbye to him, but like Luuk said, she wanted to catch up when he returned, and the invitation to her wedding was still on the table for him and his family, which was in Krakow, Poland. They both said their goodbyes and wished each other good luck.

Ted took out his passport from his coat pocket and started to slap his torso where the other inside pocket was. He knew he was missing the boarding pass he hadn't received. He saw a text message from Simon Taylor saying he was sorry for the delay and had emailed the boarding pass. Ted checked the contents and went through the quiet airport forecourt of check-in. He was looking forward to buying a pint of draught beer and reading the news article Sander and Luuk had recommended about the previous case. He navigated the electronic board to check the desk he needed to book his suitcase in for the flight.

Ted went through the roped-mazed walkway to the desk where an attendant was available. He placed his luggage on the weighted conveyor belt and slid his passport and open phone screen on the top of the staff's desk. His service weapon was unloaded in his luggage in a locked, hard-sided container. He declared the firearm and ammunition to the airline and the airline worker. She quickly inspected the container to ensure it was completely secure, not to allow the gun to be accessed quickly. Thankfully, before he left the town house for the airport, he used a double combination lock on the zip, as suitcases that can be easily opened were not permitted. Once she completed the firearm check and Ted handed over the declaring documents, the bag moved along the motorised belt to its destination.

She looked at this passport and up at Ted's face for comparison.

"Have you been to Athens before, sir?"

"Yes, I have once."

"Have a great time."

Ted smiled. "Thanks. I'm sure I will."

The desk attendant gave back his passport and phone. The phone was still open on the boarding pass. He looked at the one-way ticket on his screen and thought about when the empty return section would be filled with a date.

Chapter 5

T HE RED FLASHING LIGHT from the airport tower in the distance became overshadowed by the bright golden glow from the airport LED light fixtures surrounding the car park of aeroplanes resting for the evening. Although there were often flashes of green and red lights from the wings and tail end of the planes manoeuvring through the tarmac towards their designated runway. Ted found a seat in the bar area of the terminal after a speedy journey through check-in and security. Above him was a row of lights on the ceiling, running from the window gallery back towards the terminal's interior, with long thin rectangle shapes that looked like you were being sucked into a vortex. He picked up a ham sandwich to tie him over from *La Place* for the evening flight. He thought it was best to eat now rather than use the trolley service on the plane. He had a container of Triazolam (Halcion) in his hand luggage, as he planned to sleep on the plane if he could.

After seeing a doctor in the Dutch capital, Ted was prescribed the pills for the lack of sleep he was suffering with. However, he was hesitant to use the drugs regularly to avoid addiction. Ted thought the accompaniment of a pint of Amstel beer would make him sleepy for the flight naturally and wasn't planning to drink the cans of beer on the plane, no matter whatever deal they had onboard. Before Ted found a seat in the near-empty airport, he picked up today's edition of *De Telegraaf* from the refreshment shop. The last copy before the rack would be refreshed with tomorrow's news.

Ted rubbed his hands together, removing the crumbs from his fingers into the empty brown bag, crumbling the paper into a ball and placing it on the table with the nearest bin a few metres away. Ted reached for the cold draught pint of beer and took a large sip, which hit the spot. Placing the cold glass on the beer mat, he went for the paper and unfolded it, glancing at the front cover. Ted observed the Dutch wording matching the photographs on the outside. Although he had worked in the Netherlands for nearly two years, he wasn't fluent in the language, as many colleagues spoke English. However, from what he had learned, he loosely translated the front cover, which covered a variety of news articles. One column included a suspected drunk driver who killed six German tourists and injured four others at a ski resort in Italy. Another was about a man who killed one person and wounded two others in a suburban park in Paris before being shot and killed by police.

As he read those new headlines, he thought about his words before: *In beauty, there is always darkness.* Inside the elegant city of Paris and among the snowy mountain hills were beauty, but also darkness, negativity, and even death. Finally, he reached the section that covered the case from his previous investigation in Amsterdam, which Sander had told him about. Ted saw the article's page number included in the newspaper but became distracted by the section below, which depicted a Chinese man wearing a mask in Wuhan, China. He moved on from the information, licked his finger, and turned the pages until he reached the section he wanted and began reading by using an app, which translated the words captured on his phone camera.

Dangerous Organised Crime Group exposed in the vast Sex Trafficking operation.

January 04, 2020

An operation to track down a dangerous organised crime group that crossed international borders through the heart of mainland Europe. Police authorities from Amsterdam, Germany, Hungary, and Romania worked together to track down organised crime boss Marius Lazarescu in his own country.

Sander Meyer, the chief of police for the Dutch Korps, confirmed to De Telegraaf *that Marius Lazarescu had been arrested and was in custody. The task force, which took place on June 10, was the latest stand of Operation Hawk, which originated from the Dutch Korps investigation into law enforcement response to modern slavery and human trafficking. Around 45 victims had been identified, and suspects were arrested following a week-long law enforcement operation targeting sex trafficking across the continent. How the operation task force was gathered and the intel came to light is unknown. Some speculate that there were underground operatives, but Chief of Police Sander put it down to prior hard investigative work from the operational team.*

Marius Lazarescu was arrested in a public park in the Romanian city of Timișoara. The investigation brought them to the town following another OCG member from Budapest. Unfortunately, that suspect was murdered by another member, who was shot dead from a self-defence perspective in the same park. The task force that brought him down comprised officers from cross-border police forces and Europol detectives. Later this year, Marius Lazarescu will be trialled in The Hague in the International Criminal Court. He had been charged with conspiracy to transport individuals under 17 against their free will, conspiracy to transport individuals under 17 with the intent to sell and engage in illegal sexual activities, and conspiracy to commit sex trafficking of individuals under 18. Mr Lazarescu has also been linked with several historical murders and assassination plots throughout the last five years of ongoing investigations. It's unclear what additional charges will be brought to Mr Lazarescu at this stage in the investigation. It is also unclear if a plea bargain will be made in agreement between the defence and prosecutors for an exchange or concession of information. Mr Lazarescu is on current suicide watch and monitored 24 hours daily, with a high-security presence.

Lewis Hewitt, the British Ambassador to Budapest, was able to comment on the events in Budapest. "Following the operation, which successfully halted the progression of a much profitable business for organised crime groups, we can confirm that the operations team rescued thirteen young women from Budapest's modern slavery and sex trafficking operations. We totalled another twelve liberated from their horrors, including those from Amsterdam, Berlin, and Romania. Other members of the OCG groups were arrested and will stand trial. Some of those didn't stand trial because they were killed by trained officers in firing exchanges, which we deemed self-defence. We will ensure that those gang members get brought to justice with the mountain of evidence still forming throughout this investigation. Although it seems the curtain is falling on the investigation, I assure you this is only the beginning. We are working hard with cross-border forces, Europol, Interpol, and the FBI to continue the fight. We will continue working in the heart of our city and continental Europe to gain a foothold in this difficult and somewhat complex crime operation where these gangs target young girls for greed."

The victims' names and all public records have been hidden from the media for safety reasons. Although, those girls have now been reunited with their families and loved ones after their tremendous ordeal. Those girls' homes span the globe and multiple continents. The names of the

OCG members have also been hidden from public records, as the investigation is still underway.

It is speculated that this chain of crimes reaches bordering continents and within the realms of highly public figures within significant countries worldwide. They declined to further comment on approaching the partnered authorities leading the investigation.

We cannot disclose the German company brought into the analysis of sex trafficking offences for legal reasons. The company manager was coerced into supporting the OCG in their criminal activities.

There was a special note to several officers who lost their lives during the difficult and complex case, and we've been assured that those names will be released and those officers will be truly honoured and respected during the trial later this year.

The aftermath of one of Europe's most successful operations in the fight against organised crime was on a much larger scale than ever seen. However, sadly, this is one piece of the puzzle within a maze of illegal operations across the continent, a needle in a haystack. The depth and distance of this root problem are unknown at this moment.

Once Ted read the article's last line, he heard the overhead announcer state that the gate for his flight to Athens was opening and for passengers to proceed immediately. Ted became welded to the article, just like he became in the investigation. His thoughts cascaded his mind with the faces of the girls Ted met alive and those less fortunate. A drop in his stomach became uncomfortable when he recalled the two girls; they were too late to save in Romania. Amanda Coleman and Toni Laurent were their names; they infiltrated his mind daily, even at night when he tried to sleep. He didn't know where they were or even if they were alive. In a moment of selflessness, Ted hoped maybe they weren't alive, so their nightmare could be over. Although various authorities still hunted for them, there was still hope of rescue; no matter how slim the chances were, someone was still looking for them, even if it wasn't Ted's jurisdiction.

However, he knew he needed to leave that behind him and allow those actively working on the case to do their part. Ted had a duty to his new investigation and to find justice for Daniel Belfield and why he was shot dead. He stood up from his seat and saw the location upon the line that ordered him to proceed to the gate.

Chapter 6

Athens

THE PLANE LANDED SMOOTHLY in Athens, ten minutes ahead of schedule. Ted had a window view and admired flying at night time. The cabin was quiet, and the smoothed light gave flight travel a better ambience and quality. The view down was mostly blocked by clouds across mainland Europe. Although there were little pockets within the clouds, he could make out small towns and cities with the illuminated orange lights. The earth's floor was bright, with lights through the clouds on the descent. The area mass of its lights was large enough to estimate Athens, and Ted thought he could see the outline of the Acropolis standing tall over the city. At that central point, the lights continued until they reached a shade of black, which engulfed a large surface area—the Aegean Sea. The Aegean linked the Mediterranean Sea between Europe and Asia, with its Greek islands floating within the Aegean's mass.

On the ground, Ted spotted large and small international and domestic passenger planes as they taxied to their designated parking spot. Connecting to countries around the continent and different continents around the world. Some smaller planes were run by Aegean Airlines, serving other smaller Greek airlines travelling to Rhodes, Crete, and other islands. Athens Airport, situated east of the city, was the main airport for Greece, with Thessaloniki Airport Makedonia being the most northern.

The plane stopped at its apron to unload its passengers and their baggage. His phone buzzed in his pocket as he stood up and ducked underneath the overhead shelves due to his height. He needed to be vertical from his seat to allow blood to flow into his legs from the limited movement on the plane. Simon messaged to say he was waiting in the arrivals lounge and asked if he needed caffeine from the all-night vending machine. It was one in the morning now Greek time, and he was partially charged from sleep but thought a hint of coffee would hit the spot no matter where it came from, so he accepted.

He caught the passenger bus that connected the somewhat abandoned plane in the middle of the open airport parking space and dropped him and the other passengers off at the airport doors. He texted Rose, updating her that he had landed safely as he swiftly moved through baggage collection and security. His only delay was the long walkway from the new satellite departure and arrival terminal. He walked through the last automatic doors, which depicted two bottles of Alfa beer as they opened. Through the small crowd of people gathered to welcome their family, friends, or businessmen, Simon was waiting in dark trousers and a green coat jacket holding two cardboard cups of coffee. As he looked up, he had short brown hair, was clean-shaven, and was slightly smaller than Ted.

"Good flight, Ted?" Simon said, offering him his coffee.

"Thanks. Don't know. I slept most of it. Yours?" Ted replied, taking his first sip of coffee.

"Great. I just got in over an hour ago, checked in, showered, and returned for you.

"Any updates from the authorities?" Ted said.

"No, I tried to check in, but they said to head over tomorrow morning first thing," Simon said, finishing his coffee.

"Strange."

"Very, but all will be clear tomorrow. We've got rooms at Hotel Sofitel next to the airport for a few hours. We will also have hire cars available tomorrow morning for our stay."

"Thank you for sorting this out."

"Don't mention it," he said, taking the lead towards the taxi rank outside. Simon offered to take one of Ted's bags. Ted handed over his rucksack for Simon to hold as they made their way through the departure terminal to the outdoor areas.

"How did Rose take it?"

"Okay. They're going home to England with the kids to make it easier."

"Already? Shit. Sorry about this."

"Don't worry, we have a job to do. I'll sort it out another day."

Simon looked back at Ted with empathy.

"Listen, I understand where you are coming from. Antonia and I were the same. She liked being away sometimes in different locations, but the next thing she missed home and family badly. Eventually, I made my way through the ranks and got lucky with my job now."

"Lucky?"

"Well, I was working in Rome when she fell pregnant. Planned, not planned, that kind of thing. I saw this job application and thought I'd pursue it as a career progression I got an interview and got the job."

"But you've been with the NCA for over twenty years. You were more than qualified for it."

"Maybe. Anyway, my point is, it's hard; you're not the only couple to go through this, and you won't be the last. I've seen people get divorced, have affairs, quit their job, and all those things. I'm not saying that will happen to you, but you get my point."

"Yeah, I get you."

"You've just got to see what happens. Allow them to be at home, and look after yourself for now. Let's focus on this. Focus on Daniel Belfield."

"Yeah, you're right."

They made their way outside with the gust of air reaching them with a hint of a chill as it brushed their faces. The surrounding roads around the designated exit point were quiet, with no taxis on standby.

"What's your hunch then for tomorrow morning?" Ted said, looking around.

"I'm not sure. I think maybe something he was investigating got him killed. It could be gang-related, maybe."

"Why do you say that?"

"I'm not saying it is similar in any way, but there was an assassination attempt on a senior officer in Paris and one of our ILOs about four years ago. They were driving in a vehicle when a convoy appeared from behind. One of the cars overtook the officers' vehicle and stopped in front of them, and the other stopped behind the bumper to box them in. Some men got out with guns and were about to enter the vehicle when a police car on the same road spotted them, spooked them, and they left the scene without going through with their plan."

"Everyone was okay?"

"They were."

"What were they investigating in Paris?"

"Organised crime groups. But there was a link to high-ranking officials."

"What happened?"

"The senior officer investigating with the ILO wanted to drop the investigation shortly after the scare, said there wasn't enough evidence."

"And they stopped because he said?"

"Well, he was right; they didn't have enough evidence. But he blocked any rebounds on the investigation. Then that was the end."

"What happened then?"

"Nothing. He retired a year later and went wherever he went to enjoy the rest of his remaining years."

"Doesn't sound right to me."

"No, but nothing was proven in terms of corruption."

"Were there any further assassination attempts?"

"No, we moved the ILO out immediately."

Ted nodded to the ending, allowing his mind to wander to the possibilities behind Daniel's murder. The night sky was a black dome with white freckles of light glistening in the sky. He started to clear his mind of the case, allowing his body to rest again before heading to the hotel. Simon waved down a taxi, and the vehicle pulled into a pickup point, and the driver exited the driver's side, lifting the boot to help with the bags. Simon was like Ted, working across Europe and other continents as an ILO, and their acknowledgement of each other was through brief conversations or emails they had been CC'd into. Shortly before Ted's first anniversary working in Amsterdam, Simon was appointed senior officer after a successful application and started communicating more with his managing ILOs. Naturally, Ted and Simon's interaction grew over various forums, and interest matched from supporting the same football team, love of music, and similar social activities. Although Simon was pushing fifty years old, they still had a connection beyond friends.

The journey to the hotel was short. Upon entry into his hotel room, Ted rolled his suitcase over to the bed with his bag over his shoulder. He unpacked fresh clothes for tomorrow and removed his toiletries and toothbrush from his bag. Once he had freshened up with a shower and propped his morning clothes for the following day, he reached into his bag for his wireless headphones. He climbed into bed and worked his phone to a music app, finding a playlist he had created. This wasn't his usual routine for nighttime when he was in attendance of other people. This was the moment he had to himself, his own self-care therapy. Recently, Ted struggled with his thoughts and sleep patterns due to the previous case. It was a phenomenal success in the authorities' exterior world and the media. Yet, inside the interior shell, he struggled to comprehend the positives when dark circumstances occurred. Darkness within the beauty. When he closed his eyes at night, and during periods of rapid eye movement, he returned to the nightmares in which two girls were still actively participating in real life—Amanda and Toni. He lay under the bedsheets and turned off the bedside light. He clicked play on the screen for the track of choice, with the screen displaying a song with a misspelt wording of Siegfried:

Frank Ocean – Seigfried.

The song's meaning wasn't personally connected to Ted because it was speculatively about a metaphysical break-up song between Frank Ocean and his rumoured brief affair with another man. Individual lyrics smoothed and delved deep into his mind for all that. The poems struck a chord of connecting emotionally and understanding people deeper when his emotions were so entangled within him. Relating to peers was the sometimes unnatural act Ted portrayed when people underlined him to fit into a mainstream society rather than Frank's unique idiosyncrasies. He rested well as the song finished, transitioning into its next track. His eyes started to become heavy and closed almost immediately.

Ted approached the metal container and lifted the black plastic lid carefully. He froze and saw the pale white body lying on their side. She had ginger hair and a red stain on her throat, which had stained the rubbish bag she was resting on. Another haunting memory from the previous case consumed him. His eyes opened instantly. The room's brightness was the same, as if his eyes were closed. He reached for his phone and saw the time display on the screen following a slight eye adjustment from the screen's light. It was thirty minutes before his seven o'clock alarm set off. He decided he would get up now and prepare himself for the day. He was anxious to discover why everything was so secret about the case. He lifted the sheets and sat upon the edge of the bed, turning the bedside light on. He stood up from the bed and placed the bedsheets neatly in their position, which they were in when he first entered the room. He left the burden of their fates within the sheets for now.

Chapter 7

T ED SAT WAITING WITH his baggage in the hotel lobby with a fresh coffee from the hotel's free machine. Simon appeared from the hallway door, surprised to see Ted prompt ahead of the arranged meeting time. Simon got himself a coffee from the coffee machine, an americano, and they proceeded to the hotel entrance with their bags. A taxi met them outside the hotel doors and took them to the rental car building within the large industrial area of the airport. Once they received their five-door hatchback cars, they began their fifty-minute drive from the airport to the Hellenic Police Headquarters. HQ. was situated in Athens and northeast of Lycabettus Hill, across the road from Apostolos Nikolaidis Sports ground, home to Panathinaikos FC.

They approached the building, which would be best described as Athens's equivalent to Scotland Yard. On approach, the building had large blocks as its foundation and white pillars holding the fort above. A towering block emerged from the middle with square windows giving a familiar look to the game *Minesweeper*. Palm trees stood tall at the front of the building before a side exit led towards the rear of the building, where underground parking was available. They navigated through the parking area and found an empty spot not too far away from each other. Exiting, they walked across the parking lot to the elevators across the underground complex.

"What floor is it?" Ted said as they entered the empty lift.

"Floor six, they said," Simon said, pressing the button.

The doors closed, and the elevator started ascending through the floors until the designated floor was reached. They were quiet on their ascent, pondering the information and personnel they would meet beyond the lift's metal confinement. Simon exited first and turned right out of the short corridor that led to the main control room, which included numerous desks with computer screens and officers working on them. The square windows ran alongside the room's walls, looking out onto the main street and stadium below. One of the officers hovering over one of the workers at their desk saw Simon and Ted enter the room, looking for someone, waving them down, and approaching them. Simon and Ted smiled at the man, who looked like one of importance with his black boots, navy trousers, and jacket to match, complete with badges and sewn embroidery, which identified his rank. His hair was light brown and fair, but noticeable signs of balding and receding hairline were clear. His complexion showed signs of middle age; his skin was looked after but worn, possibly under the stress of the job over the years.

"Good morning—nice to see you both. I'm Police Deputy Director Andries Iraklidis."

"We spoke on the phone," Simon said in a statement rather than a question.

"We did."

"I'm Simon Taylor."

Andries and Simon shook hands.

"How did you know it was us?" Ted asked in the middle of the introduction.

Andries laughed.

"Well, you are both strangers to me. You looked lost, and you look British," Andries said, taking a step back to take them both in.

Ted wasn't sure how he looked British or what constituted the description, so he moved on.

"Fair enough. Nice to meet you," Ted said, offering a hand.

"Nice to meet you two. First of all, I'm sorry for losing your officer—our officer, too, may I add," Andries stated in a sombre tone.

"Thank you. I'm looking forward to hearing about the information surrounding it so we can get straight to work with the investigation," Simon pressed.

Andries nodded at Simon and turned his attention to the other unintroduced man.

"Sorry. I didn't catch your name?"

"Sorry, I'm Ted Chester, the new ILO for Athens; nice to meet you."

"Nice to meet you, too, Ted. I look forward to working with you, although it comes sooner than we thought. Shall we all go into my office?" Andries said with a welcoming smile, opening his arms to the door behind him.

Andries sat down, and Ted noticed he was slightly overweight, with his belly pressing out through his white shirt, catching the table as he sat down. Andries offered them coffee and some breakfast goods in koulouri and koulourakia on a communal table outside his office. The former was a circular bread encrusted with sesame seeds, and the latter was a sweet Greek dessert made from butter-based pastry and a hint of vanilla. They both accepted the coffee and the offer of koulourakia as they both missed breakfast due to their eagerness to leave early. Andries stood up, collected the treats, and made his way back into his office, which was in the left-hand corner of the office, giving a ninety-degree view of the main street and its side-street corner.

Andries placed a tray with two small plates, each with one of each treat and black coffee in both cups, with a small shot glass of milk. They took their seats grabbed their coffee cups, adding a splash of milk, and left their baked goods on the plates next to their cups.

"So, how were your flights?" Andries said in an attempt at small talk.

"Good," Ted replied, sipping his drink.

"Good—a little bumpy for me, but we both arrived separately late last night," Simon said.

Andries nodded, looking down to his side. He immediately cut straight to the point as he raised his head to make eye contact with the two officers.

"I'm no good with small talk. So let's get straight to the point. Again, my deepest condolences to you and our dear friend again."

"Thank you. I'm sorry to be blunt, Andries, but I'm eager to find out what needed to wait and what you couldn't tell us before?" Simon said.

Andries leaned back in his chair, which creaked as he did so. He put his hands on the back of his head, took a deep breath, and then leaned forward towards them again, clasping his hands under the desk with his elbows resting on the armrests on either side of his chair.

"I believe he was working on something that got him killed."

Ted stopped mid-sip. Emptying some of the contents from his mouth into the cup while hearing the statement. Andries noticed the transfer back into the cup as he and Ted locked eyes, but Simon pressed on, distracting Andries's judgement.

"What makes you think that?" Simon said, leaning forward with interest.

"It's too much of a coincidence to not think it. He's been here nearly two years and helped us with organised crime groups, murder, and robbery. He's done excellent work, no trouble at all, but..."

"But?" Ted said.

Andries took a deep breath.

"Maybe I could have done more..."

"Andries, please explain," Simon pressed.

"He came to me a few months ago about corruption in the force. A severe matter. When he first started, he saw police lieutenants taking bribes from civilians to avoid getting small parking fines. He told me about those officers and internal affairs dealt with their disciplinaries. Some of those have been let go from the force—fired."

"So do you think it is revenge from those officers?" Simon said.

"No, I don't think that..."

"So how is it connected?" Ted asked.

"Daniel believed it was much higher than just lieutenants. He was already working with the Hellenic Police internal affairs unit investigating corruption cases among police lieutenants. But there were more than just rookie officers or lieutenants; he believed senior officials, including those in this building, were accepting bribes from traffickers. Look, we have huge problems with the Albania Mafia here, and I think it's connected to his death."

"Albanians?" Ted and Simon said simultaneously.

"Yes. They control a large part of billion-dollar sales of cocaine in Europe. These groups also often export other immigrants from the Middle East and South Europe to Greece and control the working-class districts in West Athens. The nightclubs, bars, and strip clubs are laundering money into them."

"So, let me get this straight; he was investigating the department or individuals within the department and links to organised crime. Did you know what exactly?" Simon said.

"It all started when he came into this office and told me he was anonymously going to the affairs unit. I told him to go. It's the correct procedure with this huge scandal he was apparently uncovering. He said it was too dangerous for him to share the information with me yet, so I never knew the full details. Daniel didn't trust us anymore; maybe he didn't trust me, and even I don't trust people in the authorities either. Still, I trusted Daniel," he said passionately, pointing his finger towards the office door.

"Is corruption a big problem? Can we trust these people here at the moment?" Ted said, pointing his head towards the war room.

"Citizens don't have faith in the police. They think everyone is corrupt. Still, we do have good officers out there."

"I just think if there is a corrupt officer, will they try and stop us with our investigation?" Ted asked.

Andries let out a puff of air and nodded slightly.

"That's the risk we may have to take—maybe they'll make a mistake, and we can find them, or we will have to investigate pushing a rock up a hill with them on our backs to make it harder."

"I've seen corruption before; how bad has it been here?"

"Well, in my time, the big ones, as you say," Andries said, using his index and middle finger for quotations before continuing.

"There was a discovery a few years back, in 2015. Santorini Police officers were only performing minor rudimentary checks for passengers travelling from Asia, Africa, et cetera, to see if they were using forged documents, which was the normal routine. Later, we found out they were taking bribes on certain passenger names to allow them into the country. The gangs gave the names of those who would be let through illegally. In another case, two police officers from Thessaloniki HQ. They were suspended and later jailed because they took bribes to allow women to enter mainland Europe from the Middle East—as young as *eleven years old*—for trafficking. There's more, but you can read about it on the news if you wish."

"So, do you think the Albanian Mafia murdered Daniel?" Ted said.

Andries leaned back on his chair again with his hands together, swivelling in his chair but looking back at them.

"I believe so. At the murder scene, we found a 9×19mm bullet standard for a Beretta Px4 used in the Albanian Land Force."

The Albanian Land Force was the land force branch of the Albanian Armed Forces. Founded in 2000, their main mission was the defence of the independence, sovereignty, and territorial integrity of the Republic of Albania, and known to have participated in humanitarian, combat, noncombat, and peace support operations.

Andries paused and looked each officer in the eye before continuing.

"Do you want my opinion, honestly?"

Simon and Ted glanced at each other before nodding their heads toward Andries.

"Of course," Ted said.

"I think he was investigating the corruption, and someone noticed he was getting close to something, maybe too close. They wanted to cut him loose quickly. Either someone within the department or through the Albanians or both."

"I'm fully onboard with the corruption theory. However, just check all bases; couldn't it be Albanians and not police officers involved?" Simon said.

Andries tilted his head, not revealing the theory had been explored.

"Good theory. I guess we will have to find out."

The room fell silent momentarily as the officers thought about the possible avenues.

"No witnesses to the shooting?" Ted continued.

"A few people say they saw the man with a balaclava on making the shot, but he was gone as soon as the shot was fired. Not many heard the gunshot because of the music, so we don't have much."

Ted nodded, knowing that would have been the first route of investigation. Interviewing witnesses, but if the balaclava masked the suspect, it gave nothing fruitful at present to reinterview those witnesses.

"Is Daniel's girlfriend okay?"

"Not really. She has fears for her life, but we have police protection for her around the clock. We need to ask her a few more questions. Then we would be able to let her go back home to England. Not forgetting Daniel's body once the autopsy has finished."

"Any news on the autopsy?"

"Results should be in today, I hope."

Ted nodded and felt sympathetic towards Daniel's girlfriend and what she must be going through losing a loved one, something Ted had never experienced, whether a partner or family member.

"There's more. Two days ago, our Police Sergeant Christos Masouras was involved in a hit-and-run off duty. He had his seat belt on, thankfully, and he was alone. Few bumps and bruises, but he is off recovering this week. Christos was Daniel's partner on the case."

"How did the hit and run happen?"

"There was a junction just north of the city—this 4x4 came into side of him, hit Christos's driver's side at high speed. Drove off, licence plates were fake; we lost them on the CCTV and ANPR cameras."

"Did you note it as suspicious?" Simon asked.

Andries's faced became confused.

"What do you mean?" he asked.

"Was Christos working with Daniel closely when he reported his theories to internal affairs?" Ted said.

"He was. Why?"

"Have you spoken to Christos recently?" Ted said with urgency.

"No, I haven't," Andries said with a worried face.

He got up from his seat and walked towards his office door, opening it and standing in its doorway.

Andries shouted to the room full of officers in Greek—which could only be assumed to be him—asking if anyone had heard from Christos. Ted and Simon turned to the window, looking at the officers facing Andries. They shook their heads. Through the glass, one of the female officers lifted her work phone, typed in some digits, and pressed the phone against her ear. Andries hurried to his desk to pick up his mobile. Ted and Simon looked anxiously at each other and at the pacing of Andries. He worked the screen for a few seconds and then placed the phone up to his ear. Twenty seconds must have passed, and the deputy director's face whitened as the rings continued unanswered. He lifted his chair again, approached his open door, and stood in the doorway again.

"What's going on?" Simon frantically asked.

Ted watched Andries become increasingly agitated in his movements as they both stood to observe the tension.

"Eliana, can you try his emergency contact?" he said in English.

"Yes, his girlfriend, I think it is. What's wrong, boss?"

"I don't know," he said, looking back at Ted and Simon in the doorway.

Ted saw Eliana, a young female officer working the corded phone again on the desk. She placed it to her ear, and Ted watched her remain silent, staring down at her keyboard and constantly flipping her pen from tip to end in her hand. She lifted her bottom lip and shook her head, placing it back in its holder.

"Skatá!" Andries shouted.

"Pardon?" Ted said.

"Sorry. We need to go right now," Andries said, collecting his belongings off the desk. The three coffee cups would go cold, and so would the baked goods.

"Eliana, Manolis, get a car to Christos's house now! Anyone else spare can join us, too," Andries said in the main room.

"You want us to take our cars?" Simon said, leaving the office.

"No, you both come with me. Do you both have your weapons?" Andries said, looking back as he reached the door to the hallway.

"Yes, we brought them over," Ted tapped his waist where his holster was under his jacket. Simon also nodded to confirm he was armed.

"Good, I have a bad feeling about this," Andries said as he pushed the door open to exit the war room.

Ted agreed with Andries's words. He had a bad feeling about this, too.

Chapter 8

CHRISTOS AND HIS GIRLFRIEND'S apartment was situated south of the city, halfway between the Athens Riviera and the central point of the capital. Asyrmatos was a neighbourhood of Athens located on the west slopes of Philopappos Hill, with its ancient Greek mausoleum overlooking the area. Christos's apartment block was made of concrete, with tiered balconies created for affordable housing, but their designs had stood the test throughout the decades.

The front door was underneath the overhang of the building's concrete structure. Police Sergeant Manolis Pelas and Eliana Abulafia stepped out of their vehicles with their weapons drawn. Ted, Simon, and Andries were next, taking up the rear as they approached the electric front door with a keypad that allowed communication to the apartments. There was a keylock entrance, which wasn't helpful without the corresponding key. Manolis pressed a button on the keypad, and a continuous buzz noise played back. Once the noise stopped, a male voice was on the other end of the pad. He spoke in Greek, and Manolis returned the conversation. A clicking noise was followed by a loud metal bang from the door. Manolis opened the door, and the other four officers entered the premises cautiously.

"Which floor is it?" Ted said, holding his weapon as they approached the stairway.

"Second floor. Apartment six," Eliana said.

They went up the first flight of stairs and proceeded to the second. Andries was ahead of the group, with Eliana at the side, aiming at the area in front. Simon, Ted, and Manolis brought up the rear of the group. The man Manolis buzzed through the communication device was in apartment eight and standing in the doorway with his Zimmer frame. He was a frail old man with olive skin and a leather look. Eliana instructed him to go back inside for safety, lowering her weapon as she confronted him to defuse his worry.

Apartment six was in sight. When they approached, Andries moved to the right-hand side of the door, with Eliana joining him. The others took up their positions to the left.

"No landlord around to let us in?" Ted said.

"Didn't check, but no time," Andries replied.

"The old-fashioned way then," Simon said.

"I'll do it if you give permission?" Manolis said, looking at Andries.

"Do it."

Manolis was similar to a Greek god. He was muscular, and his face seemed chiselled from God's hands. His jet-black hair was slung back with gel, and his beard kept so perfectly. He reminded Ted of Yannis Philippakis, the lead singer of the band Foals, who was of Greek heritage. Manolis knocked on the door and waited a few moments before trying again. There was no response, nor no sounds from the apartment. Just complete silence.

Under instruction from Andries, Manolis used his strength, stepped back, and flung himself forward, raising his foot high and using his arms to gather momentum. In one thrust, he crashed the bottom of his black boots onto the door handle. The door swung open and hit the wall behind it, creating a loud bang that would have disturbed anyone in the apartment complex. The door started to slowly creep back towards them, but Manolis used his forearm to keep it open as he entered. The hallway had a wall on each side and opened into the lounge and kitchen area on initial viewing. Everything seemed clean and presented nicely. There was no sign of damage or struggle within the apartment.

Manolis took the first steps into the hallway, aiming at the space in front. He continued his forward steps towards a corner of the room with an office table, computer, and keyboard, giving all clear for the open space as he turned back to search for the officers. Eliana checked the kitchen area with a U-shaped barrier of fitted surfaces with cupboards underneath. The area was clear; she lifted her head towards the entrance, noticing two doors on either side of the hallway. Ted and Simon were on the left-hand side, holding their aim towards the door, and Andries took a right, backed up by Eliana and Manolis. Ted stuck his left hand up, extending all five fingers; he dropped his thumb, index, and middle, initiating the countdown. Once his hand became a fist, both doors opened instantaneously. Ted and Simon entered the bathroom, which seemed relatively well-kept and showed no struggle. There was a bath and shower combination, a toilet to the right and a sink to the left. Everything was clean, and as it should be, the towels perfectly propped over the towel rail, seemingly undisturbed. Ted announced the all-clear but didn't hear anything from the adjacent room as the moments passed.

Approaching the door leading back into the open plan area, Manolis exited the other room with his hands in disbelief and his gun holster on his waist. After what he witnessed, someone who seemed powerful and strong looked weak and defeated. Manolis stepped aside as Simon and Ted approached the room. Within the large square-sized bedroom was a bed at the head of the room, with two bedside tables on either side. A dressing table to the right accommodated a mirror and chair.

On the far left was a large wardrobe for clothing arrangements and other clutter pieces.

Eliana leaned over the bed, towering over a stretched-out woman lying on her back. She was motionless, and her skin was pale white. On first inspection, there didn't seem to be any patterns of blood from her or on the bed. Andries was radioing that the woman was deceased, and so was another figure who Andries was soaring over. Andries moved to the side in his stride, revealing a man sitting on the floor with his head propped against the wall, tilted to the side. A wound on the forehead indicated a gunshot, and the combination of his dead body holding a gun in his hand characterised suicide. Eliana stood straight, backed away from the bed, and left the bedroom to find Manolis.

Ted and Simon lowered their weapons and placed them back into their holster. Ted walked around the bed towards the women as Andries still occupied the man's space. On approach, she was white as the sheets she was lying on, and a pillow was propped up against the side of her face, indicating she may have been smothered to death.

"Is this Christos?" Ted asked Andries.

"Yeah, unfortunately," he replied sombrely, peering over his dead body.

"This is the girlfriend?"

Andries didn't reply. He just turned to Ted and nodded gloomily.

"What do you suspect?" Ted said, looking at Andries.

"Albanians."

"Yeah?"

Andries moved back from Christos's body in disbelief, and Simon approached and knelt to look at the wound without tampering with the body. He followed his line of sight down to the weapon and examined the body. Simon wasn't an expert. However, he was taking in the first initial counts in person before the forensic investigators arrived.

Andries paced the bottom of the bed and placed his head into his right hand, harshly rubbing his forehead with his thumb, index, and middle finger before stopping to compose himself.

"He wouldn't have his service weapon at home; it's kept in a lock-up at HQ, so it's not his gun. The gun there looks like a Beretta Px4, which could be similar to the one used on Daniel. The serial number has been ground on the side from inspection, but we can send it to the lab for analysis. We can extract the bullet in our lab in the city to see if the bullet matches Daniel's, too. But my guess is that it will match," Andries said.

Simon examined the gun to where the serial number would have appeared and gave Ted a nod to confirm. Andries asked Simon to take pictures of Christos's body and passed him a pair of gloves and a plastic bag from his back pocket to dispose of the gun.

"Always carry these?" Simon asked.

"No, but I had some today."

Simon nodded, not knowing how to respond.

The evidence left at the crime scene would be left to the experts, but with the careful process of non-contamination, they had started identifying and acquiring potential evidence. The following stages, analysis of the evidence, and report production, would be left to the experts.

Ted quickly glanced at both bodies, but something wasn't adding up from the crime scene that was produced.

"Not done a good job of making it look like murder with the partner and then suicide with Christos, have they?" Ted said.

"They're not scared, so they're not bothered what we think; it's like a little bit of fun to them."

Andries's face turned pale white, and suddenly he turned to exit the bedroom. Ted wandered around the bed to look at Christos's body as Simon zipped up the bag with the gun inside. The officers were huddled outside as Ted passed the opening, embracing each other over the tragic news of one of their colleagues. Simon held onto the bag as he leaned over to look at the woman on the bed.

"You can see the bruising on her neck. It could be strangulation. We won't be able to tell until postmortem, so I think we can disregard the pillow," Simon said.

"And he definitely didn't shoot himself with how he is holding the gun," Ted said.

Simon nodded in agreement.

"I don't know where we'll start with this. Take a picture of the girl before this place is locked down for evidence," Simon said.

Simon passed him and headed towards the exit of the bedroom. Ted stared at Christos, then shifted his attention to the girlfriend. She was in her early twenties, just like Christos, and had long black hair, which was slightly curled. She had a white T-shirt top and a black cardigan over that. She wore dark blue skinny jeans, and her feet were bare. He held his camera phone up to her body and took a few pictures, capturing the broader view and some up-close showing the bruising around the throat. He took the photos, looking from the camera view to one with his own eyes.

He had sudden flashbacks to the previous case, and his head spun as he lost balance on his feet. He closed his eyes and shook his head to shake the images from his mind. He placed a hand on the bed to steady himself before breathing deeply and exhaling at seven-second intervals. Before something caught his attention, he recovered his breathing regulation and his balance and returned to his intuition. Ted noticed her hands and became intrigued by what he saw. Her fingernails were broken—two on her left hand and four on her right. He frantically searched the bed and knelt on the floor to investigate stray nails.

"You okay in here?" Andries said, reentering the room.

"I'm sorry if I forgot to say I'm sorry for your loss," Ted said, kneeling up, looking at Andries with his full attention.

Ted returned the favour just like Andries had done for Daniel, but Ted didn't know Daniel personally like Andries knew Christos; he knew his words meant more. Andries's face became confused by Ted's current actions as Ted began to use the torch on his phone, illuminating under the bed.

"Thanks, Ted. But, are you looking for something down there?"

"Some of her nails are broken. I didn't see any near Christos's body, so I'm looking around the bed, but I can't find any."

"I'll start looking out in the lounge and bathroom," Andries advised before exiting the bedroom.

Although Ted continued his search in the bedroom, it did not prevail. He couldn't see any under the bed, on the sheets or surrounding areas. Ted stood up to exit the room, pushing his hand up inside his jacket sleeve and using the sleeve to close the door behind him. Without even turning to face the open plan, Eliana shouted across the room from the kitchen unit.

"I've found some here."

"What is it?" Andries asked.

"It looks like nails," she proclaimed.

"How many?" Ted said on approach.

"Three or four."

The team manoeuvred their way to the kitchen space, positioning themselves by the edge of the units and looking in at Eliana on her hands and knees.

"Five... six!"

"Good work," Andries said.

"So, they killed her here in the kitchen?" Simon said.

"Maybe. Maybe she put up a fight."

Ted took a picture of the apartment room and pulled up a scenario in his mind.

"I think... she runs into the kitchen to grab something to defend herself. They get her, and she fights back here, breaking her nails. They take her into the bedroom and strangle her, or they do it here," Ted said.

"Could be," Eliana said.

"Then eventually dump the body onto the bed. But when do they shoot Christos? Before or after the scuffle?" Ted replied.

"Only the killers and the dead would know that. Still, I'm sure forensic may give an estimate possibly," Manolis said.

Andries's phone vibrated in his pocket, interrupting the conversation. He reached into his jacket to answer it. He spoke in Greek and quickly ended the call.

"Forensics are here," he said, walking over to the apartment door. A ring reverberated through the apartment. Andries pressed the panel on the door with his gloves, allowing the forensic officers in. Andries walked back to the kitchen by-passing the team, taking in the apartment's view while placing his hands on his hips.

"I'm going to set up a meeting with the internal affairs team. We need to know what Daniel knows right now. This is only the start—they will continue to silence anyone who knows."

Ted walked over to Andries and held one hand on his shoulder.

"If these criminals are this ruthless, I need the names of everyone involved in investigating the corruption. Their lives are in danger, even ours now."

Andries stared back at Ted with fear in his eyes.

"I'll get you them right away."

Chapter 9

T HE MIDDAY SUN WAS in full winter bloom. It wasn't giving its full Mediterranean heat, but a slightly chilled temperature perforated the clouds. The team returned to the police HQ, and were to meet in the boardroom. Ted and Simon sat alone, after only grabbing coffee refreshments, as their appetite for food wasn't present. Andries would join them momentarily, with the members of those investigating Daniel Belfield's original investigation into corruption of senior officials, not before informing his team of the news surrounding Christos and his partner's death.

Discovery at the scene by the forensic team confirmed the female body in the apartment to be Cassandra Argyros, twenty-two years old, the partner to Christos. There were no signs of intrusion, as the door was locked inside when Manolis initially forced entry for the officers. Access to the balcony was possible but was ruled out due to the hardship of the climb and drop. The registered keeper of the property was a landlord called Angelo Sotiriou, who only lived a couple of blocks away from the apartment and had CCTV available on the front door entrance. Ted and the officers witnessed the video footage, showing a man approaching the entrance to the building wearing a balaclava and using black spray paint to cover the only camera available on-site. As he covered the lens, they saw the feet of two other people approaching before the blackout was complete.

Ted and those initially in the apartment search were joined by additional officers appealing to neighbours for anyone who may have seen the men entering. None of the residents witnessed the men, which added to the mystery of how they entered the apartment so silently. Further investigation showed the keypad was activated to open at around 22:02 the night before, which correlated with the time stamp on the video, the exact moment the men arrived at the door in disguise. Speculation grew about where the masked men had gathered access to open Christos's apartment door and if they had access to the keylock outside the apartment. Officers questioned the neighbouring residents whether any CCTV was available from the other apartment entrances. They were unsuccessful, not due to the lack of it, and due to the positioning of the camera. The CCTV on the street level only showed the inside entries at the door level and did not show anything exterior to the building. Most residents were inside, with their windows closed during winter, abandoning their balconies if lucky enough to have one.

A local resident was walking his dog around the same time as the time stamp, witnessing three men enter a black vehicle before it sped away. Unfortunately, he didn't have his long-distance glasses on to check whether the car had a registered licence plate or the make and model of the vehicle. The next step was to investigate traffic and ANPR cameras in the city for a car fleeing the scene at a similar time, which was currently being examined. The forensic officers' initial inspection confirmed that Cassandra had died from compression of the anatomical neck structures, leading to asphyxia and neuronal death. The nail placement in the kitchen assumed she was strangled while fighting against the intruder or intruders. The nails were placed in separate evidence bags for further analysis in the lab for any DNA that could be matched through the Greek and foreign databases; speculation suggested the former wouldn't bring anything relatable.

Christos's death was ruled as a fatal bullet wound to the head, and he died instantly. On initial inspection, suicide was ruled out due to the gun positioning, making it a one-in-a-billion chance for his final resting position to be like he had pulled the trigger on himself. The evidence of another party's involvement was unquestionable due to the CCTV evidence, and if bullet confirmation was that of a 9×19mm bullet, then Albanian involvement was highly probable.

Andries took longer sharing the sombre information, which was expected, before he entered with a queue of other officers, finding a free seat at the long wooden oval table. Ted watched each officer enter the room as everyone took their seat; Andries closed the door and took his position next to Ted. Everyone looked around at each other with unsteady news of new strangers and devastating new developments until Andries broke the ice within the group.

"Ted, Simon. Here are the people working alongside Daniel on the case," Andries said, stretching his arms out towards the small crowd gathered.

Ted nodded and pierced his lips together as if to smile.

"Thank you for taking time out of your working day to meet with us. First of all, I want to offer you all my deepest condolences for the deaths of Christos, his partner, Cassandra, and Daniel Belfield," Ted said.

Ted paused, watching the officer's reactions to his speech. They were straight-faced, and he grew unsure how the interaction would proceed, but he pressed on.

"I'm Ted Chester, the new ILO for Athens, and this is Simon Taylor, the senior officer in the European division. I'm under the notion you've all been notified of the current developments surrounding Daniel, Christos and his partner, Cassandra, after this morning's discovery before you came in here?"

The team nodded and said that they had been briefed in the main room by Andries. They introduced themselves to Ted and Simon as the officers working alongside Daniel to investigate corruption in the department and links to Albania OCG members over the last few months. Two members of the internal team included Superintendent Savvas Kritsikis and Detective Investigator DI Angelika Bafa. Savvas was a middle-aged man with spectacular whipped-back grey hair that would light up the darkest room and had an impressive shine as reflected off the light. Angelika was much younger—possibly around late twenties—slim and more capable of chasing criminals than Savvas, but Ted assumed he was now the brains of the department after a career of physical intervention. Angelika had long blonde hair in a ponytail, which fell at the middle of her back, built with muscle and tattoos on her short-sleeved shirt.

Hector Baros was the last person to enter the room; he was small in size, with short jet-black hair and a moustache remaining the only facial hair he had. Hector's role as police constable was a rank below Demetri Nomikos, the police major subordinate to Andries. Hector led the charge for most of the officers on the main floor of the building. He'd been in the force for seven years, working his way up from sergeant, lieutenant, and now constable, which was different in name to many police force career progressions that Ted was used to in the UK and the Netherlands.

The superintendent of the internal affairs team, Savvas, explained that Daniel had come to him about his suspicion after speaking to Andries and Hector first. Savvas explained Daniel was prompted to the conclusion when immigrants coming into the country had their documents signed off by police officers at Athens airports and some island departments such as Crete, Rhodes, and Santorini.

This intel came to light when Daniel investigated a fight in a strip club just west of the city a few months ago. It was a routine disturbance that he investigated, and upon routine documentation checks, he identified fake IDs and tracked one particular set of documentation back to Athens airport for a woman from Saudi Arabia. He worked through interviewing and investigating the other girls that night and saw similar forged documents from Georgia, Russia, Morocco, and Israel. He then privately investigated the departments in Crete and Santorini but believed the police officers had been paid off to keep quiet about it, as no one was forthcoming in his line of questioning after the document's discovery, and it was deemed an easy mistake to make. Savvas explained that Daniel initially believed it was a huge hunch but knew something mistrustful of the professionalism of some officers and came to the affairs team about it.

"Did you investigate?" Ted pushed.

"Of course, and we still are. We got close to a lead, and then Daniel was murdered, and now Christos and his girlfriend."

"What was your lead?"

Superintendent Kritisikis extended his hand across the table to Hector Baros, the police captain.

"Daniel worked closely with Christos and me. Daniel told me about someone in the department possibly paying other officers here or elsewhere to sign off fake documentation for incoming immigrants. Daniel did his investigation and came to me about it, then I told him to go to Andries about it, as my senior and then the internal affairs team. When he did, Daniel became obsessed with studying the incoming passengers to Greece who ended up in the clubs and brothels with these fake passports, tracking them to the other island's departments. He was here late at night, in the office and out investigating, too.

"The night before he was murdered, he went out to a strip club where a girl who had come from Georgia worked part-time. She tried to run, but he caught her. She works part-time at another venue in the same west city area. Daniel offered her money for information and told her he wouldn't investigate her false documents if she told him what she knew. She disclosed that she had regular visits when working at the brothel from someone she thought was a police officer. He hid with a cap and requested to turn the lights off, but she never asked him anything. She just did what he said. Her suspicion arose when she thought she saw a badge when he placed his items on one of the bedroom dressers."

"Has anyone questioned her?" Ted said.

"I wasn't aware of this," Andries interrupted.

"It was new information. Daniel gave it the day before he was murdered. We were going to investigate together, but he made me swear to keep the information to ourselves to keep the girl safe for the time being."

The room became tense—it seemed information sharing wasn't forthcoming. Ted thought Daniel might have told Hector to keep the new information secret for the present, but did Daniel do this because he suspected someone in the department or even closer to the case? Ted thought Andries's response was interesting, but he was Hector's senior—he was expected to know this intel. Ted observed Andries's annoyance, but that seemed to quickly subside.

"Okay, sure. Sorry, please continue," Andries offered.

"We're going there tonight to question her where she works; unfortunately, we don't have a home address for her," Hector replied.

"Can I come with you?" Ted said.

"Sure." So far, Ted felt unsure about the cooperation between the officers in the room.

"Did the mystery man or officer ever communicate with the girls when he visited?"

"Daniel said the girl he visited said, like, 'Do what I say, or I take you back to where you came from.'"

Ted nodded to himself rather than to Hector's statement. It confirmed if that confession was true, someone within the Greek police force was taking financial bribes from gangs to allow immigrants to enter the country, and the officer knew it and was a team player in the illegal activity.

"Would it be someone high up? Surely an officer or sergeant wouldn't have the authoritarian power to corrupt airport officers?" Simon said.

"I don't know. Money talks in many ways. Money is power. Sergeant signs off documents normally at the airports; they don't need senior figures unless told by someone senior. It could be anyone in the department or another department or location," Angelika said.

"So, what's next?" Simon replied.

"Well, we can't just go looking at everyone pointing the finger. We need to get evidence before building a case and going after someone. If it is someone in the department, the investigation may spook them. The girl at the club could be a good starting point. Why don't we go see if we can get a description of some kind?" Hector asked.

"Sure, sounds like a good start. Is there anything Daniel left regarding paperwork or information?"

"No, just what he mentioned to us. He was going to get something official over to us. Still, he never did—well he couldn't... *can't*, should I say. Sorry."

The last part of Hector's comment hit hard to those who knew him most and stopped the flow of conversation. Ted pressed on.

"So, is this everyone who knew about the investigation and those involved?" he said, searching the table.

"Yes, this is it," Hector replied.

"Well, I will need to tell the Police Director Nikolas Konstantinou, my boss, about this. I can't hide it from him. He is the head of this entire building," Andries interrupted.

"Okay, no problem. Where is he?" Ted said.

"He's helping escort government officials to Hellenic Parliament today. There are rumours of protest groups forming against the proposed Macedonia deal; he is leading the safe arrival of those visiting."

"What is the situation there with the protests?" Simon said.

"Well, I didn't want this to be a history lesson. Still, the name Macedonia has been disputed between Greece and the Republic of Macedonia for around the last twenty years. The name dispute was an issue between Belgrade and Athens. The former Yugoslavian Republic of Macedonia declared independence from Yugoslavia in 1991. Athenian citizens claim its territory of Macedonia lies across the border from FYR Macedonia. The Greeks have used the name since the times of Alexander the Great. The new proposed agreement of FYR Macedonia to North Macedonia is controversial for Greeks because it uses the same name as a neighbouring region in northern Greece, if that makes sense?"

"Sure," Ted responded.

"So possible protests. Will this affect our task force size?" Simon said.

"Possibly—we have the Army on standby, too, for the protests, but we would want to keep this investigation as small as possible. We don't want other officers risked."

"Of course."

"I know we can't have additional forces for the investigation. But do we have protection for everyone in this room?" Ted said.

"Protection?" Angelika queried.

"Yes. We have three people dead because of this. It seems to me whoever they are, they're not going to stop if it means uncovering their whole operation or the officers involved," Ted responded, looking at Savvas and Andries as he spoke.

Ted was concerned for the officers involved, although knowing Simon and himself were now deep-rooted in the investigation, he knew his life could be at risk, something he didn't know before accepting the transfer and leaving his family at Schipol Airport.

"I will speak with the police director when I see him about what we can do, but for now, I'd suggest working in pairs, never alone, and make sure you lock your doors at night," he said with a serious face directed at everyone in the room. The room nodded silently.

"What time does this club open where the women worked?" Ted continued.

Andries caught eyes with Ted before his gaze was distracted by another officer.

"I'll have a look," Hector said.

Hector picked out his phone, worked the keypad, and waited a few seconds before confirming eight o'clock as its opening time. Ted looked at his sports watch and saw it had just turned midday. Before visiting the girl at the club, there was plenty of time to investigate other routes.

"Did he give a name for the female worker?" Ted asked.

"No, he didn't."

Ted nodded to himself. Daniel wouldn't have wanted her name passed to anyone in the department, even those he trusted. Ted asked the question to see if anyone would slip with her name, but no one was triggered. Everyone in that room was a suspect in Ted's eyes, and maybe even some who weren't in the boardroom. Daniel's secrecy gave the investigation its living breath, even though Daniel had lost his.

"Well, we have time to plan. Like Hector said, the club doesn't open until eight; we have other lines of enquiry," Simon added.

"We could visit the music venue and see the forensic pictures to see if you can get another angle. They have CCTV running there and here in the office. The officers seized evidence through the night and early this morning," Andries said.

"Yes, please. We will review the CCTV there. Will forensic reports be back from Daniel, Christos, and Cassandra by then?" Ted said.

"Like I said, they're a top priority. I can take you to the music venue, and we will see if they're back by the time we return."

"I'll come, too," Simon said.

"Very well. I'll see if I can get hold of the director or leave a message before we go from my office about your protection request," Andries said as he rose from his chair to exit the boardroom.

Ted turned his attention to the internal affairs team.

"Do you need anything from us at the moment?" Ted said.

The superintendent let out a large breath before he replied.

"Just keep us in the loop. But my advice... I'd just say, be careful, Ted."

Ted didn't know whether to take the statement as advice or a threat, so he just nodded to play along. Ted had to be open with himself and suggest that no stone was unturned and no person was left out of the suspect pool. Even if that meant being cautious with information to the police deputy director, Hector, or the internal affairs team involved in the initial corruption investigation. Ted didn't want to be sat in the boardroom another minute longer. He wanted to get out of the building and see where Daniel Belfield's last moments were before he was murdered.

Chapter 10

ANDRIES, TED, AND SIMON rode in one vehicle to the music venue, which held five thousand ravers only a few nights ago. Although this time, it was abandoned as it once was when its clothing company owners ceased to trade many years ago. They had driven East of Athens towards a city quarter in Vyronas called Kareas. Just off one of the main roads through the area was a track that led to a disused industrial area with multiple warehousing units. One of which was now hired out to hold huge music venues. Andries explained on the drive over that Daniel was a huge house and dance music fan. Daniel spoke with the officers about his experiences at Warehouse Project in Manchester and one of his favourite artists, Duke Dumont, who played on the night he was shot. The attendance wasn't just random; it was a birthday present from his girlfriend, who was also in attendance.

Ted asked how Daniel's partner, Joanne, was coping and discussed interviewing her after visiting the venue. Andries said he would contact the team back at the station to reach out to her to arrange for this afternoon if she felt up to it. She was waiting in Athens for the police to release the body before she and Daniel's body returned home to England and his family.

They arrived outside the warehouse, where they were greeted by a man as they exited the vehicles. It was a young security police officer who was guarding the facility. On approach, Andries spoke to the man in Greek, and the security officer lifted the police tape so the three men could duck underneath it to access the interior. They navigated through a long tunnel-like corridor that still had its separative metal barriers, presumably to create a queuing system. Once the barriers ended, open doors led into a big hall with various stages and drinks bars.

"It's through the back here," Andries continued. "There's an even bigger area for the main acts, where Daniel was found."

They made their way through the first main hall, Ted feeling a chill in the air as he manoeuvred through. The cold January season for Greece lingered in the city after the blizzard-like ice and storm just a month ago. The heap of snow was still on the roofs of buildings and the grounds of unkempt houses and facilities around the city. Although, that was soon to disappear with a January heat wave on the horizon in the upcoming days.

As they entered the main hall, a large, padded cover was on the right, creating a wall draped across a large metal barrier-type fence. When the room opened into an enormous empty space beyond the drapes, various concrete pillars held up the roof. Adjacent to the open space was the view from the DJ stage, complete with a large stage from the padded metal fences that created a safe space for its acts between their sets for the ravers. The stage was empty and gave an eerie feeling that roamed around the venue's atmosphere from the night of the shooting.

"He was found just over here," Andries added as they followed.

Approaching the area around seventy yards away from the stage, almost in central view, they saw four small yellow signs with the numbers three, four, five, and six. There were red stains on the concrete floor where blood had not drained but evaporated most of its moisture.

"So, the body was found here, I presume. What else did they find?" Simon said.

Andries held a green file that he opened, unclicking the binder in the middle and lifting out a photograph. The forensic photo contained an image of Daniel lying on the floor in the exact spot they were observing. Ted felt harrowed by the photograph depicting Daniels's dead body, lying flat on his back with both arms resting on either side of his head. The four yellow signs were also on the photo after the forensic officers placed them, preserving the spots where the evidence came to rest. Ted took the photograph and held it before him. Andries was standing over the yellow signs as he narrated the findings in the photograph.

"Three was where the blood accumulated as it exited from the wound. Four was a small trace of gunpowder which was found by forensics. Five was a spatter of blood, which we've confirmed was from Daniel and no one else. Lastly, six was a small strand of wool that they found. They're still working on it for any DNA fibres, but we will see if we get a match on our system; we may need to go wider if it's the Albanian Mafia, as we will probably not have them on our system. One of the witnesses didn't see the shots happen but thought he saw someone with a wool face covering walking through before the shooting, maybe our mystery man in a balaclava."

"He didn't see a face?"

"He said he was very drunk when he saw it happen. He only remembered because the guy pushed past and knocked his drink. But the witness said he definitely had a mask on. Most of the ravers were probably high off God knows what aswell."

"Okay, anything else?" Ted asked.

"As I said before, the gunpowder and bullet came from the Beretta."

"The connection between the Beretta and the Albanians is strong then?"

"It is, but I'm not sure we can trace it."

"And if the witnesses saw nothing, and if the wool strand doesn't show anything, we're pretty much stuck here," Ted said, defeated, searching the venue for anything interesting.

"Indeed. That's where we are," Andries said as he placed his hands on his waist.

"Can we check the CCTV?"

"Of course," Andries said, standing up straight. "I think it's going to be our best bet if we can get the shooting and exit timing and possibly track anything on the ANPR out on the main roads."

"Did you view it already?"

"We did at the office last night, but we couldn't spot anything on the footage, as it was pandemonium a few minutes after the shooting, with large amounts leaving simultaneously. No one leaves before the mass exodus happens."

Ted and Simon still wanted to witness the CCTV and give another set of eyes. Even to confirm what had already been authenticated. They made their way back into the first initial hall of the warehouse complex. A set of temporary scaffolding steps led to a large container of rooms running across a gangway with makeshift offices. The police had taken the memory card containing the night's CCTV back to the station, but the CCTV was saved onto the computer's hard drive, making it accessible for the officers in attendance. Ted hit the power button on the screen and navigated his way through the home page and multiple files until he found the initial CCTV footage. The files were in Greek, and Ted relied on Andries's finger movements to select the correct files.

"When were the gunshots reported around?" Ted said.

"We had initial reports of 11:40 PM, some said 11:45 PM and some close to midnight on our interviews, but we had the time stamp at around 11:46 or 47," Andries said.

"I'll run the tapes from 11:35 PM and see what we get," Ted said.

Ted let the tape run through the first time and saw a view of security guards patrolling the front gates on-screen. There wasn't much happening apart from conversations between the guards. One or two groups of people entered the complex, arriving late for entry, but were let in after showing their tickets on a mobile device. The time stamp reached 11:47 PM when some of the spectators from the event hurriedly made their way through the doors. Ted continued to let the tape play as multiple groups surged towards the exit doors, with security guards confused and becoming frantic with the predicament.

"We can't tell who's who here. Even if we had a description, it's hard to see from the back of people's heads," Simon said.

"What do you propose? We've looked at the video a few times and can't tell Zeus from Zeus," Andries said.

Ted paused the feed and lifted his right hand, resting his chin upon it and rubbing his stubbled beard.

"I'm going to play it again and let it run. See if the second go brings anything new to the frame."

He clicked on the rewind button at the bottom of the screen, rewinding it back to 11:35 PM, and then pressed play. Ted wasn't sure if anything new would be caught on the second viewing, but it was worth a shot. He believed he was focusing slightly too much on the exit and the guards loitering. He kept his eyes on the bottom of the screen for if someone came into view as they walked from the long walkway. The time was 11:44:56 PM, and Ted noticed a rapid movement from the bottom of the screen and clicked pause. This caused Simon and Andries to lean forward more intently at Ted's actions.

"What did you see?" Simon said.

"Look here," Ted said as a surge of adrenaline entered his body.

Ted hovered the mouse at the bottom of the screen and clicked on the live time bar, dragging the footage back a few seconds. Even ever so slightly, the screen showed the figure of a man. A man's head came into the shot on the tape and sharply returned to where it had come from, moving back out of the image. The man was only in the video briefly, but it was a new investigative angle.

"Who do you think he is?" Andries said.

"Could be no one, but could be someone?" Ted said.

"What's he doing?"

"I'll play it again and see if we can get a cleaner visual of his face on the turn, but it will be difficult. Is there CCTV on the fire exit by the toilets?"

"No, but we have CCTV at the front of the building showing the front yard. There is a passageway from the fire exit that joins a side exit into the yard, though. What are you thinking?"

"Do we have the feed for the other exit?"

"It's back at the station."

Ted banged his fist on the table in frustration. Ted replayed the feed, moving the time frame bar back every time the man appeared.

"I can't get a visual on his face. He's smart and keeps his head down."

"What are you thinking?"

"If this is our man. Maybe he knows there is a camera there and turns back to use the other exit, which may camouflage him."

"Or maybe he forgot to take a piss?" Simon said.

"Maybe."

"Did anyone see this man on the outside footage?"

Andries shook his head.

"I don't think so. I think if he was outside, it may have been with a rush of people and hid him from our suspicions."

Ted nodded at the response and pondered at the screen a little longer, but knew there was nothing further to discuss. He was anxious to look at other footage quickly and wondered if Joanne would be willing to speak with him about Daniel's activities. Ted turned to ask Andries if he had any updates on the matter.

"I'll call to see if Joanne got back to us," Andries replied.

"Thank you. I'll shut this off now and meet you out front."

Andries made his way out of the office and down to the ground level to make the call back to the station regarding Joanne. Ted rewound the tape to a blurred, uncovered face. Ted grabbed his phone and opened his camera to take a picture of the person.

"What are you thinking, Ted? I can see your brain going," Simon said.

"Can you?" Ted said, rubbing his forehead.

"Yeah, are you okay?"

"I'm fine. Why?"

"I just worry about you. You've been through a lot recently. This isn't an easy job; you're constantly moving, and sometimes that breaks down family relationships and emotions are affected by the job—I need you sharp, Ted. The first job in, and you've already seen a lot, that's why we got you that time off after you finished in Timişoara. I'm here to help, but if you need more, I'm sure they will have a counsellor here to talk to."

"I'm fine, Simon, don't worry about me. We've got a job to do."

"I know, but listen, Ted. I haven't told you this before, but I didn't really want to, but I was stationed in Sudan in 2002 after being stationed in Europe for a few years before that. I was there when there was the Darfur genocide. I witnessed the devastation of what happened and needed serious counselling once I finished posting there. I kept it inside until I finished my posting, breaking down on the plane home to England. It's best to talk, Ted—it's the best thing I ever did."

"Thanks, Simon, I'll think about it."

"Thanks, Ted, promise me you will."

Simon rose from his seat and tapped Ted on the shoulder, holding his hand still in that position. Ted nodded back at him and perched to a standing position to follow Simon out. Ted pondered for a few seconds about support on the nightmares he was experiencing during sleep. Instantly pushing those needs to the side and concentrating on the case, he followed Simon out of the control room, focusing on his next move to keep his mind off the terrors that haunted him.

Chapter 11

THEY RODE BACK IN Andries's car, discussing the man in the video and the next moves in the investigation. Andries confirmed that Joanne would be available and could make her way to the station voluntarily this afternoon to be reinterviewed by Ted. Andries offered to stop at nearby van vendors selling delicious Greek gyros with various fillings. Although hungry, they thanked him for the offer but decided to get back to the station to view the tapes and interview Joanne promptly; then they would think about food. The day would be one that would extend into the night, with the visit to the club scheduled later.

As they entered the war room, Eliana announced from her desk that Joanne was waiting in one of the interview rooms. Ted was surprised by Joanne's eagerness to attend the station, which caught him off guard; he thought he would have some time to review the CCTV footage first. Ted would leave that to Simon and Andries initially, and Ted didn't want Joanne waiting for too long.

"I'm going to go in," Ted said, turning to Simon.

"Need me to come in?" Simon said.

"I'll speak with her—she's probably spoken to many people already. You two review the tape."

"Don't worry, I'll have a look now with Andries."

Simon walked off down the hallway, while Ted reached for his phone and sent Simon a message that contained the picture of the man he saw on CCTV to cross-reference. Ted explained they would need to start the tape from 11:35 PM again like they did with the front exit. If the same man came out from the fire exit passageway shortly after he was spotted initially, it could have been possible that he didn't want to be spotted on CCTV and was indeed involved. As Ted clicked the send button and observed the grainy picture of the man, he noticed he wore a black jacket, although its fabric couldn't be determined. He had black hair and a pale complexion, and Ted caught one side of his face on his turn. His eyes looked so menacing and evil, though blurred. Ted's gaze was interrupted as Eliana stood up from her desk and asked who was conducting the interview with Joanne. Ted confirmed he would and followed her down the corridor to one of the interview rooms.

"How is she?" Ted asked as he moved towards her direction.

"As expected, in shock still. I'd warn you to go easy on her. She has been through a lot, you know," she replied as she led the way.

"Of course, thank you, Eliana," Ted said, smiling at her.

She returned the smile and asked if Ted wanted a coffee for the interview as they walked through the corridor towards the interview suites. He had missed breakfast and declined lunch, so he needed the caffeine as fuel to be ready for the interview with Joanne. He accepted the request and asked for milk, no sugar. Eliana said she would be a few minutes, left Ted at the interview door, and informed him Joanne was already nursing a freshly made cup.

Upon entry, he saw she was already sitting in a chair behind the table for interviewing suspects. He could understand the difficult scenario and environment may not help her, so he wanted to feel comfortable with her in some way first.

She was small, and her long hair reached just below her shoulders. It had been half-brushed, but there was no effort in maintaining it. She wore an open puffer jacket with a grey hoodie underneath. It was clearly visible that she had been crying due to the eyeliner smears, and the accompaniment of used white tissues on the desk confirmed that.

"Afternoon, I'm Ted Chester. Thank you for coming in on the short notice. I'm here to help with the investigation regarding Daniel." He extended a hand as a welcome.

She returned the gesture, and they shook hands across the metal table.

"You're English?" Joanne said, shocked but seemingly more at ease.

"Yes, I'm here investigating with the Athens department. Another officer and I are from England and are here helping with the investigation. I know you've had multiple people interview and question you about what happened that night. I'm sorry, but I will need to ask you a few more questions and update you on the investigation from this morning, if that's okay?"

Joanne nodded as she took a sip from her drink.

"First of all, I'm sorry for your loss. I know you sitting in this environment again doesn't help when processing what's happened either."

Joanne took another sip from her drink and didn't respond. There was a knock on the door, and Ted instructed the person to enter. It was Eliana holding a cardboard cup with fresh coffee inside. Ted collected the cup, and as she exited the door, Ted noticed her scrunch up her face as if she was in pain as she closed it behind her. Ted was confused by Eliana's actions but returned to his seat and faced Joanne again.

"I know you've probably gone over questions like, *What did you see?* or *Do you remember seeing anyone?* and the like... so, I will update you on what we have this morning, unless you've got anything new to share with me today?"

"No, sorry. Like I said, I just remember seeing him on the floor when he fell. It all happened so fast, you know? I looked around, but all I saw were people still dancing and smiling, and most hadn't even noticed what had happened."

"Right, yes, I understand."

"Do you?"

It caught Ted off guard. He attempted to comfort her, but he had no logical clue about loss or grief; he hadn't experienced it in his lifetime from a personal perspective. They both locked eyes. The initial comment brought a serious tone to the glance, but it slowly faded as both understood the nature of the situation.

"You're right, I don't. But I understand how you may feel and the emotions behind it."

"Sorry. I shouldn't have said that."

"Don't worry. No need to apologise," Ted replied, waving it off.

"What's the update? Have you found who did this?" she said, pointing her finger at the table.

"No, we haven't found who has done this yet. However, we have found someone of interest that we wish to speak with. May I show you a picture on my phone?"

"Sure."

Ted reached into his jeans pocket and brought out his phone. He saw a message from Rose on the screen, which he would respond to later. He opened his photo file and enlarged the photo of the man from the CCTV. He turned the phone around and placed it flat on the table before her.

"It's not the best picture, and I know you said you didn't see anyone, but do you recognise this person?"

She studied the photo and shook her head.

"Sorry, I don't."

"It's okay, don't worry. I wasn't expecting you to."

"Is this who you think killed Daniel?"

"We're not sure. From the incident, we had a loose time frame of 11:35 PM to 11:50 PM. We watched the tape from the front entrance, and shortly after, we saw the first person walk towards the exit. He turned back, which is captured in this picture. About a minute later, the hordes of people exit the venue. We want to know who he is—it's just a hunch at this stage."

She continued to study the picture and started to nod.

"He must have done it," she said, picking up another tissue and wiping her tears.

"We are not sure. If he was involved, he might have been one of several people involved, or he may have been alone. Or this may not even be the person. However, we currently have two officers who I've been working with this morning studying the outdoor cameras."

Her face was leaned downwards as she wiped her tears.

Ted continued. "I want to ask, do you know where the toilets are in the main hall? Did you notice a fire exit?"

Her head lifted towards Ted.

"Yeah, people went out there to smoke. I grabbed some air for a few minutes before the main act came, and we both did. It was cold, but when you were inside, it was warm, thousands of bodies near you."

"What time did you go out to smoke?"

"I'm not sure, maybe an hour before Duke Dumont came on."

"Which was?"

"He came on at eleven, so maybe ten?"

"Okay, thank you."

"Why?"

"We will review the footage and see if we can spot you two. Then look for anything suspicious."

"You think we were being followed all night!"

Ted lifted his hand to calm her down after her outburst.

"We can't confirm that. Still, anything is possible."

Joanne looked down at the table, searching for the words to speak. Ted noticed the life was exiting from her body as they spoke; he needed to finish the interview, but he had a few remaining questions.

"I won't be much longer, Joanne. Did the fire exit lead out towards the front of the warehouse?"

"Yeah, it did."

"Well, the other officers are checking the CCTV to see if this man exited that way shortly after. We think he may have known CCTV was at the main entrance and backtracked to find another exit."

Ted took his first sip of coffee, injecting that much-needed caffeine into his bloodstream. He was unsure how to change the interview angle without repeating the same questions, avoiding unnecessary stress, but he needed something else from her.

"Did Daniel tell you what he was working on?"

"He didn't."

"Nothing at all? If he did, I need to know."

"No, he didn't."

"Okay, no problem," Ted replied, feeling compelled to press on, and he did. "Joanne, I can't tell you everything—I shouldn't. However, the reason why I was desperate to speak with you is that there has been another victim or victims this morning, which we believe is connected to Daniel and what he was investigating."

"Oh, God, who?" she said, holding her hands up to her face.

"Do you know Christos Masouras and his partner Cassandra?"

Joanne removed her hands and shook her head.

"Christos is... *was* a police sergeant with the department and worked with Daniel."

"He kept his work and home life separate—well, from me anyway."

"Okay. I'm only telling you this so you understand if you knew anything Daniel knew, you could be a threat."

"To who?"

"We don't know at this time. We are investigating."

She was shaking her head in disbelief. It looked like she was fighting back the tears of anger that were building up behind her eyes.

"When will I be able to go back home with him?"

"I will update you as soon as we get the forensics back from the lab. They are with Daniel now, and he is a priority."

There was a knock on the door. Ted momentarily rose from his chair and excused himself before exiting the room. Simon and Andries were in the hallway, returning from viewing the CCTV viewing.

"How is she?" Simon said.

"As expected. What you got?"

"We viewed the CCTV from outside. Started the tapes at 11:44:56 PM from when the man retraced his steps back into the venue. Around 11:47, we saw the first people coming from the main entrance below the exterior CCTV. However, at around 11:46, we saw the same man exiting in the distance where the opening from the smoker's area opens out into the industrial quarters."

"It's him?"

"Yeah, it's him. We took CCTV from the smoker's area and saw the same man walking away about thirty seconds after we first saw him enter the shot at the entrance, then turn back again. We've contacted the other warehouse facilities to see if we can access their CCTV to see how he gets away from the location."

"We missed him last time because we didn't see him at the front camera entrance," Andries added.

"Great. Also, could you check the smoker's area from around ten o'clock? Joanne said she went outside to the smoker's area to get some air. Maybe see if anyone suspicious is following them both."

"Okay, will do," Andries said.

"I'm going to update Joanne on this and let her go. Could we have someone follow her as she drives home, so she gets home safe?" Ted said.

"I'll get Police Sergeant Krystabelle to see her home," Andries said.

"Thanks."

Simon and Andries headed back towards the video room as Ted held his hand on the interview door before entering. He felt a slight kick of energy flow through him, and he wasn't sure if it was the instant coffee he had drunk starting to take effect. Although, he knew it was a much-needed kick-start in the investigation. Ted knew Joanne would be safe on her return home with Kyrstabelle watching over her, but Ted knew he was alone for now.

Chapter 12

TED FINISHED THE INTERVIEW with Joanne and told her she would receive protection from a police follower on her drive home but reiterated that her life wasn't in danger. Although Ted felt guilt about the promise, he couldn't guarantee that statement because of Cassandra's fate. Left alone in the hallway, Ted took out his phone to read his wife's message and replied.

We are back at my mum's now. How's Athens? X

Glad you're back safe. How are the kids? It's a busy case x

They're good. They're doing well studying from home, but I am happy to be back in England. I think they want to stay here for a while x

Okay, we will talk about it when you return. Keep Safe x

Okay, love you x

Love you too x

A surge of anxiety built up in his chest like a knot getting tighter and tighter with every thought. He opened his lungs, took a large breath for a few seconds, held it, then exhaled slowly out of his nose. He did this several times in the corridor, allowing his thoughts to be submerged and controlled. Suddenly he stopped when he heard footsteps behind him from another officer walking past the junction for another corridor. He took a forward step inside the long hallway and continued moving towards the main room. Eliana popped up from her chair behind the desk when he entered the main room.

"How was she?" Eliana said.

"She was okay. We gave her some updates on the investigation, but I feel she didn't know any more from what she told officers originally. Could you do me a favour unless you're busy?"

"Yeah, sure, I was just filing these reports."

"Firstly, are you okay? I saw you look uncomfortable when you left us with the coffee before?"

"I'm fine, yeah, it's nothing."

"Sure?"

"Yeah. What was it you need me to do?"

"Do you have social media?"

"You want to be my friend or something?"

"Nothing like that. Have you got Twitter or Instagram?"

"Yeah... but why?"

Ted sat on the edge of her desk, looking down at her as she sat down again. She was looking up at him, intrigued by his approach. She had green eyes, which he became fixated on before breaking away from them and pointing at her personal phone on her desk.

"I need you to search social media for the other night at the music venue. I'm sure pictures of the body will have been posted on the internet. We can look for that, but I'm more interested if there are videos of the music to see if we can catch anything. Do you know if that's been done already?"

"Well, I'm not on this case of yours, am I? So, I'm not sure if it's been looked over."

"You can be on the case if you want to, unofficially for now. You were there at Christos's apartment. I saw you were upset..."

Eliana's eyes wandered across the room and down by her side.

"You want justice, right?" Ted pressed.

"Yeah," she said with her arms folded, but her eyes were searching for something still. He thought about his response and also the decision he was making. Bringing her into the investigation was another life on the edge of danger. However, he couldn't do this all alone. It was risk either way; she joined the investigation, and the OCG knew, or she was a part of the OCG's task force.

"Listen, I don't trust anyone yet, so take me trusting you any way you want, but I could do with your help..."

"And why do you trust me?"

"I don't know yet. But if anyone officially questions you first, you can either say I asked you or say you did it on your own instinct and get the praise?"

"Okay, fine, boss. I never get much praise, so let's go with that."

"Thanks, let me know how it goes."

"Am I looking for anything specific?"

Ted stared at Eliana as she waited for a response. He wondered whether he should mention the mystery man. He reached for his phone and looked around the room to ensure no one was nearby.

"You're looking for a man."

"The suspect?"

"Maybe," Ted said, navigating his phone screen.

Ted opened the photo of the man on the CCTV footage and showed Eliana; she studied it and lifted her head back up to Ted.

"Can I send this to you?" he asked.

"Sure, I'll give you my number."

She worked his phone and sent the message to herself, even creating a new contact called Eliana.

"Thanks; see if you can find him in the footage," Ted asked.

Ted manoeuvred back towards the corridor, and entered where Andries and Simon were reviewing the outdoor surveillance of the industrial area.

"Anything?" Ted asked.

"Nothing. We have looked at several different feeds from the facility units. We all see people moving through these different avenues toward the main road after the gunshot. Still, we don't see that man," Andries announced.

"He may have gone a different way?"

"Possibly, but we don't see him," Simon said with defeat in his tone.

"However, we checked the main roads after the shooting. There is a petrol station that we will retrieve footage from today; maybe it sees somebody exit there."

Ted nodded, but more to mask his disappointment. He told Joanne they had something from the CCTV footage, but it seemed it was fruitless and undermined the hope he had given her. Andries turned in his seat to face Ted to give a different route to their conversation.

"I should have an update on the forensics this afternoon with Daniel. If we are all cleared up, we can release the body. Still waiting on updates from Christos and Cassandra, too; they shouldn't be too long after."

Ted nodded at the information, which gave him some hope. The room fell silent before Ted proceeded.

"Eliana. She good?" he said as he sat down on the empty chair, straddling the seat rather than the standard customed approach to sitting.

"Er, yeah, why?" Andries said.

"Eliana just said she was going to search social media to see if she could spot anything different on the night. Using people's posts and videos to see if it gives us anything new."

"Shouldn't she be filing reports?"

"Yeah, but she knows what's happening and seems a good detective. Let us see what she finds."

"Okay, well, I'm..."

Ted raised his hands to protest and reject any disagreement that may come.

"She said it; I didn't ask her. Don't worry, I'm not telling your officers what to do," Ted lied.

Andries relaxed again as he built up an argument and settled himself.

"Very well. Nikolas isn't going to be happy. He doesn't want too many officers on this case."

"Well, we don't need to tell him yet."

Andries gave Ted a look of *Don't get me into trouble*, but ended with a nod of approval.

Ted stood from his straddled position.

"Can we go to the strip club earlier and see if anyone is around? We are kind of sitting here doing nothing," Ted said.

"We can, yes; maybe we could catch the owner. We can grab food on the way—you two haven't eaten yet?" Andries replied.

"That would be good," Simon said.

"Yeah, I don't think I can last on brown liquid for much longer," Ted said.

"The club is about thirty minutes away, just west of the city. I know a place on the way near Pedion tou Areos, a city park that does great souvlaki. You tried it before?" Andries said.

"Yeah, love anything Greek," Ted said.

"Let's go. I'll grab Hector, too," Andries said as he stood from his seat and lifted his coat from the back.

"Hector?" Ted asked.

"Yeah, why not?"

Ted paused for a few seconds before nodding. Andries smiled back at Ted.

"Let's go; this is my treat."

On the drive over, Andries and Hector talked deeply about the loss of their officer, Christos. They explained to Ted and Simon that Christos had been in the force for three years, starting as a voluntary officer and then a probation officer, before joining as a police sergeant. Andries explained Christos had a bright career ahead of him and would be deeply missed by all in the department.

The forensic reports were priorities for Christos, Cassandra, and Daniel, and jumping the queue from civilians' deaths remained unanswered in the city. Andries rang the laboratory on the ride to Pedion tou Areos to press the urgency. The chief medical officer Kostas Basinas explained they were finishing their reports this afternoon on Daniel. At the time of the call, Kostas had pulled away from the final stages of Christos and Cassandra's autopsy. Andries, eager for an update, pressed Kostas for any update he could provide. Kostas determined that Daniel and Christos's deaths were down to 9×19mm bullets, possibly from a Beretta Px4 as the first assumption. The bullets taken from the bodies didn't include any further discovery.

Although disappointed, Kostas explained that unless the shooter carved his name into the bullet for the police to find, they wouldn't be able to trace it back. Other forensic experts were observing if the cases recovered at the scenes included fingerprints deposited during loading, but nothing was showing on the shell. Kostas further gave a professional opinion on the positioning of Christos's body as it concerned suicide as a cause of death. Kostas quickly dismissed the cause and agreed there was no possibility that the positioning of the body and the gun would be deemed good enough for death by suicide verdict. He further explained that the gun must have been planted after his death and he was shot by a third party.

"Now, Cassandra..."

"Sorry to interrupt. Hector here—I have a quick question."

There was quiet over the Bluetooth device.

"Sure, go ahead," Kostas finally stated. "Would you exclude the possibility of Cassandra killing Christos and then killing herself?"

Ted looked at Hector sitting on his right of the back passenger section, screwed his face and then glanced towards the Bluetooth device for an answer.

"I'm just thinking of alternatives. Maybe money issues at home or an argument," Hector added.

Hector had been at the apartment and seen the bodies' positioning. Ted was confused as to why he had the theory behind his questioning. Although thinking longer about his question, he understood why he may have asked it to clarify the situation, for if and when it went to court.

"I've been doing this for ten years, sir. Of course, I've thought about it, but I didn't mention it because I would disagree. It's impossible."

Hector slumped back into his car seat, embarrassed on observation. Ted pondered on Kostas's response about watching too much TV. Convicting criminals wasn't something Ted was knowledgeable in. Still, he'd seen a series about an American defence lawyer who worked in the back seat of his car, using manipulative tactics to distract and discredit the prosecutor's cases.

"What about Cassandra?" Andries regained the expert's attention.

"Yes. Cassandra, as I just mentioned, did not kill Christos, in my opinion. She could not fracture her larynx to cause these life-threatening injuries herself. If she had managed to do it with another object, that object would have been near her body, and she wouldn't have been able to breathe, as the direct impact caused a break in her voice box, giving her only a few minutes of air remaining. Whoever did this was not found in the apartment."

The car rode silently as they increasingly got closer to their pitstop. The information explained was known to the team; their theories matched Kostas's and the initial observations. However, hearing them officially from a professional made the destruction and the evil act much more real.

"Do you have any more for us?" Andries asked.

"I always leave the best till last. You should know that."

"What have you got?"

"Well, we examined the fingernails in the apartment, and that's where my third-party involvement comes in. DNA revealed Cassandra and a little bit of Christos ever so slightly. There was DNA under the nail, where Cassandra may have fought back against her attacker, scratching him. We gently took the DNA under the fingernails for DNA typing with sufficient care. However, we didn't find a match on the Greek system, but I recommend you send it out further afield once you get my report. Also..."

"Great news," Andries said.

The atmosphere inside the vehicle was electrified, even awakening Hector from his embarrassment.

"Did you examine the fabric found at the music venue?" Ted continued.

"Also! As I said, we found a match," Kostas finished.

"A match?" Ted pressed.

"The fabric inside the music venue matched DNA inside the apartment. If I believe from memory, it was something they brushed off a glass container in the kitchen."

"Same as under the nails?"

"No, it wasn't. A different set of DNA. Like I said, I'll send you my report as soon as I finish."

"Okay, thank you."

"You need anything else?"

"Thanks, Kostas—that's all for now."

"No problem, I'm going to go back now and stitch them up."

Andries disconnected the call.

"Seems nice," Simon said.

"I know; but he is good at his job, so they can keep paying him," Andries said.

The vehicle started to drift towards the pedestrian walkway and decreased in speed.

"Are we stopping?" Ted said.

Andries turned in his seat to look at the back section.

"Food time."

Once they arrived, they sat inside the small restaurant just by the city park entrance. It was a small but locally run food business called Tēniakó. The wooden tables were lined with plastic red and white coverings. It wasn't busy approaching the limbo period between lunch and dinner at 3:35 PM. Simon and Andries ordered the lamb souvlaki with a side of fries. Ted and Hector opted for the chicken version with a side of halloumi fries, and all opted for the water to accompany their drinks. The food was inhaled shortly after being brought to them at the table.

The case had moved fast from this morning's arrival at the office that they barely had time to stop and refuel, and it was a welcomed relief. Andries talked about his three sons and the current progress of a messy divorce he was going through with his wife of ten years. Simon diverted from the conversation and asked Ted about the current case in Amsterdam.

"You heard anything from your people at Europol about the case in The Hague?" Simon said.

"No, Luuk would call me when he had an update on the trial," Ted said as he finished his water.

"Fingers crossed," Simon said.

"Is this the Timișoara case?" Andries said, breaking his attention.

Ted hesitated, "Yeah, it is—how did you know?"

"How did I know? It's in the news. But I read about it when it all went down in Timișoara, saving all those girls, the pursuit in Budapest Park. Wow! That's a major case; you should have said you were involved! Looks like we have a celebrity here!" Andries said, looking around to catch the diner's attention.

Ted went red in embarrassment but remained straight-faced. He tried to seek Simon's attention to sarcastically say thanks.

"I didn't mention it because I don't think it was relevant to the case."

"Sure," Andries said with stretched arms.

"There were many people involved in that case, equally as important as me or each other," Ted said, placing his hands on the table. He continued.

"Also, it's an ongoing investigation, so we can't be talking about it. None of the officers' names are released, so please keep this to yourself, even my name."

"No problem," Andries said, raising his hands in defence.

"Sorry, you know how it is."

"No, I understand. But if we have you on this team, we have a chance with this case, right? We've had officers here and probably across Europe talk about this officer who cannot be named—Ted Chester—who led the pursuit through Europe to catch the gang, and you did it. Never been done before on such a large scale."

Embarrassed about the praise, Ted just returned a nod.

"You have Simon, too, yourself and other officers who want justice for Daniel—that's all that matters. The case I did last year was made harder by a mole in the police force, and we seem to have the same here as Daniel suspects, so I'm treading cautiously with the information I gather."

"How did you get the mole in your last case?" Hector said.

"A hunch, something wasn't right after the first operation in Amsterdam. But I had the wrong guy all along. I got the right guy when he got desperate, but I connected the dots before it was too late."

Andries nodded before smiling, as if holding something.

"You saved one of our local girls, you know, Ted?" Andries said." One of them was from here?"

"Yeah, she was called Alexia. Went on holiday with her family to Budapest for a few days to visit their Hungarian grandmother. She went with her sister, too, and the sisters went to a club on a Friday night. Simzpla Kert, I think it's called? Her sister escaped from two men who got Alexia out in the street. Then a few days later, you found her in Timişoara. We'd only started contacting the authorities in Hungary, and then she was found."

"How is Alexia?" Ted said.

"She is good. Her parents like to update us from time to time. She always asked to thank the people who saved her in person. But of course, I knew there was some block on information and said if we could, we'd let her know."

"I'm glad she is doing well," Ted smiled.

Ted felt a warm embrace from within him, hearing about Alexia's story and recovery. Although he did remember the few names that would remain in his mind for a long time, Alexia escaped him from Timişoara, probably because he knew she had made it.

"Shall we go?" Andries offered to Ted as he stared out on the street.

They raised from their seats, leaving the empty plates on the table.

"Efcharistó!" Andries shouted to the old man behind the counter.

"Ta léme sýntoma afentikó," the man replied.

They reached the car, which was parked outside the restaurant.

"What did he say back to you?" Ted said, holding his hand on the door handle.

"See you soon, boss," Andries said as he opened the car.

Chapter 13

THEY ARRIVED AT THE strip club building in the western part of
Athens, in the neighbourhood of Gazi. Gazi-centred industrial
and gasworks buildings with contemporary art spaces and concert
venues for indie and jazz music, quintessential tavernas, global eateries,
and independent bars and clubs. They exited the vehicle, taking in the
building's exterior, which displayed a black wooden frame above its
old brickwork depicting two LED-shaped girls dancing on a pole, with
Toys Strip Club in bold white lights in the middle of both.

They reached the front door, which was locked when Ted reached
the handle to open it. Understandably, the opening hours for customers were eight o'clock in the evening, and it was just after four. Ted
looked up under the archway where the door was situated. There was
a CCTV camera, and he pointed it out to Andries to raise his badge.
Ted knocked on the door loudly and waited a few seconds. A ruffle of
noises came from behind the door, the metal turn of the lock clicked,
and the door opened ajar.

Ted saw a man balding from the crown of his head through the
crack. He was around forty to fifty years old with a tanned complexion. He spoke Greek to Ted, who stepped back to allow Andries to
communicate with the man. They talked to each for ten to twenty
seconds, not in a confrontational tone, but very content throughout.
The man nodded and opened the door for the officers to enter the

premises. Upon entering the premises, the man locked the door be-hind them with a key. The balding man moved ahead as they walked through a darkened hallway that led to another set of doors.

Within the hallway was a tall chair with a raised single platform that looked to be where a person would greet anyone who entered the premises. A money box was resting on the platform's top, and a notebook was presumably used for entrance fee records. The man opened the second set of doors where music was played—*Doja Cat, Candy*. When Ted whispered to Andries, the officers were a few yards behind the man.

"What did you say to him?"

"I said we wanted to check his CCTV for someone who visited here last Friday and who he spoke to."

"And he just said yes?"

"Not exactly. He asked whether we had a warrant. And I said I'll show it to you when you show me valid business insurance," Andries replied with a wink.

"Nice."

They entered the second set of doors that opened into a vast hall with a reception area to the left. A long bar was on the right, with stools running along its front. In the middle of the room were chairs facing a stage with two poles at either end. The man led them to the building's far end, heading towards another set of doors for staff only. There weren't any other staff except the man and a few cleaners mopping the floors in preparation for tonight's opening hours.

Andries and the balding man began to converse in Greek. Andries translated for the others as he led them down a series of corridors.

"He says we're in luck; the video would have been wiped after tomorrow night, as they only keep the footage for seven days unless there's trouble."

Eventually, the balding man broke away from the route to a specific door. He pulled out his key from the string strap on his belt and flipped it into the keylock, turning and unlocking it. The man nodded and held his hand to the open door for the officers to enter. The room was small, with a storage unit containing folders and boxes on the left and a table on the right with a chair and computer. The computer had a series of wires exiting from the hard drive to other various computing units. The man sat in his chair and fired up the computer hard drive, which turned the screen on. A few moments passed as he navigated through the loading screen and the initial folder searching when he entered his password, moving his body to block it from view.

"Ti óra? the man said.

Andries puffed out in annoyance and then asked the man in Greek if he could speak in English to save him from having to translate again.

"Okay. What time?"

"Around opening time, or maybe just after eight in the evening."

"Okay, I can set it up here for Friday at eight and let it run for you?"

"Great, is this the entrance point camera?"

"Yes, where the second door is."

"Were you working last Friday?"

"Yes, I was."

Hector approached the man, towering over his seated position, showing Daniel's service photograph from the police station.

"We believe this man was here on Friday. Do you know him?"

"No, sorry, I see many people, but no detective spoke to me," the man said, looking up.

"Okay."

The man looked around the room sheepishly and lifted himself from the chair to mobilise an exit.

"I leave you alone. If you need me, ask."

"Okay, thanks. We will come to find you if we need to ask you any more questions."

The man rose from his seat and held his seat to whoever wanted it. Andries offered a hand to the chair while looking at Hector. Hector took the seat as the man exited the room and pressed play on the feed, watching it for a few minutes as a few early customers entered the building to pay their fees. He clicked on the time frame bar and dragged it forward, keeping a close eye on the screen as it fast-forwarded. Hector stopped the frame and pressed rewind slightly to something that caught his eye.

"Here he is," Hector said, pointing at the screen.

It was Daniel Belfield on the screen. The still frame was him in the corridor between the two doors. Hector clicked play, and Daniel continued walking through the corridor and out of shot.

"Does he have a file or app for the interior cameras here?" Simon said.

"Let me look before you get him," Hector said.

Hector paused the feed and minimised the screen. The previous document file screen was still open, and Hector returned to a page that displayed multiple files marked in Greek letters. Hector double-clicked on μπαρ, which he indicated meant *bar*. He opened a media player that showed the bar feed, and forwarded the time frame to the same time Daniel exited from view on the first camera. Hector pressed play, and the view took in the entrance point and the few customers buying drinks at the bar for their evening ahead. Daniel entered the bar premises and stopped by the reception area. He spoke to a man who looked like the man who showed them to the CCTV office.

"Is that the office guy there?" Simon said.

"The feed is a little grainy, but it looks like him," Hector said as he paused.

"Lying to us already. I'll get him back in here to see if he remembers this," Andries said.

Andries exited the room in the hunt for the man.

"Just play it a bit more," Ted asked.

Hector pressed play again on the video to see how the next moments would play out. Daniel showed a badge to the man, who then looked agitated. Eventually Daniel was ushered by the man, following him through the main room and out of view as they headed towards the staff door like the man did with the officers.

There was a noise outside the office room, and the door opened, allowing Andries to enter. The man was behind him, and Andries shut the door as they both entered. Andries stood before the door, creating an intimidating situation for him. The man looked worried as he looked at the officers in the room. Hector rewound the feed to show the man himself and Daniel walking across the bar area.

"This guy spoke to you on Friday," Hector said, pointing his finger at the screen.

"I don't know," the man said.

"Don't play dumb!" Andries said.

"Look, I don't know anything!"

Ted turned to face the man, who made a few steps back, resulting in the man becoming sandwiched between the shelving unit and another desk. The wall was behind him, and Ted was now facing him, enclosing him into the tight corner.

"What's your name?"

"Nikos Tsipras."

"Nikos. This detective came in to investigate illegal immigrants who were entering Greece. Some of which he traced back to this club.

You know exactly who this man is and why he was here. So, you're going to tell me now what he said to you and who he met that night, or we shut this whole place down right now," Ted stated.

The man's face turned into panic. He looked for an escape. Still, there was none; it was hopeless. He conceded.

"Look, you can't shut us down," Nikos said, searching towards the other officers.

"Why? You're breaking the law already; give me one good reason," Andries replied.

The man let out a sigh, took a deep breath and explained.

"Listen, I just let the girls work here; I look after them. They come here and don't have work, and I say, okay, come and work."

"The girls?" Andries said.

"Yes, the girls," dropping his head.

"You don't check their documents?"

"Yes and no."

"So you know these are illegal workers?"

"Yes and no."

"Yes and no? You'll have to explain, Nikos."

"I don't employ them; I get told who is employed. I just do the day-to-day running of the club. I don't get involved."

"Who employs them then?"

"Some guys."

Ted interrupted, pointing at him, "Stop messing around here, tell me now!"

Nikos lumped his head down to his chin, breathed, and looked back at Ted's eyes.

"I don't know their names; they own this part of the city. The bars, the clubs, you know. No names were given. We don't ask questions.

We just say yes and let the girls work. They collect their money, nothing else."

"Are they Albanians?"

The man's face turned from a defeated look to horror as he stared back at Ted.

"Do you want a seat, Nikos?"

Nikos nodded and took a seat on the chair by the desk. He sat on his hands, slightly rocking back and forth. Hector stood up and offered Ted his chair, which Ted took to face Nikos and sat down. The other officers backed away towards the walls to make it less intimidating.

"Did the officer, Daniel, come here to ask you about legal workers?"

"Yes."

"Did he speak to anyone else here when he visited?"

"Yes."

"Who?"

"A girl. A girl called Cleopatra who works here part-time and part-time somewhere else nearby. Same owners."

"Cleopatra, her stage name? No real name?"

"Yeah, stage name, and I don't know her real name."

"Do you know what Daniel asked her? What time does she arrive tonight?"

"He brought a photo that looked like Cleopatra walking through an airport, and I recognised her. He threatened to shut me down just like you guys. She is working tonight; she would be here at seven."

Ted looked at his watch. It was nearly five. There wasn't enough time to return to the station to return back to the club; it would waste precious time, so he had a better idea.

"Do you have her address?"

"We don't give out those details, the protection, you see."

"Nikos, you will give us her details, or I will shut you down, do you understand me? We are police officers. We are not here to hurt her or you."

Nikos paused and nodded, conceding the information was in the storage boxes or on the computer files. He took a step forward and nodded towards the computer. Ted stepped back, and Nikos took the seat. He worked the files and double-clicked on a Word document with a photo attached and their name as the title. Under those was detailed information, including address and ID documentation, and evidence of probable fake credentials they used to enter the country.

"Print that for us, please," Ted said.

Nikos worked the keyboard and brought up the print screen.

"éna? One?"

"Please."

He clicked the button, and the printer fired up, and within seconds, a black-and-white picture printed out with Cleopatra's information. At the top of the page was Cleopatra's black-and-white image. Ted held the printout up and compared the photo from the airport arrivals. The woman looked no older than twenty years old. The club photograph showed a mug shot of her face. She had jet-black hair, thick black eyebrows, and an Arabic complexion. Her eyes were light blue but overshadowed by the tired complexion underneath her arduous journey. Ted asked if Nikos knew where the girl originated, as he couldn't trust the documentation mentioning Iran and the name Daria Hussain before him. There was a ringing noise that came from inside the room. It was Andries's phone, and he stepped out of the room to answer it.

"When was Cleopatra here last?" Ted said, turning back to Nikos.

"Yesterday was her day off from us. So Monday."

"Two nights ago, okay."

"Listen, do you need anything else? I need to get back to work," Nikos said.

"Last question. Do the Albanians come to the club often?"

"To collect their money."

"When?"

"Every Sunday night."

"What time?"

"Around ten."

"Were they here this Sunday? Do you have the tapes for then?"

Nikos laughed, then quickly stopped, giving a look of forgiveness.

"What's so funny?" Simon asked.

"Sorry."

"Do you have the tapes?" Simon pressed.

"They delete them. They are smart."

"We will take them anyway if you can give them to us. We will return them when we are done with them."

"Do we need them? The man said they deleted them?" Hector asked.

"No stone is unturned, Hector. You should know that," Ted explained.

Hector slowly nodded while Nikos navigated the storage unit for the correct videotape.

"I think we are done here, guys," Ted said, looking at Simon and Hector.

They returned a nod as Andries opened the door to re-enter.

"Forensic reports are in on all of them."

"They'll be leaving the labs for the day now, won't they?" Hector said.

"They've sent me the report. If we are happy with it, we can release the bodies to the loved ones."

Nikos extended a hand to Ted, which contained the videotape. Ted took the tape and thanked him for his time as he manoeuvred to the door.

"Shall we visit Cleopatra?" Ted said to Andries.

"Yeah, you and Hector want to take this. Simon, you can read the report with me back at the station."

They all agreed, leaving Nikos alone in his small office space to his thoughts. Andries opened the door again, allowing Ted and Simon to step out, followed by Andries himself. Hector caught the door before it shut, still inside the office space. Standing underneath the doorframe, he looked back at a nervous man.

"We will be back," Hector said as she shut the door.

Chapter 14

AFTER EXITING THE CLUB, Andries and Simon returned to the police station, hitching a ride in a nearby police patrol car. They returned to process the day's activities to gather no real purpose but new murder enquiries. They left Ted and Hector to interview Cleopatra or Daria in her apartment, deciding that four officers would have been overwhelming and intimidating for her to be helpful anyway. Ted and Hector made their last turn in the Skouze Hill region, located north of Athens. They hoped the worker would still be home so they could question her on her conversation with Daniel a few nights ago. Ted had elected to drive, assisted by the built-in navigation system to plan his route to the apartment, although Hector offered diversions to beat rush hour traffic. Ted's phone vibrated in the cupholder, which he had connected to the car's Bluetooth device. The car's display screen showed a number that started with +30.

"That's internal affairs, I think. I recognise the number," Hector said, looking at the screen.

Ted answered the phone by pressing the green phone logo on the wheel.

"Hello, it's Angelika Bafa from the internal affairs team."

"Hello, how can I help?"

"Have you just been out with Andries and Simon?"

"Yeah, why?"

"They've just come back. Said they'd been out and went straight into their office. Are you hiding anything from us? We are meant to be working as a team?"

Ted looked at Hector as he pulled into a car space on the road where Cleopatra's apartment was. Ted gestured to ask, *What shall I say here?* Hector shrugged his shoulders. He then pointed his index finger upwards as if he would respond.

"Are you going to answer me?" she insisted.

"Hi, Angelika, it's Hector."

"You in on this, too?"

"Look, Angelika, no one is leaving you out of this. Ted went to the warehouse where Daniel was shot and instinctively went to the club to see if we could get anything from the girl he spoke to a few nights ago. She wasn't there, but we got her address. That's where we are heading now."

"And?"

"We're at the girl's house now, just outside and about to go in and speak to her. Andries is reviewing the forensic reports in the office now."

"Okay, do your questioning, but bring us in on this, okay? Starting tomorrow morning. I'll go easy on you, but Superintendent Kritsikis won't be okay. Daniel came to us, and we had to investigate. Don't be going lone wolf on us; it's too dangerous."

"Sure, we will let you know how the conversation goes."

"Okay, thank you."

Ted jumped into the conversation.

"Who checked Daniel's apartment, by the way, after he was found at the gig?"

"Saturday morning, when Joanne went home to collect some belongings. She reported that her apartment had been burgled and ransacked, too," Angelika said.

"I was never told that. Nor did she tell me that when I spoke to her," Ted mentioned.

"Did you ask?"

"No, I didn't. I suppose she may have told the story so many times she felt she didn't need to."

"You've only been here a few hours; I suppose you'll catch up with the information. Andries and the police major oversaw the inspection of the apartment and a few other officers. I'm sure there is a report you can get off Andries."

"Okay, thanks."

"Why do you ask?"

"I only ask because I wondered if something is connected in the apartment report. Now, you say the burgled apartment makes me think whoever it was wanted something from Daniel."

"Maybe so. Joanne said the jewellery was taken; it could have been a coincidence. So anyway, you'll keep us in the loop?"

"Yeah, we will, sorry," Hector said as Ted thought deeply.

The phone call disconnected, and Hector looked at Ted, turning off the engine.

"What's up?" Hector asked.

"Did they not find anything in Daniel's apartment related to the case?"

"I don't think so. Like Angelika said, jewellery and a few broken objects were taken. I was off duty Saturday, so I wasn't phoned in or updated about Daniel until Sunday afternoon when my shift started."

"No problem, we will investigate it at a later date."

"Shall we go in? She will be leaving soon," Hector said, looking at his watch.

"Yeah, sure."

They both exited the car and were surrounded by the high-rise apartment complexes that lined the streets. The area looked like Christos's apartment, lacking renovation and care, with paint cracked along the exterior walls. Ted unfolded the paper from his jacket pocket and looked at the address. He knew he was looking for apartment seven on the metal box, which contained a buzzer for each resident. He found apartment seven, which had Daria on the label.

"Daria," Ted said.

"Real name or fake?" Hector said.

"Let's find out."

Ted was about to place his finger on the buzzer when a man appeared from the front door. The man turned the lock and opened the door exiting the building. He was spooked when he saw the two officers standing at the door, but Hector opened his badge and told him in Greek they were there to speak to someone and not be alarmed. The man was in his forties and looked to be in some sort of overalls and possibly going out to work for the evening. The man held the door open for the officers to enter, and as he moved away, the door closed, leaving the officers alone in the hallway.

"That was easy," Ted said.

Hector didn't reply, just offered a smile and nod. They worked their way through the initial hallway, and navigated up the stairs to the second floor, where apartment seven was situated.

"You can't jump from this floor, can you?" Ted said.

"You'd hurt yourself."

"I thought so."

"Why?"

"Just in case we have a runner."

They approached the door to apartment seven, and Hector knocked on it. A peephole looked out on the corridor from within the apartment. Hector stood before the door with a badge held up towards the hole so the occupant knew it was the police for additional reassurance. Although at the same time, Ted thought it may spook the resident due to her illegal status. Hector knocked on the door again and waited. Ted pointed at the door to indicate he heard something behind the door. It was unclear what the noise was, but a voice filtered through.

"Esee tee thelis?"

"We are the police. We just want to have a word in English. Is that okay?"

"What is it you want?" the female voice repeated her first question.

Ted and Hector looked at each other, thinking how they would get her to agree to speak with them inside without using force.

"It's about the officer who came to see you at the club."

"What about him?"

"He's dead."

There was a clunk sound behind the door, and the door opened. Through the crack in the door, the woman from the photo appeared: Cleopatra. The woman looked more glamorous in person than on the ID paper. The ID paper was probably taken when she arrived in Athens instead of when she was getting ready for work. She had long black hair and was average height with a small thin frame bordering anorexic. Hector stepped in first as she walked back into her apartment. Ted followed and closed the door behind him. The apartment was basic, with a bathroom on the right of the space. Then there was a lounge and kitchen area with a bunk bed in the far corner with the bed on top and an office space underneath. Two sofas and a glass coffee table in the middle faced each other. One of the sofas backed onto a glass window with a glass door leading to a balcony. As she took the other, the woman offered them a seat on one of the sofas. Ted looked down at the view of the road they parked on.

"Is it Daria Hussain?" Hector said as she sat down.

"Yes."

Ted turned as she revealed it was her real name.

"This is Hector Baros, and I'm Ted Chester. We are..."

"You're English?"

"Yes, I've come to investigate Daniel's death; he was an officer stationed in Athens by the British government. So, I'm helping investigate his death with the Athens police force."

"Okay. So, what happened to him?" she spoke frantically.

"We want to ask you a few questions about your conversation with him first."

"I didn't do it if that's what you mean!" she shouted.

She stood up from the sofa, pacing backwards and forward.

"It's okay, Daria. Take a seat," Ted said, pointing out the sofa she was sitting on before Ted moved away from the window and took a seat with Hector. With his movements, they watched her return to her seat.

"Am I in danger?"

"We wouldn't say so. We think what Officer Belfield knew got him in trouble, and we need to understand what it was."

"How can I help?" she said with a worried look.

She was wearing a blue silk dress with fishnet stockings and no shoes. She was leaning forward with her arms on the legs covering up her midriff area.

"What did the officer ask you that night at the club?"

"He... said he knew I was here illegally."

"Okay. What else?"

She was silent as she seemed to contemplate her thoughts.

"Look, Daria, we are not here to arrest or investigate you. We are just concerned about what happened to the officer. If you cooperate, we will see what we can do for you, but we can't promise anything. But we won't threaten you with deportation if you don't speak to us."

She grew relaxed with that comment and took a deep breath before speaking.

"I told him I was offered a chance to work in Greece by some people in my home in Iran. They said they knew people who could get me into Europe. I could start a life where I could be successful, you know? Provide for my parents and live a good life. I had to pay for some documents for travel, and they took me to Greece, no questions asked. We got through passport with no issues."

"How long have you worked here in Athens?" Ted said.

"A few months now."

"Did you start work here when you arrived?"

"When I arrived here, they provided me with accommodation in my name and a job. I didn't know this was the job at the club, but I was told I couldn't leave, as I had signed a contract for everything. I'm so stupid," she raised her hands to wipe the tears from her eye.

She leaned forward to pick a tissue from the box, dabbing her eyes and smearing her mascara.

"It's okay. Take your time."

"No, carry on," she said as she placed the used tissue on the table.

"Thank you. Were there any other girls who arrived with you?"

"Two others, but I've not seen them since. They were from Turkey and Lebanon, I remember."

"Okay. The officer said you told him about a man you thought worked for the police force, who regularly visited you at your other job."

Her face changed to shame as she started to look away from the officers towards the front door. Ted knew this was possibly the cue to trigger her fight or flight response.

"Sorry, we have no judgement here, Daria. We fully understand your situation and the hardships you are facing. We can protect you after we leave. We will contact our department and ask for protection. We can try to help."

Realistically, Ted wasn't sure if he could offer protection for everyone, but it may have been a safety net the victims could cling to open up about their information.

"I think he is a cop. He started visiting a few other girls and me in the... other places I work. He never took his cap off or sunglasses when he entered. We get regulars who do that, so it is not odd behaviour. They have wives, girlfriends, and families. They don't want to be seen. We respect that, and it is business for us. If the man never wants the lights on when we do it, we leave them off. However, this guy. I've noticed a few times that he had this leather thing that I think is a badge. He leaves his phone, wallet, and that leather thing on the side. After a few visits, I noticed it and thought he was a cop. But if he was going to arrest us, he would have done it already, so I thought nothing of it and saw him as another customer."

"The other girls noticed this, too?"

"Yes, some."

"Does he still visit?"

"I've not seen him since last week. He normally comes once or twice a week."

Ted looked at Hector. He returned the glance.

"When did he start visiting?"

"Around three months ago, some of the girls who have been there longer than I said."

"Okay, thank you. Do you have the other girls' names?"

"Do I have to give them?"

"Please. These will be kept between us."

"Okay, sure. Amira and Ayat were two regulars he visited."

"Thank you," Ted said while making a mental note.

"Do they work at Toys Club or the other venue?"

"Just the other venue."

Ted nodded, and then turned to Hector.

"Just show me your badge a minute, Hector."

"Why?"

"Please."

Hector lifted himself from the sofa and reached into his pocket, presenting his badge.

"Did the badge look like this that the man had?"

"Yes, just like that."

"It's not me," Hector explained.

"Sorry, Hector, I wasn't suspecting you. I don't have a badge, so I used it as an example. Besides, Daria doesn't recognise it to be you," Ted said, looking toward Daria for clarity.

"No, he was older than you."

"How much older?"

"Not sure, maybe ten years, maybe more."

"Okay, thank you, Daria. I don't believe my partner here is the mystery man, but these badges are given to the Greek police department, confirming he may be an official in the department."

Ted's mind wandered briefly as he thought about the older officers than Hector. Andries, Savvas looked older, maybe even Nikolas, whom he had never met. Although there may have been officers in other departments, too, worth noting.

"Thank you, Daria, for the information. Can you remember anything else?"

"It was dark, and I can't remember too much."

"Any smells from him?"

"Just aftershave, but we always get that."

"What aftershave?"

"I don't know, sorry."

"Did he smoke?"

"No, he didn't."

Ted pierced his lips together. He didn't know what else to ask her, and he was annoyed he didn't bring any photographs of department officials so that she could try to remind herself of the mystery man. Although he knew he had been running with the investigation for only one day, he was playing catch up. He thought about finishing the interview and restarting tomorrow with the new approach.

"Do they have CCTV at the place?"

"Yeah, but it gets deleted. Unless something happens, we never keep the footage—client privacy."

"Can one of us or another officer come to you tomorrow with some pictures of officers who may match your age description? It may help us identify the man you saw," Ted asked.

"I don't know. I'm working all night and then all day tomorrow."

"You won't need to come to the station; we will come to you. When do you normally wake up from a night shift?"

"Around eleven."

"So, say twelve, noon here?"

"I need to leave around twelve thirty, so make it quick."

"Okay, let's say just before twelve?"

"Sure."

Ted turned to Hector, "Anything else?"

Hector shook his head, and Ted asked Daria if she had anything else to say, which she declined. The two officers rose from their seats and thanked her for her time, before exiting Daria's apartment.

"She's a key witness," Ted said, exiting the front door.

"Do you think she would recognise the person from the photo if she never saw them fully?"

"It's worth a shot. Can you arrange protection?"

"I'll see what I can do."

"We're going to need it. If she is dead, she won't be telling us who the mystery man is."

They reached the parked vehicle, with Hector taking the driver's seat. Hector navigated the heavier traffic heading back into the city centre. While en route, Ted updated Angelika on the interview with Daria and their planned second visit tomorrow, which Angelika would also attend, to add a female influence to a much male-dominated conversation. Ted made another call as they manoeuvred through the streets of Attiki, heading towards Pedion tou Areos, the city's largest public park. Ted called Simon, announcing they were close to Leof Alexandras, the main east-west thoroughfare running through the northern part of Athens, with the police HQ at the end of the long avenue stretch. The call ended, and Ted lay back in his seat, watching the pedestrians walking along the avenue and observing the traffic-ridden row of cars crawling along the other side of the road. He looked to the left-hand door, searching through the driver's side wing mirror, witnessing the traffic halting from where they had passed.

Suddenly, he saw a black Mercedes pull into the central reservation and peculiarly overtake a car. The Mercedes lifted slightly from the flat central reservation and overtook the slow-moving OPEL vehicle, whose loud horn roared through the traffic. Hector jumped momentarily in his seat, hitting the brakes on the car. Ted's movement to turn around to look through the back window was harder due to the harsh braking. In one quick movement, the black car swerved across a lane and exited out of sight down a sideroad.

"Jesus. Who was that?" Ted said.

"Crazy driver, maybe," Hector asked.

"Yeah, you're right."

Ted turned around and rested back in his seat as the vehicle began to travel along the avenue again. He was trying to remember if he'd seen the black Mercedes before.

Chapter 15

I T WAS APPROACHING HALF-FIVE in the evening, and the central office back at the police station was half-empty. Ted saw Andries and Simon still in the main office through the partially drawn blinds. Sergeant Giannis Bakais was packing his rucksack as he prepared to leave after his shift. Sergeant Manolis Pelas passed Ted on the way out and said he would see them tomorrow. He wondered whether Giannis and Manolis looked older than Hector, but he pictured them at similar ages, not the older suspected officer. Ted knew he would go insane if he became suspicious of everyone male in the male-orientated police department. Across the room, Eliana was still working at her desk, and Ted felt a sense of guilt fill her, as he knew she was probably still working because of his orders. Hector reached his desk, loading his computer to check communications that had come in for him during his time away.

"You're not still here because of me, are you?" Ted said.

"Yeah, it's all your fault," she said defensively.

"Sorry."

"It's okay. I love not being paid for overtime." She smiled sarcastically.

Ted smiled back, knowing she had her sense of humour but was not angry with him.

"They don't pay you?"

"Budget cuts. Still affecting us from the economic crash," she said again with a plain face.

Ted wasn't sure how to take her responses. He wasn't sure if it was an attempt at humour or if she was seriously annoyed with him. He asked how she got on with the social media searches.

"I searched Twitter, Instagram, Facebook, and other sources. I saw many pictures of the music event, you know, normal stuff. I didn't find anything from the initial gunshot. I saw lots of pictures being shared of Daniel's body on the floor, which the social media companies are struggling to remove; it spread so fast."

Ted turned around to where she was sitting, pulled up a nearby chair, and sat beside her, looking at her computer screen.

"So, what did you find?"

"In some photos, I noticed cameras on the stage and some in the VIP booths at the back of the warehouse. They have companies or freelance photographers that take pictures of the gigs and the artists for music magazines or the warehouse venue companies for marketing. Photographers sell them to earn their wage."

"You know a lot about that?"

"My ex was a freelance photographer who did this, so I knew about freelance photographers then."

"Was your ex there that night?" Ted continued.

"No, he moved abroad. I don't know where—we lost touch."

"Okay, so can you access these freelance photographs?"

"That's what I was doing when you came in. Some I've found on websites, but nothing I can see yet of the gunshot. I rang a few, and they said they were uploading them tonight or tomorrow morning. They said they would send us a file, too."

"Good work. When are you going home?"

"Shortly."

"Good, I'll let the guys know in there."

"It's okay; they already know."

He thanked her again as he stood up, moving the chair back to its original place. He entered the office where the three officers were now sitting. Hector had entered during Ted's conversation with Eliana, and there wasn't a seat free for him, so he stood by the door.

"You get friendly there or something, Ted?" Simon said.

"Just work. She is searching the internet for the venue's photographs, social media, and freelance pictures."

"I'm just joking. She updated us; good work from her. Andries said so himself."

"Yeah, we will allow her to continue her work with us. But remember, if she gets involved, there may be a risk."

Ted perceived the situation much more profoundly and became annoyed that he had potentially brought danger to the fact that she was now involved in the investigation, although a small part.

"I understand," Ted replied.

"Right, I was just telling these about the report on our victims. Daniel, a gunshot wound to the head, killed him on impact. Toxicology showed no signs of drugs, just a small trace of alcohol, which he was consuming during the event. Maybe two or three beers, which matched Joanne's recollection. Christos was similar in terms of the gunshot wound. Dead upon impact. Bleeding and damage from the pressure waves resulted in brain swelling and instant death. They've ruled out suicide—it's a setup, basically. Cassandra's report was strangulation, as we thought. No other causes. Oxygen to the brain was cut off, and there were compressions to the carotid artery, resulting in cerebral ischemia. Crushed trachea, death by asphyxia."

"What about the DNA?" Ted said, folding his arms.

"That's the good bit. As the forensics said, we don't have a match on our system for the DNA found under the nails. But we have contacted the Albanian authorities to see if we can access their system; they are studying the nails now. However, good news. Another person with identical DNA was found on the wool at the music venue and a water glass inside Christos's apartment, which had been brought up unknown on our system. Maybe Daniel's killer."

"Unknown?"

"We collected DNA for a murder investigation in Vouliagmeni around six months ago, twenty kilometres south of the city, on the Riviera. A businessman and his wife were killed, and jewellery was taken. No witnesses, no evidence, and no leads. CCTV on the property captured three masked gunmen entering. They disabled the security unit and CCTV to get into the panic room and steal their wealth and lives. We found a hair strand inside the panic room that didn't belong to the occupants, and we've never had a match to it since, until now."

"So, the same person. Maybe the same gang suspects in Daniel and Christos's deaths?"

"Looks that way."

"Did you speak to internal affairs? They called Hector and me when we were on our way to question the girl," Ted said.

"Yeah, Angelika rang me upset. Hector told me about the girl you questioned and going back tomorrow. You need internal affairs to go with you tomorrow?"

"Yes, I informed Angelika after we finished up with Daria."

"Did Hector ask about protection for the girl?" Ted said, looking towards Hector.

Hector shook his head.

"Sorry, I was going to," Hector mumbled.

"Protection?" Andries said.

"She's a prime witness in this. We need to ensure she is safe."

"Look, I rang the Police Director Nikolas Konstantinou about the officers involved, and he said he can't spare anyone. They've lined up the protests for Saturday, outside parliament and throughout the city. He needs all the men in Athens and Greece on this, so there are no riots or intercity wars. Call it bad timing, but he can't spare anyone. All of us will probably be taken off this task force temporarily."

"Ted, if we are lucky, you'll still have us two and maybe another officer or two. It's not ideal, but it's politics. Once the protest is over, it's back to normal," Simon said.

"Looks like we'll need internal affairs after all. Surely they won't be officiating the riots," Ted said.

"That's right," Andries said.

"The CCTV," Simon offered, as a change in conversation towards Andries.

"Yes. We reviewed the petrol station's CCTV outside the main road's industrial units. We didn't spot anything out of the ordinary. However, there was a black Mercedes that was parked in the forecourt of the petrol station. We know this because we ran the tape before the shooting, and it pulled up around thirty minutes before the shooting and left ten minutes after. We can't see what happens when it's stationary because it's out of the camera's view. The station worker didn't notice the car and saw nothing suspicious either."

Ted was connecting the two dots in the case. Although small, it gave him a jolt of energy.

"Did you get the plates?"

"Already tried. Fake—nothing comes up with what we have."

Ted stared at the floor beneath him as the rest of the officers turned to face his racing mind, which was so ever present on his face.

"What is it?" Andries said.

Ted raised his head and started to pace the floor.

"On the ride over, on the main road from the city park to here. As we turned, I saw a black Mercedes acting suspiciously, and then it sped off. It could be a coincidence or something."

"What spooked it?"

"Well..." Ted said.

"Ted saw it, and it caught my attention, so I braked sharply. Then they must have seen us. Or it could just be nothing," Hector explained.

"Interesting. We will see if we can pull CCTV from the park to match. What time was this around?"

"Five ten, fifteen maybe," Ted said.

"Okay. Well, you've made good progress today; go home, get some sleep, and let's go again tomorrow. I'll see if I can get any night officers to drive by Daria's from the club to check the area is okay," Andries said.

"Thank you," Ted said.

That was the cue to leave. The three other officers rose from their seats and exited the office, with Hector shutting the door behind him. Simon exited Andries's office first and turned to face Ted just before the row of desks.

"I will stay behind here with Andries, Ted, but you head back. You've got the address for it?"

"Yeah, what are you doing?"

"I need to check in back home about our latest updates. I may need to conference call in one of the rooms."

"Okay, I'll head back. Sure you don't want me to wait?"

"Yeah, the same floor as you. It's next door to The Frogs Hotel. Just off Iroon Square in Psyrri. I'll be an hour or so."

Ted noticed Hector at his desk, who closed the zip on his bag, flung it over his shoulder, and hurried towards the office door, mumbling goodbye as he walked out.

"He's in a hurry," Ted pointed out to a lone Eliana.

"He's an Olympiacos fan. They are playing tonight," Eliana said as she rose from her chair, shutting down her computer screen.

"You a football fan?" Ted asked.

"Sort of; I played it when I was younger."

"Did you?"

"Yeah, but my parents are fans. My Father's team was Maccabi Haifa, and my mother's family was Sevilla fans in their local region. So either of those, but I'm not passionate about it."

"Nice," he said with a smile.

"I would ask if someone would take me home, but everyone has gone. I've got my car in the garage, and it won't be ready until tomorrow morning," Eliana said.

"I guess I can."

"Thanks, Ted."

"So, are you far away?"

"Fifteen minutes away."

"Great, lead the way. I've just got to make a call," he said, offering out a hand for her to go first.

Ted looked back at the empty main room. Andries was still in his office, with his curtains drawn for privacy. Eliana had walked ahead and caught the lift, starting to make its way to the underground car park. Ted remembered an important part of the investigation into Daniel's death and returned outside Andries's office. Ted knocked first and was told to enter the room, he presumed, as Andries thought it was another Greek officer.

"Oh, Ted, sorry, I thought you'd gone home."

"I'm going now. I wanted to ask, do you have the report on Daniel and Joanne's apartment?"

Andries squinted his eyes and opened them again, expressing the memory returning to him.

"Oh, yes, I'll give you the report tomorrow morning."

"Thank you."

Ted exited the office, picking up the pace as he crossed the main workroom. Ted opted for the stairs to make his phone call without the lift signal interference. Ted was making a call to the internal affairs team on his way down the car park.

Over the phone, Angelika specifically detailed the plan for tomorrow morning to meet with Daria at her home, now with her company instead of Hector's. He arranged to meet Angelika in the office in the morning and go out together to meet with Daria at noon. He also updated her about the black Mercedes and the CCTV recovered from the petrol station, but the conversation stopped as Angelika was heading through her front door to see her daughter on her third birthday. As the phone went silent, he touched the last step before the double doors into the car parking level. His mind drifted towards the Mercedes at the petrol station, and his curiosity grew with each step he took in the underground garage towards his car. He had one question as he saw Eliana standing in the car park waiting for him: Who was driving the Mercedes?

Chapter 16

T ED'S HIRE CAR CLIMBED Rovertou Galli, a steeply inclined road heading northwest towards the Acropolis of Athens. Rovertou Galli began off one of the main streets that ran south from the temple of Zeus to the Aegean Sea. Once you met the ocean, you could head towards the Piraeus Harbour or the Athens Riveria. The Harbour, rebuilt during World War II, was the largest in Greece and the primary connection between Athens and all Greek Islands. On the other hand, the Riveria was a coastal region of suburbs running from Piraeus to Sounio, which reached the southern points of Athens's landmass. Rovertou Galli was layered in white and cream apartment blocks with overhanging balconies shadowing the street below. Diverting off at every junction were side streets with similar surroundings. During the peak seasons, the traffic built up in the areas and could become overwhelmed with vehicles, especially coaches full of tourists coming to and from the Acropolis.

Ted pulled into a parallel space on one of the side streets off Rovertou Galli. He hit the brake slowly, bringing the car to a stop. Ted applied the handbrake and tapped the driving wheel.

"Here you go," Ted said.

"Thank you," Eliana said.

"Do you need a lift tomorrow?"

"I'll sort myself out. My car will be fixed tomorrow."

"Great, take care."

She opened the passenger side door onto the pavement and turned back to shut it. She hesitated and leaned forward into the open passenger side window towards Ted.

"So, are you going to walk me to my door?"

"Why, is it a bad area?" Ted said back to her, looking around.

"There are bad guys out there, remember?"

The passenger door shut, and she started to walk ahead along the pavement. Ted was confused about the request. She was striding forward and out of view behind the row of parked cars in front. He opened the driver's side door onto the street and exited quickly. Ahead, Ted noticed she had stopped and knelt on the ground as if picking something up that she had dropped.

"You move fast," Ted said as he approached after a short jog.

Eliana knelt, offering her hand to a black-and-white cat who was vocal with every stroke. The cat stood on his back legs, headbutted her hand, and dropped again. Its tail was towered high with a slight bend at the top, symbolising a question mark.

"The cat yours?" Ted said.

"No, it's a stray."

"Is it a big problem here? I remember reading that there are many stray cats on Greek islands."

"It's a big problem. The mainland and the islands are inundated with stray and abandoned cats. They survive through the kindness of tourists or rubbish bins in the peak months. But during the cold seasons, they survive because of us."

"Us?"

"The locals. A lady called Eirini works for a charity in Athens, looking after and neutering stray cats. She helps support them and offers them homes to those who can adopt. She gives these kittens a second chance."

"That's nice. I have a cat at home. I don't think she would last five minutes out here."

"Some of these cats have nine lives. They've been through a lot in their short lives. You need to have nine lives to survive here."

"Is that the same with policing?"

"Sometimes," she responded without lifting her head.

Eliana put her hands on the cat's cheeks, rubbed them softly, and scratched under the cat's chin. Suddenly, a metal banging noise came from one of the alleyways up the street. The cat remained in its position, but its head turned back to face the noise. Several cats appeared underneath cars and other craters in the road and scarpered towards the alleyway from which the noise echoed. The cat Eliana was playing with was enticed by the noise and disappeared through the alleyway like the others.

"Dinner time," she said, standing back on her feet.

"Who feeds them?"

"An old lady in that apartment. She gives them all hope, like Eirini."

Ted nodded and understood the sentiment behind it. He knew there were charities back in the UK, but he was touched by the hearts of the locals in the area.

"This is me," she said.

She pulled out her key and pierced the keyhole to the front door, turning it in one motion. She walked through the door and held it open for Ted to enter. They made their way up the two flights to her apartment door. Upon entry into the apartment, Ted took in the interior of it. On the right and left was a door, and in front of him was a huge open space with a lounge area, kitchen, office space, and a bunk bed in the corner, with space underneath to sit, very similar to Daria's apartment.

"Nice place," Ted said.

"Bathroom is on the right as you come in if needed."

"I'm okay, thanks," Ted said, holding his right hand up.

Ted walked over to the window and took in the view of the street he had parked on.

"So, you said your mother is Spanish, and your father is Israeli?" Ted said as he turned his eyes towards her.

"My mother and father aren't together anymore. Apparently, they both wrote down a name they liked for a girl and freakily, it was Eliana. Eliana in Hebrew and Spanish means *My God Has Answered*."

"That's cool."

"Yeah, it's the only thing the two could ever agree on, and now they're divorced."

"Sorry to hear."

"They split when I was young. She remained in Athens, where they met, and he returned to Israel but visited me regularly. Now I go out to him because he is getting old. He's had some health issues."

"Is he okay?"

"Yeah, he's had heart problems and gets weaker each time I see him, but he is okay. Thank you."

Ted studied the apartment's interior and asked if he could sit on the sofa, facing inwards from the apartment window. She agreed and offered him a beer. He was hesitant about the offer. He had only been working for one day and needed to return to his temporary accommodation to unpack, make check-in calls, and refresh for tomorrow.

"Only one—I know you'll need to go. Just a peace offering for the lift home," she said.

He looked at her as she stood with her hand on the fridge. She was staring back, waiting for the response. He saw her in the police station, but there were multiple people he was interacting with. This time he was alone; he noticed her standing—she was tall, with long legs shown off through her jeans. Her long dark hair flew down to her shoulders, and her green eyes pierced into him. He didn't know what he was thinking and thought maybe the case was opening his mind to strange thoughts.

She waited intently, still demanding a response.

"Just one, please."

"Alfa okay?"

"Great, not had that for a while."

"You had it here before?"

"Not in Athens but in Kos many years ago."

She closed the fridge door holding just one beer.

"You not having one?"

"I don't drink beer."

"Why do you have it, then?"

"Just in case I bring someone home who does."

"Is that often?"

There was silence between them as they stared at each other. She broke away first to grab a bottle opener from her kitchen drawer next to the sink.

"Sorry, don't answer that."

She walked over to him and held out the bottle opener. Ted reached out for it, manoeuvred it with his other hand holding the bottle, and flipped up the lid. She held out her hand for the empty cap, and he placed it in the palm of her hand.

"It's okay, and no, it's not often," she said, returning to her kitchen.

"Sorry," Ted said.

"Sorry I don't bring anyone home?"

Ted laughed with embarrassment and began to turn red in the face. She smiled back at him and laughed as she threw the bottle cap into the waste bin. She leaned back against the high-raised worktop.

"It's okay, I'm just playing. I don't need anyone. It's just my dog and me."

"Where is your dog?"

"He's at a neighbour's. The old lady across the way didn't have much company after her husband died, so she looked after him when I was at work. I normally wait until around six because the lady gives her dinner around now," she said, looking at her watch.

Ted looked at his watch, which displayed 17:45. Ted took a long drag of the cold beer, drinking a third of it in one pull. He wasn't a midweek drinker, but he could appreciate a nice beer when he tasted one, and this one was one of his favourites.

"I best get going and let you get your dog."

"I'll walk out with you."

"Can you walk me to my car?" Ted said jokingly.

She returned the comment with another smile back at him, locking eyes again.

"Where shall I put this?" Ted said, waving the half-empty bottle.

"Just leave it on the table. I'll sort it later."

"Thanks again."

"This isn't me coming on to you or anything. But if you and Simon need a place to stay, the sofa is free. Just in case anything happens, you know."

"Okay, thank you. I'll keep it in mind."

She nodded back at him as she held her apartment door open. He nodded back at her and smiled as he exited. Immediately, he turned around to face her again.

"By the way. Be on the lookout for any black Mercedes."

"Why?"

Ted froze with the question. He didn't want to scare Eliana, but he did want to make her aware of the suspicion surrounding the unknown vehicle.

"Could be important to the case," Ted said with a smile to ease worry.

"Okay, sure."

He turned and headed down the hallway towards the exit, realising that she had also exited but wasn't following him. He turned slightly and saw her walking through the same hallway in a different direction, assuming she was retrieving her pet.

"What's your dog's name?" Ted said back at her to catch her attention.

"Zeus," she said, moving her head forward.

Ted made his way down to the street level through the apartment complex. As he entered the driver's side door, his thoughts changed to reality. He needed to navigate his way out of the side streets onto the main road back to his dwelling, just north of his current location in the Psyri area. When in his apartment, he would phone his family back in England to check in on them and redirect his mind.

As Ted placed the key in the ignition, he noticed a young woman across the street with dark hair and a tinge of red flowing through it. She was knelt down facing away from Ted, with a cat carrier by her foot, which was in view. Then she turned her body back around, and Ted noticed her large red-framed glasses and kind face. She was holding a mangy-furred white cat that desperately needed attention. She carefully placed the patient, calm feline into the carrier, closed the latch, and locked it inside. She lifted the carrier and turned to look down the street, moving a few steps before opening her small hatchback car and placing the cat cage on the backseat of the car. Once the woman entered the driver's side door and was seated, she turned on the engine, pulled out of the space, and the vehicle disappeared down the street. All the while, Ted wondered if the red-framed woman was Eirini giving the stray cats of Athens their chance of survival. Giving the felines their nine lives.

Chapter 17

TED PARKED IN THE underground car park off one of the many side streets in Psyri. According to the map app on his phone, he parked around two hundred metres from his apartment. The vibrant area of Psyri offered streets full of eateries, live music, and bars that stayed open late with DJs or more traditional musicians. He was fast approaching Iroon Square, which had cover for outside seating from the various tavernas surrounding the squares. A few locals enjoyed a drink and food as it approached six thirty, with dark starting to submerge the sky. There was still a chill in the air, but the locals wore jackets or coats to embrace the cold while smoking their cigarettes outside, as others decided to eat inside.

Simon had texted Ted as he reached the square to say he was leaving the office shortly after finishing his calls with his bosses back home in the UK, offering to eat food at one of the local restaurants in the square, which Ted agreed to. Ted reached his floor and walked along the hallway until he found his apartment door. He picked the key out of the envelope and placed it into the door lock, turning and opening it. He entered the property and guessed Simon's room was two doors down due to the row of even numbers on one side of the building.

Ted moved his suitcase into the bedroom, started unpacking some of his clothes, and hung them on the available hangers in the wardrobe. Upon entering the kitchen area, he opened the fridge and saw a pack of six bottles of water. He ripped one out of the plastic packaging and downed the water in one. Once he finished it, he placed the empty bottle on the side. There was no milk in the fridge, so it would be black coffee for the morning unless he managed to go shopping after or before dinner.

In his loneliness, his mind started to race with the thoughts and possible scenarios of the case. Ted was always involved in his work, and his mind rarely switched off from the end of his shift. He knew crime didn't stop when he clocked off for the day and hated that he would be resting while criminals were still out there. Ted looked out the window, which overlooked one of the side streets. The building wasn't near the square, so observing it and the covered seating areas was problematic from the opened window, which had a raised fence to stop one from falling. Overall, the apartment was better and cleaner than he expected. It wasn't big enough for his whole family to have come here, even if it was temporary, but he knew it was makeshift due to the transient nature of his visit. He saw a few men on his partial glimpse of the square, some on their own and some in groups smoking, reading the newspapers or drinking half-pints of beer accompanied with a glass of water.

He moved away from the window because he knew he had an important call to make to his family back home. He worked his phone and pressed the call button on Rose. He paced around the apartment, looking at the interior and taking in the space as it rang.

"Hello," Rose said.

"Hello, you okay?"

"Good, yeah, you?"

"Yeah, I'm good. How are the girls?"

"Yeah, good, just missing their dad."

"Are they there?"

"Yeah, I'll get them now."

Rose shouted their names on the other end of the phone, and there were squeals of excitement, which warmed his heart and crushed it simultaneously.

"They're here now."

There was a moment when Ted heard ruffled excitement in the background.

"Daddy!" Ivy said.

"Dad!" Florence said.

"Hey. Am I on speakerphone?"

"Yeah, you are," Rose said in the distance.

"Great, how are you?"

"Good. When are you coming home?" Florence said.

"Soon enough, girls. But I have to work, you know this."

"Dad—you will come to England?"

This gave Ted pause. He knew they had moved, but they were further away.

"I will. I promise when I can."

The girl's voices faded into the background to some inaudible mumbling, and Rose's voice came through clearly.

"Hang on one moment, kids. You can speak to him again in a moment... Hi, Ted."

"Hey, everything okay?"

"Good. They are happy. Missing you, but settled. We couldn't stay there alone with everything going on with them."

"I understand. Sorry... everything has been so rushed."

"Well. It's your job, and I know what it comes with."

Ted smiled to himself.

"Thanks, Rose. Thanks for everything."

"Did you say bye to Sander?"

"We did. Was over the phone, but she understood. She actually agreed with our choice."

Ted nodded down the phone, grasping the device tightly.

"Yeah, it's for the best."

"Maybe we will come out when we are ready. We want to be with you for the school holidays in Greece, the sun, the food," Rose laughed.

Ted smiled at the prospect of them spending time together, not just like before, but with the option of a summer destination being on their doorstep for the kids and Rose to enjoy.

"Sounds great, Rose."

"I'll put the kids back on."

A conversation was occurring down the other end of the phone, met with excited screeches.

"Daddy, Daddy," they said.

"Hey, kids. How's Grandma?"

"She is good! We've had macaroni cheese for tea," they both said.

"Amazing. She makes good macaroni cheese, doesn't she?"

"The best!" Ivy said.

"How was Evie going home?"

"She went into the plane's base," Ivy said.

"Bless her. Still, I'm glad she is with you and not alone in our old house."

"She would be lonely," Ivy said.

Ted smiled at their caring nature, that some touched his heart.

"Listen, I have to go. I've checked into my apartment, but I'll FaceTime you soon, yeah?"

"Yes, please, Dad."

"Good. Listen, is your mum there?"

"Yeah, she is. Bye! I love you, Dad."

"Love you, too, and you, too, Florence."

"Love you, Dad," Florence said.

"Love you, too, see you soon."

There was a moment of ruffling as the girls' voices went into the distance, and Rose changed the phone back to the normal speaker. Ted returned to the open balcony, looking at the square before closing its door.

"They miss you."

"I know."

"We miss you."

"I know, I do, too."

He noticed the arrangement of people had changed under the canopies. There were just a few tables of people starting to eat their dinners for the evening under one of the heated lamps. The man reading the newspaper and one of the beer drinkers had left. Once he closed the balcony door, he went to the coffee machine. He lifted his right shoulder to balance his phone between his shoulder and ear to keep it in place. He lifted one of the coffee pods from the side, holding it in his hand.

"We will talk about it when you get back but keep safe, Ted," Rose said.

Suddenly, there was a noise at the front door. Ted dropped the pod into the machine without closing the lid and moved away. He made his way over to the door. He checked his watch but wasn't sure if Simon had made it through to Psyri with the traffic, found parking, and walked over to the apartment in this time. Another noise sounded like the door handle being moved, which alarmed him. He was sure it wasn't Simon who was outside this door. There was no possible way he could have made it unless he didn't have a signal when he initially sent the message.

"Hey, listen, I've got to go," Ted whispered.

"What's up?"

"It's okay—speak soon."

There was a response from Rose on the other end, but it wasn't audible to him as his focus had shifted to the door. He placed the phone into his pocket and crept towards the peek hole to look outside. Looking through the small glass window, he saw a man outside his door, seemingly trying to work the door lock. Ted took another step forward while keeping his eye through the hole. The movement caused the floorboard to creak, encouraging the man to look up.

As the man looked up directly back at Ted, he recognised the man at the door as the same one reading the newspaper in the square. The prospective intruder studied the door before him and then investigated the peek hole as if looking directly back at Ted. He had short black hair and a Mediterranean or Eastern European look on his face. He had a tattoo on the side of his left eye, but Ted couldn't tell what it was—possibly an eagle, the symbol of Albania.

The man became startled and moved away from the door, then exited from view down the corridor. Ted reached for the lock, turned it, and slowly opened the door, peeking around the frame and into the corridor. He saw the man running through the hallway towards the stairs and out of view again. Ted felt the weight on his belt to indicate he was armed. He set off down the corridor running to catch up with the man who looked around mid-twenties and five years younger than Ted. The man swiftly descended the stairs with pace as Ted started to descend the one flight. The man moved to the front door, pushing it before the door started slowly closing on its latch from a previous exiter.

Before it locked, Ted saw the closing door ahead of him and caught it with his hand. He pushed his body between the small gap and was now on the side street. He looked right and left and saw the man going through the canopy covers in the square, looking back as he ran. Ted urged his arms and legs to make him run fast through the light crowds as he gathered momentum. Ted saw a small walkway through the sheltered tables as a shortcut rather than the man's journey around the seating areas.

Exiting the square, he began moving through the middle of the road, in and out of the slow oncoming vehicles. The vehicles beeped their horns and flashed their lights as pedestrians looked on as he sprinted past them. Ted was gaining on the man until a car pulled out of the side road, throwing him off and making him divert onto the pavement to continue his pursuit. He felt the lactic acid building in his leg due to his exhausting running speed.

Ted walked through the crowds building upon the pavement until he reentered the road to continue his pursuit. The man increased the gap between them as he reached a slight turn in the road, obscuring the view beyond the bend. He disappeared momentarily, which prompted Ted to run faster to try and close the gap. Ted was moving along the bend when the man reappeared. The main road was ahead, which was much busier than the side streets they had been navigating.

The man ran across the busy road dodging the car traffic as their horns blared and their headlights illuminated the streets in the night. Ted quickly surveyed a gap in the traffic and caught it perfectly, crossing the road without reacting to the drivers. Upon crossing the road, they entered Monastiraki Square. The square was illuminated with bright yellow lights from the surrounding buildings. The yellow-lit Acropolis was towering over the square on Areopagus Hill. The square was crowded with people venturing to various amenities and using the nearby transport network. Next to the mosque was a beige building with tall windows arching at its peak, the nearest transport station in the area.

The man maintained his pace through the square, weaving into the Monastiraki train station interior. Ted saw the runner disappear through the open door and behind the building wall. Once Ted entered the train station, he saw the man heading towards a set of stairs that descended underneath the ground platform he was standing on.

Up ahead, the man brushed past two people who tumbled to the floor. He composed himself and passed a row of metal posts with yellow electronic check-in devices for tickets operated by touchless cards. Due to the man's stumble, Ted closed in on him, passing the ticket posts himself. The man was rapidly descending the first flight of steps, which led to a platform with two more stairs running off it, giving the option of either platform. A noise from beneath the stairs reverberated underneath his feet and through the walls. With the sound of a train incoming from a distance, the fleeing man had to choose which platform to join. Suddenly the man turned right, manoeuvring down the steps to his chosen platform. He reached the platform, signalling trains running south towards the Port of Piraeus. The platform was crowded with workers commuting home and football fans wearing red and white football tops and scarves. The train pulled into the station and slowed on its approach as Ted made the last step, descending onto the platform. A gust of wind blew through the platform as the train powered to a steady stop, with the loud sound of screeching metal as it broke. The train reached its stop, and the passenger doors opened.

Ahead, the man merged into the crowd of people exiting and about to enter the carriage, and Ted was trying to maintain visual through the bodies. The M1 train was a row of silver aluminium box carriages with two sets of doors on each and completed with orange lining on its exterior side. There were five carriages; with a quick glance, the man reached the last one before darting inside at the furthest door away. Ted walked to the nearest carriage doorway, one foot on the train and one on the platform. He kept his eye on the furthest door for any signs of movement. The train made a ringing noise to indicate the door was shutting. The man didn't get off the train, and at the last second, Ted brought his right leg into the train. The train doors closed, and the carriage began to jitter as it gathered acceleration and speed.

On the screen above Ted's head read *Neo Faliro*. The station stop was unknown to Ted, but he presumed they were heading southwest of the city due to the football fans heading towards the Karaiskaki Stadium. The train reached top speed as Ted flashed through the crowds of people in the carriage. Ted manoeuvred through the first carriage with three more carriages left until he was sure to face the man, thinking about his next move as he went. Suddenly, the train started to slow down, and an announcement in Greek indicated to Ted that the next station was fast approaching. Ted was at the end of the last carriage looking through the door. Ted couldn't see the man's face but saw a few similar figures facing the other way at the front of the carriage. Ted pushed the handle down, releasing the lock on the door. Ted pulled the door open and stepped through the connecting door, allowing him to enter the last carriage. Ted scanned the interior and saw a man in the distance looking back attentively as he entered.

It was him.

Throughout the pursuit, Ted tried to remember where the familiar face was from. He knew the man from his apartment window, sitting in the square pretending to read the newspaper, blending into the furniture around him. However, that wasn't the only time he had seen him. Ted reached for his phone and flicked through the gallery of accumulated pictures, focusing particularly on the CCTV still he took at the music venue. Without encouragement, the man turned and glanced out the sliding doors. Ted looked up from the photograph and at the man in the flesh. It was him indeed.

The train began to brake with more force, and Ted could see the gleaming stone reflecting the station's lights as the train entered the platformed area. Ted wasn't going to reach the man in time within the carriage, so he had to go on foot again. Ted positioned himself at the nearest door to him that would exit onto the platform. The man ahead was doing the same at his door, holding his hand on the button that released the door. Ted pushed through a few people by the door wearing red and white shirts to ensure he could exit first.

The train came to a complete stop. Ted maintained a visual on the man, who returned the stare; then Ted heard a noise coming from the door's illuminated button. It became a standoff between two men until the fans' intervention, one fan trying to press the button to open the doors. This triggered the man to hit the button and open the passenger door. Ted imitated his move, and they became two greyhounds being released from their starting cage with a dash to the finish line. Neo Faliro was an old but modern station with blue pillars running along the platform, holding up the steel structure and providing cover. There were three platforms with a train line running between each one. At the end of each platform was a set of stairs inclining to a raised platform that ran to the station's exterior, where Poseidonos Avenue's coastal road was situated.

The man began sprinting through the platform, reaching the stairs. Ted wasn't far behind, and closed in on the distance as the crowd formed near the stairs. The man shoved through the accumulation of moving people on the stairs, pushing people to the edges.

"Move! Police!" Ted shouted.

The large mass of people moved towards the edge of the railings, allowing Ted to ascend without becoming forceful. Ted lost visual as he reached the stairs' peak, and the man shifted his body to the right and out of view. Before building up his speed on the open concourse, Ted reached the last few steps. Ted could see the man exit the station complex and enter the upper tier of multiple walkways where the stadium was situated.

Ahead the man navigated the pavements through the sea of red and white-clothed fans, with a sprinkle of fans in Panathinaikos green. Ted followed the man as he curved around one corner of the rectangular-shaped stadium. The man was still scurrying through the crowds of fans on the path, missing them by an inch. Ted was still fixated on the man, unaware of the fans coming from his side towards the stadium. Ted lost control of his balance as he collided with a male fan. Ted managed to keep on his feet, using his hands in a leaned position to push himself back up into a standing position. Ted lost the momentum of his speed and wasn't sure if he could regain that position with the remaining energy.

Ted and the man he was pursuing were heading towards the other side of the stadium. The area was much quieter than the station side, with fewer fans flooding the pavements around the Karaiskaki Stadium. Along the edge of the stadium stood tall metal red-like crane structures curving over the top of the stadium. As they progressed around the stadium structure, Ted could see up ahead to the end of the walkway, which led to a road. Ted was applying his remaining energy to keep up with the man.

Still moving at speed, the man pulled out his phone and placed it against his ear as if to answer a call. He kept his momentum but was moving without direction as he started moving his head, as if looking for someone. He entered an area north of the stadium, with its surrounding area bare from the busy forecourt they'd darted through. The area was filled with wooden telephone lines, grass wastelands, and an unkempt road used as a drive-through.

Suddenly, a black Mercedes screeched down the road and pulled up alongside the man, breaking harshly upon the approach. The passenger side door swung open, and the man flung himself into the vehicle while the car gathered speed with the door still open. The door shut as it approached the junction at the end of the road, narrowly missing an oncoming van coming from one side of the road. Ted pulled out his phone and tried to navigate his camera app, keeping a steady hand with the adrenaline coursing through his body. He snapped the vehicle before it turned and went out of view. Ted found the phone number for the Police HQ, dialled it into his phone, and pressed the call button. He was sure someone on the night shift would be at one of the desks to answer the call.

"Police Lieutenant Christodoulopoulos."

"Hello, it's Ted Chester."

"Hi, Ted, you okay? You seem out of breath," she asked.

"Yeah... you could say that. Can you run a plate, please?"

"Sure."

Ted put the lieutenant on the loudspeaker as he searched his gallery for the photo. Ted asked if she was on nights, which she confirmed. Ted read the plate, the colour, and the model of the vehicle. He placed the phone back onto the regular speaker and waited a few seconds as he caught back his breath.

"Nothing here, Ted. Although there is a note to say this vehicle was found near the shooting scene at the music venue. Is this connected to Daniel's death?"

She read the information back to Ted to ensure it was correct. Ted confirmed it after relooking at the photograph himself for reassurance.

"It is, thank you."

"Anything else I can help with?"

"No, that's great, thanks."

Ted disconnected the phone, squeezing it hard until his hand turned white. He placed it back into his jeans pocket and made the journey back, retracing his steps to the station. He knew the black Mercedes was involved in the murder of Daniel Belfield—he was certain.

He reached the station's premises again, passing and observing the football supporters as they approached the stadium turnstiles. He went down the steps back onto the station platform again, waiting for the next train back to the city. Ted's phone buzzed in his pocket. As he lifted it out, he saw on the screen that Simon was calling. Ted forgot that Simon was checking in himself and had plans to meet up, but Ted hadn't told him about the chaos he was caught up with.

"Where are you, Ted?"

"We're being followed, Simon."

"What do you mean? Where are you?" Ted looked up at the timetable board for the next train.

"Near Neo Faliro Station. Meet you at Monastiraki Station in thirty minutes. I'll explain it all then."

Ted disconnected the call before Simon could reply. He slipped his phone back into his pocket and walked over to a raised bin connected to one of the blue metal poles on the station's platform. He kicked the chest hard. It wasn't enough to loosen its position against the wall, but enough for everyone near to pass judgement on him. Ted didn't care what the station goers thought; whoever was behind Daniel's death was after Ted now.

Chapter 18

T ED ENTERED MONASTIRAKI SQUARE just thirty minutes after his hunt with the man. This man was now the suspect in the murder of Daniel Belfield, and Ted used the short journey to vent his frustrations upon himself on losing him. Upon exiting the train, Ted searched for a friendlier man, Simon Taylor. The night had fully formed, and the square was embraced with illuminated artificial yellow light. Across the square's tiled flooring was Simon, who stood next to the Ottoman-era Tzisdarakis Mosque. Simon spotted Ted approaching him and spread his arms as he took a few steps forward.

"What's going on, Ted?"

"We're being followed."

"Yeah, you said that. Explain what happened."

"When I got to the apartment, I rang Rose. I was standing in my apartment looking out of the window onto the square. I noticed a man sitting there, and then that man was trying to get into my front door. I'm sure he is the same guy on the CCTV at the music venue!"

"Where is he now?"

"He's gone. I chased him through the neighbourhood and then into the station there," Ted turned his body briefly to point at the train station behind.

"You lost him in the station?"

"No, I followed him from this station and journeyed to the stadium. I lost him when I think the same black Mercedes picked him up, and here I am."

"Shit. So you think they're on to us, too, then?"

"Looks that way. Whatever this is, someone doesn't want us to investigate or find the truth. I don't think the man wanted to speak to me. I think he wanted to stop us from carrying on with our investigation into Daniel's death."

"We can't stay in that apartment tonight. They know we're staying there. I've rung Andries before you arrived, and he said there is an apartment near the police station that can be used; it's used to hide witnesses."

"We can't trust anyone, Simon."

"We have to trust someone, Ted. Not everyone is a bent officer in this city."

Ted stared at Simon as he pondered on the two of them going on alone.

Ted stopped pacing and looked at Simon directly.

"So this guy... you think?"

"I think the guy I chased was the same guy we saw on the CCTV at the venue."

"Are you sure?" Simon said with wide eyes.

"I'm confident, but we need CCTV from the stations or the stadium, so I can get another look and maybe a facial recognition from the Albania police force."

"Sure. We will get those."

"We will call Angelika from internal affairs. She is someone we can trust. We will check the CCTV and see if we can identify the man."

"What about asking Andries or someone at the station to look at the tapes?"

"We can't trust them, remember?"

"Okay, Ted, sure. What about the safe house? I've already called Andries—I don't know where we can go tonight."

Simon pulled the buzzing phone from his trouser pocket and pointed at the screen with his other hand.

"It's Andries."

"Answer it on the loudspeaker."

Simon pressed the screen twice, and Andries was on loudspeaker. A constant humming sound came from his line as if he was driving on a busy road.

"What happened?" Andries asked.

"The Albanians know we are investigating them. They tried to get me in my apartment. Someone told them where I live. I think it's the same guy we saw on the CCTV at the music venue," Ted said.

"Whoa. How can you be sure of all of this?"

"Andries. They knew where I was staying. Someone followed me, or they were given location information."

"I booked these apartments myself, so I didn't tell anyone about them, Ted," Simon replied.

"Yeah. I don't know where you're staying. Only you and Simon."

"He's right, Ted," Simon reassured.

"Someone is following us and knows then," Ted said.

"Okay. Simon said about the safe house, you can stay there. I can make arrangements now," Andries replied.

"Don't take this personally, Andries, but..." Ted said.

"Yes?"

"We can't trust you or anyone in your unit."

"I won't take it personally, Ted. I understand, I really do, but I'm on your side. If there is someone corrupt, we will find them. Have you spoken to internal affairs?"

"I'm going to get in touch."

"Okay, I'll see you tomorrow, yeah? Where will you go tonight?"

"We will work it out."

Ted nodded, and Simon ended the call. They both stood in the square under the illuminated mosque and passed by many people using the square to reach their destinations.

"Where will we go tonight?"

"Let us get our bags and take the cars. We'll find a hotel."

Shortly after closing his eyes, the darkness projected the harrowing vision of Ted walking through a disused building with rows of bodies lying on their back side by the side. An old wooden chair faced the wall in the room's far corner. Positioned on the chair was a figure whose posture was slumped forward. The person was dressed in dark clothing, and on Ted's approach to the chair, he saw the person wearing a hoodie covering his face.

Ted reached out his hand and placed it on the top of the person's head, gaining a grip on the hoodie. Just as he was about to lift the hood, Ted saw spots of blood forming on the floor beneath the chair between the trainers of the unknown person. Ted lifted the hood in one motion to reveal a man slouched with his head forward. Ted pushed the man's shoulders back, sitting upright in the chair. The blood was draining from Vladimir Balan's neck, and his eyes were staring wildly back at Ted from the seated position. Vladimir was the undercover operative Ted had embedded into the Hungarian and Romania OCG that ran sex trafficking operations across Europe. He managed to escape the clutches of the OCG and was presumably living a second life under the radar of any police official or criminal activist.

Ted felt warm and drenched in sweat, his mouth dry. It was as if someone had poured a glass of water on his face, and the moisture was warm and sticky. He saw his sports watch resting on the bedside table in the darkness. He reached out for it to check the time. It read ten to six in the morning. It was a pleasant sight, as he knew he could rise from and start the next day of investigations. Although he was glad he could leave, he had just endured the nightmare in his sleep. The brief heartwarming delight was slightly distracting from the harsh and imminent reality.

Chapter 19

MORNING BROKE ABOVE THE high-rise apartment blocks and lit up the fronts of buildings, roads, and walkways with its winter glare. Simon and Ted stayed at the Hilton on Vassilissis Sofias Avenue, within the Hilton Area, adjacent to the Kolonaki and Pangrati neighbourhoods. The time was approaching six twenty in the morning on Ted's sports watch, and he knew he needed to leave immediately and meet Simon downstairs. He had risen from the bed, showered, changed, unpacked some of his belongings into his temporary wardrobe, unloaded his toiletries, and rowed along the sink's surface.

After Ted and Simon left Monastiraki Square yesterday evening, they returned to their compromised apartments to collect their belongings and cars. In the apartment, Ted rang Angelika from the internal affairs team, who was leaving her home to dine out with her boyfriend and daughter in the Plaka area of the city. Ted and Angelika discussed the mystery of the man who attempted to break into Ted's apartment and how they could unveil the man from the CCTV recordings. Ted explained the movements and the locations where the foot pursuit occurred from Psyri towards the stadium. Angelika said she would make some calls to the police force and the Hellenic Railways Organisation for opportunities to source the CCTV from both train stations to find a still picture of the man Ted was pursuing.

Ted also traced his steps from the police station to the apartment via Eliana's through his memory but didn't see anything suspicious about his journey; he didn't even witness a black Mercedes that he had become on high alert for.

Shortly after the call with Angelika, Ted rang Eliana, asking if she was safe or had detected anyone suspicious outside her department or on the ground level outside. She confirmed she hadn't detected anyone lurking outside and was curious about why Ted asked; he explained how the events unfolded shortly after he left her apartment and became relieved she was safe and told her to be alert.

As the sun rose, Ted and Simon entered the Police HQ's main room separately. On the drive over, they were fending off morning traffic even in the early hours. The morning officers began their shifts, exchanging follow-up information with the night shift staff. Ted noticed Andries was sitting in his chair, seeing him through the open blinds lining the office window, staring out onto the main room. Across from Andries sat a man dressed in uniform. Ted approached the office when Andries noticed them both and raised his hands to wave them through. Upon entering the room, Andries rose from his seat and held a hand towards the mystery man, who remained seated and unphased by their entrance.

"Ted, Simon, this is Police Director Nikolas Samaras. Nikolas, this is Ted Chester and Simon Taylor from the British agency," Andries announced.

Ted was eager to meet Nikolas and ask questions regarding the Daniel case in person. Nikolas turned his head, looked up at the two officers who had entered, and nodded slightly towards them, unphased by their appearance. Ted noticed the difference in urgency to meet one another, with Nikolas having none at all. Ted recalled previous officers he had worked with and their huge egos blocking any chance of a working relationship. Ted got the same vibe from Nikolas in the few seconds of the introduction. Nikolas looked much older than Andries, with his medium-cut black hair, speckles of grey hair on view as a sign of ageing, and a clean-shaven face showing off his chiselled jaw, which became more edged when he tightened it. Nikolas remained facing Andries as Ted and Simon took free seats on either side of the police director.

"Are you okay, Ted?" Andries said after the events of last night.

"Yes, I'm okay. Any news on the CCTV?"

"Yes, we will get to that. We have officers working on it at the moment. We should have some results this morning."

"Okay, what did you find?"

"Where did you sleep last night?" Andries replied.

Ted ignored the question. Not out of spite—he didn't want to reveal where they were staying. Ted wanted to press on and break down Nikolas's hard exterior. He noticed Andries dodged his question about the CCTV, so he played the game.

"Do you know what Daniel was investigating, Nikolas?"

Nikolas turned his head towards Ted and gave him a glaring stare and a long pause.

"Yes," he finally responded.

Nikolas turned his head back, facing forward again towards Andries.

"You know this affects your department?" Ted pressed on.

"I'm very aware."

"We will expose the corruption."

Nikolas not only turned his head, but his entire body towards Ted. Ted felt slightly intimidated by Nikolas's stance; although both sat, their height was similar. Nikolas's jaw tightened before he replied. Ted caught a glance at the sharpening jawline as it clenched. Ted knew he was annoying Nikolas every time he did it.

"We can't have you running your own investigations. This is Greece, Athens, our ground. Not someplace back in your homeland," Nikolas said.

"We were sent to investigate the death of a British ILO on foreign soil, and that is what we are doing. He was investigating corruption in the police force, which got him killed," Ted said.

Nikolas tightened his jawline again in the stare-off with Ted. Simon noticed the tension and attempted to defuse the situation.

"I don't want to start us off on the wrong foot here, but like Ted said, we are investigating the death of Daniel Belfield. Andries here has been excellent in supporting the operation, and we need that to continue to reach our conclusion and find out what happened," Simon said.

Nikolas was unmoved by Ted and Simon's defence and remained silent while returning to his original position. Andries took the compliment from Simon and nodded but offered nothing more. Nikolas was the first one to break the silence.

"I understand. It's unfortunate what happened to Daniel. However, as police director, I must protect the public and tomorrow's upcoming protests... Andries and Angelika have already informed me about your request for more officers, Eliana. However, you may understand I'm swamped arranging the reassurances of public safety. After today, no officers will be available to join you in your investigation. All officers will be on the ground tomorrow and Sunday. We're even drafting in the Army and Special Forces to assist. You understand the severity of this operation?"

"I understand the politics behind it and fully comprehend you need officers to protect your city from potential protests turning sour," Simon said.

"How about the severity of corruption in your police force?" Ted interjected.

Nikolas lifted his left hand and held it over his mouth, resting his shaved moustache in the *U* shape of his thumb and index finger, seemingly lost in thought.

"When you have the evidence, I will help support it."

"Evidence? We have an ILO dead, and Christos Masouras and his partner were murdered. We have Albania connections involved with the gun and bullets at the scene. A man came to my apartment yesterday evening, and we have a connection with a black Mercedes appearing wherever we turn. It can't be clearer, police director."

"You have an Albania connection, with no evidence and word from beyond the grave that has been filtered through many officers' word of mouth. We have internal affairs working on this anyway. If you argue again, I will pull everyone off this—do not underestimate me."

Ted shook his head in frustration. He bit his tongue at his thoughts and decided to filter them for the words he would speak.

"Is it evidence you need?"

Nikolas remained facing forward, placing his index finger on the desk but remaining forward facing.

"You get the evidence and present it to me. I will support you after the protests."

"Ted," Simon said, holding his hand up.

Ted changed his conversation pattern. Nikolas was hard as nails, with an ego that wouldn't be able to leave the office door. Still, he needed something from the exchange to help his cause in the investigation.

"How about I just take Hector and Eliana?" Ted interjected.

Andries looked confused with the request and changed his view from Ted back to Nikolas, who remained silent, looking down towards the floor.

"You just asked for Eliana before," Andries said nervously.

"I need all officers, as I've already explained to you—sorry," Nikolas replied, offering a brief exchange of eye contact.

"Okay, how about Eliana? Just one of them?" Ted replied.

Again, there was another silence as Nikolas thought about the answer. This time Nikolas turned his head towards Ted, looking at him for much longer.

Ted noticed his jaw had tightened again.

"Just Eliana. If this keeps you out of my way for the time being, Detective Chester," Nikolas said with a hard stare.

Ted nodded. He knew he wasn't going to get much more from Nikolas. Ted knew the protests were important to Nikolas and in order to contain the city's risk factor. Ted fully understood he must be under immense pressure to ensure the safety of government officials, the public, and the city.

"Thank you," Ted said.

There was a moment of silence that deafened the room. The only noise was the officers outside in the main room working. The first move was made by Andries, who stretched his arms out, leaning back in the chair in one motion.

"So, the CCTV."

"What do we have?" Ted asked.

"We pulled the CCTV from the city park when you said you passed through. We saw Hector's car, and then maybe two or three cars behind us, we saw the black Mercedes. Here is a photograph."

Andries pulled a photo out of a paper sleeve on the table. Looking at it, he turned it around for Ted and Simon to see before placing it flat in front of them. Ted and Simon edged forward in their seats to take a better view. Nikolas remained unmoved by it but remained fixated on the piece. Ted scanned the image and saw a grainy shot of the black Mercedes. The licence plate displayed IHA-4320.

Andries explained that IHA was a prefecture where the car was registered, in this case, Athens. The night shift officers' investigation discovered the car was a rental car from Avis, located south of the Plaka district. The day officers who received the information from the night shift workers offered to attend the rental building this morning to ask questions about the individuals who made the rental car payment. Andries requested they hold off until Ted and Simon were informed of the information this morning. Ted was keen to make a cross-reference to the car outside the stadium. However, he knew from experience that licence plates could be changed instantly, or multiple cars of the same make and colour were used in the OCG operation.

Ted took out his phone while Andries narrated the night shift activities. He searched through his recent gallery photographs. The latest picture that had been taken was the one he was eager to look at. Ted photographed the speeding vehicle as the man he had pursued entered the car by the stadium yesterday evening. Ted compared the two photographs and felt a bolt of energy course his veins. Without asking, he took a still image picture of the A4 size printout before Andries took it away, placing it back inside the paper wallet. Ted held onto his phone and looked at Andries with a smile.

"We have a match."

Andries looked surprised in his returning gesture, then directed the same facial expression to Nikolas, who remained straight-faced when offering his reaction.

"Okay. This still proves nothing with your opinion on corruption and Albanian links, but find out who is following you, and we will see how we move forward. Together," Nikolas said sternly.

"Sure. Angelika is working with the train stations to retrieve the footage of the man to see if we can get a facial photograph."

"Okay, great news," Andries said.

"I'm guessing the licence plates at the petrol station doesn't match these?"

"They don't, but it could have been changed or be another vehicle. However, the one at the petrol station we know has fake plates because nothing has returned on it."

Ted nodded as he absorbed the response, then suddenly remembered he wanted to obtain the reports to check the details of the burglary at Daniel and Joanne's apartment on the night of his murder.

"You two searched Daniel's apartment after he was killed. Do you have the report on what you found, so we can review that, too?"

"It's been filed by Andries and Hector. You can find it in the case reports," Nikolas replied.

"I'll give it to you—don't worry, I've not forgotten," Andries offered.

Ted noticed Nikolas give Andries a cold stare. Andries returned a look but suddenly broke away, staring down at his desk and then towards the partially opened blinds, which showed the main room. Nikolas used both hands, slapping his thigh and raising in his chair.

"I must go and prepare for the weekend. If you need anything, ask Andries."

Nikolas was already holding onto the handle near the door when he looked back towards Ted and Simon. He moved back between the two officers before finally resting on Ted's shoulder.

"Remember, don't run this city on your own. You update Andries on what you know, and he will tell me. If you don't hear from me, that's good. If you do, you've gone too far, and this will be stopped. I've got a city to protect and a reputation to keep."

Ted felt angry but didn't want to push his thoughts too far. He faced Nikolas gawking directly at him as he looked down upon Ted.

"With all respect. There are only two of us here. We could have tens or hundreds of police officers or agency detectives running the streets of Athens, trying to find the killer or killers involved. Be lucky; in your view, we haven't."

Nikolas's face scowled back with no response. He opened the door and exited, with the door closing gently behind him. Ted noticed he ignored the working officers in the room as he exited, focusing on his phone screen and navigating whatever he was doing. Andries held both hands up and looked at Ted and Simon.

"Sorry about that. You see what I have to deal with daily. He can be hard work, but when he got higher in his career, he became cold in his approach. Before that, he was a great officer, you know. The best in the division."

"I understand. He could add a smile occasionally; it wouldn't hurt," Ted said sarcastically.

A silent awkwardness filled the room. Ted turned the phone around in his hand to see the screen. He had his phone on silent, turning it to that setting before entering the police HQ building. In the last three minutes, he saw five missed calls from Savvas Kritsikis from the internal affairs team and many more from Angelika Bafa. Ted jolted from his seat, leaving Andries and Simon on edge.

"I've got to make a call."

"What's wrong?" Simon said.

"I don't know."

Ted pressed the return call for Angelika, and she answered the phone after one ring.

"Where have you been?" she stressed.

"I was meeting with Nikolas and Andries about the Daniel case. What's wrong?"

There was a moment of silence over the line before she replied.

"Daria, the woman you interviewed yesterday. She's dead."

Ted closed his eyes while holding the phone to his ear. He felt a large pit in his stomach.

"What's happened? How did you find out? We weren't meeting her until noon."

"After you gave me the address, I saw it wasn't far from where I live. So, when I drove past there this morning, I saw an ambulance and a police car outside the apartment. I pulled over to see what the situation was. She didn't turn up for work last night and was reported missing by her manager around ten o'clock last night."

"Thank you for letting me know. Savvas rang me. Was it about the same thing?"

"Yes. He wants a meeting with us all about the next steps. This is serious, Ted. We need to move quickly."

"Okay, let's make it happen. When?"

"This morning at HQ. We're heading there now."

"Okay, see you shortly."

Ted disconnected the phone and lowered his hands, resting them on his leg and taking a deep breath.

"What's wrong, Ted?" Simon said.

"Daria, the girl from the club, is dead."

"Is that who you interviewed with Hector last night?"

"Yes, that's four dead now. Internal affairs want to meet. I think someone saw us drive there yesterday and silenced her."

"They came for you last night, Ted, too."

"I know."

Ted fell deep in thought, looking out the window behind Andries, which showed the view of Lycabettus Hill towering in the backdrop. Ted knew the severity of what Daniel was investigating but didn't truly understand the danger involved. However, that realisation was forming in his mind. He was in danger, and so were Simon and anyone else involved. Those involved in the corruption were covering their tracks quickly and effectively.

Simon's comments hit hard. He managed to hear the intruder at his apartment door and scare him off through the pursuit, but unfortunately, he lost him by the stadium; he regretted that even more now. So easily, he could have been one of the lives ended to cover up the investigated crime, just like Daniel was. He knew he would need to be careful with those around him—he needed to find those responsible quickly before more lives, even his own, were lost.

Chapter 20

TED AND SIMON SAT in the boardroom, eagerly awaiting the arrival of the internal affairs team. They both sat in silence, drinking from fresh, steaming coffee cups, observing the outdoor city view as the sun pierced through the cluster of clouds in the sky. The next few days began a winter heat wave in the Greek capital and across many islands in the country's southern parts beyond the Aegean Sea. Temperatures of nineteen degrees were about to embrace the city over the weekend, with the already heated protests lingering for the days ahead. Angelika Bafa and Savvas Kritsikis from the internal affairs team entered the room with their own steaming coffee in a polystyrene cup. The door shut behind them, and the duo took their seats across from Ted and Simon's position.

"Andries joining us?" Ted asked.

"We saw them in the corridor; he's got to do some planning with Nikolas for the protests," Savvas said.

"Sure."

Savvas nodded and then looked towards Angelika, sitting next to him. Angelika carried a paper file, which she opened, plucking the papers from inside and placing them onto the table. The top page, from his view, looked like a police report that was in Greek. She shuffled the pages and pulled out a similar-looking sheet and a collection of photographs underneath. All the people sitting in the boardroom were staring at the papers as Angelika placed them on the table, one by one rotating them so Ted and Simon could take a better view.

"Here is the report on Daria Hussain, who was found this morning at 07:02 AM by her landlord and colleague."

Ted reached for the document and started to read it. It was a police report with a stamp and signature in the top left-hand corner to indicate it had been translated into English and all information was correct. Angelika continued.

"Daria failed to report to work at the club last night, and one of the dancers, Anita Yalom, drove to her address early in the morning, around 06:05 AM, shortly after her shift. Anita entered the apartment as one of the residents headed out to work. She knocked on Daria's door, and there was no answer there and no answer on her mobile, which she called and messaged many times throughout the evening and night. Anita went downstairs towards the office on the ground floor and found the landlord entering his room from the front door entrance."

Ted could hear Angelika reading the report, but he was reading further in front than he was speaking. The information indicated that Anita told the landlord that her friend Daria didn't report for work last night and was worried about her welfare. The landlord agreed to use one of the master keys he kept with him for all apartment rooms in case of an emergency, used only when the resident was locked out of their apartments. Upon entering the apartment room, they both noticed signs of an altercation. They reported a lamp smashed and lying adjacent to a coffee table, some wine glasses were broken in the kitchen area, and some metal cutlery lying scattered on the floor next to a plastic cutlery tray.

An adjacent door was the bathroom, and the report stated a horrible truth upon its opening. Within the bathtub was the body of Daria.

Her eyes looked toward the door as if pleading for help or staring at the person who murdered her. However, she was beyond saving. She sat upright in the tub with a description of clothing that Ted had seen her wearing the evening before. Her skin was pale and cold to the touch. The report continued to suggest that the cause of death was an exposed hypopharynx following a cutthroat, haemorrhage, shock, and asphyxia from aspirated blood. She had coughed and choked on the blood that had entered her lungs, resulting in it having foamed and dried around her mouth. Ted finished the report, and Angelika relayed the gruesome part of Daria's death in audio form, which was more beneficial to Simon. Ted's mind raced to when he left Daria's apartment and whether he remembered seeing anything unusual. Ted couldn't remember, and he hated himself for it.

Savvas interrupted Angelika as he finished the report.

"Now you've heard that, please tell us what you know, Ted, so we can understand everything clearly before it gets worse," Savvas said as he leaned back into his chair, allowing Ted to unravel the events.

Ted spoke with great detail about his first meeting with Andries and then the concern about Christos not being in contact with the department on his leave. Upon entering Christos's apartment, they discovered the officer and his partner, Cassandra, dead. He recalled the crime scene visit at the warehouse facility and the CCTV they viewed with the mysterious man who avoided the front exit. The visit to the strip club, the CCTV showing Daniel visiting inside, the conversation with the club owner, the money collection date, and the visit to Daria's house. Lastly, he recalled the unknown male lurking around his apartment door and the foot pursuit towards the football stadium, where Ted lost him, and added the black Mercedes to the narration. The affairs team sat plain-faced as they absorbed the information from Ted's lone investigation, taking a few seconds to process it.

"I appreciate you finally updating us on the investigation," Savvas said.

"Sorry, I didn't know who to trust. I still don't," Ted pleaded.

"It's okay. I understand."

He paused for a second before delving deeper into Ted's story.

"You mentioned that the owner said on Sundays, people come and collect the money from the club? That would be an excellent start, but that is a few days away. However, the owner may have told the gang about your little visit and that Sunday collection may not happen."

Savvas took a sip from his coffee mug and looked disgusted.

"This coffee is cold and shit."

"Wish they did Starbucks nearer to our office," Angelika added.

"That's for people who love Instagram and posing. A Coffee Island, Coffee Berry, or Mikel Coffee will do. Not this grainy, muddy water," Savvis said, swirling the liquid around his cup before continuing.

"Anyway, sorry, Ted."

Ted smiled from his outburst. He hadn't tried Greek coffee chains but would do so if he could. He didn't mind a Starbucks but knew the caffeine levels weren't high enough for him, and he wasn't one for those Strawberries & Cream Frappuccino photo opportunities. He saw a side of Savvis that differed from his professional outlook—a sense of humour, a hint of normality.

"Erm. Yes, where were we?"

"The Sunday collection at..."

"Sorry, yes. You're right, the owner has possibly spooked them, and it could be any day or time now; they may change their pattern."

"Could we force their hand? Shut them down? Pending investigation for connections to organised crime? Illegal immigration? Let's be real here—people know we are on to them; we stop this specific point of their activity..."

Ted shook his head and interrupted.

"No. There may be someone there who knows more than we are being told. The club owner, of course. Maybe even this Anita who works there. Someone at this club or the other place Daria was working may be able to identify the suspected officer."

Savvas lifted his index fingers towards his mouth as the officers waited, and he pondered which words to respond to.

"Okay, we keep it open on the basis you think it will be significant to the investigation?" Savvas said.

"Correct. If the owner fully works for them, they won't be there on Sunday."

Savvas nodded before replying.

"Okay, well, we will leave the option on the table. I might get one of our affairs officers to keep an eye on the club to see if there is any suspicious activity."

A momentary lull crossed the room as the officers reached for their cups of mixed reviewed coffee and took a sip.

"Who is working on this case with you, Simon?" Angelika said.

"Us two," Simon said, pointing at himself and Ted.

"Eliana and Hector partially, but Hector has been taken off because of the protests," Ted followed.

"Andries, too, of course," Simon said.

Ted realised at that moment he had asked for police officers to protect Daria, but it seemed likely this hadn't been arranged due to her death. He tightened his eyes, and the team noticed his confusion.

"Something I don't get. I asked Hector to order police patrol on Daria's house. Was this operation still active last night and in the early hours?"

"I don't know, Ted; I can find out for you," Angelika told him.

"Please."

Angelika cleared her throat. This caught the attention of the room. Savvas and Angelika looked among themselves, communicating as if their expressions were Morse code.

"I want you to do me a favour, Ted," stated Angelika.

Ted raised his eyebrows as if to say *proceed*.

"Don't bring Andries or Hector in on this anymore. Try to keep them out of the loop, so to speak. Hopefully, the protests will do that naturally."

"Why?" Ted said, piquing his curiosity.

Savvas interrupted.

"We don't know, but we have been running our investigation and have a shortlist of potential suspects. We just need to gather the evidence to strengthen our claims. That's all they are, claims."

"Who do you have on your list?"

Angelika searched Savvas as if to seek permission to speak.

"What is it?" Ted pressed.

Angelika gained a nod from Savvas to proceed.

"There may be speculation to suggest that someone close to the case is involved."

"Like Andries?" Ted asked.

Ted knew there was an officer in the department who had the potential to be involved with the OCG and the department's corruption. However, he never saw it as Andries, someone close to the case, or close to Daniel. Someone whom Ted had to trust as he entered the unknown of this investigation.

"We have a list of suspects; it's not just Andries, let me tell you. We just need to tread carefully. There is a fox among the hens," Savvas added.

"So it's just speculation at this point?" Simon asked.

"It is, I'm afraid. We know, for example, through conversations with people and rumours. Andries is going through a divorce; Hector took on a second job in a bar a year ago. I don't know if he still doing it now, and other officers have taken it upon themselves to take second jobs, and some have previous gambling and addictions. Could be nothing, could be something."

"What about the officers that may have taken revenge on Daniel finding out about them taking bribes from the public with minor offenders?" Ted asked.

"We are aware of those offenders, which are on our list, too."

"Do you think the officer was threatened? The gang threatened them and their family to participate in organised crime activity?" Ted asked.

"Maybe so, yes. Nothing is out of the question," Savvas agreed.

"It could simply be that the money offered was too large to refuse," Angelika added.

A few nods cascaded the room, adding to the rumours of monetary problems with some officers, forced to take second jobs.

"So, what's next? We have another dead victim and no leads; we need to move forward quickly," Simon asked.

Ted pointed out the report on the table, containing the details of Daria surrounding her discovery early this morning.

"Can I have a look?"

"Sure. Here."

Angelika reached inside the file on the table and picked through the sheets until he pulled out the pages, which were set on a bonded link. She slid the papers along the wooden table until they reached Ted. Ted was searching for any interviews that had taken place with any witnesses to the crime. He used his index finger as he slowed down his skimming technique to study carefully any keywords he was searching for. His finger stopped, and the reading intrigued him greatly.

"There is a passage that says someone saw a black Mercedes fleeing the scenes in the early morning?" Ted glared.

"Yes, a woman in her late sixties couldn't sleep, so she watched reruns of TV shows she enjoyed and heard voices on the street. Got up to see what was happening, heard a few car doors close, and it sped off down the road."

Ted continued to read as the state of Daria's discovery was narrated below. He skipped the details as it was relayed to him before, but the image of the black Mercedes entered the front of his mind.

"Did anyone get the reg?"

"We are waiting on a call now from our team. They searched the cameras in the area when the woman heard the potential suspects. We should have an answer any time now," Angelika explained.

"Police and forensics are doing a thorough job, too, so we will have their report as soon as it's ready," Savvas added.

"I'm sure they are. Also, Hector was with me during Daria's visit. Have you spoken to him?" Ted asked.

"We will, don't you worry. I'm waiting for higher powers to allow me to investigate more abruptly."

"Nikolas?"

"Yes, I will meet him today and discuss my intentions."

"Great. Any leads on the CCTV at the train station?" Ted reimposed.

"We've contacted the Albanian State Police Force this morning and are waiting for a response; they're searching their systems, but no luck so far," Angelika said.

Ted turned to Simon.

"Who is the ILO in Albania?"

"One step ahead of you all. I've already sent the details to our ILO in Tirana, Elijah. He will get back to me as soon as he has anything."

"Here we go," Angelika said excitedly as her phone vibrated in her pocket.

The room went silent as all eyes focused on her facial expression as she began communicating with the person on the other end of the phone.

"Aha. Yep. Give it to me."

Angelika grabbed the nearest pen, snatching it from its position and furiously started to write on the outer part of her report file.

"Thank you," she spoke as she placed the phone away from her ear.

"Good news and bad news," Angelika announced, placing the phone beside her.

She continued while everyone in the room grew pressed to her every word.

"The bad news is we don't have a location on the vehicle. The good news is that we have the licence plate connected to a lease vehicle owned by a rental company in the city. Our team is now running through the city's and our limited ANPR cameras for the location."

"What's the licence plate?" Ted asked urgently.

Angelika glanced at Ted, then at the file she just wrote on.

"A black Mercedes. Licence plate IHA-4320 owned by Avis rental company."

A surge of energy flowed through Ted's veins, forcing him to stand up impatiently. "Lets go."

Chapter 21

A SMALL INDENT IN the pedestrian walkway allowed space for one car to park. Fortunately enough, the car space was available when they reached their destination. The rental car office was located north of Leof. Andrea Siggrou Road was flooded with other rental car companies, littering both sides of the buildings surrounding the dual highway. Avis's rental car office was hidden behind a selection of roadside trees, allowing viewing of Hertz, Ansa, and Bazaar until the Avis sign was eventually spotted. Ted knew the area from the other evening when he drove to and from Eliana's house, as their current location was at the bottom of Rovertou Galli.

Entering the offices, the room felt larger in its interior than its exterior shell, reminding him of the tardis in the *Dr Who* television series. The interior included a small waiting area on the right side, with a water tank and a tower of polystyrene cups for customers. Upon the left was a barrier from the front door to the middle of the room, secluding the waiting area from the fully operational staff members. A selection of four tables was occupied by one staff member working on each with their computers, but no customer was in sight. Maybe it was the time of the year, with minimum visitors or the fierce competition with other neighbouring companies led to the quiet working day.

Ted surveyed the staff members, who all looked at the quartet of officers entering the building, wondering if they were there to hire a vehicle and save them from their boredom with some riveting drama. Ted noticed one staff member, whom he guessed was mid-twenties, with surfer long blond hair, sitting in a blue shirt, with the top button undone and tieless. The man glanced up and seemed to nervously return to work while the other staff smiled as a friendly greeting. The end of the barrier led to a walkway along the back wall, containing toilet facilities, what seemed to be a restroom for the staff members, and a single office, presumably for the branch manager.

Angelika reached the office's open door, spoke in Greek, and entered. The window that allowed a vantage point to look inside was blocked due to the closed blind partition. Simon entered the room, as did Ted and Eliana, just after he glanced back at the blue-shirted man he was sceptical of. Their eyes briefly locked before the man dropped to his computer screen again. Ted kept an eye on him as he closed the office door behind him and went out of view. Inside the office, a man sat small and hunched behind a large computer screen.

"English?" Angelika asked the man.

"No problem. We have many English tourists, so I can do that."

"I'm Officer Angelika Bafa from the Hellenic Police Department."

Angelika turned her body to face Simon and Ted to introduce them. The man was still sitting behind his desk, looking up at the four officers, slightly intimidated.

"This is Officer Ted Chester and Simon Taylor; they're from England, and we are investigating something that has brought us here, and I'm wondering if you can help?"

As he reacted, the man's intimidated look continued with a sprinkle of confusion.

"S-sure," the man stuttered.

"May I?" Angelika said, pointing at the free seat in front of the desk.

"Yeah," the man said, extending his hand to approve.

Angelika took one of the seats and pointed for one of the other officers to take the other free chair. She soon realised the height discrepancy and decided to stand instead.

"What's your name, sorry?"

"Kostas Vouvali."

"I forgot to ask, are you the manager? I just assumed."

"Manager?" the man asked, confused by the English word.

"Boss, Afentikó."

"Sorry, my English is good but not excellent. I'm second in office, do you say? The Afentikó is out of the office on holiday."

"Okay, but you can search your system for information?"

"Sure."

"Do you have a vehicle registered to your company with this licence plate?" Angelika asked, handing over a small piece of paper with the information regarding the black Mercedes IHA-4320.

Kostas took the slip and placed it on the side of his keyboard. He worked the mouse, manoeuvring through the open windows he had on-screen. He entered the information into the corporate system and clicked enter, revealing the results.

"We do. Black Mercedes E-Class Sport. Currently out on rent at the moment. If I remember correctly, it's two vehicles, actually."

The officers glanced at one another with concern that multiple identical vehicles were being used by the OCG. This would add complexity to the case, as they wouldn't know which Mercedes were being used or had been used for which crime.

"Looks like we've got more than one to look out for," Ted said to the room.

Angelika towered over the screen while Ted and Simon remained standing. They took a step forward, standing snugly behind each seat.

"Does it say who you rented it out to?"

Kostas's thick eyebrows raised high.

"That's strange," he said with a puzzled expression.

"What is it?" Angelika pressed.

Kostas peered over his company screen and back at the screen.

"It's not here," he said, looking back at the four officers.

Ted looked down at the floor as he continued to feel peculiar about the man sitting at his computer screen in the main room.

"What do you mean?" Simon asked.

"It looks like it's been changed. The information has been deleted," Kostas said, peering towards the closed door.

"So you can't tell us who is renting this vehicle?"

"I can't... I don't understand why he..."

Ted lifted his head after Kostas's statement and looked back at the closed door with a flurry of thoughts flooding his brain.

"Why he what?" Angelika pressed.

Ted moved over to the blinds to gain a view of the office. He placed his index and middle finger within a small gap in the blinds, lifting the section upwards to gain a small letterboxed view of the office and focusing solely on the nervous-looking man's workspace.

"Mario deleted the information a few days ago."

"Does Mario work here?"

"Yes, he is out there now. Starting about three weeks ago."

"He's not there anymore," Ted replied, witnessing the empty chair.

Ted quickly moved away from the blind and reached for the office door, flinging it open in one motion and powering through. The noise of the door hitting the internal office wall caught the attention of the other three workers, who lifted their heads over their computers to gain a better visual.

"Where has Mario gone?" Ted yelled, pacing towards the front door, pointing at the empty chair.

"He said he was taking an early lunch break after he finished his report," one of the workers replied.

"How long ago did he leave?"

"You've just missed him, only just now."

Ted pulled back hard on the door, and then pushed through the door onto the street. Ted pivoted his head left and right, searching the pedestrian walkways along his side of the road. There was no sign of the man. If the worker was right and the man had only left a few seconds ago, he would have been spotted on the walkway unless he'd managed to sneak into an alleyway behind the rental car buildings. As he gave up hope, many cars passed the dual carriageway. He searched across the road for a sign of activity, but the man wasn't there.

Suddenly a mixture of two mechanical noises gave Ted his next move. A loud horn came from a vehicle across the carriageway, clearly frustrated by something. The large trees on the side of the road blocked Ted's view as the car stopped suddenly. The car horn noise, long and drawn out to begin with, became intervals as the driver made his point of annoyance. The line of the trees broke, giving Ted a view of the worker running across the street, reaching the pavement. As the man approached it, he looked back momentarily and locked eyes with Ted as he began to step out into the street. The man gave the same nervous look when they first locked eyes in the office building, and then he disappeared behind the high-rise building blocks.

"Ted, where has he gone?" Simon shouted.

"He's gone down that road," Ted replied, running across the road, catching a break in the traffic.

Simon shouted a response, but Ted couldn't hear it as the traffic horns started to fire up again as Ted reached the other side of the road. Unbeknown to Ted, the man had entered Athanasiou Diakou Road, a side street to the main carriageway. It held no significance, as it was a dead end; however, one could venture around the L-shaped road back towards the Rovertou Galli Hill. Although, there were many hiding spots along the route, side street exits, and various cafés, hotels, and shops. Ted managed to reach the road in time for him to witness the man enter the side street, which led towards the Plaka area of the city. Ted reached for his phone and used one of the communication apps to share his live location with Angelika to help guide her in her vehicle. As the man crossed Dionysiou Areopagitou Street, adjacent to the south slope of the Acropolis, Ted realised he was entering a large pedestrianised area. Ted knew Angelika wouldn't be able to drive into the small narrow walking streets of Plaka but would have to circle around them both until they reached the outer rim of the area. For now, it was Ted and Mario alone.

The man ran across the cobbled walkway, which was lined with pop-up stalls selling a variety of different goods. Those streets were busy with bustling pedestrians, catching a glimpse at the foot race as they stormed past the junction onto Frinichou. The distance between the two was reducing, with Ted being the better runner on this occasion. The Holy Church of Saint Catherine, the centuries-old Greek Orthodox church featuring weathered columns from an ancient temple, opened the vastness of its reach. Mario darted left, weaving through trees and the towering columns to slow Ted down.

Suddenly, Mario was given three escape options, and he chose Adrianou. When those restaurants offered Alfresco dining in the height of summer, a narrow one-way system had become a temporary opportunity again due to the winter heat wave. The walkway ran around the grounds of the northern boundaries, which held the Acropolis on top of its rock finishing due south of Psyri. Mario became desperate to stop Ted and began to slow down and increase his exertion by throwing chairs and temporary stand-up menus down in his path. The pedestrians and other obstacles acted as chicanes as they bounded through the tightly packed streets.

Suddenly, Mario shifted his weight to the right and entered Kidathineon. A similar street to the last, littered with souvenir shops, cafés, and tavernas, towered with cream buildings on either side. Ted had caught up to Mario within a matter of metres when a group of people exited one of the cafés, colliding with Ted as he powered through. He exchanged an apology to the group and two young men who had fallen to the ground under his moving force. Ahead, for the first time in a few minutes, Ted could see the movement of cars crossing left to right and right to left in the distance, indicating the main road was approaching as they exited the pedestrianised area. The distance between the two was much larger than when he'd followed him through the first packed street, but Ted was gaining on him faster than ever. Mario was starting to tire. The suspect had reached the end of the pedestrianised area, which led to Filellinon Road. This road was similar to when he exited the rental car building, busy in its nature. The road was between Plaka and the National Gardens, near the Hellenic Parliament, where the organised protests were due tomorrow. Ted was hopeful Angelika could help support him on the motorised roads.

He reached the busy street, witnessing Mario running along the pedestrian pavement before entering the busy road, spotting a break in the oncoming traffic. Ted briefly looked down at his phone to see Simon had shared his location, presumably in the exact vehicle as Angelika. He opened the app while observing the runner stepping into the road. The marker showed Simon was on Filellinon approaching south, the direction he was running towards at that moment. Ted edged towards the end of the pavement, taking one foot onto the road's tarmac. He saw a break in the traffic from the south, all the while trying to spot Angelika's vehicle.

Suddenly, there was a loud roar from a vehicle. The mechanical noise didn't come from Angelika's oncoming car but from the north. As Ted stepped onto the road and looked left for a clear run, he saw the black Mercedes licenced IHA-4320 accelerate at high speed, bulldozing Mario as the front bumper collided with his body. Mario was flung into the air as the front grid of the vehicle shattered his legs. The roaring black car sped up after impact, and Mario's body skidded along the roof and landed head-first onto the tarmac as the vehicle accelerated away.

Ted glanced at the shadow of the person behind the wheel, whom he was sure was staring directly back at him. He couldn't work out his face, but he was sure it was a male. Ted turned his attention to Mario, lying motionless in the street. His eyes searched the sky for hope while life was draining from his body. Blood was pooling around the base of his head as Ted knelt next to him. Ted reached for his mobile phone and rang emergency services, 112, and then Angelika to update the other officers on his location and the Mercedes. Ted knew instantly that the man's life was ending; even an ambulance rush wouldn't get to Mario's needs quickly enough to help him. Ted placed his hand on Mario's shoulder, shaking it slightly to keep his eyes open before he slipped towards the inevitable light.

"Who are you working for?" he shouted.

Mario opened his eyes slightly.

"Mario, who are you working for?"

Mario started to mutter, but blood was escaping from his mouth simultaneously. Ted tilted his head down, turning his ear towards Mario's mouth.

"Mario!"

"To Afentikó," he muttered slowly and so quietly.

Ted lifted his head as he stood, looking down at Mario's desperate face, taking in the full view of the man's life disappearing. Ted locked eyes with Mario as more blood exited his mouth and began dribbling down his cheek onto the tarmac.

"The Boss," Ted whispered back.

Mario's eyes closed.

Chapter 22

FILELLINON WAS CLOSED IN both directions, and pedestrians were urged to avoid the crime scene. Those who witnessed the motionless body took videos and photographs as police officers arrived to cordon off the scene and bring some order to the incoming media footage that would submerge the internet and the city's news again. Angelika, Eliana, and Simon exited their vehicles, quickly crowding around the dead body, which Ted remained staring at. The bloody pool turned a dark red as the sun hid behind the high-rise building on the main road.

The piercing alarm of incoming service vehicles penetrated the area, covering the shouting and questioning from onlookers on the pavement. The two officers approached Ted, standing as if overlooking a loved one's grave, never diverting from its stone stature.

"Was it the same vehicle?" Angelika announced, holding her phone to her ear.

Ted nodded to confirm. Angelika shook her head, demanding the officer on the phone follow the vehicle on the ANPR cameras. Once she finished, she placed her phone into her trouser pocket and exhaled deeply. She looked down at the tarmac where Mario lay.

"Did he say anything?"

"To Afentikó."

"The Boss? What does that even mean?"

"I don't know. It could mean anything."

Angelika touched her hips as the other officers investigated the body.

"What a mess this is. Nikolas and Andries are not going to be happy."

Ted ignored the comment and reached into the dead man's pocket, reaching for the credentials he had in his possession. He opened the brown leather wallet and found his EU Greek driving licence card. Ted scanned the licence. The wording was in Greek letters, which he didn't understand. However, he knew from his UK driving licence where some of the identification points were. The name read Mario Martinaj, with a date of birth of 19th January 1993. There was an address towards the bottom of the photo identification card, which was challenging to locate. However, Ted noticed the word *Athena*. The Greek spelling of Athens, so he knew his address was nearby.

"Who is he?" Simon asked, leaning over both Ted and the body.

"Mario Martinaj. Think he lives in the city."

Ted remained crouched, observing the card. He had not yet searched the place of birth, which he assumed may have been in Greece, but he was unsure.

"Where is Kruje?"

"Albania," Simon replied.

Ted smirked, rising to his feet, still fixated on the driving card.

"Of course. He gets a job at a car rental, so they can use him to delete records, access cars, and provide their own plates. Cover themselves up and hide."

"Thankfully, they slipped up, and we got the plate, which led us to Mario."

"And Mario is now dead. Don't be surprised if you never see that plate again on the camera."

Simon nodded in agreement; he knew it was time the OCG changed tactics and became incognito again. Angelika scanned the identification document so she could ring back at the police station for someone to check the name on their system. Once the information was gathered, she waited a few moments before the officer relayed them.

"He's not coming up on our system with anything. He's clean."

Ted bit his bottom lip in frustration.

"Nothing at all?" Simon pressed.

"We can look at further information, education, when he moved to Greece. However, there is nothing on the system. He must have been educated in Albania. We will need to contact them to see if they have anything."

"Sure, yeah. See what it brings up," Ted replied.

"Let me make a call to the ILO in Albania. Speed some things up a bit," Simon said as he stepped away from the group.

As Ted watched him move out towards the pavements, an influx of public servants infiltrated the crime scene. Ted noticed some officers were piling out of vehicles and rolling out police tape using the lamp posts and trees that lined some of the sidewalks to place a barrier for those looking. Paramedics rushed out of the front cab, holding their medical bags in bold red uniforms. One of the medics entered the rear of the ambulance, obtaining a large, folded screen that allowed privacy and coverage for the body preservation from media broadcasting. The forensic team would be en route once the paramedics announced the death on arrival.

Ted watched the first paramedic at the scene check Mario's pulse before checking his watch and presumably reporting the obvious. At that moment, the large protection screen masked the lifeless body, as if the stage performance on Broadway had finished, and all but the rapturous applause was missing. Ted broke away from the view, witnessing Simon on his mobile device, presuming to be the ILO.

"Angelika? Who did you speak with when you sent the information to the Albanian authorities?"

"Inspector Kejsi Çela. Policia Kufitare department," Angelika announced.

"What's Kufitare?"

"Border police tasked to patrol the state border and migration."

"Not the first time you've spoken to him, then?"

"Well, let's say we've had similar for a while, even before this happened. In Greece, Albanians constituted the largest migrant community within its borders. Some Albanian immigrants applied for asylum, some failed and remained in Greece illegally."

"Not your first rodeo. Have you got his number?" Ted pressed.

"You want to speak to him now? I've just told our officers to contact him," she said, confused.

"Sure. I've got nothing else to do; we're at a dead end, literally. Can I have it, please? I want to speak to him personally."

Angelika nodded and gave Ted Kejsi's office and personal number so he could store it within his contacts. Ted began ringing the number provided.

"Inspector Kejsi Çela. Policia Kufitare department. Who am I speaking with?"

"It's Ted Chester. I'm an International Liaison Officer working in Athens..."

"You Brits work fast. I've only just spoken to one of your officers."

"Angelika's officers?"

"Yeah."

"Do you have an update on the information given?"

"Jesus. Wine and dine me first. I've literally just sat down from getting a coffee."

Ted smirked at Kejsi's response but was unsure if he had already gotten off on the wrong foot, allowing for dismissive or refusal to cooperate from Kejsi. He was about to apologise before the inspector saved his blushes.

"Listen. Sorry, it's been a busy day. I'm happy to help, I was just about to ring the officer back at your headquarters to update him, but I can also update you if it makes the chains of command flow quicker?"

"Sorry to be so forward with you. It's just we are losing a battle here with these gang members. If you can give us any update, that would be appreciated."

"I heard one of your officers is dead. Well... a few, if you don't mind me being so blunt."

"Yeah, you are right."

"Well, I'll help you the best I can to help you get these scumbags. So, Mario Martinaj. Born Kruje. 19th January 1993. He was in and out of the education system and family homes. His parents were drug addicts and died when he was nine or ten, but he was already filtering around different foster homes and adoption centres. Not the best of upbringings..."

Ted glanced over at where his body was, feeling sorry for him as he lay cold on the ground. A victim to the system and one that life chewed up and spat out to defend himself, and in a less developed country, he only knew the horrors he had previously faced. A boy with no home would reach out for safety and comfort, which may have been those in the wrong crowd.

"He entered our system around fourteen, minor theft charges such as shops, and that got bigger as he grew into an adult. Turning into the robbery of houses, jewellery, and cars. We have information that links him to the Sinaloa Cartel. Sacra Corona Unita. Società foggiana. He was only a small piece of some of the major Albania gangs and Mafia groups here."

"Do you have any information on him travelling here?"

"We don't—you may on your system. However, he may have used a fake ID or illegally accessed the net. Who knows."

Ted understood that may have been the case. He knew nothing about the case's direction but now knew Mario's backstory, which left an eerie feeling.

"Does that help? I know it's not what you wanted, but we are still working on the man's identity at the train station. The camera footage isn't great, so we are trying to see if we can get any digital experts to help clear it up a bit. I think some of your officers there are trying to do something, too."

"No problem, let me know if you hear anything."

"Understood. I'll let you and Angelika know of any updates."

Ted disconnected the phone without replying. He saw Simon reapproaching the group, and Ted was keen to see if he had anything new from his contact.

"Any news?" Ted pressed.

Simon shook his head.

"He's out on a case; he said he would call back when he could. He said officers are working on the CCTV footage, but it's too grainy to cross-reference it on their system."

Ted pierced his lips together.

"You?" Simon asked.

"Yeah. They said the same about the CCTV. We got news on Mario," Ted said, nodding towards the erected protection screens.

"He was passed through the foster system, and things didn't work out. He got into crime, probably groomed or found safety with the gang, and now he's..."

"Poor kid."

Angelika overheard the conversation and followed up with her own update.

"We're sending an officer to Mario's apartment now and see what we can find. We're getting a warrant written up now."

"Good. Do you have guys working on the CCTV here too?"

"Yes, we do, but it's hard work. We hope to have a better-quality photo for you in a day or two. The tech guys are on it."

Ted noticed Eliana wasn't within the circle of officers. She had picked out her phone a few yards away, taking it from her trouser pocket and turned her back to the group. He kept an eye on her while she communicated to the other person on the line. She held one finger over her vacant ear, trying to hear the person through the external circus of noise on Filellinon. Ted blocked out the sounds within his vicinity as he focused on her and grasped the last few sentences as she turned back.

"Ah, ah. Yeah. Right. Thanks for the update. Keep us posted if you hear anything else."

She dropped her hand while holding her phone, making her way back towards Ted.

"What was that?" Ted asked inquisitively.

"It was an officer from the switchboard at the police station. They take calls from the public. They are getting reports of a car fire in the Rouf Exarcheia area of Athens."

"Where is that?" Ted asked.

He didn't know the area of Athens, evidently. Rouf was located west of the Athens centre, between Piraeus and Petrou Ralli Avenue.

Rouf was named after a Bavarian businessman who, during Otto's reign, bought large areas in this location to make a farm. Eliana explained the background of the area to Ted before revealing more details.

"No plate yet, but they've identified..."

"A black Mercedes?"

Eliana nodded. Ted pressed his mouth together as he thought about the news, shaking his head and clicking his fingers in frustration.

"They've covered their tracks. Quickly, may I add."

"Officers and firefighters are in attendance now; they say it's recoverable. But whatever is in there will have been destroyed. Get this—no plates on the vehicle at first glance."

Ted exhaled and grew impatient with the situation.

"We've got dead officers, dead witnesses, and no leads. We're not getting facial recognition back on our suspects."

"It will come soon. We are expecting updates soon," Simon proclaimed.

Ted shook his head, not due to Simon's comment, but more so the overall situation. It was bleak, at a dead end. Ever since he reached Athens, he'd been rushed around with the wave of activity and deadly situations. He needed a moment to look over the whole timeline and timescales, gain a handle on it, and see if there was a small fragment that could open the entire investigation.

"We need something else, something new. Some sort of breakthrough."

"Like what?" Simon asked.

Ted looked down at his watch; it was approaching midafternoon and was still no closer than he was when he arrived, with the chaos that had come with it.

"I don't know, but we must look over everything."

Chapter 23

TED AND SIMON'S BOARDROOM was quiet before the storm a few days ago. Now, it was very different. They sat in the boardroom deliberating over the story of the investigation so far. Over the last few hours since the foot pursuit which led to Filellinon, there had been a few updates from the aftermath. The Greek firefighters extinguished the black Mercedes fire before further damage was created from a potential blast if the flames reached the petrol tank. The only concern was when the tyres exploded, throwing off burning debris, but the area was well cordoned off before. As first feared, the fire left only the bare metal shell of the vehicle and no other potential evidence in its interior.

The last marker the ANPR camera received was the vehicle heading west, northwest of the Acropolis and Psyri area. What happened between that last capture and the burnt-out car was unsolved. Officers scrambled to contact local businesses for their CCTV footage but showed no indication of why the plates disappeared or where the men headed. The area where the burnt-out vehicle was positioned was unseen by any CCTV. The location was between St. Basil Greek Orthodox Church and PAO Rouf FC's Rouf Municipal Stadium. Witnesses saw the car starting to blaze but not the initiation or any suspects within the quiet area. Due to the vehicle's location and the lack of

CCTV in the area, officers assumed the OCG had prior knowledge that the area had no surveillance coverage.

An earlier search of Mario's apartment revealed it grotty and unkempt. The entire flat didn't appear as though it had been raided by anyone. So far in their search, they found a few bundles of notes, each containing one thousand euros. Not serious amounts of cash, but money stashed, nonetheless. Residents within the apartment complex stated Mario wasn't a problem for neighbours. He was quiet and reserved whenever he was living inside his own accommodation.

While Ted occupied the boardroom, Angelika visited her internal affairs department to liaise with Savvas. Their team had digital expertise in obtaining information regarding possible CCTV or facial recognition from the train station, which was close to being thoroughly analysed on their corporate and internal systems. They were closing in on the possibility that the team may be able to provide better footage of the suspect to share with the Albanian authorities sooner rather than later.

The boardroom door opened swiftly, and Angelika and Eliana entered.

"Here are the reports you wanted off Andries earlier. The burglar report from Daniel's property. I've translated it through our system; some words can be slightly off, but it's good to read," Angelika said.

So far, Ted knew that apartment was reportedly broken into and ransacked during the night of his murder. Senior officers attended the apartment but couldn't specifically say what had been taken or what the robbers sought. Joanne suggested on first viewing that some of her jewellery had been taken, but nothing else seemed out of place, apart from the furniture being tipped over and other broken furnishings.

"No more updates on what was stolen?" Ted queried.

"No, there isn't, apart from some jewellery. Some were left, so I don't think they were after that. They just took it for monetary value."

"Joanne didn't know what else was stolen since this report was made?"

"No, just what was mentioned. She gave no other updates... Page four, I think you'll find that."

Ted flipped a few pages to find the corresponding page held together by a paper clip in the top left-hand corner. The information in question was merely a few sentences long, confirming what Angelika announced but in an expanded, extreme form. Ted tapped the page with his index finger, searching for something to provide a new alternative.

Angelika spoke, offering support on the information.

"I've read the report so I can summarise. The report details the on-duty officers who searched the property with Nikolas and Andries. Nikolas and Andries attended, as they'd been on-site at the music venue throughout the night and were transported to the house once Joanne reached home after being questioned to get some fresh clothes, and reported the burglary. Some witnesses in the apartment heard noises, but no one saw their faces. They wore masks, and a white Renault van was used in the getaway with no plates attached. CCTV was investigated in the surrounding areas, but a few white Renault vans were driving that night, none without plates. Nikolas closed the case for now."

"Probably trying to push it to one side before the protests."

Angelika looked back at Ted with an awkward glance.

"Okay, so nothing in the burglary report," Ted said as he closed and filed the pages neatly before gliding them back across the table.

Ted continued.

"I told Hector to request officers to circle Daria's apartment. Did you check to see if this was ordered?"

"It was. I checked the logs from that evening, and one of the officers on duty received that order."

"So, how did Daria's murderers get inside unseen?"

"Good question. But there is a valid answer. Unfortunately, a roadside accident tragically involved a few University of Athens students. Sadly, some died on the scene. Officers were requested to support, and the officers had to leave their posts."

"So why wasn't there backup support for Daria as requested when the officers left?"

"We don't have unlimited amounts of officers, Ted."

"She would still be alive."

"I agree. But I'm saying that Hector made the order, and unfortunate circumstances led to the apartment becoming unprotected. So he didn't fuck up or cancel the order or anything."

"Yes, I understand. Someone must have known it was unmanned, though."

"You could be right, Ted. Or someone else was watching the whole time after following you around."

"Also true."

Ted felt consumed by guilt, not knowing he was being followed, leading to Daria's death. On the other hand, Daria was a person of interest, and if someone close to Ted knew that, they might have already had plans to silence her. Ted moved on.

"Anything on the facial recognition from the train station?"

Angelika's face beamed.

"What?" Ted asked.

"Thought I'd leave the best till last. Well, hopefully, we get the DNA too before long," Angelika grinned as she checked her watch.

"The digital experts think they've cleared up the photograph to the best of their ability. They've used AI-based depixelators."

"What's that? Can't they use Photoshop or something?"

"I asked that at the beginning. But they said it only smooths the edges and makes the picture blurry. AI trains millions of images and places the missing pixels into the photo." "So what's next?"

"We've sent it to Kejsi for analysis; they will find him if they have him on their system. We've not had a hit so far on our system, but any time now, I assure you."

Ted felt his phone vibrating in his pocket. The reach for his trouser pocket alerted the rest of the group.

"It's Kejsi," Ted said, looking at the incoming call.

"I hope this is it. Answer it on the loudspeaker," Angelika asked.

Ted did as instructed, answering the call and selecting the speaker-phone option.

"Hi, Kejsi, it's Ted. You're on loudspeaker to my British colleague Simon. We also have Angelika on the internal affairs team and Officer Eliana Abulafia."

"Hi, guys. I'm delighted to say we have a hit on your facial photograph at the train station. Mateo Berisha, and he is known to us."

"In what capacity?"

"He was arrested in 2016 for importing illegal small arms into Greece as well as drugs—heroin specifically—and a couple of charges for exploitation of prostitution. He came back to Albania and served his sentence."

"How long did he serve?"

"Three years. Came out only eight months ago."

"And straight back into the fire."

"Here in Albania, he is known to us before 2016. Drug trafficking, prostitution, weapons importation, and even fraud and robbery charges."

"No murder?"

"No, nothing here with murder to our knowledge. Do you think he killed your officers?"

"He came for me. But I don't know if he pulled the trigger on the others. We are waiting on DNA."

"Okay, I'll let you know if we get anything else. But we have nothing recent."

Angelika stood up from her chair and answered her mobile device, hovering by the boardroom door, covering who it was on the phone.

"Listen, thanks, Kejsi."

"No problem, I'll do some more digging, man. Speak soon."

Ted wasn't sure if Kejsi was a young hipster Albanian inspector or if Kejsi was just using slang because Ted was British or different. Either way, he was grateful. Ted witnessed Angelika head back towards the desk at which they were sitting.

"We got an update on facial recognition. Confirming it, Mateo Berisha. They had an arrest on file for 2016, as Kejsi said. Nothing more," Ted explained.

"Anything else?""Nope.""I've got one better. The DNA."

"Mateo's?"

Angelika nodded.

"It matches the DNA fibres found at the music venue, among the scene where Daniel's body was found. I think we know who the shooter is."

"Witnesses said there was only one shooter, right?"

"Yes, multiple witnesses stated that."

"Okay, so we've got our shooter. Now we have to get him."

"Yes. Not only do we have him linked to this crime, but we also have a crime in Vouliagemni on the city's Riviera. A businessman and his wife were killed. A hair strand was found at the scene, and now we have a match to the DNA strand at the music venue."

"This happened after he was released from jail?"

"Yes. It seems he rejoined the same OCG or moulded into a new one."

Ted looked at his watch; it was closing in on half four with the day almost escaping him.

"What can we do now?"

"Nothing at the moment. We've got the name and the DNA—we just need to get our officers who aren't being used for the protests, some on our team, to check CCTV and other cameras in the city."

"We are chasing shadows while people are dying!" Ted said, banging his fist on the table.

"We've got a few things to work on. I'll get Mateo's information out to all officers on duty. Let's deliberate tomorrow morning, and the station will be quiet. If Mateo's face shows up, we will be the first to know," Angelika suggested.

Ted moved from the table towards the window, gaining a vantage point to look down at Apostolos Nikolaidis Stadium across the street. Noticing the pedestrians below, he realised one of the officers had been mute during the exchange. He turned to see her sitting in her chair, slightly dipped, leaning back like a school teenager disengaged from a lesson.

"Eliana?" Ted asked.

Eliana turned her head to look at Ted, then raised in her seat to sit properly.

"Yeah?"

"You've been quiet. Everything okay?"

This brought attention to her, and all the officers were looking in her direction. She glanced back at each officer before returning her explanation to Ted.

"I just want it to stop. I just want to get these Kariólis!"

Eliana was looking deeply into Ted's eyes as if pleading. Ted nodded.

"We will."

The room agreed, although they weren't sure of the investigation's actual outcome. Angelika was the first to lift from their perch, explaining she would deliberate with Savvas about their barrage of updates. Once she left, Simon turned to look at a standing and contemplating Ted, still seeking answers from the traffic below after his exchange with Eliana. She glanced up at Simon, who caught her attention to initiate he wanted to speak to Ted. Once she left, Simon spoke to Ted.

"Wanna grab a coffee somewhere else than here? I'm sick of this grainy crap."

"If you don't mind, I've got to make some calls. One to back home and one to Luuk about the case," Ted requested.

Simon lifted his hand to surrender.

"Sure. Maybe I should do the same. But I'm still going to get that coffee. You want anything?"

"No thanks."

"Hope your family are all well, and keep me updated with the case."

"I will do."

Simon left the boardroom, leaving Ted alone. Without hesitation, he reached for his phone to begin a duo of calls. Earlier in the day, he had received a text message from Luuk Vesser back at Europol asking whether he was available for a phone call to discuss an update on the Hawk case. Although incredibly eager to receive an update, he knew it would be best to call home first to his wife and family. He navigated his phone and pressed video call on his contact Rose. The phone answered after only a few rings.

"Hey, Rose, how are you doing?" Ted asked.

"Not good, but I'm okay. How are you?" Rose moaned.

"I'm okay. What's wrong?"

"I've been unwell—been sick this morning."

"God, you okay?"

"Yeah, I'm fine now. It just happened suddenly."

"Not pregnant, are you?" Ted said with an awkward smile.

"No, it can't be that!"

A momentary lull in the conversation developed. Ted's mind raced to the possibility of her symptoms correlating to one answer. Ted noticed she glanced to her side, then smiled as loud, high-pitched noises filtered through the screen.

"Daddy, Daddy, Daddy!" both of Ted's daughters cried.

"Kids! How are my special two?"

"Good. We miss you, Dad," Ivy said.

"It's only been a few days!" He said with a smile.

"I know, but we saw you for ages over Christmas. We got used to it."

"Well, I will see you soon, okay? Make sure you are behaving."

"We are," they both whined.

"Have they, Mummy?"

"They've been great, and as I'm ill, they've been helping with housework, too!"

"That's my girls!"

"Evie brought in a dead mouse today," Florence announced.

"Did she?"

"She did; she's never done it before."

"Probably because she didn't go out much with being a city cat. Now she is in the countryside where you are; she has the whole fields to herself."

"I don't like it when she brings mice in," Ivy stated.

"I know, but it's in her nature to hunt."

"I suppose," they pouted.

"There are loads of cats here in Athens."

"In people's houses?" Florence asked.

"Yes, but on the streets, too."

"But it's cold—why are they out on the streets? That makes me sad."

"They live there; they're stray cats."

"Can we help them?" Ivy prompted.

"Yeah, I'm sure we could. Maybe not in person, but a friend said this woman helps stray cats. Feeding them, ensuring they are healthy and even finding them homes. We could make a donation when I see you both next?"

"Yeah, yeah!" Ivy rejoiced.

"Like a million pounds and save all the cats!" Florence demanded.

Ted and Rose both laughed at their daughter's eager naivety.

"Maybe not that much, but we will give what we can. Anyway, I've got to go and get back to the case. I will speak to you soon, okay?"

"Okay, Daddy."

"Love you both."

"Love you, too," both replied.

The girls moved out of the shot, leaving Rose's face to fill the camera screen. Her long brown hair flowed along the two vertical points of the screen like a picture frame, and her green eyes pierced through the screen. His weakness.

"Are you sure you are okay?"

"Yeah, I'm fine. I don't think I'm pregnant, but I will do a test to ensure. I need to go to the shop to get one, but not today; I don't have the energy. Maybe over the weekend when I'm better."

"Yeah, probably just to make sure. Rule that out. Have you thought about seeing the doctor?"

"Yeah, but I don't want to waste their time. I'll see how I am in the next few days."

"Yeah, sure. Anyway, I've got to go now."

"How's the case?"

Ted looked up, pondering a good reply. One that showed things were going well.

"Complicated."

"One of Ted's generic answers. Well, keep safe."

"Thank you. Love you."

"Love you. Goodbye, Ted, speak to you soon, okay?"

"Of course, goodbye."

The call disconnected, and Ted felt warm inside for the first time since he arrived in Athens. His next phone call was to return to his previous roots. He pressed the call button when reading Luuk's message for Luuk to answer promptly.

"Hey, Luuk, how are things?"

"Yeah, good, yourself? How's Athens?"

"It's complicated."

"Always complicated. Any news on the suspects?"

"We've got some leads, but nothing concrete. Chasing shadows while people are being hurt."

"Sorry to hear, Ted. I hope you get the bastards."

"Me, too. Do you have an update on the Hawk case?"

"Yeah, there's been a breakthrough in Dubai. Interpol and the police had a tip-off last night from a high-end restaurant worker about suspicious activity regarding a group of men eating with a young woman."

"What was the tip-off?"

"The worker said the men were very controlling, and the women didn't seem to be present, but were sort of distracted when he served them. Distracted with their thoughts, scared even of those in attendance with them."

"Are they following the men?"

"They are. They've been following the men in their flashy Rolls Royce vehicle today. They're keeping tabs, but nothing out of the ordinary so far."

"Did the restaurant have CCTV? Did they get a look at the girls?"

"They did. I've seen it—it's not them, Ted. Sorry."

Throughout the conversation, a sense of energy triggered Ted's veins, but that subsided once Luuk confirmed it wasn't those two lost girls in Timişoara.

"Keep me updated, Luuk."

"I will do, Ted. Keep yourself safe."

"You, too."

The phone disconnected; Ted placed the mobile on the desk and took a seat. The call was a welcome distraction and encouraging from the perspective of a possible lead into the disappearance of the two girls in Romania. However, in a split second, the prospect evaded him as he became entangled in the complexities of his current investigation. He began to rub his eyes, knowing the day's shift would end with no further breakthroughs that warranted celebration for the weekend that approached.

The boardroom door opened. Ted thought it was Simon returning with his Starbucks, but it wasn't. Travelling from one side of the room, Eliana approached Ted, towering over him, looking down as he stretched, leaning back on the chair. Ted caught her in his vision and turned to look up as she spoke first.

"We're going out for a few drinks after work for Christos and Daniel if you want to join the team? I think everyone's going. They need a distraction from the case and tomorrow's big protests."

Ted checked his watch; it was 17:30. He knew the day shifters were working an extra hour to prepare for the protests and complete any pending paperwork they couldn't labour through over the weekend.

"What time is everyone leaving? I'll ask Simon what we are doing and let you know."

"I already spoke to him, and he is coming. We will leave around 18:30; some officers must change before we all leave."

"Sure, sounds great," Ted returned with a smile.

Ted watched as she left his vicinity and headed out of the board-room. His mind wandered back to the present case. The protests would be an unwelcome distraction to the city. However, he sensed this weekend could be a distraction to those involved in the corruption and one Ted would be ready to pounce on.

Chapter 24

THE CITY'S NIGHTLIFE WAS overblown, with pedestrians on the tight sideroads in the city's heart. The officers began their evening in Six Dogs before going to Dude Bar near Monastrikaki. Six Dogs was situated just off Athinas, the main road that stretched from Monsatrikiaki Square to its south towards its northernmost point at Omonia Square. In the height of the summer, Six Dogs was the cultural centre with its open secret garden and thriving scene of groovy and laid-back tunes. During the winter, mainly the indoor area was used to accommodate punters. However, the unexpected temperatures allowed the evenings to be cool, with the need for a jacket. The outdoor area enchanted the open spaces with its lit candles in their mason jars, which the officers took the opportunity to embrace the chill evening air.

There was a short walk to Dude Bar, where Eliana and Ted walked to beat the crowds and gain a seating area for the officers. Upon arrival, there was excellent music, with the sound of obscure funk and soul, accompanied by artwork that made you feel like you were inside a Quentin Tarantino movie. Eliana and Ted were quiet when they walked over to their destination, only engaging in small talk. Meanwhile, Ted filled his mind with thoughts about the case and remained highly alert to his surroundings. He surveyed every area around him on the walk, checking pedestrians and vehicles as they passed the busy streets.

They both entered the bar and found a booth in the back corner of the room.

"Can I ask you something?" Ted said as he took his seat.

The question caught Eliana off guard, and she sat down in the chair and shrugged her shoulders.

"Sure."

"I was going to ask now before everyone else arrives."

"Ask away."

"Once or twice, I've seen you in pain. Holding your stomach. You don't need to share it, but I just wanted to ensure you were okay?"

"I can tell you, but let's get a drink first."

Ted and Eliana studied the drinks menu and selected them as the waitress came over to take their orders. She opted for a pear vodka and ginger ale while Ted ordered the draught Mythos. The waitress brought the drinks and placed a napkin on the table with the glasses resting on top. The server also placed two small glasses of water and a small bowl of crisps to accompany their drinks. Eliana reached for her glass and pressed it against her lips, taking a sip of her drink and removing it before speaking.

"Have you heard of endometriosis?"

"No, I haven't. What is it?" Ted said as he took a sip.

"It's like tissue similar to the womb lining. But that tissue grows in other places like the ovaries."

"And it causes you pain?"

"Yeah, in my stomach area."

"Is it severe pain?"

"Yeah, it can be. Sometimes it's not as intense, but sometimes it is. It just depends."

"Is there treatment?"

"There are painkillers to help with short-term pain, but I don't take them because of previous injuries I've had."

"What do you mean? You can't take painkillers?"

"I can, but I choose not to. I got hooked on them because I had cross-country injuries after finishing school. So I decided not to take them after relying on them for so long. I was popping them like Skittles. But other things help, but it's mostly surgery. I'm going through hospital appointments to arrange biopsies, scans, et cetera."

Ted stared at her as she finished the rest of her drink in one action. She pulled her face as the fluid went down her throat.

"Sorry," she said.

"Don't mind me. Another one?"

"Yeah, sure. Thanks."

Ted ordered another round of drinks for the table, although he had only taken a few sips of his beer. He opted for the bottle of Mamos beer, which he hadn't tried before. As the waitress left the table, Ted saw Simon, Angelika, and other off-duty officers enter through the front door. Eliana turned around to catch their attention with a wave, and Ted did likewise. The queue for the bar was big, and Ted thought the group would be waiting a while for their drinks. Although he could tell them it was table service, too, he didn't.

"So how's your family with you being away?" Eliana asked.

"It's tough."

"Could you not just be with your family? Family, what's important."

"I wish it was that simple," Ted said while sipping his beer.

Eliana turned her body to view the bar and then returned to Ted.

"They aren't getting a drink any time soon. So tell me. Why is it not simple?"

Ted sipped his beer. It was a long drag, and he gulped down the remaining contents.

"I feel if I don't have this job, I will slide off the world's edge, you know? It keeps me balanced."

"Does something trouble you?"

Ted took a deep breath through his nostrils and sighed.

"You could say that."

"Go on," she said, offering her hand for Ted to continue.

"It's stuff from when I was younger, you know. At school and college, I didn't really fit in."

"So, Ted Chester, the guy involved in solving a major crime investigation on sex trafficking. He was the biggest success in the world and didn't fit in in school?" Eliana said with a laugh.

"Yeah, and it affected me. This job gives me a focus, a purpose. Distracts me from those moments I have."

"What about your kids? This purpose of yours."

"Of course, they are my purpose. But this job gives me a greater drive, a reason to..."

"...live."

"Yeah," Ted said, staring back as she finished his sentence.

They both exchanged a smile.

"Have you ever watched *Blade Runner*?"

"Which one?"

"The one with Ryan Gosling."

"Yeah, I have," Ted said, sipping his beer.

"You remind me of him. Officer K."

"Well, thanks. Good looking guy," Ted said with a smile.

"Ha. Ha. Very funny."

Eliana touched the rim of her glass with her index finger while beaming at Ted.

"What are you trying to say?"

"What I'm saying is he is. He doesn't show emotion, but he has it deep inside him. He can't show them or let others know he has them or he will be destroyed. You remind me of that."

Ted gazed at Eliana blankly, but inside, he understood every word she said. In the movie, Officer K intentionally had minimal emotions because he was a replicant or clone who wasn't supposed to have a lot of them. They still felt them but did so differently than humans.

"I see what you mean, the comparisons."

"When I first saw you, I thought you looked lonely. But you looked like a good Joe."

"Like the scene," Ted said.

"Yeah. You had a purpose, just like Officer K."

Ted looked down the bar towards the gathered officers before searching back towards Eliana.

"Are you not lonely?" Ted asked.

Eliana pouted her lips together and shook her head.

"No. I have my dog, and I watch a lot of movies."

Ted took another sip of his beer and raised his eyebrows.

"Listen. But you should see someone you know? Talk about it," She asked.

"Not you aswell." "Pardon?"

"Sorry. Yeah, maybe I will. This is my first time speaking about it, so it's a start."

"Speaking out about it is always the most challenging part. Besides, this is the first time I've spoken about my endometriosis, so we both made the first steps."

Ted nodded back and thanked her, and the conversation came to a lull.

"I will hang out with my colleagues if that's okay. We need each other after what happened in the past few days."

"Of course, go, please. I'm going to head back, I think, anyway. Don't drink too much," Ted said with a smile.

"I won't. But I'll be heading to get some loukoumades afterwards if I do."

"What's that?"

"Fried dough balls with honey and cinnamon, the classic is the best."

"You'll have to show me them sometime."

"If you are here for two years, you must learn to love them. Just watch the waistline. You won't be able to catch many criminals if you have a belly."

"I'll make sure I try it out."

They both smiled as she raised from her seat in the booth. She grabbed her drink from across the table and looked down at Ted.

"You're a good man, Ted, don't beat yourself up about it."

Ted looked up at Eliana and nodded, raised his glass, and clinked his beer over the table.

"Yamas."

"Yamas," he replied.

Ted watched her walk away towards the other end of the bar to greet her colleagues. His attention turned to the beer in front of him. There were around two-thirds of the content left. He had an outpour of emotions and feelings in that booth not too long ago. Emotions had been bottled up inside him for so long.

Often in his past, he had thoughts and desires to drink into oblivion, so he could forget the day before and bring forward the day ahead by passing out. He always remembered when he was much younger, a little boy. His father was working his regular night shifts at a chemical fire station control room, and their next-door neighbour, who became an alcoholic after his wife and daughter left and facing eviction from his home, knocked on the door one night. The man was far from aggressive when Ted's mother answered, but young Ted sat at the top of the stairs witnessing the pain and desperation in the man's face and the tremble of agony in his voice. Pleading for help, young Ted was scared, and his mother rang the paramedics to help the man. The memory of that man's agony was printed in his mind forever. He never wanted to be like that man, no matter what. Ted didn't want to become the man who had fallen into the dark abyss.

Ted looked at the beer bottle before him, twisting it in his hands on the coaster. His grip loosened, and he shimmied out of the booth, leaving the remaining contents in the bottle. Ted walked through the bar area and headed towards the door, keeping his eyes on the floor, not to make contact with anyone. As he exited, he smiled at the fact that he had turned down the remainder of the drink after his outpour. He felt proud and lighter after exhaling some of his difficulties. He was focused. He was ready.

Chapter 25

Ted reached for the spherical door handle. It was slimy to the touch and cold. The room around him was dark and grim. However, a light emitted from underneath the small gap between the bottom of the door and the ground. The light was shining from the next room, and this intrigued Ted. He reached for his holster, situated to the right of his belt, lifting it out, and aimed it ahead of him. He began to turn the door handle and lock to gain entrance to the lit room. Ted felt for the door's direction, learning it inwards to the next room. Ted raised his weapon as he entered the room.

It was a large white space with a bright yellow light shining from the ceiling. The brightness was so blinding that he couldn't even see the light fixing with his eyes. Central to the room was a metal frame with a tarpaulin sheet covering its entirety. Ted walked cautiously towards the object, with his weapon still lifted, aiming in front of him. Ted looked over his shoulder momentarily, back into the black abyss where he came from. Upon approach, he reached for the sheet and quickly lifted the tarpaulin from the metal framed trolley, flying from right to left over the frame and falling to the floor. On the metal bed were two naked grey-skinned bodies. He took a tentative step forward towards the pair to seek their identity. His body tensed, and he felt a sharp pain in his chest. One girl's long black hair and the other's blonde hair were the only colour displayed before him. Ted identified them as Amanda Coleman and Toni Laurent. Ted leaned in closer towards Amanda, who was on his near side, placing both his hands on the cold aluminium slab.

Ted heard muttering in the distance; he couldn't determine what the voice was saying. Then those voices were closer as if coming from within the dead bodies before him. Suddenly, both girls' heads turned towards Ted's direction, with both sets of pale grey eyes staring deep into his soul. Ted's body jolted backwards, propelling him to land on the floor before the momentum laid him horizontally. Suddenly he felt a force drag him below the ground's surface and into a dark abyss. Ted was awoken from his dream, with his mobile device's noise vibrating by his side. He reached for his phone frantically to wake up in the process.

"Ted."

Ted began to come around from his deep sleep, rubbing his eyes to help with the transition.

"What time is it?"

"It's 6:20 AM."

Ted sat up on the bed and continued to rub his eyes, shirtless and with grey joggers on his lower half.

"What's up?" Ted said, finally gathering his full sight.

"Daniel Belfield's girlfriend Joanne has called the police station to say she's found something."

"What is it?"

"A media file, USB stick. She thinks Daniel has left it."

The update instantly shook him, and he became alert as he emerged from his sleepy state. Before he reached for his polo shirt, he reached for his jeans, which would replace his joggers.

"Let's go."

Ted looked around the lounge area and listened for any noise within the rooms from inside the apartment.

"How did you sleep, Ted?"

"Alright."

Simon filled him in with the information in much finer detail on the ride. Joanne visited the couple's locked storage outside the city centre early Saturday sunrise to search for any valuables she could collect to take home to the UK with her. Daniel and Joanne moved to Athens after a stint in Madrid, moving their lives and everything they owned with the need for extra storage. She was travelling home later in the evening but planned on getting up extra early to retrieve most of their essential storage for the time being, ahead of the protests brewing in the early hours.

Upon her arrival, she noticed a storage box that was alien to her. Once she opened the box, inside was the emptiness of its holding, except for one small item. Inside the box was a USB stick labelled *WATCH ME*. Joanne immediately called the police station, to which Police Sergeant Mikolas Lykaios took the call. Mikolas contacted Simon and the internal affairs team about the discovery early morning, and they immediately made their way into the station, just like Simon and Ted.

Ted rang Eliana, who answered after a few calls. She had returned from her walk with Zeus and was already driving towards the station in her vehicle. Once she arrived, the three of them entered the boardroom and were met by the internal affairs team, primed and ready with an open laptop and a projector. As they entered the room, Savvas asked Ted with his eyes.

"Why is she here?"

Ted read the facial expression and reassured him.

"She's with us, and she is good."

"Okay, fine."

"Where's Joanne?" Ted asked.

"She returned home to carry on with packing. She didn't want to be here when it was played or get caught up in the protests forming."

"Has the autopsy been completed, and is the body ready to be released?"

"Yeah, they've done everything they needed."

Ted nodded and took his seat with the rest of the team.

"She's not seen any of this tape?" Simon asked.

"No. She brought it here this morning after calling Mikolas on the phone. She couldn't face it."

There was a collective nod from Simon and Ted back to Savvas.

"Okay, I'm ready," Ted said.

"Same here," Angelika agreed.

Savvas adjusted the laptop's positioning, and the media file showed a still face of Daniel Belfield facing the camera. Daniel had short brown hair with a slight quiff and a kept beard and exhibited a face of trouble. The video started, and Daniel spoke in his Northern English accent.

"I'm Daniel Belfield. Date of birth, 4th July 1989. Today is 2nd January 2020. If you are watching this, I believe I'm in great danger. I've made this video hoping that if something happens to me, the intel I have gained so far can be used to continue this investigation beyond what I have managed. This video has been kept in my storage unit because I know no one knows about it. Except myself and Joanne. I've discovered significant corruption in the police department in Athens, which I believe is connected to gang-related activity, possibly from Albania. The gang are smuggling in fake documentation and people via the airports and maybe the ports of Athens, which I think are undetected because the documents are being read as accurate. Or, of course, bribery is being made in monetary payments, so airport control and officers turn a blind eye. So far, this is speculation. Through the clubs in the city, I've visited and conducted a series of interviews with some of the workers. Through these interviews, I believe one avenue of transport is that the gangs are also using small boats off the south coast of Greece. I'm investigating the whereabouts of this location to uncover the gang in person. This is the next stage of the investigation.

"If you watch this, I won't give away any of my sources because I will not want them endangered. I believe the officers working with me on the case are also in danger, serious danger, so I'm trying to do this by myself for now; however, I've started to reach out to others for support. Christos Masouras and Hector Baros, but I feel they will be put in danger."

Everyone in the boardroom was fixated on the screen as the film played. Daniel's face became more fraught and anxious with every word he spoke. As he spoke, he moved his eyes away from the camera he faced and dropped his head to show the physical stress he was under. He used a large force of energy to lift his head back up to face the camera and the detectives in the room.

"I've been looking at this for the past three months. I've seen low-level stuff out on patrol, but this is much bigger, and it's starting to overwhelm me now. Giving me sleepless nights and making me obsessed with the case. I need some time off to loosen up; tonight, I'm looking forward to releasing some stress... Shit. What am I saying? Anyway, this is what I have so far. I will update the USB drive if I find out more information. If you are watching this and something has happened to me, I believe this is someone in the department trying to bury the truth. I can't prove that yet, but I will try my best. Over and out."

The video froze on a close-up of Daniel as he reached for the recording device to cut the feed. Ted witnessed the sombre emotions of the personnel in the room. The internal affairs team sat silent, glancing at the blank screen and bowing their heads. Ted looked toward Simon, who was obviously affected by the video, and his posture relayed the bleak reminder of Daniel's death. Ted felt for Simon with his more personal affiliation, which Simon had with Daniel on a much more professional level. Ted was the first to break the bleak atmosphere with the metaphorical knife.

"What are we thinking after watching the videotape? Anything ringing out to anyone?" Ted said, aiming his questions toward the internal affairs duo.

Savvas lifted his head and looked toward Ted. Ted turned his head towards the internal affairs team across the table before continuing.

"He mentioned documentation and money being shipped from and to the south of Greece. Who told him that information? I wasn't aware of this?" Ted said, looking at Simon for assurance.

Simon returned a slight shoulder shrug as he raised his bottom lip over his top to assure Ted that he was clueless.

"May I?" Angelika said, looking towards Savvas.

Savvas replied with a wave as he rested them on the table's edge.

"Daniel said when he went to the strip club. The one you visited. He spoke to Daria and talked to another girl called Maya Beridze. When she landed in Athens, Maya heard one of the men say about money and passports being shipped to an island in the south."

"Was it further investigated?"

There was silence. Then Savvas leaned forward and spoke out.

"Simply. No, it wasn't. We didn't have an exact location, nor did he get any more information from Maya, and he told us the news only a few hours before he went out to his music venue with his girlfriend where he was... you know. Besides, he said it was one way they were transported out of hundreds."

The room paused momentarily before Savvas broke the sombre mood.

"If you were his boss, Simon, why didn't he tell you?"

"Simple. He didn't trust anyone, didn't want to put me in danger, maybe. I don't go around holding my officer's hands every day. They're trained officers, and their judgment is exceptional. I don't need to worry about their day-to-day investigations on a minute-by-minute basis..."

Simon paused. His announcement provided self-evidence that Daniel was a well-trained investigator. Although, the facts showed he was murdered, and Simon knew there was nothing he could have done to prevent it, yet he would carry some conscious blame.

"He is trying to say that we don't update our boss daily. We write weekly reports on our updates, but Daniel never mentioned anything about the corruption," Ted interjected, looking at Simon for an answer.

"Ted is right; Daniel never told me."

"Now, what do we do?" Eliana asked.

"We need to speak to Maya and anyone else about identifying the man who visited the brothel. The apparent police officer," Ted said.

Ted pointed at the screen, displaying a black screen once the screensaver power commenced.

"He also mentioned officers involved are in danger. Us, internal affairs, and Hector. Where is Hector anyway?"

Savvas was about to answer when he stopped in realisation, pausing for a few seconds before glancing at Angelika.

"He's at the parliament building protest, policing it with Andries, Nikolas, and the rest of the department," he replied.

"We won't have access to their communication link, will we?" Ted said.

"No, we won't. You think he's in danger?"

"I do; the distraction could be an idea for the OCG to cover any tracks. Cause chaos. Can you ring his mobile?"

Ted turned to Eliana and ordered her to call his number. Her face became confused with the demanding order.

"Are they going after Hector?" she asked.

"Ring him, please, Eliana."

She was still bewildered by Ted's order again, although more softly spoken, and she actioned it. She worked the screen to pick out Hector's mobile number, looked up at Ted, and stopped.

"Actually, he won't have his phone."

"How come?"

"Security. If there is potential unrest, they won't have their mobile in case it is taken. It stores personal information, phone numbers, et cetera."

"Okay. Try it, please," he said urgently.

Eliana worked the screen again, pressed the phone to her ear, and waited seconds.

"Straight to voicemail."

Ted closed his eyes.

"I could try Andries. Will he have his phone?" Simon said.

"He will do as senior for emergency usage," Savvas added.

"I'll ring him," Simon replied.

Simon navigated his phone, and the phone began to ring. Simon selected the phone call to be on the loudspeaker.

"Can you explain to me what's wrong?" Eliana asked.

"I shouldn't have brought you into this. Those involved with Daniel and his case have been targeted, and we still could be."

Eliana's eyes descended to the central point of her body. Her face lifted when Andries answered the phone on speakerphone after only a few rings. The background noise was deafening, with the sound of people protesting loudly and the voices of nearby officers shouting inaudible orders.

"Andries, it's Simon."

"I'm busy here, as you can tell. What's wrong?"

Simon paused whilst Angelika leaned forward over the table from her seated position and flicked her dark hair back to project her voice towards the mobile device.

"Hi, Andries, it's Angelika from internal affairs."

"Internal affairs? Simon, why did you call?"

"You're on loudspeaker with a few other officers and me."

"Sorry, what did you say?"

The booming noise outside the parliament building interfered with the conversation. Angelika repeated her announcement of who was present, with Simon sliding the phone across to her, so she could speak much louder into the phone.

"I can hear you now. That's better," Andries said.

"We've retrieved a self-video of Daniel Belfield on the day he was killed at the music venue."

"A video? Where... I mean, what did he say?"

Ted squinted, trying to vision Andries's reaction to the videotape. Angelika was doing the same across the table.

"He specifically said Christos Masouras and Hector Baros were in danger because they were helping him with the investigation, and Christos is already..."

Angelika paused on her last few words. Ted lifted himself from the chair and walked around the oval table to gain a better projection of his voice.

"Andries. This is Ted. You need to pull Hector out of there now for his safety."

"Do you have intel that his life is in danger?"

"We don't, but we believe it is from what Daniel said, and these people have been following me and others and have already killed two officers and other citizens."

There was a pause from Andries as the background noise reverberated through the boardroom still. Ted was not sure if Andries had his order or if he was reflecting.

"I can't pull Hector out, and I'm under strict orders from Nikolas to keep all personnel here for the remaining duration of the protest today. He said if anyone pulls out or breaks rank, he will give out discipline or worse. We don't want the fuss, the paperwork, and it keeps people up late writing it out."

"Is Nikolas there?"

Again, there was another pause. This time, it was for a time of reflection, longer than the previous.

"He is."

"Can you put him on?"

"Hang on a minute."

Ted still hovered over the phone, waiting for Nikolas to introduce himself. Tension in the room was edgy and full of anticipation. As they cleared their throat, a sound projected through the phone, one that seemed of annoyance.

"Police Director Nikolas Konstantinou speaking."

"Police director. I'm going to cut to the chase. We need you to relieve Hector Baros of his duties at the protest. We believe his life is in danger."

"Everyone's life could be in danger here, and it's a large protest that could turn into a city-wide panic. Around three million people live in the city of Athens, and that's a lot to protect. Don't you understand that we need every officer, especially Hector Baros's experience and expertise? Unfortunately, I will not allow your request. Besides, you already have Eliana; isn't that enough for your investigation?"

"With all respect, this is a murder investigation at a challenging time for you and the city—I get that. But it's a murder investigation of a British officer. We are here to do our job. However, this investigation links to corruption in your very own department. Daniel Belfield made a videotape before he was murdered, saying his life was in danger, and he is now dead. He also mentioned on that tape that Christos Masouras and Hector Baros's lives were in danger, and now Christos and his partner are dead. So, too, a dancer at the club and others."

"Where is this videotape?"

"We have it here. It was found by Daniel's partner Joanne."

Another pause of reflection came, this time from Nikolas.

"This is an order. Do not interfere with Hector. I will need to see this videotape once the protest is finished. Carry on with your investigation away from the Hellenic Parliament, and I will arrange a meeting to discuss the next steps."

"But..." Ted said before he was interrupted.

"I understand your concern, Ted. Still, I assure you Hector is in the safest place with surrounding officers," Nikolas replied.

Ted stood frustrated with the response. He stopped as he saw the raised hand of Superintendent Savvas as he stretched his fingers slightly. It didn't seem to be an order to stop talking but a supportive gesture.

"Savvas here. Let me be clear—it's the perfect opportunity to make an assassination. Crowds, coverage, perfect escape routes."

"I assure you we have the whole area covered, and there will be no assassination attempts on my officers. Your request is not granted. Is there anything else you wish to speak about except this matter?"

"Nothing else, no," Ted said, shaking his head.

"Well, I'll speak to you later."

The phone disconnected, exchanging the roars from the protests to the silent matter of the room's space.

"What can we do?" Angelika offered.

The room remained silent, significantly contrasted, apart from the underlying rumble outside the boardroom window as people marched towards the protest area beyond Lycabettus Hill and the parliament building. Ted started nodding to himself while tapping the table's edge with his fingertips.

"What are you thinking, Ted?" Simon asked.

"We get Hector ourselves."

"But you heard. He will give out disciplinaries, maybe even force you off the case yourself," Angelika said.

"Let him try it. This is our investigation. He can't stop us. I'll bring the whole British Army if he doesn't allow us to get these bastards."

Savvas smiled and looked as Ted began to pace the boardroom floor. Ted returned a glance back.

"I won't let him stop you, Ted. I agree we go get Hector ourselves," Savvas replied.

"That's right. We're not losing another officer from this," Angelika said.

"I've always thought of a career change anyway... joking," Eliana added.

They exchanged a nod as everyone rose from their seats. As Ted stood up and pushed his chair under the large boardroom table, he glanced out the wide-open window and down to the street below. He saw people holding Greek flags and chanting in their mother tongue. He pictured the crowds congregating outside the parliament building. If the OCG intended to use the crowds to take out Hector, Ted and the team would need to pick out a potential hitman from the rest of the public. He wasn't sure how they would be successful before it was too late, but he knew they couldn't fail. Not just because there would be an officer's life in the balance, but a whole city, too, if riots erupted from a fatal police shooting.

Chapter 26

TENS OF THOUSANDS OF Greeks lined the streets dressed in the blue and white, their nation's colours, and some held the same-coloured flag. Many travelled around the country to rally against the accord naming the ex-Yugoslav state of North Macedonia. This decision would allow the people of North Macedonia to call themselves Macedonians rather than North Macedonians. Those attending were peacefully protesting outside the Greek Parliament building. The Hellenic Parliament stood under the watchful eye of Lycabettus Hill, which towered in the distance. The installation finished construction in 1843, designed by the German architect Fredrich von Gartner. Initially, it served as the Royal Palace for the Greek King.

At ground level, Greeks held picket signs expressing words such as *Losing our Values, Don't sell out Macedonia, My Father Fought for Macedonia*, and *There is only one Macedonia, and it's Greek*. Most of those not in attendance had decided to live with the decision. Still, those lining the streets outside the Greek Parliament had not and were calling for Prime Minister Kyriakos Mitsotakis Tsipras to declare a referendum. Among the masses, the front exterior of the parliament building ran along a road called Leoforos Vasilisis Amalias. The road connects the city's north towards a major highway junction, leading south to the port of Piraeus. Beyond the road stood Syntagma Square. The square was lined with trees, bare from the winter season and green square spaces. The square was where Athenians rose up against King Otto of Greece in 1843 to demand a constitution. Some hundred-eighty-odd years later, similar disapproval was gathering. Modern times allowed the construction of an underground metro station to open in 2000, conforming to four tracks.

Ted, Angelika and Savvs took the short metro ride from Ampelokipi to Syntagma Square. Upon exiting the train doors, the crowds spilt from underneath the foundations of the protest itself. As they manoeuvred through the pedestrian metro tunnels below to the open area, the thunder of chants and objections grew louder with every footstep. Eliana and Simon went beneath the police station to gain access to a vehicle. This would allow them to be on standby and border the edges of the protest while being fully mobile. As the duo rose from the metro station, engulfed in the chaotic scenes, Ted received a text saying Eliana was southwest of his position. Ted replied to the message to confirm the update and received another update from Simon stating he was positioned north of the protest near the Academy of Athens.

The trio took the short steps, which were much longer to navigate, with the crowds filling the walkways. They couldn't even see the small white pillars and black railing between the road and its pedestrian edge, used for safety from the drop-down to Syntagma Square. Once they led themselves to Leoforos Vasilisis Amalia road level, between the crowds and the waving flags, they could see the Hellenic Parliament's front. The off-peach colour was only a minor feature of its German creator. Showing off its three floors, fourteen windows ran across its front, with seven windows on either side of a central point. The central point was extended outwards, with ten pillars acting as foundations. The Greek flag stood proudly at the very top of the building, and foremost for everyone to see. Approaching the building, one would need to climb a set of symmetrical steps, either left or right, which would allow one to reach the forecourt of the building.

Ted pushed through the tightly packed crowd to get close to his destination, believing he was standing on Leoforos Vasilisis Amalia, briefly seeing the tarmac beneath his feet. He was met with looks and stares from on-goers at his eager movements, and some protestors oblivious to Ted, with their passionate chants and powerful movements knocking Ted into the next person. Angelika and Savvas were not far behind when Ted saw the row of police officers standing behind the stone wall, looking out at the crowd from the forecourt. Ted searched the area for any suspicious activity but was unsure what he was looking for. He saw the masses of people around him, their faces, but everyone looked different, normal even, protesting their beliefs like everyone else.

Suddenly, Ted recognised someone in the crowd, pushing himself through the tightly packed area. He was male, with short black hair and Eastern European features. Ted could only see him from the side as he advanced through the crowd. The man was nudged into the crowd and turned to see where the push came from. Instantly, Ted saw his facial front, which was recognisable to him. Ted felt his heart pound out of his chest and begin to rise in beat; it was the man at his apartment door a few nights ago.

Ted tried to reach for his mobile in his pocket but couldn't get a grab of his jeans pocket through the tightly packed crowd. He looked back briefly and saw Angelika struggling to get through. Ted couldn't muster a gesture back to Angelika or use his voice to communicate, so he turned immediately to get a visual of the unknown man. Ted saw the man fixated on the forecourt above the street level. Ted turned his attention to the raised platform to see the officers ahead. There were possibly twenty or more officers of different ranks observing the protests, with many armed guards before the steps to stop any invasions of the inner walls of the Hellenic Parliament. Ted spotted Andries and Nikolas, but the Eastern European man wasn't staring at them; with a brief glance, Ted could see the man was fixed on Police Captain Hector Baros. A force of energy rushed through his body as he began to push through the crowd with much power. Angelika saw Ted move with intent and began to do the same to keep up with Ted's position. Ted reached for his phone and looked down through his tight space as he still managed to propel through the crowd. He searched for Angelika's number and pressed the call button, and she answered immediately. A roar from the crowd in real-time and through the earpiece caught him off guard.

"Angelika, can you hear me!" he roared.

"Just about—what's wrong?"

"The man who came for me is here. He is going for Hector!"

"So what do we do?"

Angelika couldn't hear Ted's response through the beginning of another chant from the crowd, but she thought she heard a swear word. Ahead, she saw Ted move with a great purpose as if he were swimming powerfully through the crowd, using his arms to leverage a sprint finish. Further ahead of Ted's position, she saw the man he was aiming for; he was yards away from the police wall of armed officers with a good sight of the stoned wall up in front of him. The man raised his arms, exposing a pistol, using both hands to hold it above his chest, pointing out his target, taking aim at the row of officers on the raised court. Ted noticed one or two protesters saw the man holding the weapon, and the panic on their faces was real; he nosedived into the armed man as he pulled the trigger, causing Ted to fall on top of the man as they skittled down two other pedestrians. Within that moment, the gunshot tore through the air, and the horde turned into disarray.

The armed officers began to walk forward, protecting the parliament building area and blocking entry from the pedestrians trying to escape the panic. Angelika was flung back as the crowd stampeded away from the edifice. Ted tackled the man to the ground; the hold of the man's weapon was loosened, and the gun flew onto the floor in an unknown direction. Ted began to wrestle the man's strength as he attempted to overturn Ted's advantage of being above him.

"Who do you work for?" Ted shouted.

The man's eyes were full of determination to not be stopped. Ted held a grip on his upper arms, holding him down. He briefly glanced for assistance from Angelika, but she was not nearby.

"Who are you? Why did you come for me?" Ted continued.

They locked eyes as the man pushed back against Ted's resistance and held against him. Ted felt a force from the man as he fought back with true aggression. The man lifted his right knee up into his groin area. Ted let out a big cry as he lost his strength. He lost grip of the man's hands, who drove them both into Ted's chest. The various pain points caused Ted to lose focus, allowing the man free use of his hands. The man raised his hands towards Ted's eye socket, grabbing his hands on his cheeks and pushing his thumbs into his eyes. Ted felt the pressure on his eyeball, automatically pushing himself backwards, using his hands to move the man away from his eyes. Ted fell onto the ground, watching the man stumble momentarily and search the ground around him, which was still full of stampeding Athenians. The man gave up; he looked down at Ted with piercing evil eyes, turned, and began to run through the crowd.

Ted saw him break free through the crowd, ploughing through people as they stood. A moan came from Ted's body as he rose from his position from his chest bone and groin, as did a tingling sensation around his eyes. He blinked a few times to regain his vision, which was temporarily hazed. Ahead the man was fumbling through the crowd, but the crowd was depleting, allowing Ted a clearer run than the man had. Ted saw the sun gleam on the gun's metal on the ground. He diverted his forward momentum to reach down and collect the weapon to use whilst Ted's pistol remained in his holster.

His focus returned to the suspect ahead, increasing the gap between the two. Ted's body was driving with adrenaline, and his vision was clearer. Ahead the main road was emptying, with many people spilling down the steps towards Syntagma Square and its metro station. Protestors had gone west back towards the centre of the city, and others north and south. Suddenly, he saw a black Mercedes with blacked-out windows in the distance heading towards him. This was surely the second vehicle in their operation, Ted thought. Its speed was roaring as those fleeing jumped out of the way to avoid being hit. Ted held his service pistol out but couldn't get a clear shot of the suspect for the pockets of escaping groups ahead of him. Ted used his phone to dial the number for Eliana, who was in the position he was heading.

"I need your vehicle right away!" Ted shouted as he took quick breaths.

"En route now. Turned onto Leoforos Vasilisis Amalias from Zeus's temple," Eliana replied.

Ted kept the phone line open as he lost ground on the rapidly escaping suspect. The Mercedes reached the suspect and turned ninety degrees so the door was positioned directly before the man. The man opened the passenger side door and flung himself into the space as the vehicle crossed the tram line to flee down Leoforos Vasilisis Amalias. A few moments later, a police vehicle headed towards Ted's location on the other side of the road.

"Here now," Eliana said.

"See you."

"Okay—get in quick!"

The car made a similar turn across the tram line, which ran through the middle of the road, and the passenger side door flung open. Ted caught the movement right, so when Eliana hit the accelerator, he was forced back into the car seat. Ted closed the passenger side door and moved into a more comfortable position.

"You okay, Ted?"

"I'm fine."

"Where do you think they are going?"

The car they were pursuing was a few hundred metres ahead, accelerating fast, forcing pedestrians from the protest to mount the pavements. Ted looked across to Eliana but towards the driver's side window to his left, taking in the row of greenery, which was the National Garden, acting as a public park for the City of Athens. Looking to his right, he saw the building and apartment blocks lining the street. The side streets would lead to the narrow cobblestone of Plaka, where Mario was mowed down. Directly ahead were the open roads of Athens, which connected to many exit points with vehicles and pedestrians, and that worried him.

"I don't know, but we can't lose them."

Eliana took the statement as a direct order. She pressed her foot hard down on the accelerator.

Chapter 27

THE ROARING METAL OF both cars manoeuvred through Leoforos Vasilisis Amalia as the road passed the National Gardens, running parallel to the road, heading towards a crossroads. The pursuing vehicle hit one hundred forty kilometres per hour as it tried to maintain the distance between. The car being chased was weaving in and out of traffic, narrowly missing the concrete barrier separating one side of the road and the central tram line. Fortunately for the public's safety, no trams were running along the road due to the blockade of pedestrians outside the parliament building, which was one of the destinations on the tramline route. The crossroad head gave two directions: One to the left, which headed onto Leof Vasilissis Olgas, leading towards Panathenaic Stadium, flowing between the National Gardens and the Temple of Olympian Zeus; the other option was the road directly in front, which sailed around the Temple towards Hadrian's Arch.

"What happened, Ted?"

Ted summarised the events. Once he finished his narrative, the Mercedes screeched at speed, swerving towards the left exit at the last second, colliding the passenger side door with the front of an Opel Estate car motoring through the junction.

"What's that way?" Ted said, holding onto the handle above the passenger side door.

"Panathenaic Stadium."

Panathenaic Stadium was an open-area stadium made only entirely from marble. After numerous transformations, it eventually became the home of the first modern Olympic Games in 1896, but the natural materials it was made from remained.

Eliana mirrored the direction of the black Mercedes, this time avoiding any near-collisions. Leof Vasilissis Olgas was a two-way road with a raised central reservation lined with winter plants and metal poles holding up the tram electrical wires above the road. The route the two racing cars were riding along split into three sections. The middle section had a tram track and a small raised area to divide the two sections for vehicle transport.

"I've got to make a call."

Ted reached for his mobile using his free hand. He worked the screen, and Simon answered a few moments later.

"Ted, you okay? What the hell happened?"

"Is Hector okay?"

"I don't know. Where..."

Ted hung up immediately since Simon didn't have the information he needed. He searched for Angelika in his contacts and rang again.

"Ted, where are you?" she shouted over the noise of chaotic pedestrians.

"Pursuing the shooter. Are you okay?"

"I'm okay. Everyone turned when the shots were fired, and I got pushed down and crushed. But I fought my way back up, thankfully. Savvas is here too."

"Did you see Hector after the shooting?"

"I didn't see anything, Ted; like I said, we were on the floor."

"Fuck!" Ted took a second to compose himself and continued. "Can you call Andries or someone to check he is okay? The shooter aimed for him before I took him down. I don't know if he got the shot or not."

"Will do, Ted."

Ted disconnected the phone, throwing it into a gap under the media system in the central area of the dashboard. Ted glanced across at the speedometer, pushing over one hundred ten kilometres per hour, as he gripped tighter on the handle.

"You've done this before," he said.

"I like fast cars."

The words didn't fill him with ease as the pedestrians flashed by the window watching from the pathways.

"Just don't crash, please."

"I'll try."

"Thanks."

"We need backup," Eliana added.

"How are we going to get it?"

"Well, I have a plan."

"What does that involve?"

"Crashing."

"How is that a plan?" he spoke firmly, looking across at Eliana, who was fixed on the road ahead.

"Call it being spontaneous," she replied.

Eliana reached for the comms device holster with her right hand, which was attached to one of the air vents and pressed to button to speak.

"This is Police Sergeant Eliana Abulafia. I need backup. I'm pursuing a black Mercedes, licence plate IBH-9920, south of Leof Vasilissis Olgas, heading towards the junction of Leof Vasileos Konstantinou and the Panathenaic Stadium. Urgent backup required."

She released her finger and continued to navigate the road with her left hand while Ted looked worried, gripping the handle above much tighter than before. A voice crackled over the radio from someone back at the police station.

"This is sergeant Pietr Samaras. We will try to get some backup on the route, but the protests have turned ugly at the parliament building. Rocks and stick-wielding are being used, and fireworks."

"God damn it!" Eliana shouted while slamming the top of the steering wheel with her left palm.

"Thanks, Pietr; please keep us updated. We are in pursuit," Ted intervened.

"Over. I will update you as soon I can," Pietr signed off.

Eliana slammed the comms device back into the holster but missed, leaving the device to dangle freely from the vent.

"I like it better when you have two hands on the wheel."

Ted looked at Eliana, who ignored the comment. Eliana was focused and silent as they approached the junction of Leof Vasileos Konstantinou, which ran east to west from their location. The Mercedes ahead turned left at high speed, running a red light, forcing two passenger vehicles to turn into each other to avoid the collision with the Mercedes, stopping before both of their front bumpers met. Their car horns deafened the inside of the car as they passed them. Eliana navigated the junction at a similar speed, but the intersection was clear this time, allowing the pursuing car to make up valuable ground. In the distance and fast approaching was the Panathenaic Stadium. Eliana quickly turned her head towards Ted's direction before turning it back to face the road ahead.

"Here's the part where we crash."

Ted glanced at Eliana and back toward the road ahead. Ted knew it was the only way to stop the high-speed pursuit.

"You ready, Ted?" she asked.

"Ready."

"Just hold on to something."

"Good job, I already am."

Ted looked at Eliana again, whose eyes were fixed on the Mercedes ahead with pure intent and determination. Like a home missile would on its designated target, the red button was about to be pressed. He looked up at the handle he was holding to ensure his fingers were still purchased into the nook. A yellow-striped hatch marking appeared, separating the road and the pavement. The Mercedes entered the hatch markings, and the pursuing car's front bumper was now level with the boot of the Mercedes.

Eliana was steadying the steering wheel with both hands when suddenly she swerved to the left and swung the steering wheel hard back across her, jolting the car right and into the side of the Mercedes. The impact lifted the front of the vehicle, and as it glided, the Mercedes climbed over the low concrete pillars that protected the pedestrian walkway from vehicles, tumbling over the pillars and rolling three hundred sixty degrees, still sitting back onto its wheels. The car was damaged, and the hood was dented inwards from the roll. The driver and passenger's doors opened, and the suspects began to flee toward the stadium. Eliana slammed on the brakes and turned the car into a stationary position, blocking the most significant gap between the concrete paths used as an entry point, just in case they backtracked on their position and reentered the vehicle.

"You okay?" Eliana said, looking over at Ted.

"Still breathing."

"Good, follow me."

Eliana and Ted exited the vehicle raising their weapons in an attack position as they crossed the forecourt, pursuing the suspects ahead of them. The suspects jumped over the small marble barrier entering the stadium, bypassing the cubicles containing workers taking entry fees for the stadium's visits. The two men powered through the open space, running past a family taking photographs of themselves posing on the celebratory podium for third to first place finishers. They entered the running track within a barrier around its edges, allowing for pedestrian movement during sports activities. Up ahead was a slit in the border, and a large opening, underneath the seated section, on their left.

"What's under the stadium?" Ted said.

"A gift shop and an exit point."

"We need them out in the open."

Instinctively, Ted fired a few shots towards the tunnel entrance, aiming low, checking first for any nearby tourists. The bullets from Ted's weapon forced the suspects to turn away from the tunnel, jump the barrier, and climb up the marble steps. The roaring shots caused panic in the tourists watching as they fled the area.

Both suspects managed to reach the first level of the spectator's area and take a perch behind a small raised marble barrier, shooting off rounds toward Ted and Eliana below. Ted followed Eliana in taking shelter behind the walls that separated the track, before they were exposed to the wrath of the suspect's gunfire.

"What now?" She asked.

"I want these alive, but I'm not sure it will end that way. Any news on the backup?"

Ted and Eliana flinched as the bullet rattled against the barrier, protecting them. Eliana reached for her radio attached to the pocket of her work uniform.

"This is Police Sergeant Eliana Abulafia. I need backup. The pursuit with Mercedes licenced plate IBH-9920 is now a foot pursuit at

Panathenaic Stadium. Two suspects, shots fired. Fear for public safety. Urgent backup needed."

More gunfire sprayed the back of the wall they were protected by as they awaited an update.

"Pietr Samaras here. We have two officers on their way, I've managed to get them away from the parliament building to take general city watch, and I'll send them to you. Three minutes out."

"Thanks. Over."

Eliana removed her finger from the communications button.

"God knows what's going on there, in the city."

Ted turned his body to peer over the top of the barriers, ducking back down again to avoid gunfire from the men above them.

"They've got the height advantage."

Ted weighed up his options: They could wait and ride out the wave until the backup arrived, or they could approach and attack, but there was a huge risk of exposure. Suddenly, an opportunity was presented to the covered officers. A jamming noise came from both of the guns. It was ever so faint, but it was noticeable. At that moment, the continuous firing from their position stopped. Eliana perched herself on one knee to fire back, still using the wall as cover. Ted managed to do the same but didn't return any more, just observed their movement and behaviour. Ted noticed they remained covered behind their marble barrier. The two men were animated and began to expose the top of their heads as they seemed undecided on their next moves. Ted perched higher, lifting his chest over the wall to get a better look while holding out his weapon in preparation to fire.

"What are you doing?" Eliana shouted.

Ted didn't look down at Eliana's covered position. He started to mount the wall—that was their cover.

"Ted, get down!" Eliana ordered.

"They're out of ammo."

Ted climbed the wall, locking eyes with the two suspects ahead of him. They peered over the wall with horror in their eyes, rose from their positions, and began their escape.

"Freeze! Stop where you are and put your hands on your head!" Ted demanded.

Ted focused on the man he knew while the other suspect climbed the Pantheon steps. Ted held his weapon out, with no returning fire from the suspects. Eliana followed cautiously behind, using Ted as a shield almost as she approached the stairway.

"You got the driver?" Ted asked, not diverting his gaze on his own man.

"Got him," Eliana locked eyes as the driver climbed the marble steps, sidestepping from Ted's protection.

Eliana took the first step, aiming her weapon on an incline towards the moving target.

The driver was now situated towards the peak of the spectator's stand and the stadium's outer ridge. She rose slowly, focusing on the suspect while her finger touched the trigger. The man reached the remaining step and panicked as the climb disappeared, leaving only a horizontal option of left or right. The man succumbed to the situation. He turned to see an encroaching Eliana with the barrel of her gun intimidating his position.

"Get down on your knees now!"

The man contemplated his options, possibly thinking about an escape, but he was cornered and caught.

"Get on your knees now!" she ordered again.

The driver lowered himself and began balancing on one knee with his hands raised above his head. Eliana enclosed on the suspect with her final steps neutralizing him with the handcuffs she kept in her possession. She lowered her weapon into her holster, grabbed the man's hands behind his torso, and locked the cuffs.

Below, Ted held his weapon, homing in on his target. The man stood on the first level path and ran horizontally along the stadium's south side. Ted ordered him to stop once more. The man took his final steps before turning back slowly, positioning himself in the open space of the stairwell on a large marble platform.

"Get down on your knees!" Ted ordered.

Ted noticed Eliana witness the exchange from above, with the suspect sitting on the top step, watching the events unfold. Ted's target was exposed on the platform, ignoring yet another call from Ted to surrender. Suddenly, the man's right arm moved slowly around his jeans as if reaching for something slotted around his lower back. Ted homed in on the movement, focusing on what would appear from his back and what the mysterious action would bring. Ted rested his index finger on the trigger, remaining focused and ready. The man didn't break his stare towards Ted all the while. Ted glanced back at the man's face instead of his waist. The man was smiling.

"Ted! Gun!" Eliana shouted.

The man raised his right hand, exposing the gun for only one-thousandth second. The man didn't bring the gun past his waist before the gunshots fired. The man fired his weapon; the bullets cracked the marble flooring below him as his knees crumbled. Ted's pistol fired only two shots, entering the chest cavity and neutralizing him. The man dropped the weapon to the floor and fell back, lying on his back. The wounds seeped through the man's black T-shirt, flowing to the floor, creating a pool around his torso. Ted kept aim at the man as he approached. He glanced up at Eliana, holding her suspect on the shoulder as if to restrain him.

"Are you okay up there?" Ted asked.

"Yeah. You?"

Ted didn't respond. He advanced towards the body, keeping aim. Ted lowered his weapon, deciding the man was no longer a threat. Ted knelt, reaching over to him like he did outside the parliament building. This time the man was in no position to fight back. Ted placed both hands on the man's T-shirt, grabbing him gently and lifting him to a seated position. The man whined as he was lifted; blood exploded from his mouth and down his chin, showing off his once pearly white teeth, now smeared with blood.

"Who are you?" Ted asked.

No response, and the smile before had vanished.

"Who do you work for?"

The man's face was unresponsive, but his eyes were genuinely different. The man's eyes stared up at Ted with fear and intimidation, far from what Ted had witnessed before in his previous encounters. The man's breathing started to fade, and his eyes slowly closed.

"Where are the medics?" Ted shouted to gain Eliana's attention, tapping the man's face to keep her awake.

"On their way. Any minute now," Eliana shouted from the peak of the arena, searching towards the main road for any vehicles approaching.

The wounded man's eyes closed, and his body went limp and heavy as Ted held him. Ted let go of him gently, resting his dead body on the marble floor, which had stood for over one thousand years and was now stained with red blood pooling from his bullet wounds. Ted stood over the body, tightening his fists and whole body, physically shaking, before letting out anger and frustration.

"God damn it!"

His voice bellowed across the stadium's domain. He composed himself without dwelling on the moment before speaking more neutrally.

"It's too late," Ted said to himself.

Ted turned his body to look towards the main road, holding his hands on his hips. He saw the beacons of blue light approaching in both directions of Vasileos Konatantinou.

"They're here, Ted!" Eliana shouted.

Ted kept his hands on his hips, searching out towards the road. The area became overshadowed by the police sirens and the commotion of people entering the stadium's ground floor.

"He's dead," he replied.

"Sorry, Ted," Eliana offered from above.

Ted glanced up at Eliana, hovering over her still-seated suspect.

"It was either them or us."

Ted knew he wouldn't get answers from the man who tried assassinating him and Hector. There would need to be another way he discovered the truth.

Chapter 28

THE POLICE BACKUP AND medics arrived at the stadium grounds approximately three minutes after the fatal shooting. Ted took pictures of the dead body to send to his ILO contact in Albania. Alongside the names found within the wallets of Amar Veseli, the arrested man, and Mateo Berisha, the man he shot down. He walked over to the arrested suspect, sitting on the floor, leaning against the marble barrier, and ordered him to look up towards the camera so his picture could be taken. Ted was going to engage with Amar, but the rushing paramedic took away the moment as he began to check over the suspect.

Shortly after the medical support finalised their report and saw that the detained man had suffered no injuries, Eliana indicated more officers were arriving in their cars on the main street they had pursued on.

"Maybe it's calmed down at the parliament building. We've got reinforcements."

As the first officer arrived, Ted marched over with purpose, demanding an update about Hector. However, upon his approach, he realised Eliana was wrong to assume the quieter nature of the protests. It was the known officers to the Daniel case, not anyone additional. The two internal affairs members had made their way to the stadium with Simon and the two backup officers whom Pietr had summoned.

"How's Hector?"

"He's good. I think you may have saved him, Ted. One of the officers witnessed your tussle and thought he saw a bullet embedded into the side of the parliament building before they ran for cover inside," Simon said.

"How do you know?"

"Officer Daphne Anagnos here was told Hector was safe on their team's radio."

Ted nodded at Daphne, who smiled awkwardly back.

"Thank you."

Ted felt a sense of relief, clear to place that fear from his mind. Suddenly, Ted's phone vibrated in his hand. Once he looked at the screen, he saw Elijah calling him, but Ted wasn't sure if he'd done the search that quickly.

"Ted. Some graphic pictures you sent me there. The dead guy. Mateo Berisha."

"Knew that one. You know Inspector Kejsi? He informed us of him before. Although, do you have any news on him? We knew about his arrest in 2016?"

"Stole my thunder a bit there, but anyway. Apart from that arrest, nothing new."

"No problem."

"Did he murder Daniel?"

"We're not sure yet, but we don't know who was behind the trigger."

"Damn."

Ted focused on the slumped man, resting on the marble stone with the handcuff behind his back.

"What about our other guy, Amar Veseli?"

"Born in Korçë, here in Albania. However, nothing on the database, I'm afraid. However, there is a connection between the two."

"How so?"

"Amar was a prison guard at I.E.V.P Fier prison here in Albania."

"Where in Albania is that?"

"It's around thirty kilometres inland from the western coast of Albania. One of the largest prisons, holding around 850."

"Did he make friends with him on the inside?"

"Maybe, or threatened him, we don't know. Amar didn't help Mateo escape because Mateo left early on parole."

"When did Amar leave or resign from his job at the prison?"

"I'll find out for you."

Ted pondered the new information. He wasn't sure if it would bring answers to the case, just a tick box filled on how the two were acquainted.

"Sorry I can't help you anymore, but I'll keep you posted if I find anything. Keep me posted, too."

"I will do, thanks anyway."

"No problem, call me anytime."

His adrenaline levels were peaking, and he didn't want to stop but keep the case's momentum gliding along. He looked for Angelika and confronted her.

"We need to test these against the DNA found. Test Amar to see if there are any connections to the shooting. If not, maybe Mateo is our killer."

"We will do. Forensics are arriving now; they will take swabs from Amar and return them to the lab."

Ted nodded back.

"Any news on the licence plate here?" Ted said, pointing at the vehicle in the distance they had forced off the road just before.

"Nothing. It's fake—nothing on the system is showing up. ANPR have picked up a few hits tracking back out towards the Piraeus area, but nothing before that. We can run the road CCTV back and see what we find."

"You won't find anything, but appreciate it if you do."

Ted glanced around for his next officer, searching back and forth.

"Are you okay, Ted?"

"I need to check with someone to see if Amar is on our system. Amar was a prison officer in Albania, in the same prison Mateo was held."

"Really?"

"Really."

Ted saw Eliana standing there discussing the events with a male officer making notes on his pad but interrupted them mid-flow.

"Eliana, sorry. Who's the officer back at the station you called?"

"Pietr Samaras. Why?'

"I just need him to check something for me."

Ted walked away from the crowd to get some quiet near the tunnel, which led to a gift shop area, once home to the staging route athletes would take from the changing facilities, which was almost gladiator-like.

"Astynomikós Pietr Samaras."

"It's Ted Chester, ILO; Eliana rang before..."

"I know. Are the officers with you?"

"They are, thank you... Listen, do you have an email? I want to send you two photos and two names to check something for me, please."

"Sure."

Pietr announced his email address at Ted's request and placed him on the loudspeaker as he composed the email. Ted filled the silence with small talk.

"Any news on the parliament protests?"

"Everyone is safe. There are a few injuries in the crowd, but nothing major from the crush. The issue now is if there are rioting and robberies of businesses. The Army is thinking of martial law tonight."

"Right, okay. You got the photos and names?"

"I've got them now. I'm just searching the names now... Jesus... just saw the picture—everything okay?"

"Everything is fine, don't worry."

Pietr was working the keyboard in the background, which echoed the quiet, empty police office.

"Luckily, we have some volunteers in today on the phones, or I wouldn't be able to help you."

Ted smiled, eager to hear the results of the police database search.

"Right, I've a hit. Mateo, 2016, arrested for importing illegal small arms into Greece, and heroin, and a couple of charges for exploitation of prostitution..."

"Okay, I know that one, so that's good. Amar?"

"He has two convictions on a note here. One is minor, drinking while driving, but his charges seem to have been spent, although they shouldn't be."

"How do you mean?"

"Well, he had a drunk driving offence issued seven months ago, but it says it's been served, the licence given back. However, he wasn't jailed."

"Does it give a reason as to why his offence was served early?"

"That's left blank. I'll try to investigate, but it may mean contacting the Judiciary of Greece to see if any appeals were lodged, and it's the weekend; we won't get a response until Monday at least."

Ted was scratching his head metaphorically about the revelation. It seemed someone had done exactly the same as Mario did to the car rental company system, to Amar's offence. It had vanished. Amar served his sentence early by completing community service-type punishments, or he lodged an appeal, but he would have thought that information would be kept on a police database. The other option was the data was altered, allowing Amar access to his own transportation and not raising suspicion if ever caught, thus helping support the OCG.

"Thanks, Pietr, that's good information."

"Happy to help; keep safe."

"You, too."

The phone disconnected. Ted held the phone to his ear for a few seconds, digesting the new wave of information. He felt his grip vibrate on the handheld device. He dropped his arm to see the screen and saw Elijah's name appear on his home screen with a text message below.

"Amar was released from his duties at the prison on gross misconduct offences. Unfit due to the influence of alcohol."

Ted replied with a gesture of appreciation for the update. This meant to him that Amar had a drinking problem. Amar might have lost more than his job when he was fired, and Mateo was his guardian angel, leading him into a life of crime. The theory surrounding his driving ban being expunged was becoming more of a reality.

Breaking into Ted's peripheral vision appeared Officer Daphne Anagnos. She was almost as tall as Ted, sitting around six feet as she stood beside him.

"Officers have searched the vehicle. They found three Beretta Px4 pistols, a crate of ammunition, and a bag of cash, I'd say at least forty thousand euros by estimate."

"Thanks, Daphne."

"Forensics will take samples and take them away for further analysis."

Ted nodded to Daphne as she walked back towards another group of incoming officers just a few metres away.

A few officers overheard the conversation, meaning Ted didn't need to relay the message.

"Where do you think they got the cash from?" Eliana questioned.

"If I was a betting man, I'd say the club. They made the pickup this morning. Beat us to it. Can we get someone to go to the club and interview the owner, the cleaners, or the neighbourhood to see if they saw anyone or anything? Even check CCTV in the area for the same vehicle?"

"I'll go and take any officers we can spare," Eliana asked.

"Thanks, I'd go armed heavy."

"Always."

Ted turned to see Angelika, who was staring intently at Ted. He was sure it was an intimidating glance, or a genuine question morphed into a seriously contented face.

"What are you going to do?" Angelika asked.

Ted broke away from her demeanour and searched for the slumped Amar on the ground. Angelika followed Ted's directions and saw the same apprehended suspect before they locked eyes again.

"Can I have a minute with him?" Ted asked.

Angelika stared into Ted's eyes cautiously, biting her bottom lip and finally nodding.

"Sure."

Ted was confused by her toned response.

"Everything okay?"

"Everything is fine. I told you waiting until today would bring some answers, right? I'm just ensuring you don't go rogue on us now."

"I won't, don't you worry."

She pierced her lips as if to smile and walked away in the direction Daphne took to gather a more formal update regarding the vehicle search and recovery.

Ted walked over slowly, aiming at Amar as his head slumped. He locked eyes with Amar for a short duration. Amar looked up, his arms still behind his back in handcuffs. Amar almost showed a cocky nature as Ted knelt down to get to eye level, offering a smirk. Ted was knelt down on his right knee, his left hand holding the floor for balance. The man's eyes were a wild brown, with flashes of green mixed in. Ted decided to make the first move as the silent stare intensified.

"Amar Veseli. I don't know if you will answer the first question I ask, but by doing so, this can be much easier. Do you understand?"

There was silence from Amar. Ted wasn't sure how good his English was. Eliana had given his Miranda rights in Greek shortly after Ted shot down Mateo, but Ted didn't stop to see if Amar had understood. Ted decided to give it a shot.

"Okay, Amar. Here it goes. So, we know you worked as a prison officer at Fier prison."

So far, Amar was motionless. Either trying to give no reaction, or he couldn't understand English. Ted noticed his long thick black hair and thick eyebrows with stubble to complete his facial features. A few scars on the right cheek, either from a wound or a fight. Ted glanced upon these before moving on, not yet knowing if Amar even understood the language he was using.

"When you were at Fier prison, you met Mateo over there," Ted continued, pointing to the screen protector behind Mateos's body.

"We know you were—you are an alcoholic. You probably lost everything, right? Your job? We know about that. Any girlfriends? Family?"

Amar's face gave a demoralised expression, as if unlocking a traumatic memory. Ted knew he understood every word he was saying.

"You moved to Greece. Mateo helped you? You continued with your drinking problems. Got done for drunk driving. Then you were banned from driving. That ban got shortened, God knows how. And here you are now. Deep in this mess you are in."

Amar's lips started to tremble, his eyes grew wild, and he wrestled the cuffs as he sat on the concrete flood. Ted held a firm grip on his shoulder to keep him in place and comfort him.

"Amar, stop. Listen. I can't promise anything, but if you want to live, you help us. You talk at the station. We won't kill you, but they will."

Amar searched left and right, looking for gang members surveying his position.

"It's just officers and medics. You're safe."

"Please," the man pleaded.

Ted looked down at the ground, picking up a small granule and squeezing it between his thumb and index finger before throwing it back to the ground. Ted lifted his head and saw Amar's eyes search for Ted for safety.

"So now, will you talk?" Ted asked.

A stare-off occurred for a few seconds, and both intensified within each other. Amar broke away for a second, overseeing the forecourt one last time, then reverted back to Ted. Amar nodded.

A talking suspect was the luck Ted needed.

Chapter 29

Amar Veseli waited anxiously in the interview room, handcuffed to the chair he perched on. Meanwhile, Mateo Berisha rested within the confinements of a cold storage unit in a city forensic laboratory. Eliana, Simon, and a few other officers congregated inside the viewing room behind the one-way window view of the interview room, holding cups of instant coffee for the exhibit.

Angelika came rushing down the corridor with her mobile device raised in one hand and the paper files carried low in the other for the interview.

"We've got DNA analysis back," she announced as she arrived at Ted's position.

"What they got?"

"The DNA found at the music venue, and Christos's apartment matches Mateo Berisha. We've found our shooter."

Ted nodded. One of the central mysteries in the case was potentially revealed, but there wasn't a man alive to proclaim justice for it. He was dead on a metal slab. Ted was gutted regarding that outcome, but there were other answers to divulge.

"Let's see what Amar's involvement is," Ted said, flicking his head towards the door.

Ted entered the interview room first, with Angelika following behind, observing the two men on the other side of the table. Amar sat slumped in his seat, awkwardly trying to lift himself upright for the questions he would face. The other man was young-faced, and in his early twenties, Ted suspected. Kostas Vasileiou, Amar's lawyer. He had already introduced himself to Ted and other officers before he was given access to his client for a few minutes to prepare their action plan. Amar was willing to answer Ted's questions but wasn't sure if the baby, clean-shaven lawyer would have changed his direction in those five client-privileged minutes.

Once the two officers were seated, Angelika asked if Amar and his lawyer were ready to proceed. Kostas announced he was as he opened his notebook and began to scribble on the page. Angelika reached for the tape recording and announced those present in the room, the time and date, why Amar sat in the chair, and the charges he faced. Angelika gave Ted a nod to proceed.

"Let's start with a simple question. Your name is Amar Veseli?"

Amar nodded sombrely.

"Thank you, but can you please speak for the purpose of the tape? Just to note, Amar nodded once I asked the question."

"Yes, that is my name."

"Where were you born?"

"Korçë, Albania."

"You have good English."

"I studied in school and got top marks for it. I was smart." Amar smiled to himself.

"Okay. What education certificates do you hold, and what occupations did you hold while living in Albania?"

"I was educated in Korçë; I went to Shkollë E Eesme or secondary school. I passed my Dëftesë Pjekurie, or exam, to access higher education. I studied Public Service Management and dropped out after the third year."

"How come?"

Amar shrugged his shoulders and took his time to compose his answer. It was as if he was having flashbacks, and his eyes wandered as the emotion seemed to affect his speaking ability. Amar leaned in to whisper to his lawyer. His lawyer leaned back, catching the words. Ted couldn't hear what Amar was saying. The lawyer nodded, reached for the cup of water on the table before Amar, and lifted it towards Amar's lips, tipping it slightly. Amar took a sip, then another, before the lawyer placed the cup back on the table.

"Is it necessary for him to be cuffed?" the lawyer asked.

"Absolutely," Ted replied with no hesitation.

Kostas raised his eyebrows and began to scribble on his notepad again. "Amar?" Ted prompted.

Amar replied immediately. "My girlfriend at the time had our first child, and I needed to support her, so I took a job at the supermarket as a security guard and then at Fier prison because it paid more. That's why I dropped out."

Ted researched Korçë prior to his interview with Amar, learning the city was one of the largest and most important cultural and economic centres in Albania. Although this didn't deter anyone from impractical and criminal thinking due to their location, he thought it may have been the latter of his two theories. Ted was luring Amar into a false sense of security, beginning to lightly ease him in before going on the attack.

"In Fier prison, is this where you met Mateo Berisha?"

Amar remained quiet and had a calm nature in his answers until this moment. His face became tight and contented rather than relaxed and open to the questions about his upbringing.

"Amar. You were in a vehicle with Mateo Berisha over an hour ago. We also know you worked at Fier prison when Mateo Berisha was imprisoned. It's not rocket science to assume this is where you met?"

Amar shrugged his shoulders.

"Amar, remember what I told you when you were on the ground arrested? You want to remain alive. You will tell us what we need to know."

The lawyer's face looked vexed and outraged, lifting his head from the notebook he was buried in.

"Are you threatening my client?" he questioned.

Ted raised his arms, lifting his bottom lip.

"Not at all. This next moment..." Ted said, wiggling his index finger to the room around them.

"This will save your client Amar if he answers these questions. He has many bad men after him now they know he is here. Amar seemed willing to speak to me before; what's changed since you walked through the door here?"

Amar tilted his head and remained mute, staring towards Ted but somewhat through him. Ted thought the presence of the police station may have altered Amar's willingness to confess anything if he knew one of his seniors was a police officer or director. The lawyer sat nervously after the last note about Amar's safety but continued to scribble in his notebook. Kostas looked fresh out of university or some graduate scheme representing suspected criminals. Due to the circumstances, Ted thought he must have been a trusted lawyer to be recommended for this case, or maybe no one else was available. Angelika pulled out the evidence folder and picked out an A4 sheet.

"Officers found this." Angelika held out an A4 photograph, offering a glimpse towards Amar as she placed it on the table before him.

Ted spun it around to give Amar the full vision of the boot of the Mercedes car.

"Do you recognise it?"

The photograph depicted the three Beretta Px4 pistols, the crate of ammunition, and a bag of cash, which was eventually counted to fifty-five thousand euros.

"This was found in the black Mercedes recovered at the scene inside Panathenaic Stadium. You, the driver of that vehicle, and Mateo reached the stadium by fleeing from where Mateo opened fire towards officers outside the Greek Parliament building. First, tell me why Mateo was opening fire outside the parliament."

"I don't know," Amar muttered.

"You don't know?"

"Amar. Remember, we can help you," Angleika said.

"You can't save me! Someone working inside your department is making the orders; they'll probably have orders to kill me here!" Amar yelled, standing up, still cuffed.

Kostas leapt from his chair, scuttering towards one corner of the interview room. Angelika and Ted stood up in defence. Ted heard the door handle of the door jerk. "It's okay, don't come in. It's under control."

"Are you sure?" a voice said from behind the metal structure.

"Yes. Everyone is going to sit back down and remain calm," Ted said to Amar and Kostas.

Kostas nodded and edged towards his seat, keeping eyes on Amar, who was slowly steadying himself into his seated position again. Once the four returned to their seats, there was a period of silence as everyone gathered their thoughts.

"Amar. Are you ready to continue?"

Amar turned to look at his lawyer Kostas, who was staring at the table before him. Ted was beginning to believe he was the spare part in all of this; the lawyer, although qualified, was swimming in the big ocean of crime and wasn't sure what to do.

"You don't need to answer," Kostas offered.

Amar gulped. Then nodded.

"I'm ready—I will answer your questions."

"Good, Amar," Ted said.

"But you promise me something," Amar said.

"Yes?"

"You protect me."

Ted nodded. "We can do that. However, Amar, you must understand that this doesn't mean there will be no criminal charges against you. You are involved in a gang who have murdered and attempted murder to their name and other things. We will need to know your involvement in this also."

"I know."

Ted offered a nod. "I think before, DI Bafa asked why Mateo was opening fire outside the parliament. If you could answer that, please?"

"I don't know, but I was ordered to pick him up and escape once he did it. We met yesterday to discuss the plan. Mateo would take out an officer, Hernandez or Hector or something, and I would be the driver. That's all I ever do, really, the driver."

Ted saw the irony in that fact as he was charged multiple times for drunk driving.

"Who gave the order?"

"A guy comes and goes, calls himself Dardan; I don't know him that well. I work for Mateo—whatever he says, I do."

"Did you ask Mateo why he was ordered to shoot an officer?"

"He said the officer was a loose end."

"Was he a loose end because he was investigating the corruption on the police force and getting too close to your gang?"

"I don't know," he said with a shrug.

"Don't lie, Amar."

"I don't know! I don't know what was happening. Like I said, I just get told what is happening, and Mateo tells me what to do."

Angelika broke into the conversation to change its direction. "Where did the money retrieved from the car come from?"

"The clubs in the city. We collected the money through the night and this morning."

"Don't you normally do that on Sundays?" Ted interjected.

Amar's eyes squinted in confusion. "How do you know?"

"Why did you collect it early?"

Amar exhaled loudly and then adjusted his hands as the seated position became uncomfortable with his handcuffs behind his back. "Mateo told me we were collecting the money early. Said the police were on to us and knew the collection date had been given away. Said something about police were visiting one of the clubs."

Ted's mind wandered to when he and other officers visited the strip club during the sunlight hours. The collection date of Sunday was mentioned, and if Mateo knew the operation had been compromised, then either one of the corrupt officers had given this information to the OCG, or the strip club owner passed on the information to the OCG. Ted knew Simon was present with Hector and Andries, both officers who could be cause for suspicion, minus Simon.

"So what happened? Did you go into the club?"

"We went into all of them. Last night, through the night and this morning."

"Did you go to Toys Strip Club?"

Amar squinted his eyes towards Ted in a confused way. As if Ted had revealed Amar's secrets. Amar started to shake his head, and his eyes widened in realisation.

"Did you and your officers visit this club? Talk to the owner?" Amar asked.

Now Ted became confused, and so did Angelika. They turned briefly to look at each other, then swiftly returned to face Amar.

"Maybe something happened there. Something that Mateo said before he went in and when he returned from the visit," Amar said, looking down at the table as if envisioning the moment.

"What did Mateo say?" Ted pressed.

"Erm. He said something like, the cops are sniffing around the place. Hold tight. This may take longer."

"Anything else?"

"No. Only when he came out," Amar raised his head, staring directly at Ted.

"What did he say, Amar?"

"He said it's taken care of."

"Ted," Angelika said.

Ted turned his body, holding his right hand on the back of the seat, facing the mirror behind him. He flicked his head as if to signal a response to Amar's answer regarding the welfare of those who may have been inside the Toys Strip Club late last night.

"I know, but we're not finished yet."

"What time did you visit Toys Strip Club?" Ted continued.

Amar lifted his bottom lip, trying to recall his movements through the late night.

"Around 04:00 AM? Maybe just after, I don't know exactly."

"Was that when it closed?"

Amar shrugged his shoulders.

"I don't know, I wasn't checking the opening times. I didn't see anyone."

Angelika lifted from her seat quickly, causing one side of the room to watch her movement. Ted remained focused on Amar, as Angelika announced to the tape recording that she was exiting the interview to investigate Amar's narration from last night, leaving the three in the room. Ted was sure that police officers would make their way to the club within the next few seconds, with paramedics in that convoy.

"How did Mateo seem when he came out?"

Amar had zoned out. Possibly trying to recall the moment Ted was probing him on.

"Amar?"

He shook his head lightly, bringing him back into the room.

"He seemed a bit different, I don't know."

"Did he say anything else? Did you ask him what he meant by 'taken care of'?" Ted said, raising both hands, emphasizing the quote with his index and middle finger.

"I didn't ask. But thinking back, he seemed tenser after that trip."

"Did you make any more trips after?"

"Just two, I think. I drove and never left the vehicle; he went in each time."

"Where did you go afterwards?"

"I drove to my apartment; he gave me some money and took the car. I don't know where he went—home or to see his boss. He told me to be up in the morning for the next instructions."

"And here we are."

"I didn't hurt anyone," Amar pleaded.

"Maybe not, but you are deeply involved in this mess. Tell me this. We have Mateo's DNA at the scene of the music venue and in the exact location where an officer called Daniel Belfield was shot. Did Mateo pull the trigger?"

Amar's body language changed. His shoulder dropped in the chair, and he'd lost strength in keeping his body rested in a seated position.

"He did."

"Were you there?"

Amar slowly nodded.

"What was your role?"

Amar sniffed his nose, trying to avoid the answer, wasting time but making noises with his nose and mouth. Searching the room for an escape or something to focus on to kill time.

"Amar?"

"Are you going to protect me?"

"Depends what you say."

"I was a spotter."

"Explain."

"A group of us were spotters. We were told the target would be at the music venue tonight. He saw a picture of him and looked out for him. There isn't much CCTV in there, so we had to use our eyes. Some waited by the front doors, some inside. I was inside by the toilets and saw him, so I followed him. To the bar. Through the dancing crowds. I followed. I told Mateo..."

"How did you tell Mateo?"

"Phone. Text."

"Did you give the order?"

Amar clinched his jaw together tightly, raising his head to look upwards while breathing slowly but deeply.

"Let me explain something first. How I met Mateo."

Ted opened up his right palm to signal to continue. Ted felt a vibration in his pocket as Amar continued his story. Ted reached for his phone to reveal the text. Angelika's message stated they were en route to Toys Strip Club.

"Mateo was a leader in that prison; he had his own protection, gang. He noticed one day that I had been drinking. He threatened to tell the guards and have me fired. I couldn't be fired; I have... *had*... a family to provide for. He said if I did things for him, he would keep it his little secret."

"What things did you do?"

"Nothing sexual. He had me bring things in. Phones, drugs, weapons."

"Did you get caught?"

"No," Amar laughed.

"He had the guards on his payroll, too, sometimes," he continued.

"Okay, so why did you get caught drinking?"

"My manager caught me off guard, saw me drinking in the toilets and smelt it on my breath. I begged for a second chance, but apparently, someone else had seen me, and he was checking if it was true. I lost my job, my family."

"So, how did you meet Mateo after he was released?"

"A man approached me in the supermarket and told me he knew I was poor, with no family and had a chance to earn some money. I said yes, and then I met Mateo again. He threatened to hurt my child and... his mother if I didn't."

"So he forced you to work for him?"

"Yeah."

"Did he say for how long you would work for him?"

"He said he would tell me, but my son would be safe, and his mother."

"He approached you in Albania?"

"Yeah."

"Did he say the work was in Greece, Athens?"

"He did."

Ted was piecing the puzzle together on how Amar and Mateo came together professionally, although under hostage. Albanian organised crime in the Hellenic Republic was a serious concern. The Albania Mafia controlled approximately fifty percent of human trafficking, eighty percent of the retail distribution of heroin, and ninety percent of the importation of illegal small arms in Greece. Crimes committed by Albanians amounted to fifty percent of armed robberies of homes and businesses in the country. Mateo was a controlling figure in the gang, but with previous experience, Ted knew there were big chains of command up the food chain. Amar was useful to Mateo—even under his control—but was dispensable at any moment.

Ted felt sorry for Amar as he stared back at him, somewhat shaken by his confession. Although Ted felt sympathy towards this man, Ted knew he was an accessory to murder, among other crimes. At this point, Kostas had given up writing and stared blankly at the page before him. Amar's conversation and the tape recording would prove he was guilty and involved in the OCG's criminal underworld, and this was just the tip of the iceberg.

"So, Amar, before you told us about how you met Mateo."

Amar braced himself, adjusting himself in the seat, perhaps uncomfortable with the cuffs forcing his hands behind his back.

"Did you tell Mateo where Daniel was located?" Ted continued.

A single tear fell from Amar's eye, falling down his bony cheek and onto the table's surface. Amar dropped his head, tears trickled from his face, and a slight moan came from his mouth, producing mucus in his nostrils. Ted had one burning question in his mind, though.

"How did you know he was going to be there?"

"One of your officers, they said. The officer told our guys he would be there, and he was."

Ted forgot about anything else, searching the table before him for some narrative or answer. He thought it must have been an officer close to Daniel and the corruption case. The internal affairs team? Hector? Andries? Or someone else. He repeated the names in his mind hoping one would stick, but he couldn't fathom a conclusion.

"Did they say who the officer was?"

"No," Amar replied, wiping his nose on the clothing fitted over his shoulder.

Ted knew it wouldn't be that simple. Suddenly there was a knock on the interview room door. Ted reached for his phone to check if any other messages had been received, but there were none.

"Come in."

The door opened at full tilt, and in came Eliana, flustered.

"Can you come outside for a second?"

Amar and the lawyer looked concerned, lifting their heads to peer at Eliana over Ted. Ted grabbed the chair's armrest and lifted his body quickly to stand, announcing the interview would be halted. Ted reached for the red button to stop the recording, sidestepped speedily, and propelled himself to the door to follow Eliana outside.

"What's wrong?" Ted said, reaching for the handle to close the interview door.

"Officers have arrived at the club."

"And?" Ted pressed.

Eliana closed her eyes and tightened her lips.

"Mateo must of got the money and killed the..."

"The owner," Ted finished.

Ted closed his eyes and began to pace the corridor. He clenched his fist tight and banged the bottom of his fist against the wall.

"Fuck!"

"That's not all."

Ted unclenched his fist, turning to face Eliana more calmly, but no less intimidating as he waited for an answer.

"There's good news. We know who the other girl is who Daniel was talking to about the case."

"Who is it?"

"Maya."

"Where is she?"

"She's alive."

Chapter 30

Nikos Tsipras's lifeless body was positioned in front of the bar space inside the Toys Club. He lay on his front, arms and legs stretched out in various positions, just like the novelty dead body outlined in white tape. Red blood stains soaked his previously cream-white shirt, accumulated from five gunshot wounds to the back as he attempted to escape from the shooter. Officers who had arrived at the scene searched the entire complex and found another person alive, hiding inside the owner's office behind a locked door. The person was Maya Beridze.

On approach, the officers found the door closed; she unlocked the door and surrendered to the officers before explaining the scenario from her own perspective. At the time of the shooting, she was changing in another room where girls dressed and undressed, preparing for the night's punters. The bar staff had left, and Nikos was cleaning up the various tables, stages and floor as the cleaner called in sick through the night. Officers studied the CCTV of the club, rewinding back to see the footage, extensively looking for the moment when Mateo entered the complex. The CCTV outside showed a vehicle pull up to the door with an unknown man inside, whom Amar had earlier confessed was himself. Mateo entered the unlocked club around 03:58 AM when it seemed it was closing business for the new morning, which was imminent. Mateo entered the complex and went through the passage to the main room.

Once he entered the wide opening, he was confronted by a visibly confused and distressed Nikos as Mateo distinctly aimed his gun towards him. They were communicating, but the footage didn't pick up the vocals. Mateo followed a nervous Nikos as he manoeuvred through the room towards the staff entrance. Other camera footage showed the pair moving towards Nikos's office, where they went out of view. Moments later, the couple returned, with Mateo holding a black sports bag similar to the one in the black Mercedes boot. They returned to the main hall, where they last stood together by the first set of double doors leading to the exit passage. An altercation ensued as Mateo began to shout, and Nikos nervously took steps back to move away from him. Nikos turned to run and escape the danger before Mateo raised his gun and shot him multiple times.

The gunfire blinded the CCTV screen as the trigger was pulled. Nikos's lifeless body was still and so silent at that moment that Mateo stood over him for confirmation. Suddenly, Mateo spun his body, raising his gun as if disturbed. He looked at the staff door as if he saw or heard a noise. As he paced towards the doorway to investigate, the camera footage stopped, and a black-and-white static appeared on the screen. Unbeknown to the officers, the following moments were undetected and unknown.

When Ted arrived, police officers had swarmed the premises, with forensic officers investigating the body and swabbing different objects for any fingerprints or fibres. Ted watched the body from a distance, another life lost in the entangled web of lies, corruption, and murder. Ted searched the room for the other lonely soul, alive this time.

"Is that Maya?" Ted asked.

Across the room, seated on one of the chairs included in a table set, was Maya. She leaned forward with her hands clasped together, and a long black coat resting around her shoulders. She was still in her work attire from the night before, reaffirming her police statement.

"Yeah. Maya Beridze, she was born in Georgia," Angelika said.

"Did she say any more about what happened?"

Ted had seen the videotape. However, at no point during the film was Maya visible on the screen. As the time clock was seconds from reaching 04:00 AM, in her statement, she said she moved from the changing room to Nikos's office for safety. During those movements, she dropped her phone onto the hard carpeted floor, thus making the noise that Mateo was interrupted by. She gathered her device, stumbled into the office, and seemingly shut the door. At this point, the camera's footage disconnected. The officer revealed that the security system was on a timing loop, meaning at 04:00 AM, when the club was officially closed, the camera footage would shut down and download to the computer hard drive. Additionally, this would have been a positive resource for saving electricity, as the power wouldn't need to be kept on overnight.

"Maya said she heard arguing, and then she saw Nikos and Mateo when she sneaked to look through the door of the changing rooms. She had seen him speaking to Nikos before."

"On Sundays?"

"On Sundays."

"She heard them arguing and then heard the gunshots; she ran into Nikos's office because she knew he had a lock on it and hid."

"And Mateo came for her?"

"She said he did; he must have heard the phone drop. He tried to get into the office, but she said he gave up and left."

Ted began to ponder, thinking about those moments that weren't captured.

"You've asked her about the exchange, or lack of it, with Mateo?"

"Yeah, she said she just hid in the corner waiting for him to come or shoot through the door, but he didn't. He left."

Ted nodded, accepting this was an accurate account of what occurred.

"Can I speak with her?"

"Sure, just don't talk about what happened. She made an account already, and I don't want her to relive it again today—maybe tomorrow when we take a full statement."

"No problem, I've got something else to ask her."

"Be my guest," Angelika said, holding her arm out toward her.

Ted carefully advanced towards Maya's miserable persona, playing through a careful introduction in his head. As he approached her, she looked up towards him and offered a half-faked smile through the smudged mascara on her face.

"Hi, Maya, I'm Ted Chester. I'm a British officer investigating a murder. Not this murder, but another one that happened prior."

Maya looked visibly confused.

"I know you are shaken by what happened here. I know officers have asked you questions about Nikos and the shooter, and I won't ask you again. However, can I ask a few questions about another important matter?"

"Yes."

Ted reached for his wallet and brought out a piece of A4 paper positioned inside the slot where cash notes were held. He unfolded the slip to reveal a picture of a man, then held it up to Maya.

"Do you know this man?" Ted said, holding up an image of Daniel Belfield's service photo.

Maya's eyes widened, not in fear, but in comfort and safety. She began to nod.

"Yes."

"Did he tell you his name?"

"Yeah, Daniel, I think?"

"Correct."

"Why are..."

"Daniel said he spoke to you, and we are particularly interested in something he mentioned. He said that one or two of the girls smuggled here remember arriving on an island, and on the beach, they remember seeing the wording of some artwork or graffiti that said the 'scratchy night' or something before their view was blinded by bags being put over their head."

Maya shook her head in fear and became agitated, trying to stretch up to reach her feet.

"Easy, Maya. It's okay."

Maya relaxed and sat back down again in her original position.

"He told me he wouldn't tell anyone."

"Well, Daniel was murdered a few days ago."

She sat there in disbelief, her mouth open wide.

"I don't believe it. They'll come for me next!"

Ted crouched down, now at eye level with Maya. He reached out his hand and held it upon her shoulder.

"You are safe with us. After you've done here, we will arrange to keep you safe. We won't let you go home anytime soon alone. I promise you," Ted consoled.

He turned to Angelika, looking up towards her from his lowered position.

"Sure, we can make arrangements for that. I'll make a call now." Angelika smiled, reaching for her phone before turning away to make a phone call.

"See. You are safe. Now, I've got a few more questions for you, if that's okay?"

Maya nodded her head tentatively.

"The graffiti you saw. Explain what you saw."

"I was on a boat and then a smaller boat."

"Were you blindfolded?"

"Yes."

"For the whole of it?"

"No. There seemed to be an issue with the boat. It couldn't get close enough to the shore, so we had to get into the water. We still had the bags on our heads, but I couldn't see I was panicking. It was nighttime, and the bags made it impossible. So, one of the men asked if I swam. I said yes. He said he would take it off to let me see where I was going, to swim. We were close to the beach, but it was dark, and I couldn't see much. One of the men shouted at him from the shore, and he put the bag back on immediately."

"I know it was dark, but can you remember anything you saw?"

"The car's headlights and maybe two people."

"How many cars?"

"Two, maybe."

"What about the graffiti?"

"Yes. I saw a street light shine on the wall of the building. I started to read the words, as they were big, but the bag went over my head, and I only saw the words 'scratchy night' on a colourful background."

"No other words, nothing else?"

Maya shook her head, searching the floor to see if she could recall anything else.

"Were you the only one being transported?"

"There were three of us. Me, Ayat, and Amira."

Ted nodded. The names were familiar. The girls, including Maya, had given Daniel a clue about their onshore departure location, although it was ineffectual.

"I'm sorry I can't give any more... although..."

"What is it?"

"The police officer that was visiting the club. I wasn't sure who it was. Daniel showed me a few photographs to let me remember, but I think I remember now."

Ted was surprised at Maya's announcement. She hadn't mentioned it to any of the officers, but the curveball gave Ted a jolt of optimism. He felt his jacket and trouser pockets, although he knew he didn't have any of the service photographs upon his person. Ted turned to look for Angelika, peering up towards her as she finished her phone call.

"Angelika!" Ted shouted.

She looked down at Ted's position, still crouched next to the sitting Maya.

"We've just had word that we're all good to go with taking Maya to a safe house."

Maya heard Angelika's instruction, and fear of panic filled her saddened face. The mascara and eyeliner from the night before had already been blotched and smudged down her pale cheeks.

"Where am I going?" She stood.

"Somewhere safe. You can't go home."

"What about the police station? The cells? I don't mind it there; it will be safe."

"You will be safe at the accommodation you will be given. Even I won't know where you are going. Okay?" Ted looked deeply into her innocent eyes.

"Okay," she nodded softly, searching for comfort in his.

She slowly dropped herself back to the chair while Angelika stood beside Ted. Ted raised his body to stand up tall before asking if she had photographs of the officers in the line of their suspicion.

"Yeah, sure, on my phone, I think. Why?"

"She says she knows who it is," Ted said, looking down at the key witness.

Angelika's eyes widened with suspense. She swiftly reached for her jeans pocket and brought out her phone. Angelika navigated her mobile device to the photo gallery, flicking her finger on the screen to search for the photographs. Maya sat there patiently while Ted stood there, quite the opposite.

"Are they all together?"

"They should be. Yep, got them," said Angelika, looking through the initial photos.

She selected the first photo to enlarge it to a full screen. It clearly depicted Hector Baros, but she wasn't sure of the photographs' order. She carefully gripped the phone, allowing her fingers tips to not distort the clear image.

"Okay, I'm going to show you a selection of photographs. Tell me if you recognise the man to be the one who visited you."

Maya nodded and remained silent while looking up at the two officers. Angelika kneeled down to Maya's level and held the screen in perfect view.

"No."

Angelika turned the screen so she could face it, and then flicked it ever so slightly to the following picture but didn't see the person.

"No, not him."

Before Angelika could turn it back, Maya held her hand out.

"I'll swipe it for you."

"No," she said after swiping.

She touched the screen again.

"No."

Her finger was reaching, ready for the next swipe.

"Wait."

Ted noticed her eyelids squint as she decided whether the picture would be of the officer who visited. He couldn't tell if she wasn't sure or if she was reliving the memory back in her mind from the reminder.

"Is this the person you saw?"

Maya paused for another moment before nodding.

"Yes, that's him."

She remained gripped on the one photograph, although hesitant in her voice.

"Are you completely sure?"

She affirmed, and this time she seemed sure, nodding quickly and with conviction.

Angelika turned her wrist to reveal the phone's screen and the authority figure Maya had been visited by. They both took one quick glance at the photo before making eye contact. Ted felt a pit in his stomach. He didn't have a professional or personal connection, not ultimately; he had only been here less than a week. He was more nauseous that someone could turn his back on the badge they worked for and turn to a life of crime, ending many other good ones.

She stared down at the screen without making a sound. Ted turned to see Maya looking up awkwardly at the pair's reactions.

"This was the guy who visited you and Daria?" Ted said.

"Yeah, it was him."

There was a silence between the trio again.

Maya was impatient. "Can I get out of here now? To this safe place."

Ted saw Angelika was composing herself, lowering the phone away from view.

"Yeah. If you've got everything, Angelika will make the arrangements now?" Ted asked.

"Yeah, I'll come with you now. Transport should be nearly outside. Maya, follow me out front."

"Are you calling the identity in?" Ted asked.

"I'll do it now."

Angelika turned to face the door, which exited to a corridor before the outside space. She began to walk, holding her device to her ear as she walked through the first set of doors. Maya lifted herself up to Ted, collecting her bag as she moved.

"Thanks, Ted," she said as she passed him.

Ted watched Maya chase after Angelika, who exited the complex with purpose. Ted bowed as he tried to decipher the reasoning behind everything, but he couldn't. Ted saw a pair of legs approach him, and as he raised his head, he saw Simon.

"No one else in the building—it doesn't seem like anything else was broken, destroyed. Mateo came in and out, took the money, and shot Nikos."

A question returned to Ted's curiosity as Simon finished. It started to bother him, similar to the disclosure from Maya only a minute or so ago.

"Something bugs me. Why was she kept alive?"

"Maybe Mateo felt remorse or couldn't get to her?"

"I don't think Mateo felt any remorse. He had a weapon, and I've seen this guy; you've seen him. He could have taken down that door if he wanted to. She's a risk."

"What did she say anyway to you there?"

"She told us who the officer is."

Simon stared in amazement.

"Really! Who is it?" Simon asked eagerly.

"You're not going to believe it."

Chapter 31

S TEAM LIFTED FROM THE coffee cups spread along the desk. Officers were leaning over them, not peering inside at the dark liquid, but with their eyes peeled ahead of them. Through the one-way glass was a table, accompanied by two seats on one side and three on the other. The set of three was empty, but only temporarily, while the occupants of the other two seats waited eagerly for them to arrive. Andries slumped in his chair, nodding slowly and sombrely as his lawyer tried to communicate with him to prepare for any advice to help his situation.

"We all set? They're about to start," a voice said from inside the listening room.

A few confirmations echoed throughout the room, and Andries's body flinched as the door to the interview room opened. Entering the room were Savvas, Angelika, and Nikolas. Once they sat in their seats, adjusted their comfort, and placed their folders and beverages on the table, they stared directly at Andries. Angelika reached over to the recording device, clicked the record button, and stated the time, date, and those present in the room before letting the interview commence.

"Yia tin kaséta..." Savvas began.

Ted stood frustrated at his inability to understand, and Simon shared the same thoughts.

"Could someone translate, please? Sorry," Simon asked.

"Sure, I'll translate for you both," Eliana replied as she broke her stare with the mirror.

"He's just introduced himself for the tape..."

The female lawyer interrupted Savvas's narrative, and after a quick-fire discussion across the table, the interviewers allowed the lawyer to make his announcement. The lawyer wore thick-rimmed glasses, and her long black hair was in a ponytail, resting on the back of her suit jacket. Eliana translated her response loosely.

"My name is Arianna, and who is representing Andries. My client Andries and I spoke before, and Andries will answer your questions; however, if I feel that the interview in any way will further incriminate him, I will interject and proceed Andries into a no comment," she continued, "but first, Andries would like to say something before I read this to you."

Everyone's attention immediately turned to Andries's incoming statement. Andries looked up from the table. He searched the interviewer's eyes for some remorse and understanding. They offered none; Savvas and Angelika stared blankly back at him, awaiting his declaration eagerly. Nikolas wasn't even locking eyes with the accused.

"Is he going to confess?" Simon asked behind the glass.

"Who knows?" Ted replied.

Andries cleared his throat.

"I would like to record that my lawyer advised me not to answer your questions, as it could further incriminate me. However, I've been a member of the police force for nearly twenty years and will answer all of my questions truthfully, because I did not commit these crimes that I'm charged with."

Andries finished, and briefly glanced back at the mirror and reclused, slumping in the chair again, embarrassed to be sat accused by those he led.

"You believe him?" Ted said, turning to Simon.

"I don't know. The evidence is clear, but let's hear him speak."

Savvas continued his statement from before.

"For the purposes of the tape, I, Superintendent Savvas Kritsikis, and DI Angelika Bafa are both part of the internal affairs team. Also present is Police Director Nikolas Konstantinou. Being questioned today is Police Deputy Director Andries Iraklidis. He has used his right to legal counsel, and his lawyer is present. The charges are conspiracy to assist with the murders or murder of Police Sergeant Christos Masouras, International Officer Daniel Belfield, Cassandra Argyros, and Daria Hussain. The attempted murder of Police Captain Hector Baros, organised crime group participation offences, human trafficking, and extortion, to name a few."

Savvas turned to look at Angelika while Arianna heavily worked her pen tip into the notepad. Angelika took the glance as her turn to speak.

"You were identified as the police officer who was seeing the sex workers at Cleoptra's Cove. Did you visit this building?" Angelika asked. "Photograph A is a statement from the sex worker today confirming that she matched your official service photograph to the man she saw on multiple occasions."

Andries visibly gulped. "I did."

"So you're admitting you visited this building called Cleopatra's Cove and paid for sex?"

"I did."

"How many times?""Five or six times."

"What was the reason behind these visits?"

Andries paused, reflecting on the response he was about to give, increasing the anticipation for those sat behind the glass.

"I've been going through a divorce. It was a stupid mistake; I just needed a distraction and the pressures of work. I don't drink and would never do drugs, so I... you know."

"The girl who identified you said you threatened her and some other girls, saying you were a police officer, saying that you own them, and they must do what you say unless they were to be deported or killed."

"That is a lie!" he proclaimed.

Angelika placed another sheet on the table, a photograph of Maya.

"Andries, did you visit this girl? Photograph A is a photograph of the sex worker who identified you, Andries."

Andries peered forward and briefly glanced at the picture before leaning back.

"Yes, I visited her, but never said those things."

"Why would they lie?" Nikolas announced.

"I don't know."

"Okay, so we have witnesses placing you at the club and confirming you threatened them," Nikolas continued.

"Who?" Andries pleaded.

"Other girls who worked at Cleopatra's Cove."

"But I never threatened anyone," he pleaded again, lifting his cuffed arms to exaggerate his point.

"Okay. Can you explain the money we found in your home search?"

"What money?" he said with his eyes wide.

Angelika took over the next round of questioning, allowing Nikolas to rest back in his chair.

"Can you explain the large amounts of euro notes in your home? Please take a look at photograph B."

Angelika collected the photograph from the open file, passing it to Savvas before Andries glanced at it himself. Arianna leaned forward, peering over the photograph. Her face remained unchanged, expressing a poker face. She began to make notes on her lined paper briskly before raising her left hand towards Andries.

"I cannot," Andries explained.

"Can you explain photograph C? This document contains a bank statement from your personal bank that shows cash deposits of twenty thousand euros not two days ago."

"No, I cannot!" Andries shouted. "I'm not behind this; I'm being..." he tried to continue.

"Not another word, Andries!" Arianna bellowed.

The voice stunned both rooms into utter silence.

"But I did not do this!"

Andries's face grew full of fear. He looked into the eyes of the interviewees and turned his head towards the one-way mirror, pleading again.

"I did not do this; I'm being framed!"

"Andries Iraklidis! If you ignore my orders, I will leave you to the wolves in this room and separate my role from defending you."

Andries slumped in his chair, with his head down, admitting defeat from the orders he was given. Behind the one-way mirror, the officers were stunned by the abrupt nature of his lawyer's demands. She looked petite and fresh out of secondary education in her light grey suit, white shirt, and open-top button, but she was ruthless and in control of his destiny.

"May we continue?" Nikolas aimed towards the lawyer.

She raised her right hand, which held the pen. "Sure."

"Andries, have you collaborated with Mateo Berisha, Amar Veseli, and Mario Martinaj?"

Andries hesitated, looking forward to his lawyer, who intently stared back. Andries took the order but shook his head first in disapproval.

"No comment," Andries hesitated.

Angelika pulled out another file and named it Photograph D, placing it in view of the accused side of the table.

"Can you explain the burner phone found in your apartment and the numerous messages received from unknown contacts? Some contain replies from the phone's owner stating the locations of Daria Hussain, Ted Chester's apartment, and orders to execute Police Sargent Christos Masouras?"

Andries shook his head. "No comment."

"You know this is a mountain of evidence we are compiling against you. Do you and your lawyer want to have a few minutes, so you can come back and help your cause?"

Andries looked towards Arianna for answers, but she shook her head while continuing to write notes. Andries turned back to face the question.

"No comment."

Savvas raised his right hand and signalled from left to right against his throat to cut the interview. Angelika reached for the stop button on the tape recorder, stopping to announce the termination of the interview.

"We will conclude the interview with Police Deputy Director Andries Ikraklidis. The time is now 16:56. Andries will remain in custody for now," she said before pressing the button.

The interviewers raised from their seats simultaneously, staring down at the accused. Andries lifted his head, aiming a straight face towards his colleagues, who returned a judgemental look. The interviewers exited the interview while the officers in the monitoring room exited the door to meet those outside, leaving Ted and Eliana alone.

"Thanks for translating for me," Ted said.

"No problem."

"So, what do you think?" Ted said as he turned to Eliana.

"Honestly?"

Ted nodded while Eliana bit her lip and tilted her head to process her words.

"I don't know. I can't believe it or believe it's Andries."

"I know, I know. But the evidence? What do you think?"

Eliana exhaled softly.

"It doesn't look good, Ted. It doesn't look at all. The money, the bank transactions, the visits to the sex club, like Daniel was investigating. The girl confirmed it was Andries. I just can't believe it. It must be true, but I just can't get my head around it; I feel sick."

Eliana bowed her head. She began to believe the crimes Andries had committed as she uttered them out of her mouth.

"I'm sorry, Eliana."

Eliana smiled, piercing her lips together, unsure what to reply. The door opened to the outside corridor, and Simon entered the monitoring room after quickly debriefing with the interviewers. With a whistle, Simon grabbed Ted and Eliana's attention.

"Nikolas wants to meet us all in the boardroom now."

Simon retreated towards the door, leaving it open for them to exit. Eliana turned to look at Ted with a smile.

"Looks like we've solved it anyway. For Daniel, for all of them," Eliana announced. Ted shook his head, leaving Eliana visibly confused.

"It's not over yet."

Chapter 32

NIKOLAS ORDERED THE OFFICERS involved in the case to attend a meeting in the boardroom. There wasn't an agenda to the gathering, but most assumed it regarded Andries's arrest and the overall investigation. Leaving Andries to gather his thoughts on the interview, Angelika gained an update on a few unanswered questions in the inquiry before attending Nikolas's meeting. She addressed the group, stating the two black Mercedes rental cars from Avis; both fitted with GPS, but only one was retrievable due to the other being destroyed in the fire. The one retrieved, Amar and Mateo occupied, rather than the one that was burnt out. Angelika explained the installation sometimes can be on the high-end spec cars they lease out, and most car rental companies have trackers and vans fitted to their vehicles.

The logs showed the car passed through multiple checkpoints in the story of the investigation. The car was present during the murder of Daniel Belfield, a situation at the petrol station on the main road, outside the music venue industrial complex. This collaborated with the CCTV, which didn't show a view of the licence plate, but provided a similar vehicle description to the one rented. The Mercedes was frequently parked at Amar's address, which had been raided during the interview. There were bundles of euros amounting to fifteen thousand and a burner phone with a list of numbers, some unknown and some untraceable. However, Amar was given orders from the anonymous members of the OCG and Mateo to meet and execute their violent plans. Angelika continued to inform that the department's leading mobile phone forensics experts would investigate the electronic device further.

Everyone was in their places as Angelika finished her debrief. Ted turned momentarily towards the window as the setting sun broke through the boardroom windows, illuminating the room further beyond the electronic lights above. The big yellow sun was large and bright even in the winter months. The only spoil to that moment was the cemented towering building obscuring the natural view beyond the Piraeus, the Riveria before it met the water of the Saronic Gulf, Myrtoan Sea before the Mediterranean. Ted drifted towards the sun as he sat, becoming translucent, allowing it to pass through him. In those moments, his worries and regret departed from him. He closed his eyes, feeling light and free from all negativity. His mind was blank, empty, a hollow container of nothingness, and Ted enjoyed those moments before he was interrupted by the start of the group discussion.

"How's Hector?" Eliana asked.

Nikolas smiled at Eliana.

"Yes. Sorry, I forgot to update you all. He is well. He was taken to the hospital for some checks but wasn't hit by the gunfire. He is well, and I've told him to take a few days off to recover."

"I tried calling him before, but his phone was switched off."

Nikolas dropped his bottom lip, shrugging his shoulders.

"Maybe he doesn't want to be in contact, or he wants to be switched off from what happened."

Eliana nodded.

"Yeah, true. I'm glad he is okay."

Nikolas nodded before returning to his natural resting face. He took a moment to retrace his moment and began to address the whole group.

"I'd like to thank you all for your hard work over the last few days. I've updated the police lieutenant general and police major general on the investigation, and it will be noted that everyone involved in this case will be gratefully acknowledged. We have also lost those we have lost, including Christos, Daniel, and many others. I'm glad we managed to find justice after such a difficult and emotional week for all. With the distraction of the protest, which could have been far worse than what occurred," Nikolas said, aiming his words at Ted.

"Although I must thank Ted and Simon for helping catch those involved."

Ted leered back towards Nikolas, who held the connection, before breaking away to seek other officers as he continued his lecture.

Nikolas continued his speech by detailing the next steps in gathering evidence against Andries, the areas to focus on concerning the bank transfer, money found in his apartment, apparent text messages from his device, and Maya's confession.

"So, what are we going to do next now this is over?" Eliana whispered.

"We've not finished yet."

"What do you mean?" Eliana asked, twisting her head towards Ted.

"I'll speak to you later," he whispered.

"Okay, everyone. Please let me have a moment with the British officers Ted and Simon."

As the group stood up and broke away from the table, Nikolas was peering towards the expansive windows, giving a view of the sunset overlooking the city. Once the last officer exited the room, there was a lull of silence for a few seconds. Ted and Simon glanced at each other in the awkward tension. Nikolas was the first to break it by pushing himself into a seat closer to Ted. He sat and extended his hand in the form of a warm greeting from a man Ted thought was cold and reserved.

"Thank you for your hard work and determination with this case. I wasn't very welcoming when you arrived, and I apologise for that introduction. Even though the officers here know about my personality, I should have been more welcoming in a time of great distress for you and your colleague. I hope I've received some of your respect now we have brought justice to this department and those we have lost."

Ted thought he saw a breach of a smile from Nikolas's mouth. His face was still straight as he finished his peace offering, until Ted lifted his hand to meet the handshake in the middle. Nikolas portrayed a beaming smile as their hands squeezed. Ted held a firm grip, but Nikolas's was clutching tighter. Ted offered a nod while pinching his lips, which portrayed a smile. Ted was happy there was some form of resolve for the pair and felt somewhat uncomfortable seeing a happy Nikolas, but Ted still had pressing matters.

"Thanks, Nikolas; I appreciate what you've said."

"Thank you, Ted," he replied as they lost their clasp of each other.

"Although, if you don't mind. I do have some questions still?"

"Sure."

"Sorry to stop the positivity. But what about the Albanian gangs? The man who chased me? The man who shot down Daniel and the others? We can't let them get away with it. Are you moving forward with this part of the investigation?"

Nikolas's face changed completely. His happy and positive smile was taken away from him. He tightened his jawline, the bone structure piercing through the skin. Nikolas reached out his hand to offer the seat next to him. Ted took the invitation tentatively. As he lowered,

Nikolas kept constant eye contact with him. Nikolas's nostrils visibly increased in size as he inhaled and exhaled through his mouth with such great power that it could be heard.

"I understand your frustrations," Nikolas started.

"Do you?" Ted replied sarcastically.

Nikolas's eyes widened with surprise. Simon raised his eyebrows to Ted, offering advice to stop his disagreement any further.

Ted ignored the advice and pressed on.

"I'm not being a problem for you, Nikolas. I came to Athens with Simon to help investigate, and it seems we have the man behind this in a cell right now."

"You mean, we have our man."

"Yes. But this isn't my point. Within the complexities of the case, there is evidence of OCG involvement. Scrap that; there is evidence of murder and attempted murder by this Albanian gang. This is why I'm asking you about this case of investigation. This is far from over, do you agree?"

"I agree. There are more doors to open in this investigation," Simon added.

Nikolas exhaled, searching the floor for a comeback.

"It's been a testing week for the department with protests, even the murders of their colleagues and friends. We've performed a major step in his investigation by finding the corruption within the department, and more will come."

"With all respect. I want to continue with the case now."

Nikolas stared hard into him, feeling irritation in his eyes.

"Be my guest." Nikolas shrugged.

The tension between the two intensified as the silence became eerie. Simon offered a break from the toxicity, a hand from the outer ring of displeasure.

"Listen, I want justice for Daniel and the other officers as much as any of you two do, and so do the police forces and agency back in the UK. We could have quickly brought over a dozen officers from the UK, infiltrating your department and streets investigating the case, but we didn't. We kept it low-key, and I'm glad we did. The evidence points towards Andries; it's worked if that's the case. I'm with both of you on your thoughts surrounding the Albania Mafia. Ted has been threatened by them, and he's retaliated to his life being put under threat. He's not running around the streets of Athens shooting anyone and anybody; they are coming to him, and they will still be coming for us. Although, like you say, Nikolas, we have no leads with the vehicles; they've burnt one out, changed the plates multiple times, and have probably got new vehicles altogether. We've OCG members in cells who don't know shit, some dead," Simon announced.

Nikolas seemed smug about the latter part of Simon's narration, feeling Simon had taken his side. Ted felt similarly embarrassed. However, this was far from the truth of the situation. Simon went on the attack, backing his partner and setting the ground rules, knocking the smirk off Nikolas's face with his formal manner.

"However, Police Director Nikolas Konstantinou. Ted and the affairs team in your department will continue to investigate and support the evidence collection towards the charges of Andries Iraklidis. When we see fit, we will continue to investigate any potential suspicious activity or leads we may come across with the Albanian OCG. The information will be shared from our side, and if any investigations from your team bring up any detail, you will share that information with us. As I said, I don't want to bring over an army of UK officers clogging up your desks in your police department."

At the start of Simon's second monologue, Ted observed the smirk disappear from Nikolas's face, becoming one that was unsettled. Ted noticed he was biting, clenching his teeth together hard as his jawline tightened, lifting his top lip slightly. The dialogue left Nikolas unsettled as he stood up from his position bearing down on the two officers, who remained seated. He pressed his suit jacket down with his hand to iron out the creases, occasionally moving his hand in strokes from the chest to the bottom of his torso.

"As I said before, well done, and thank you for your efforts. Now please allow us to work together. One step at a time."

Nikolas took one last glare at Ted before breaking his focus to throw a nod to Simon. Nikolas strode towards the door without offering a handshake. He didn't turn to look back at the officers before reaching for the handle, pulling the door towards him and exiting. They both watched Nikolas leave, waiting for the door to click upon its latch.

"Ted," Simon said.

"Yeah."

"The sunset looks lovely," Simon said as he positioned himself by the window.

Ted stood up and followed Simon, taking in the view. The sunset was illuminating the sky. However, the height of their position wasn't expansive enough to take in the full city view as the sun was about to hide behind the concrete buildings across the road.

They silently embraced each other as they watched the fiery ball sit in the sky, waiting to be engulfed by night.

"We must go to the roof and see it fully one day soon."

"I'm sure you will have time to see many," Simon replied.

There was a brief silence as they took in the sun's lavish orange glow.

"So what's the plan?" Simon said as he turned to face Ted.

"We've got something we can investigate. While the rest are busy here with Andries."

"So you're not going to listen to Nikolas, are you?"

Ted beamed, turning to face Simon.

"I wouldn't have listened to him anyway."

"I know you too well, Ted."

"That you do."

Chapter 33

T HE KEYBOARD CLICKED AWAY as Eliana's fingers typed in different combinations of wordings into the internet search bar and social media platforms. The wordings the smuggled girl described weren't picking up apparent matches. Links offered advice on allergic reactions while at the beach or courses of action if you gain an allergic reaction after swimming in the ocean.

Eliana was in the hot seat, working the system using different characters, while Ted and Simon watched. The suggestion of adding *Greece* to the search bar only brought up listings of unspoilt places to visit on various Greek islands. They grew frustrated—the search was nearly an hour long, and they were complaining and conceding.

"Maybe the girl read it wrong, or it got lost in translation," Simon said.

"Maybe so—we would have found something surely by now," Ted added, tapping the desk with his hands.

"I can go through social media again if you like?" Eliana offered.

"No, it's okay. We may need to regroup with this," Simon said.

"The word must mean something," Ted said frustratingly.

"Like a lyric? A famous quote?"

"Yes, try it!"

Eliana filled the search bar up, including the quote and the word *Greece*, then hit enter. The results brought up many options displaying the full quota of the wording. They searched the results listing reams of vocabulary and titled headings until they found something different from the previous results.

Eliana switched the tabs to view the image results of their search. She was drawn to one of the images that clearly depicted a wall art visual linked to a social media platform.

"Look here. It's a link to a guy's media page."

The page loaded quickly, showing a header and introductory bio above a range of gallery pictures.

"Samuel George. His profile suggests he's like a traveller's blog person."

The image Eliana selected became at the forefront of the screen within an instant as it finally loaded.

"The night is a starry dome, and they're playin' that scratch rock and roll beneath the Matala Moon," Ted said, reading the photo.

"This must be it, but what does it mean?" Simon said.

The wording was white on the side of the small building block, which seemed to be near a beach car park. The words were the centrepiece of an art design that covered the concrete wall. The painting depicted a purple and red starry night sky, with a wooden boat floating upon the waves under a moon in the top right-hand corner of the piece. The word *Carey* and the drawing signed off by Joni Mitchell were on the boat.

"Where was this picture taken?" Ted said.

"Matala," Eliana said.

"Where is Matala?" he continued.

"I've heard it before. I think it's..." Eliana stopped.

Eliana opened a new website tab on her computer, typed in the word *Matala*, and clicked enter. She began to skim-read the suggestion beneath a map of its area.

"Matala is a village located 75 kilometres southwest of Heraklion, Crete."

"Do the words mean anything?"

Eliana opened a new internet tab and entered the words into the search engine.

"Nothing of interest. It's lyrics to a Joni Mitchell song. She's a country rock, folk, and pop singer. She wrote it when she backpacked at Matala."

"Ted. Your parents were into their music. Did they know Joni Mitchell?" Simon asked.

"I never saw it in their CD collections as a kid. They had Led Zeppelin, Genesis, and Supertramp, that kind of music."

"Supertramp?" Eliana asked.

"You never heard of them?" Ted asked, searching for both Eliana and Simon's reactions.

Both shook their heads simultaneously.

"'Goodbye Stranger'? 'Breakfast in America'?"

"Nope."

"Give it a listen."

"I will do," Eliana smiled back.

Ted broke his gaze and stared at the computer screen, taking in the visual of the wall art painted onto the concrete wall.

"Okay, maybe the girl saw this. So this could be the location," Ted said.

"What are you thinking, Ted?" Simon said.

"Are there any issues with smuggling there?"

"Smuggling what?" Eliana responded.

"People, drugs, passports, stuff like that?"

Eliana shook her head to answer the question.

"We'd have to ask the local police force there. But looking here on the website, it's a small seaside village. Then around fifty years ago, a community of hippies settled there, hence Joni Mitchell's song. Then every year, they have a hippy festival. Nothing major happens there."

Ted used the next moments to focus on his next moves. He looked at Eliana, who stared back at him for a response.

"Is it quicker to fly or catch a boat to this place?"

"I'm not sure about flights; there could be one tonight, but there are some ferries through the night. It takes around nine hours, though."

"You want to go to Crete tonight?" Simon said.

Eliana worked on the computer screen, using a website to check flight times.

"There is a flight tonight at 22:30, in around three hours."

Ted nodded at Eliana and turned his face to Simon.

"We go tonight."

Simon exhaled deeply, expressing he had something to say.

"I won't be coming with you."

"Why not?" Ted questioned.

"Officially, our job is done. Besides, I've got to return to the UK. There is a situation in China at the moment with the virus there. We have an emergency meeting back in London about tomorrow's next steps in evacuating all ILOs in China and the surrounding countries."

"Jesus. Sounds bad. Should we be worried?"

"Not for now. We're just thinking ahead, although it seems to be bad there. You have this covered, right?"

"Yeah, sure."

"Officially, this investigation here isn't happening," Simon said, pointing at the computer screen.

"So, go on my own?"

"If you keep yourself hidden from Nikolas, sure. But I didn't tell you that. I'd prefer you'd go with backup, though."

Simon and Ted glanced at Eliana, who had turned around in her computer chair, moving her head from left to right to glimpse at their faces.

"I can't go."

Simon and Ted looked at each other and remained silent as they contemplated the schematics of the rogue investigation. Ted scratched his head and pierced his lips tightly as he ran a plan through his mind.

"Can you go off sick?" Ted asked, staring directly at her.

Eliana started to stumble over her words as she thought about the trouble she could get into.

"I-I don't know, if I can... I must stay..."

Ted became firm in his words, trying to convince Eliana to make the journey. He needed someone he trusted, and Eliana was that person in the small amounts of days he had been in Athens.

"The problem is, like Simon said, the investigation at the moment is over. The major piece to the mystery has been found in Andries, and everyone in the department knows it. Even the affairs team are busy investigating how this happened. Andries seems to be the one who is ordering the Albanians to do his dirty work. But the OCG are the ones carrying the murders, the trafficking. I can't let them get away with it. Besides, it's the right time. The OCG probably think they are in the clear for a few days with the department so busy now."

Eliana's head dropped as she scrutinised the plan and balanced the truth and her career as a police detective.

"They came for me, Eliana. They've murdered officers and innocent people. There is still some more truth to this. More justice, and maybe Matala is where that truth is."

"Yeah."

"So, are you coming?"

"I'll come with you."

"What are you going to do with work?" Simon asked.

"I'm off tomorrow, so that's fine. I'll call in sick the day after and hope the journey is quick."

Ted smiled, and Eliana returned one back.

"Keep safe, both of you. Please come back in one piece," Simon ordered.

They left the computer station with the mindset to prepare for their individual trips. There was still one last stone to overturn before he could rest on a conclusion to the case. Ted would have to go rogue with Eliana, keeping it secret from the department and the affairs team. He wanted to know what was waiting under the Matala moon.

Chapter 34
Crete

ARRIVING LATE INTO THE night on the island between the Aegean and Libyan Sea, Ted and Eliana checked into their single rooms, east of Heraklion Centre and only a few minutes from the airport. They arrived too late to stop by local shops or restaurants to refuel, so they made do with the airport and inflight snacks until the morning. When they arrived, they flagged down a taxi and passed the Heraklion Police Headquarters from the airport, seeing its external glow under the moonlight. During the day, the HQ towered on its high-rise hill, with views of the Gulf of Heraklion to the north and the sights of aeroplanes taking flight and touching down on the tarmac. Its perch was upon the main north freeway running east and west of the island, adjacent to the junction for the airport, offering easy access from the hotel. In the morning, before heading to the police station, they'd travelled via taxi to the airport rental car, taking a saloon car for a few days to use for their time on the island. Once they'd entered the HQ, they asked reception for the police major or captain to speak with urgently, and one of the admin officers showed them through the various corridors and flight steps to the captain's office.

"I'm Tobias Aetos. Who are you?" he asked cautiously as the two officers entered his room.

"This is Eliana Albufafa, a police sergeant from Athens. I'm Ted Chester, a British liaison officer working in Athens," he announced while they took their seats.

"Okay, how can I help you?" he said with intriguing eyes.

"If I'm being honest, we are here unofficially."

Ted estimated that the young man opposite him was around his late thirties. He had short blond hair, and was fit and stocky, with his biceps bursting out of his uniform. Scattered across the walls and table were pictures of his partner and three children—two boys and a girl—depicting their growth story. Amid the images were a few certificates or qualifications he had collected after leaving school, and those he was rewarded with during his time in the force, and through various promotions, with some news articles including his picture. He seemed a family man and proud of that; even though he was a major and a higher rank than him, Ted knew he could relate to him instantly.

"Am I going to be in trouble?" Tobias asked, looking at Eliana and Ted.

"No, you won't be," Ted assured.

"Okay, so why are you here?"

"We've been investigating a case, which is near completion. Let's say we are exploring another avenue linked to the initial case."

Tobias started to nod, but his eyes showed he wasn't following.

"Okay. Tell me exactly what you want; you're talking in some riddles," he said, pointing at them both.

Ted blew out a puff of air and thought he would cut straight to the point.

"Have you much activity concerning crimes in Matala?"

"Matala in the south?"

Eliana nodded, and Ted awaited an answer.

"Matala," he said as he thought. "Can't say there is much, no," he followed.

Ted hoped for a recent crime report linking Matala and the gang activity, but it seemed there wasn't on Tobias's first reaction.

"I mean, let me look."

Tobias leaned forward to his computer screen, working the mouse and keyboard as he spoke.

"We have the tourists that come for the hippy festival. Usually, there is no trouble. Some reports of drug use, getting high, and the odd fight. We have stolen goods from the local shops, not related to the hippies, just generally."

"Okay, nothing out of the ordinary?"

"Well, last summer, there was a foreign tourist found dead. They fell from the caves high above and were found unconscious. When the ambulance arrived, he was dead. Nothing suspicious; it was filed as an accident or suicide."

"No witnesses or arrests?"

"No, no witnesses said anyone pushed him. Few people saw him go up alone, then found him on the beach. It was in the summer, and it was hectic. Distressing actually to some people who were there."

There was a pause as Ted and Tobias locked eyes briefly. Tobias raised his hand in a *what-gives* gesture.

"Why are you here? What's really happening? Why are you asking about Matala?"

"The investigation we've conducted back in Athens has brought us here because some suspicious activity is happening on the island, and we believe it to be in Matala," Eliana said.

Ted's grip on the secret was ripped from him by Eliana. However, he wasn't too angry because he knew if Tobias didn't know about the context of the investigation, he wouldn't be too obliged to help their sole operation.

"What activity? I'm looking at the reports and can't see anything for Matala."

"We're talking about people smuggling, human trafficking into the country."

Tobias rested on his chair, bringing his hands together as if to pray, lifting his index fingers and pressing them against his lip.

"We've had migrant issues here in the past. Those travelling to Gavdos, a small island on the southern coast of Crete, but that was a few years ago. The few patrol boats have kept most of them at bay since deployment."

"We're not talking about migrants, Tobias. We are talking about gangs trafficking people—women, more specifically—through the islands, the ports, the airports, and forcefully working them in the capital for profit."

"Listen. No arguments for you here, but I wasn't born yesterday. I know that happens, but that's way above my pay grade. I've not seen anything like that here for a long time, especially in Matala. We've had smugglers hide Egyptians from across the sea in crates or small containers—Iraqis, Iranians, and North Africans—but nothing was reported."

Tobias held his hands up before continuing.

"However, it's not to say it doesn't happen, of course."

"We are looking for well-organised, dangerous gangs doing their business secretly. So that is the reason why we are here."

"Have you encountered these gangs in Athens?"

"We have."

"And you think they've come through here? These people, under their own will?"

"We have a hunch that it's here. But of course, it's not just here, but all over Greece."

"Jesus."

"We would appreciate your help. We thought it would be best to come to see you before we drive around investigating."

"Sure. Do you need me to contact anyone in Athens to help with this?"

Ted raised his hand in a gesture to stop.

"Let's keep it between us three for the time being."

Tobias looked back at Ted before nodding in agreement.

"Sure, no problem."

Ted slapped both his knees with his hands and nodded to Eliana to suggest the meeting was over.

"We best get off and leave you to your work. Thanks for your time, Tobias."

"What are you two going to do now?"

"Not sure."

"Will you be visiting Matala?"

"We will be this afternoon, maybe early evening, to look at the location."

"Do you need backup?"

"No, we should be okay. Our investigation may have spooked them, or the Matala theory could be all made up. We just want to check it out, just in case."

"I can get a patrol car to stay in the south during the evening, just in case anything happens?"

"Sure, that would be good. Thanks, Tobias."

Tobias showed Ted and Eliana the kitchen area and their working space. Once Tobias left them for their work, there were a few moments of silence as they logged into the corporate system.

"Ted," Eliana said, turning to face Ted.

"Yeah?" Ted returned the look.

"What will you do if we find the OCG in Matala tonight?"

"I don't know—I've not figured that out yet."

Chapter 35

Beyond the Ormos, Mesaras Bay reached out southwest of Matala, where the edges of Gavdos lay, forming a community of islets south of Crete. The sunset lingered in the sky, about to fall into the ocean below. Matala was known for its fantastic beach and extended cove walkways, allowing great vantage points for the sunset. Walking from the car park, Ted and Eliana surveyed the sleepy seaside village, which boomed during the summer months, especially in June, when the annual hippy festival occurred. The festival lasts three days and was founded in 2011; it aimed to keep the myth of Matala alive, attracting many people from every corner of the earth to enjoy singers and bands, participate in dance, and enjoy the hippy vibe.

On their right, they witnessed the luscious white cliffs artificially made in the Neolithic Age. Looking over the bay of Matala, they saw indented caves flowing along the cliff edge. Across from the cliffs was Matala village, complete with a selection of cafés and restaurants behind the southern part of its shore. The pair manoeuvred through the tight, narrow streets of worn artwork remains on the pavements from the last festival. They were unsure of the artworks exact location and began walking deep into the heart of the village. Since the season was still amid the winter, the town was barren, with the odd local resident strolling and a few restaurants open, supported by the local clientele. Eliana asked a few locals about the wall art, but they were unaware or disinterested; she gathered the festival and its strings annoyed some of the older generations. They proceeded to the end of a pathway that gave a view across Matala. The terminus of the path was beautiful. Offering security from the cliff edge to the right was a white wooden fence that ran from the village to the taverna. Overlooking the wall was the backdrop of the beach, its cliffs and the crashing waves coming from Ormos Mesaras.

The last restaurant on the path was called Ἡλιοβασίλεμα Ταβέρνα, Sunset Taverna, serving fresh fish, octopus, and other Greek dishes. Greeted at the end of the walkway was a wooden sign with blue painted writing *Sunset View* and an arrow pointing left. Beyond was a drop leading to a marble-like rock area. They both toyed with the idea of eating; it had been brunch time since they last stopped and ate, and the distraction from the search may help clear their minds and help them focus. They both agreed; Eliana opted to order whilst Ted walked down the steps towards the sunset platform.

He was alone with his thoughts as dusk began to form in the evening air. The weather was clear but cloudy in patches, with a strong onshore wind. Ted felt the gust upon his face as it moved through the bay, navigating through the towering rock edges above. The sea was deep blue, with a bright yellow light lining through the surf as the setting sun reflected upon the water. The crashing waves below turned white, becoming unstable; gravity tugging at their tallest, weakest points caused the crests of the waves to break apart into a mass of droplets and bubbles. He was mesmerised by the waves and the area's natural beauty. He stared into the Ormos, wanting to be taken in and engulfed by its beauty. No worries or anxious thoughts were entering his mind for the first time in a long while. He closed his eyes, embracing the sound of the waves, breathing in tandem with them, simultaneously with his body.

Suddenly, he broke from his stint of mindfulness, hearing footsteps behind him. He broke away from his calm serenity and saw Eliana holding a white bag as she navigated the steps down and carefully walked across the platform.

"How much was it?" Ted asked on approach.

"It's fine, don't mention it."

"You sure? Thank you."

She stopped and reached into the bag, then passed over a beige polyester box to Ted.

"Here you go. I didn't know what to get, so I asked them to make us a box. If you didn't know, I'm vegetarian. I got you the same, if that's okay?"

Ted took the box from Eliana, feeling the heat from the pack.

"That's okay."

Ted looked down at his box, opening the present of food containing various colours. One yemista, Greek stuffed red pepper, and a side of green battered Greek-fried courgette chips, with a section of tzatziki and small pocket pita bread for dipping.

"It looks amazing."

"Απολαμβάνω!"

They smiled and were quiet as they ate, enjoying every bite. Eliana stopped and dipped her hand into the white plastic bag again, weighted with what was inside. She pulled out two bottles of Saka mineral water and placed them in front of her. Again, she went into the bag to take out the remaining purchases. Two bottles of Fix beer. She reached for her keys with a beer opener attached to the ring and removed the caps. She passed one to Ted and lifted her beer up to touch his.

"Yamas."

"Yamas. You're a woman after my own heart bringing me food and beer."

They both took a long pull on their beer and continued consuming their meal while watching the waves move along the shoreline towards the beach. The odd slash lifted towards them from the rock edges as the waves crashed below them. The fiery red ball in the sky was dipping ever close to the horizon.

"How are you and Rose? I know you said a little the other day, but..."

Ted thought hard about her question.

"It's the distance, you know. I like this job, but it's not easy trying to do both, let me tell you."

"Why isn't she here?"

"Well, the case mostly. I wouldn't want them here after what happened to me in the apartment in Athens. But she and the girls are homesick, and I've chosen to be out here."

"I understand. I suppose I miss my father and family. The distance can keep you strong, or it can break you."

"Yeah, I understand what you mean. We will see how things are after this case; I need to sit down and speak with her about what we do as a family and include the girls in that decision, too."

"I agree. They should be involved."

There was a lull in the conversation momentarily, but Eliana pressed on.

"Nothing is perfect."

"True," Eliana replied as she tilted her head to agree, then took a drag of her Fix.

"I'd ask about your boyfriend, but I know you said you aren't together anymore."

"Well, funny you mention it. I saw he had texted me earlier today. Just working out how to reply to him."

"Yeah? What happened to you two?"

"Nothing bad, but I can save it for another day."

"Sure," he said as they gave each other a slight smile.

They both finished their meal and sipped on the last of their beer. Placing the rubbish into the plastic bag, they opened and swigged a shared water bottle to wash down what they'd consumed. Ted lifted his head, looking back at Matala Beach and the village they'd walked through previously. He noticed something that caught his attention; it looked like artwork.

"Look there! Writing along the wall."

Eliana looked over curiously. She spotted the obscured artwork, too. They walked up the steps from the platform, passed the restaurant, and wandered to the entry point down towards the beach, where the concrete wall was used as a wave defence. The waves thrashed against the cement wall and broke along the sand and rocks beneath the wall defence. Looking back at the tower fortress of Matala, there was a piece of artwork written in blue along with the cement. It was indeed artwork, but those weren't the words they searched for. The design read *Today is life, and tomorrow never comes.*

They were both left deflated with their wide-of-the-mark observation. Ted thought maybe the artwork held no significance at all. Perhaps the design they were after was washed away and painted over because of the out-of-season environment. Ted noticed Eliana had her hands on her hips, looking around subdued.

"Come on, let's walk back to the car park. See if we've missed something, or try those cliffs," Ted said.

"I don't think you can get into the cliffs; it's locked for tourists."

"You never broken and entered before? Might be able to get a bird's-eye view."

"Maybe before I was a police officer, I did."

They were silent on their approach to the car park area. Eliana stopped before they reached the point where the beach met the tarmac. She turned back to look into the ocean; Ted noticed her movements.

"It's beautiful, isn't it?" Ted remarked.

"The sunset?"

"Yeah. The best one I've seen."

"I agree."

They stood together, glancing out into the bay. The southern point of the sun kissed the horizon and began its descent into the deep blue. Once the northern tip of the sun dipped below the blue line, the sky darkened, leaving an orange tinge above. Ted turned, heading back towards the tarmac car park, with Eliana following. Adjacent to the car park was a building they passed into the heart of Matala. The complex was a public toilet, with entry points for females and males on either side. An art display depicting the Joni Mitchell lyrics was on the longest side of the rectangular building.

"There!" Ted pointed.

The artwork pictured by the vlogger on the social media website was exhibited before him.

"We've wasted all that time!" Eliana smiled.

"Well, we saw the sunset, and we ate. So not all that bad. This must be the place."

Their pace intensified, approaching the art with great haste. They reached the design, studying it with great intent and purpose.

"You think they came through here?"

He looked around the beach area to see if the view from the design would offer a crumb, and it didn't. Suddenly, something caught Ted's eye on the horizon. The sun had disappeared and was about to appear on the other side of the world, but something much smaller replaced it in the forefront.

"Do many boats come into Matala normally?" Ted said, turning his head towards Eliana.

"Just the locals this time of year, I would think, but I don't see many boats around—why?" she said, returning a glance with a confused look.

"Look," Ted said, turning his head out the bay.

A small motorised boat heading directly towards the beach was fast approaching. He couldn't make out the driver, but around three to four bodies seemed to be onboard.

"What is it, do you think?" Eliana said.

"I don't know, but we need to find out. It's definitely the wrong time of year for it to be a tourist rental," Ted responded.

Glancing around the vicinity of the beach, Ted was looking for a place to hide. They couldn't stow away in their own car; their position was too open to the beach and the exposed car park, and they thought they wouldn't have much time to escape if they met someone nearby. Alongside the high-rise cliffs that cornered the beach were the man-made caves they had seen, giving Ted an idea.

They reached the second level of the caves.

"Do you think anyone here spotted us?" Eliana asked as they reached their final spot.

"I don't think so."

"What could it be?"

"They transport the girls on this small boat... from a bigger boat, maybe?"

"Yeah. You could be right. Maybe it's them."

The motorised boat was decreasing in speed as it reached the shallow sands of the beach. The vessel hit the shore's floor and stopped only a few metres away from the beach, with the waves still rocking its old, rusted frame.

"There are people in there!"

"Wait!" Ted said, holding Eliana's wrists to stop her from blowing their cover.

Her outcry was emotional and loud, making her stand to her feet.

"Stay down, Eliana. Just wait a minute."

Ted took out his mobile phone and took pictures of the stationary boat with five souls aboard it. The engine was dead, but a new motorised noise came from below. A 4x4 vehicle entered the sandy edges of the beach from the car park. Behind that vehicle was another car, this time smaller, similar to the one he rented when he first arrived in Athens. Ted took photos of the vehicles, reviewing the snaps to see if the plates could be readable on Zoom.

"I'm going to send these to the station in Athens and Elijah in Albania and see what we can get."

The passengers were forcefully removed from the boat as the officers looked down from the rocky caves. The three females were directed through the shallow waters with one of the men from the boat while the other stayed near the engine. The distance was too great to get a detailed visual of the crowd's faces below. The pushing and shoving witnessed from the caves above showed these three handcuffed females transported against their will. Two men exited the 4x4, waiting to meet the passengers at the shoreline. Ted continued to photograph the actions beneath them, quickly viewing them and zooming in on the image. The men seemed of Eastern European ethnicity, and the females were unknown because their faces were covered with hijab-style face coverings.

"What's he doing?" Eliana asked.

She pointed down towards the small vehicle and the lone figure sitting on the bonnet of his car, watching the exchange unfold. Ted worked the camera, focusing on the man to view his face. He wasn't sure about his appearance. The solitary man didn't seem Eastern European, but that could have been a mistake by Ted as he viewed the grainy zoomed picture. However, he was dressed in casual clothes, blue jeans, boots and a polo shirt, and he seemed older than the others, with a grey beard being one of the clues.

"I'm not sure."

Ted became intrigued by the sole mystery man, then somewhat anxious about how they could continue their observations.

"What are we going to do next?" Eliana asked.

"I'm thinking."

Ted's attention turned to the beach exchange between the two men in the vehicle and the one from the boat. The men exchanged handshakes as the females stood stumped in their standing positions on the sandy beach. Ted worked the phone screen, searching for his contact at a police station in Heraklion. The phone rang a few times, but a male voice answered.

"Heraklion Police Station. Tobias Aetos speaking."

"Tobias, it's Ted."

"Hey, how can I help? Did you find your wall art in Matala?"

"We did, and we need your help."

"Go ahead."

Ted began to explain the events occurring in front of them. He briefly explained the OCG group working in Greece, trafficking people into the capital to be exploited for profit. He left out the information detailing the arrested officer Andries, who had been charged with corruption and murder.

"I can contact the Hellenic Coast Guard to see if anyone is patrolling the Sea of Crete off Notio Kritiko Pelagos?" Tobias suggested.

The coast guard headquarters was in Akti Vassiliadi, located in the Port of Piraeus, policing and implementing enforcement at sea, ports, and coastal areas, and preventing illegal immigration, among other legislation. Ted knew if Tobias was to tell the Hellenic Coast Guard about the vessel using the South Mediterranean Sea as a shipping lane for trafficking, they would want to engage instantly. The rippling effects could make the OCG aware they were being watched and conceal and convert their tactics, making them harder to catch.

"No, it will spook them. We can give the Coast Guard the information at a later date."

"No problem. What would you want me to do?"

"Do you have any officers near us?"

"Yes, I should have those officers—let me check. They've not been called to something."

"They're putting those people into the vehicle. We need to get back down there now," Eliana interrupted.

Ted witnessed both men open the vehicle's rear doors, ushering them to enter. Once inside, the two doors shut, and they retook the front seats. Ted was playing out a plan as he waited for the information. He thought about following the 4x4 containing the female passengers but knew the same results would be given to them and the patrol officers if either pursued. An interaction could be dangerous, so Ted settled on the mystery man in the small vehicle.

"We have a car with two officers north of your position. Twenty kilometres away near Mitropoli."

"Can you give them registration plates for the large 4x4 vehicle?"

"Sure, send them over."

"Will do. I want you to promise me something, Tobias."

"Depends what it is."

"I don't want you to share this with anyone in your department; I just want you to do the searches for me and tell the officers to follow the vehicle and not engage. It's just a routine job, nothing serious. Do not engage at any point."

There was a pause over the phone. Ted was sure Tobias would comply but needed to hear the words to confirm it.

"Sure. I promise."

While on the phone call, Ted sent multiple photographs to Tobias's mobile device, including the stationary boat, the vehicles, the people on the shore, and those still floating on the low waves.

"Can you search the registration for any information? Last time it went through a roadside camera. Any crimes relating to the vehicle or who it's registered to?"

"I will do. I'll let you know if I find anything."

"Thanks, Tobias."

The phone call ended. Still, Ted held the phone close to his ear. Eliana began to creep along the rocky cliff edges towards the section, which allowed access to the level below.

"Come on," she whispered.

Ted was fixed on the lone man. One of the men from the boat marched towards him, but the single man did not move to greet him. Ted shifted his view back toward the two men exchanging conversation. The man from the boat passed over an envelope, offered a parting greeting, and rushed back toward the shoreline again to take the shallow waters towards the vessel. The roaring sound of the boat started up again, and so did the 4x4 engine.

Eliana and Ted began to descend the rocky cliffs, worried that if the men decided to take a view of the wonderful cave structures, they would spot two witnesses to their operation. Ted noticed the man look briefly into the envelope and close the seal again. Upon viewing the contents, he couldn't tell the emotion on his face, but he took the short trip around the front of the vehicle to the driver's side door to reenter. Ted briskly made his way to the area of descent from the second level of the cave's cliff face. He remembered he needed to send the photos to another contact: Elijah. He could cross-reference any facial recognition picked up from the photographs, and thought it was worth a go. He sent the photographs requesting to check the systems for a match and began to take the steps down.

"What's your plan?" Eliana asked from the first-floor level.

"We follow the lone ranger. See who he is."

They had reached the first level of the cave's structure, but there was only a short drop to reach the ground level. The engine of the smaller vehicle began to roar, with both cars opting to illuminate their headlights with the dark embracing the sky. The two men were now in the boat, and it began to turn, beginning their journey into the open sea. The 4x4 vehicle began moving back toward the car park, seeking the exit. Suddenly, the smaller vehicle moved forward ten seconds after the 4x4 exited the parking area. The red taillight was bright as it weaved through the car park system and the light shower of cars parked and headed towards the main road out of the Matala.

Eliana entered the vehicle and rang Tobias back at the police station to update him on the situation unfolding. Once they'd reached their vehicle, Ted looked back at the ocean that had engulfed the fiery ball in the sky, displaying its calm dark night. He tilted his head towards the velvet night, which was painting a midnight blue colour. Many white freckles were on the black canvas as the stars began to glow. Ted relayed the lyrics in his head as he opened the door, sliding into the driver's side seat.

The night is a starry dome, and they're playin' that scratchy rock and roll beneath the Matala Moon.

Chapter 36

THE TWO CRETAN POLICE officers Tobias had contacted were pursuing the 4x4 vehicle on Road 97, filtering through Stavrakia village. Their location was East of Mount Ida, the highest mountain on the island, sitting at 8,058 feet. So far, the communications suggested they were predicted to reach the outer border of Heraklion in thirty minutes. Little was known about their intended destination, but the surveillance team kept a distance on the quiet road. The vehicles were often the only light that shone the valleys through which the road flows. Thus far, they had remained unsuspicious to the 4x4 passenger, blending in as another lonely soul on the dusty road.

Ted and Eliana were still stalking their sole man along Road 97, five kilometres behind the 4x4. Their location was a kilometre from the exit to Agia Varvara, near the Nymphs Waterfall. Eliana reached for her mobile device as Ted concentrated on the dark road ahead.

"Eliana speaking. Hi, Tobias, any updates? Okay... let me put you on loudspeaker." Eliana worked the device and announced for Tobias to speak.

"Hi, Ted, so we have the 4x4 heading towards Heraklion. We're unsure about their next destination, but thankfully, the roads have more traffic on them as they get closer to the coast, giving the officers cover. I think they may be heading to the ports, if I was guessing. What do you want us to do?"

"Are there any timetabled journeys from the ports tonight?"

"There's two. Piraeus and Santorini."

"Athens, of course. Any news on the plates?"

"Nothing is showing up on the 4x4..."

"Always the way. Anything on the other vehicle we are pursuing?"

"We got a hit."

Ted gripped the wheel tighter and felt his pulse rise.

"Vehicle registered to a Kadeem Al Numan, Syrian national. Living in Exo Lakkonia near Agios Nikolaos on the east coastline."

"Any records?"

"He has a record for fishing without a permit. The occupation was down as a fisherman during the caution."

"Maybe it was a front, or he changed his hand into trafficking."

"When did he move to the country?"

"Around six years ago. There is a note here saying his family are back in Syria."

"Trying to make a better life for his family," Eliana spoke.

Ted paused. He wasn't sure where Kadeem ranked in the pecking order. He looked subdued and menacing staring at the boat as it entered the bay. His previous employment was at sea. He thought it may have been a business used to traffic women into the island or a legitimate fishing business.

"We're going to stop this car now and update you. We need to see what he has on him and what he knows."

"Okay, sure. I'll update you on the 4x4. Speak soon."

The phone disconnected.

"How are we doing this?"

"Do these rental cars come with blue lights?" Ted joked.

Eliana clicked her fingers and pointed her index finger out, portraying a beaming smile.

"What?" Ted asked.

"Back at the station in Heraklion, I took these."

Eliana reached into a sports bag she had in the footwell of the passenger seat.

"What's that?"

"These."

She lifted out a LED light with a wire attachment fitted on a small cap on the bottom of the fixture.

"I asked one of the office reception guys when you went to the little men's room."

Ted smiled.

"Of course you did. It will come in handy, thank you."

"Want me to plug it in?"

"Be my guest."

She lifted the safety cap on the car's lighter port and fitted the USB wire to its connection. The passenger side window lowered as she reached out to hold the base onto the car's metal roof, allowing the magnet to hold it. The blue light illuminated the darkness, making the road clearer to see. Ted pressed hard on the accelerator, riding the bend in the road as the car in front rode the long straight road ahead. The man inside would have seen the lights but didn't display signs of any speed, which would turn into a pursuit. The two vehicles occupied the road as they drove through the inky valley just north of Agia Varvara. The police vehicle closed the distance on the car with every rotation of its own beacon. Ted repeatedly pressed the headlight trigger, signalling the full beams to the vehicle in front. The red brake light dazzled their view as they reached the car's bumper. The car indicated right with its blinking lights and turned carefully on the gravel, which occupied each side of Road 97. Sweeps of dust covered the air creating a dark blizzard temporarily on the side of the road. The two cars became stationary, and both waited for the other to make the first move.

"Kill the blue light," Ted asked.

Eliana reached for the wire and pulled it from its connection. The hills surrounding the road became black. Both vehicles sat silently, with headlights illuminating the space before them.

"I'm going to get out and say hello. If he drives off, you stay in the vehicle and jump over to the wheel."

"Sure."

Ted opened the driver's door and patted his belt to check that his service weapon remained in its holster. He felt the hard object through his jacket, nodding at Eliana, and she nodded back. He exited the vehicle. He trod slowly, observing the rear window and the driver's side wing mirror for any jerk reactions. The driver remained still, identical to the valley's surroundings. No vehicle headlights were to be seen, although the cicadas' screech from the long grass kept Ted on edge when he heard it. Ted reached the back wheel of the vehicle, steadily pacing while locked on the driver's side mirror for any movement. Although the darkness consumed the valley, the headlights from behind now gave a partial glimpse of the driver's face. The man's wide eyes gazed upon Ted as he reached his door. Ted tapped on the driver's side window. The darkness inside the vehicle obscured the man's identity. Suddenly, the electronic window lowered, unveiling the man inside.

"Thanks for stopping there," Ted said.

The man was puzzled by the stop and somewhat on alert, his head pivoting back and forth around the car's exterior.

"Do you speak English?"

"Yes," the man said with a nod.

The man had a grey beard, trimmed, accompanied by a moustache of the same colour. He looked around forty to fifty years old with green eyes that seemed kind, given the complex nature of who he was in partnership with on the beach.

"Step out of the vehicle, please."

"Sir..."

"Sir, step out of the vehicle. I will only ask nicely one more time."

The man reached for the lever to open the door, and there was a click as the unlock button allowed the door to open. The door opened slowly, and the man exited the vehicle with his hands up.

"Are you the police?"

"Yes. I'm Officer Ted Chester, and in that vehicle is Eliana Albufafa, an officer for the Hellenic Police in Athens."

Ted pushed the man against the car frame, the man facing his back to Ted. Ted patted him down and only felt a wallet and phone outline.

"What's your name?"

"Kadeem."

"Surname?"

"Kadeem Al Numan."

Ted asked the man for his driving licence or identification, which he said was in his wallet. Ted reached into his pocket for the wallet, lifted it out, opened the flap, and searched various cards lined in the slots. He saw a green card similar to his driving licence and picked it up to look at. Kadeem Al Numan was present on the Greek driving licence card, with his address and place of birth stating Syria.

"When did you move to Greece?"

"Around five years ago."

"Okay, I'm going to put these on you. I'll keep them loose but tighten them if you're a problem. Okay?"

"Yes, I won't be a problem. But I don't understand what I've done."

"I'll explain it in the vehicle."

Ted returned the licence to the sleeve and the wallet to the man's pocket. Ted reached for his own belt to collect the handcuffs from his belt. He tied them around the man's wrists and closed the circle, keeping them looser than anticipated. They both reached the vehicle, and Ted opened one of the back doors for Kadeem to edge into. Once Ted returned to the driver's seat, he glanced at the dark spectacle of his shadow, looking in the central driver's mirror, which reflected back at him. They locked eyes again momentarily as they tried to work each other out.

"What's in the envelope?" Ted asked.

Kadeem's face was spooked; however, he tried to hide the lie too late, lifting his lower lip and shaking his head.

"What envelope?"

Ted swivelled in his chair to get a frontal view of the suspect.

"Don't be stupid, Kadeem. We were watching you from the caves in Matala."

Kadeem's eyes widened.

"I want to get out; they will know I've been caught."

With his back edging towards the car door, Kadeem turned his body, frantically pulling at the door handle and the electronic window switch, but the child lock and electronic window safety were in place.

"Remain still, Kadeem. You're not going to go far with those handcuffs."

He started to settle back down into the position he was in moments ago. His face was still anxious with fear.

"I'll ask again. What's in the envelope?"

"I need this. I'll be dead without it. They say if I don't do this, they will stop me from sending money to my family and hurt my family. I had no choice!" he shouted, echoing across the valley.

Ted held his hand up for reassurance and hoped to calm him down. The man was frantically looking around to see if anyone was observing the conversation with the two officers. There hadn't been a headlight in about ten minutes, and with the time getting later into the evening, there may not have been too many after they'd left the area either.

"Look. Understand this."

Ted paused before gaining Kadeem's attention. The man's agitated persona disappeared as he focused on Ted.

"The men you work for. Don't need to know that this meeting happened. So, as far as they know, they don't know that we know about them?"

Kadeem's eyes tightened as he listened to Ted's speech. As Ted finished, he began to nod.

"This meeting never happened," Kadeem repeated.

"That's right. You've done nothing wrong, Kadeem, but you must do something for us."

"What do you want me to do?"

"I need you to calm down and answer a few of my questions, so we can understand what's happening much clearer. Is that okay?"

The man was finally content, and he nodded back at Ted.

"How did the men approach you?"

The man looked left out of the window and dipped his head slightly, as if he remembered the day.

"I was fishing in Mirabello Bay and..."

"Where is Mirabello Bay?" Ted interrupted.

"It's off Agios Nikolaos, the island's east coast," Eliana explained.

Mirabello Bay was an embayment of the Sea of Crete on the eastern part of Crete. It was the largest bay of the Greek islands and the fifth largest in the Mediterranean Sea, with the tourist town Agios Nikolaos overlooking the bay.

"Sorry, please carry on."

"It was late evening, and I was fishing. I saw this boat heading north towards Kalydon, near Spinalonga. So, I see them; they're about sixty metres away. Then I hear screaming from the boat, and the people on the boat know I heard it. They turned their boat towards mine, and I'm also scared for whoever was screaming."

Ted noticed Kadeem's eyes were searching the floor as he explained, a sadness to them. That's when he realised maybe the man wasn't the hardened criminal he seemed on the beach; he was also a victim.

"They come aboard and threaten me. They would have killed me that evening but decided not to."

"They asked you to work for them? How long ago?" Eliana intruded.

Kadeem lifted his head to both turned officers.

"Yes, and only this summer."

"What did they ask you to do?"

"I've never hurt anyone. Thank goodness. They use me as a... delivery man."

"And that's why you have the envelope."

"Yes."

"What did the men ask you to do when they came onto your boat?"

"They asked me to work for them, deliver essential documents to whoever they tell me to deliver them to."

"What documents? What's inside?"

"I've spoken too much—I can't..." Kadeem replied, his anxiety starting to elevate.

"I assure you that you will not be arrested tonight, and you will be safe, but you will also be watched by officers, but you must help us here. These men are very dangerous and destroy people's lives and families. Where is your family, Kadeem?"

"Back in Syria. I came here around five years ago to work and ended up fishing. It's good money, and I send money home to them, and hopefully, one day, I can bring them here to live."

"Why are they not here already?"

The man's face showed a mask of sadness as another tear fell from his eye.

"I left to make a better life, work legally, and send home money. I couldn't bring them all over—only myself—so I decided to go."

"Okay, Kadeem. Can you tell me about the envelope and what you know?"

Kadeem let out a deep breath.

"The envelope contains the passport and identification documents of the girls you saw on the boat. Each girl who comes to Crete through Matala will have documents in each envelope and the new papers they get when they arrive in Greece. I take the documents to who I'm told to take them when I receive the envelope. They send me an address, a time, and a date for the following exchange."

"Where do the girls go?"

"I don't know. But the people I give the envelopes to take the documents. That's all I know. I remember they say they use the boats, the port. The people know someone at the ports who don't check baggage, vehicles, or documents, so they do it by boat. Longer, but much easier."

"What about the coastguards? Greece has issues with immigration on Lesbos and Kos, even here. Have they not been caught?"

"I heard one of them ask the same thing, but they said they knew someone in the Hellenic authorities who could dictate the search areas and at what times."

Eliana turned to Ted with an inquisitive look.

"Andries?" she asked.

"Possibly. Would he tell the Hellenic border guards where not to look?"

"I don't think professionally. Still, if the gangs were paying him, they or he could have been paying the senior officials at the ports."

Ted turned his attention back to the back seat.

"Where are the girls coming from?"

"Lebanon, Syria, and Africa, maybe, I don't know."

Ted took a moment to process the information.

"Where are you going with that envelope?"

"I've been told to give it to some people tomorrow evening at a restaurant.

"Which restaurant?"

The man returned his answer after hesitating.

"I have it on the envelope in the car, but I looked it up while driving from Matala. A small restaurant in a small village south of Heraklion called Episkopi, around eight thirty tomorrow."

Eliana and Ted both jointly shared optimism in their eyes.

"Okay, I'm going to take a picture of the envelope, the restaurant's address, and the documents inside..."

"I can't go empty-handed; I'll be killed there and then!" he shouted.

Ted raised his hand to calm him.

"Don't worry, take the envelope with you and the contents—the photographs will be enough for now."

The man searched towards Eliana and back to Ted, nodding quickly before succumbing to the decision, as if he had a choice.

"Are the numbers saved in your phone the ones you get messages from?"

"They are unknown."

"Of course they are. Right, I'm going to leave you here with Eliana. I'm going to take some pictures, and I'm going to add my phone number to your phone and label it as Joni Mitchell. You text me any updates on tomorrow."

"Joni Mitchell?"

"You know the wall art about the starry night at Matala?"

Kadeem shook his head. It seemed lost on him.

"Never mind. Listen, when I go to your vehicle, I will ring the police and have officers follow your car. So if you don't message me tomorrow with any updates, you will be in trouble. You understand?"

Kadeem nodded as Ted swivelled in his chair to reach for the passenger door.

"Will you be okay for a second?" Ted said, looking at Eliana with one hand on the door handle.

"I can defend myself. But I think he is friendly."

They exchanged glances as Ted exited the vehicle, closing the door behind him. He was alone. The cicadas which had emerged from their underground caverns echoed across the valley, and the clear sky, freckled with stars, embraced a beautiful ambience. As he stepped towards the stranded vehicle, Ted knew the larger scale of the organisation group could be uncovered in a small village near their position. He felt he was close to the truth.

Chapter 37

THEY WERE WAITING IN the shadows surveying the area, hiding on the upper floor of the local village shop. The shop was on the ground floor, with a staircase to the left beyond a white gate. Ted and Eliana were behind one of the two separate single doors, communicating with Tobias and two officers from the Cretan police force behind the other.

Upon their arrival, Eliana enquired if they could use the apartment above for an operation but remained quiet about its purpose. The shopkeeper agreed, as long as they paid him for their rent, but they had access to coffee and snacks if required. Before their current position, they'd surveyed the sleepy day town of Episkopi during the sunny hours, still amid a winter heat wave. The village was a barren area of shelled buildings eighteen kilometres southeast of Heraklion City, but still within the Heraklion regional unit. The day hours were full of old-age pensioners, men, and women, but primarily men greeting friends and heading to local shops and cafés.

Ted and Eliana camped their car on the side of one main road into the village from Heraklion City. They'd parked outside another grocery shop situated next to a pastry shop, Δια χειρός Σεβαστής, loosely translated to, *By the hand of Sevasti*. They'd chosen a seeded top roll with cheese and homemade baklava for afterwards as their fuel for the long surveillance, accompanied by an iced freddo to keep them cool. Those who lived in the village were mostly retired or travelled from outside the town to work within it. During their surveillance, the only young man they saw was the man behind the counter at the pastry shop. Presumably, the young men and women of the village had left their parents to find employment in the nearby cities, or even mainland Greece, in Athens, leaving the older generation to roam the dusty streets.

The night before, after watching the red rear lights of Kadeem's vehicle disappear into the distance, Ted updated Tobias at the station about the operation due to take place the following day. The two police officers following Kadeem returned to his home in Agios Niko-laos and watched him retire for the night. Overnight observations concluded no arrivals or departures until the early morning when Kadeem left the property, entered his vehicle, and drove into Agios Nikolaos to shop for groceries.

Ted reached out to the two internal affairs officers, who then made the journey over during the morning after the update late last night. The investigation with Andries was ongoing; now the temptation of the meeting was too much to miss. The Albania ILO, Elijah, travelled with several armed police officers to different corners of the small village. The photographs from the beach identified the two men as having links with the Albania Mafia's higher powers and charges relat-ed to people smuggling and murder. A separate operation was taking place on the boat vessel transporting the girls and the OCG men to Port of Piraeus. Undercover officers were onboard following the group while officers were waiting for them from the port exits to follow them to their final destination in the Greek capital, and an inevitable takedown would occur.

Deep into the chilled night, the pair observed the local village restaurant Κρητική κουζίνα μουρέλο, translated to *Cretan Cuisine*

Mourelo. The restaurant sat on a triangle-shaped junction, giving exit points from Episkopi's town. Across the road from the restaurant was a local petrol garage closed beyond its opening trading hours. The restaurant was on one of the corners, pointing to the triangle. The building had three faces that held four long-standing windows, with the panels in fresh white paint. The interior was open plan with windows running along two sides of its structure.

Inside the restaurant were two seated men, who arrived on foot from the north road around twenty minutes ago. Elijah, waiting in a nearby vehicle, took pictures of them arriving to send back to his officers in Tirana but didn't initially recognise them at first glance. Ted didn't recognise them as any of the two men harbouring into Matala yesterday evening. Observations of the table where the men sat gave the impression of a meeting place, accompanied by glasses of water and a carafe of red liquid followed by wine glasses. The table was filled with meze dishes, which a young waiter had brought out only moments ago. As the men started a conversation over a glass of wine, Ted was distracted by the many felines that paraded the triangle, some with missing tails, but most were malnourished, surviving off scraps from the bin containers beside the petrol station.

Suddenly a movement from the left flew through the cool night, gliding along the village road and over the triangle. A white owl slowed its momentum and perched on one of the telephone lines. It swivelled its head, exposing its round, forward-looking eyes and sharp hooked beak. Its head turned again, absorbing the noises and sights of its surroundings. One last time, the head of the owl rotated and stared directly towards Ted's location. Its feathers framed its face, showing its ear tufts used to locate prey. Within one movement, the owl's head faced away and lifted from the cables, dropping ever so slightly before it reached the narrow village streets and disappeared from sight.

"Wow," Eliana gasped.

"There are more animals than people in the village," Ted joked.

"It's amazing," Eliana replied.

"It is a thing of beauty."

"Did anyone see that owl then?" Tobias radioed.

As soon as everyone confirmed, a mechanical sound pathed through the triangle, lighting up the central point with the bright headlights.

"This must be them," Ted said.

"Standby, incoming vehicle north on Epar. Od. Karteros - Moni Agkarathou."

Ted felt a movement in his pocket and puzzled his face as he felt a vibration in his trouser pocket. Angelika was calling; he assumed wanting to discuss something privately, not over the communication link with the team.

"Who's calling?" Eliana asked.

"Angelika."

"Angelika, what's up?" Ted answered.

"Is it just you and Eliana in that room?"

"Yeah, why?" Ted said, removing the headpiece so his conversation couldn't be echoed through the team's radio.

"Hector has been declared missing by his partner, and she hasn't seen him for the last two days."

"Wasn't he given leave by Nikolas?"

"He was, but he never came home from work."

"Two days? Why is she only reporting it now?"

"Hector told her to go and see her family in Thessaloniki while the protests were taking place. She got hold of him after the shootings, and he told her he was okay, but that's the last known contact."

"Anyone from the station heard from him?"

"No one has. They've tried to get Nikolas to report it, as Andries is out of action, but he isn't reachable either..."

"Strange. Very strange."

"But we've had a bit of a situation at the police station, too—well, let's say it put the cats among the rats."

"Hang on, the vehicle is entering the junction."

The north road leading towards Heraklion began to shine from the headlight gliding along the tarmac road. A car was fast approaching in the distance. The streets were quiet, except for the felines roaming and the few old men sitting outside the shop and restaurant smoking and drinking Fix beer. The change of scene brought anticipation. As the vehicle approached the triangle, it turned left and immediately turned right, halting outside the restaurant's premises.

"Vehicle stopped outside the restaurant, can't see the interior, maybe two or three inside."

Eliana stepped towards Ted to take audio of the conversation, which restarted with Angelika. Ted remained focused on the vehicle, watching it, but was engrossed in what was coming.

"The lady from the club, Maya Beridze. She asked the guards at the safe house if she could be taken to the police station. So she voluntarily returned to the Athens head office about one hour ago. I've only been told this information minutes before I called you."

"Why did she come in?"

"Well, she asked guards if she could speak to anyone; she said it was important. The guards refused, but she insisted. She said she said some information. They brought her in, and she waited with the guard as the area was busy and got impatient. One of the guards approached the reception officer as she broke down in tears and told the officer she lied.

"A large lump formed in Ted's throat, as he lost focus on the outside area.

"She said she lied about the identity of the man who threatened her."

"Andries?"

"Yes, she confirmed twice that it wasn't him not too long ago."

The parked vehicle door opened. The diagonal angle across the road only meant the torso could be seen, not exposing the facial features blocked by the sun flap. The man pushed the driver's door open, and the passengers exited from the two rear doors. They faced towards the restaurant, surveying the people inside, and the driver waved at the two men sitting inside the restaurant at the far side. The face of the driver was still blocked, but the only feature Ted could describe was the man's short hair and height of around six feet.

"Has anyone got a visual on the men's faces?" an officer barked over the radio.

One of the Creteian officers on the road the owl travelled through confirmed a visual, but no recognisable acknowledgement of the identities was detected.

"Ted, she said when she was in the club locked in that room, Mateo forced her to give Andries as the man who threatened her, or else she would be killed," Angelika responded.

The driver swivelled his body to survey the road heading east out of the village, closing his car door. When the door slammed shut, the man's face was in clear view as he glanced across the triangle, turning around immediately to enter the restaurant.

"It's him," Eliana spoke.

Above the shop, there was a brief silence over the phone's communication. Ted disconnected the call with Angelika to focus on the tarmac below.

"Whose him?" one of the Cretan officers asked.

"Nikolas Konstantinou."

"He played us all," Ted responded.

Ted and Eliana watched Nikolas enter the restaurant, hugging and greeting an old woman who seemed to be the owner of the local restaurant. The man and his companions reached the occupied table and exchanged handshakes and smiles as they poured Nikolas a red wine. Some officers over the radio demanded information on Nikolas, and Ted explained his role in the Greek Police Department, which gained interest from the shocking revelation.

"We've finally found our man, Ted. Now we get him. Tonight," Savvas demanded.

"We have no other choice," Ted said, staring at Nikolas conversing with his men.

"So, is Andries innocent?"

"We don't know how far this corruption spreads, but we will find out, okay? Everything will be okay. We're here now and will make this right for everyone, even Andries. If he is innocent."

The word breathed new life into Eliana's soul, checking that her weapon was ready to use if required. Ted nodded back to her, and she returned it.

"Elijah, any updates on the other men?"

"Just searching the system now for facial recognition, but we have one. One of the passengers driving with Nikolas is well known for his links with the Sacra Corona Unita. Translates as United Sacred Crown. Italy's fourth largest Mafia group hails from the Puglia region. The identified man is Amir Ismajli, who works with the Albania Mafia, and the SCU works as allies. Amir Ismajli is a *kryetar*, or underboss, you could say. Known for kidnapping, fraud, and murder, to name a few. They won't get out tonight with your guys and my guys stationed around the village."

"What do we do now?" Angelika said.

"We wait," Ted replied.

"Ted, where's Kadeem? Do you think he ran away?"

Ted forgot about Kadeem.

"I don't know, but they will be expecting him here."

"Okay, Ted, let's hope you're right."

A voice came over the communications device. An officer stationed on the outbound roads near the junction radioed an update.

"Another vehicle from the north, a black Toyota, one male inside."

"That's our guy, Kadeem."

Ted waited ten seconds before the vehicle entered Ted's vision from the high building, slowing down as it joined the triangle junction. Kadeem was holding his mobile phone in his hand, showing off the light from the device inside the dark cabbie as the car stopped by the petrol station. Ted felt his phone vibrate.

"I'm here," Kadeem said.

The light from the phone blacked out, and the brighter inner car light shone as the driver's side door opened. Kadeem stood, searching the area eerily as he closed the door and crossed the junction.

"He looks nervous," Eliana said.

Kadeem turned his head again, returning to the road before entering the restaurant. Nikolas followed his gaze this time, slowly piercing his eyes together to gain a better spectacle outside. Kadeem approached the table with speed, provoking the accompaniment of men to stand in the act of defence. The men sat down slowly after Kadeem had neutralised in his chair.

"Nikolas will know something is up. He's gonna fucked up—he's full of nerves," Eliana added.

Nikolas reached for his napkin resting on his lap and placed it on the table. Kadeem dropped the envelope on the table containing the identification documents of the Matala beach girls. Kadeem drummed his fingers on the table before speaking, lifting from his chair and leaving. The men examined the contents on the table before lifting their heads to check where Kadeem was vanishing. Nikolas shouted towards Kadeem while the other men reached for their weapons, standing in the process.

"Shit. He's going to blow our cover," Savvas said.

"All officers, get ready to mobilise," Angelika announced.

"I'll keep on Nikolas if they run," Ted ordered.

"Get out of there, Kadeem!" Eliana shouted somewhat to herself.

Kadeem reached for the door, pulling on the handle hard, sneaking through the tiniest gaps available to escape. Behind him, the men followed across the restaurant floor, holding out their weapons. Preceding behind was Nikolas searching the outdoor area for invaders while holding his gun for protection.

"We need backup near Murelo Cretan Cuisine, near the Triangle. Five are about to go on foot. Eyes on Kadeem; don't shoot Kadeem. I have Nikolas," Ted ordered.

Kadeem dropped the few steps from the restaurant to the street level. The men behind him were charging through the door. Kadeem was startled by the quick chase and abandoned heading towards his vehicle, steering away from Ted's position, and escaping down the street.

"Go, go, go, go, go," Angelika instructed.

The sound of police sirens pulsated through the village instantly while the LED light illuminated the darkest corners of the crossway. The men focused away from Kadeem, fleeing their capture, and fixed on the incoming assault before spreading into individualised escape routes. As they manoeuvred, hidden, they began to aim wildly out into the crossing.

"Shots fired!"

"Suspects fleeing on foot. Two are going east; one is Kadeem, and two are south. We have eyes on suspect Nikolas; make sure Kadeem is seen to immediately," Ted instructed, swiftly taking the steps to the street level.

Ted searched for Kadeem as he fled into the night down one of the side roads, disappearing. The remaining men from the restaurant used the vehicle to provide cover fire for Nikolas to reach his parked vehicle before they escaped down their respective routes.

Nikolas opened the passenger side door, flinging himself inside under the officers' gunfire.

"Easy on the fire; we want Nikolas alive!" Ted ordered.

Immediately, gunfire was directed towards the returning shots from the escaping men. Nikolas had positioned himself inside the driver's seat, revving the engine, accelerating forward and performing a one-hundred-eighty-degree turn, narrowly missing the central point of the triangle.

"Look, let's get in," Eliana said from behind.

Ted broke his gaze as Nikolas's vehicle headed east and turned left sharply down a side street just after the petrol station, seeking the shop owner's vehicle in front of him. The driver's side was nearest to him; he quickly reached for the door as Eliana hurried to enter the passenger side. Once both were inside, Ted floored the accelerator pedal and glided around the junction, performing the same motion Nikolas did in pursuit. Steering left, towards the right, he could see the yellow flashes of light of gunfire act as floodlights to the dark village streets, parading officers in pursuit of their men.

Ahead, Nikolas's brake lights lit up shortly before it screeched to the right and out of view from the pursuing car. The vehicle was speeding along the small narrow village lanes; however, the stretch of road wasn't long enough to accelerate at any high momentum. Ted pushed down hard on the accelerator before braking sharply and turning right at the junction, mirroring the tracks of the fleeing car. As Ted straightened up, passing a local car mechanic on its right, he distinguished disappearing red lights from the left turn up ahead.

"There." Ted pointed with one hand on the wheel.

Eliana was looking at the map device on her phone to work out the schematics of the area. Passing the garage, they noticed a row of cars along with the garage building that seemed beyond repair, with rust on their exterior shell and flat tyres. Once Ted reached the junction, he followed left, apprehensive about what was to follow or where Nikolas was leading them.

"This road up ahead leads north, out of the village," Eliana said, studying her phone.

Ted noticed the red brake lights again, indicating Nikolas wasn't heading north out of the village.

"What's down there?" Ted turned to Eliana.

"Looks like a dead end on the map. I need to make a call."

Ted knew this would be where the pursuit would end; Nikolas knew, too. Nikolas was in a difficult situation, with few choices available. Ted knew he would be desperate; it was a dangerous situation.

"Our suspect is travelling on Hersonissos 70008, turning left onto Hersonissos 70007. Likely armed. Need urgent assistance."

There was silence as Ted turned the wheel onto Hersonissos 70007. Eliana was still communicating on the phone, but ahead Ted saw the red brake lights cut out, and a figure appeared from the driver's side door. Nikolas looked back at their engulfing headlights, leaving the driver's door open as he paced through the front garden gate of a nearby house.

"Okay, thank you. Wait... suspect is pulling up and exiting the vehicle. Going on foot," Eliana responded over the phone.

She finished her phone call and was working on the screen.

"How long will they be?" Ted asked.

"They're a few minutes away and busy at the triangle."

"We can't wait for them; it gives him too much time to think."

"But officers are only around the corner."

"Yes, but what about if someone is in there? His wife? Family?"

Eliana composed herself as their vehicle halted behind Nikolas's. She looked up from the phone's screen and turned to Ted.

"Let's go; I have a plan.

Chapter 38

They both held their weapons aiming towards the front of the villa as they stepped through the open metal gate. The swimming pool gleamed clear blue from the underwater lights, and something else caught their eye briefly. A couple of swallow birds were diving and gliding along the water's surface, seeking fluids or food in the form of bugs on the water's surface.

Surveying the outdoor area only confirmed that Nikolas had entered the property or made his way down either side of the villa's paths. The outdoor space included the pool, which was raised on the left and comprised of deck chairs; they had towels propped on them, which meant the villa was in use. On the right were a white gazebo with a glass table set and six black wicker chairs, encompassed by a built-in pizza oven and an outdoor barbeque area. Ted pointed towards the front door, more as an order for Eliana to take her approach. Ted looked across the villa to his left, about to step towards the upper section of the front garden using the tight paths around the pool to navigate towards the villa's structure.

The short apprehensive walk from the vehicle detailed how Ted and Eliana would approach the villa to give maximum coverage and cover from Nikolas and anyone else inside. Eliana studied a few photographs online, providing outdoor pictures of the front of the property. Ahead was the front door, which opened into the kitchen and lounge area.

To the left, around the pool, was an outdoor covered seating area and a path that led around the back of the villa, leading to a storage unit. Beyond, there was a dead-end, with no entrance point to the estate. Eliana headed towards the front door, whilst Ted took the left.

Ted had lost sight of Eliana as she approached the front door, disappearing behind the stone brickwork, introducing a porch. Ted turned the corner and discovered the second door leading into the villa. Ted could hear the trickle of water from the pool and the fading sound of cicadas on the trees. Behind the villa's exterior, there was a clash of shouting inside. The sound of a man and a distinctive high-pitched female voice. He couldn't grasp the conversation's dialect, but it was in another language—he assumed Greek.

There was a vibration in his pocket; he reached down and lifted his phone. It was Eliana.

"You, okay?" Ted whispered.

"I think it's just him and his wife," she returned in the same low volume.

"I could hear the female voice. What are they saying?"

"I had to move away around the side because I noticed a camera on the front door."

"They know we are here anyway."

"So, he was telling her to pack up, and she was arguing why. I think he hit her and told her to do as she was told as his wife, and she was asking why... Wait."

The phone line went quiet, with the same chirping noise of cicadas laying through the phone faintly. Inside, the shouting intensified and became aggressive.

"We need to move; he's got a gun. He's telling her they need to leave now."

Ted was braced for what was to come.

"Are you ready?"

"Sure."

"Countdown from three... three..." Ted disconnected the phone and slid it quickly into his pocket. He continued the count in his head... two... he reached for the door handle and pushed down on the metal... one. The metal moved downwards, and a clicking sound came from the lock. He gently pulled at the door, and it slid open. Manoeuvring around the door, he stepped over the threshold and separated the curtains... zero. Ted held his weapon up, aiming directly in front of him. Across the lounge area was Eliana mirroring Ted's position. The lounge area had a corner sofa to the right, with a glass coffee table. Eliana looked over at Ted, who turned his head to indicate to move closer together.

"You found me," Nikolas said with annoyance on his face.

Ted and Eliana used the moment to glide slowly towards a more central point between the lounge and kitchen area for protection.

"Don't come any closer!" Nikolas began to back towards the corridor leading to the villa's bedrooms.

"We just want to talk, that's all," Ted said.

"No more steps, or I will blow her head off!"

Nikolas' gun was pressed against her neck and his arm across her chest. His wife struggled under his mighty grip, trying to wriggle free as panic filled her face from Nikolas's comment.

"Stop it now!" Nikolas ordered his wife.

She immediately ceased to fight and remained upright and still under his grip.

"Easy," Ted instructed.

"Shut up," Nikolas returned. "You've ruined all of this!" he continued, blaming Ted.

"No one needs to get hurt."

"Oh, yes, they do. I need to get out of here; let me out now!"

"We all know we can't do it, Nikolas. It's over, but we can work this out."

"No way!"

Ted knew this would be the end, but he wanted an ending to this; he wanted answers.

"Why did Daniel have to be killed?" Ted asked.

Nikolas returned without hesitation.

"He suspected too much; he was on to us. I've been in this police force for eighteen years, built a reputation, and worked hard to get to where I was. I wasn't allowing some outsider to stop that!"

"Why were you working with Albanians?"

"Don't you get it? The money. Do you think I could buy this second house, a new car, pay for my children's private school, and still have holidays based on my income? It's rubbish. After the financial crisis, we earn less money. More responsibility, and not the money to go with it."

"How did they approach you?"

"It doesn't matter! Get out of my way!"

"Officers are on their way, Nikolas. You won't be able to escape; you are surrounded. As soon as you leave this villa, they will get you."

Nikolas's eyes began to run wild with thoughts. Ted didn't want to repeat the question; he wanted the conversation to gather momentum and give them more time for sufficient backup to arrive. There was also the innocent civilian, in Nikolas's wife, to consider. Ted didn't want another blameless death on his conscience.

"Who else was involved? I know there was someone else, Nikolas. You had the Albanians come after me. You weren't watching us; you weren't telling the Albanian where to go; someone else was keeping track of me. Where I was going. Who was it?"

Eliana looked confused, breaking her gaze to look at Ted briefly.

"Who else, Nikolas?" Ted demanded.

Nikolas laughed, still holding a solid grip on his sobbing wife.

"Calista, stop crying! I swear to God," Nikolas ordered.

Calista sniffed her nose as tears poured down her face, smudging her makeup, trying to do as instructed. She looked at Ted and Eliana with pleading eyes. Nikolas regained his focus back towards Ted and smiled.

"Was it Andries?" Eliana asked.

"Andries!" He smirked before continuing. "He was the fall guy. Do you think a guy like Andries could build this? Sustain it. No way! He is *weak*, a yes man. As soon as I saw he was visiting the same place I did, I used it."

The question from Eliana aggravated him. Nikolas wanted Ted to know he was the master being of the plan.

"So Andries wasn't involved? You just used him," Ted asked.

Nikolas smiled again and shook his head.

"I had you fooled," he laughed.

"Who was it then?" Ted asked, playing through the names in his mind.

"Hector," Eliana interjected.

Ted flicked his head right to look at her, turning it back almost immediately at Nikolas, keeping his gun aimed.

"Clever girl," Nikolas replied.

"Hector," Ted stopped.

Ted knew it was true as he muttered those words. Nikolas's actions had been revealed as they stood on the marble-tiled floor as a corrupt officer; his confession concluded Andries had no part to play in the deception of the department, as he was sitting in his prison cell at this very moment.

Hector had come with Ted to interview Daria at her apartment, and the next day she was dead. Hector knew where Ted and Simon were staying in the Psyri district of Athens; maybe he wasn't attending the football match, but he was stalking Ted to see where he would end up to rest. Hector knew each step of the investigation and the key witnesses the police were interviewing. Nevertheless, there was an important question on Ted's mind.

"You tried to silence him outside the parliament building."

"That is true... he knew too much. He was a risk. He was already complaining to me about us going too far with Christos and his wife, Daria, and so on and so on," Nikolas said, with the last few words becoming a whine.

"Nikolas, there were violent clashes after the shooting; Hector shot dead could have caused mass hysteria."

Nikolas shrugged his shoulders.

"So? It was part of the plan and would cause a distraction; allow us time to frame Andries and get away until you stopped it from happening, and we had to do it another way."

"You forced the girl to confess to seeing Andries and not you?"

"Sure. They're pawns in this. Little bits of dirt between the grips at the bottom of your boots."

Ted understood the design of his plan. The confessions, framing and planting money into Andries's bank accounts, altering statements, and the phone numbers in the contact lists over the last few days. There was one last important question.

"Where is Hector, Nikolas?"

He shrugged his shoulders again.

"I don't know."

"Did the Albanians get to him?"

"Yes."

"Where is he?" Ted asked sternly.

"The bottom of the Aegean the last I heard. I don't know! I don't care. My family is provided for, and my finances are taken care of. I don't care about those getting in my way."

Ted saw the man Nikolas had become. Ted decided to press on one last time; he needed some of his remaining questions to be answered before the final act.

"How did it all pan out? Tell me what your big plan was."

"Daria told Daniel that a police officer was visiting their whore houses. Daniel became suspicious, searching places he shouldn't be and getting too close. Before they could speak to her to identify the man, I told the Albanians to kill Daniel and then Daria once Hector told me where she lived. Thankfully, I found out that Andries was visiting the same place following his divorce; lucky for me, I used that. Christos was working with Daniel. His wife happened to be there when it happened—very sad, but it had to happen."

Calista was sobbing again under the realisation of the man she had married. She was losing the will to live; her eyes looked lost and hopeless, like a lost puppy begging for help.

"Shut up, Calista! Shut up! Shut up! Shut up!"

"Couldn't you get out of this mess? Look what it's come to," Ted asked.

For the first time, Nikolas looked sombre, staring down towards the large tiled floor. Ted thought about making a move, but there was a high percentage of risk, due to Nikolas's head sitting behind Callista's.

"There could have been another way; you could have gone to internal affairs or Daniel himself. We can protect you, Nikolas."

Nikolas's face returned to Ted with a serious undertone.

"No way, there's no way out of here now. Either they'll get me in prison, or someday if I was free, that's why I need to get out of here, so please move!"

Ted became cautious. Nikolas had nothing to lose; he was desperate, which made the situation hostile. Nikolas yanked at Calista, and she screamed for help again. Ted composed himself and remained steady, as Nikolas seemed to touch the trigger with more purpose—he was ready to make a move.

"Now move!"

"You know that's not happening," Ted replied.

Nikolas gave a smirk and a small exhaled laugh. Immediately, Nikolas changed the position of his weapon, turning it away from Calista's temple and outwards towards Ted and Eliana. Ted could hear the slight echo of police sirens outside and their exterior lights shining through the lounge windows reflecting on the cream walls.

Eliana composed herself and ordered Nikolas to lower the weapon as the angle of his barrel turned toward her. Nikolas's focus was temporarily distracted as his thoughts processed the oncoming hostility. Calista's face touched the soul of Ted; he knew he couldn't make a mistake with this shot.

Nikolas accented his neck muscles slightly, leaving an opening to the right of his shoulder. Ted didn't hesitate—he pulled the trigger. As the metal pushed together, releasing the bullet booming out of the cylinder, Nikolas realised his mistake, trying to quickly defend himself with his weapon. Ted's bullet ruptured the acromion, the top outer edge of Nikolas's scapula, causing him to drag Calista and slam his body against the wall behind. Nikolas fired the pistol in defence, causing a rapture of noise within the compounds of the villa. As the gunfire echoed, the screams from the hostage pierced the ears of those inside. Ted felt a coursing pain infiltrate his body as he was knocked backwards, crashing down onto a glass coffee table. The platform smashed, and its legs cracked in half under the weight of his body.

The roar of shouting and voices was met with the blast of bullets filling the villa complex. As Ted lay there in agony, the uproar was unrecognisable. Ted became delirious, moving in and out of consciousness. His vision blurred, unaware of what was unfolding in front of him. Flashbacks played out like an analogue movie projector when he closed his eyes. The film included his wife and two daughters playing in the meadows near their home by a river. Their smiling and happy faces brought warmth to his demise. He could almost hear his family's laughter over the commotion beside him. Suddenly, he felt a strong force grip him on his shoulder. The pain reverberated around his body, and the grip tightened; it was the last thing he felt before he lost consciousness.

Chapter 39

Athens

T ED WAS LYING IN a hospital bed at Evangelismos General Hospital, classed as Athens and Greece's largest public hospital. The two bullets that entered Ted's body entered through the top of his left arm, hitting the scapula and humerus bone, breaking them, and damaging his shoulder tissue upon impact. Musculoskeletal structures made gunshot wounds to the shoulder area particularly challenging. The paramedics at the scene took Ted to Ziekenhuis Heraklion Hospital shortly after the shooting and kept him under close observation. Inside Ziekenhuis, he received urgent surgery to remove the gun fragments scattered inside his upper torso. Courses of daily antibiotics had been fed through tubes and inserted into his arm to help fight any infection within the wound. Ted had been under sedation for two days, and it was agreed that he would be transferred to Evangelismos after the successful procedure on his shoulder. Doctors reduced the sedation to check his mental state, to which Ted felt the need to open his eyes.

Ted awoke from his rested sleep to find Police Deputy Director Andries Iraklidis sitting on the adjacent bedside chair. Ted could feel his left arm tightly placed against his chest in a bandage, helping to reduce the swelling, with pillows propped underneath. He remembered the last moments in the villa in Episkopi but couldn't picture the events and those that followed.

"What happened?" Ted said.

Andries lifted his head from the magazine he was reading, and a huge smile filled his face.

"You're awake!" Andries replied.

"Andries, you're here."

"I am, but how are you?"

"I'm okay, a little sleepy. A little sore."

"I bet."

"What happened after I was shot?"

"Well, I was told what happened by Eliana and Nikolas's wife, Calista."

"They're alive?"

Andries confirmed. He continued narrating the story by explaining after Ted took the bullet to the shoulder, Eliana had regained her balance from the initial gunfire and began the cautious pursuit of Nikolas down the long corridor. Meanwhile, Nikolas was injured and dragged Calista hostage, into the main bedroom. Nikolas had positioned himself around the far end of the bedroom, possibly using one of the windows to escape. He held his gun to Calista's head while bleeding out from his shoulder.

"Eliana and Calista remember the sound of a police car approaching and officers storming the building."

As Andries proceeded, Ted closed his eyes to vividly remember the final moments before his blackout. He remembered someone grabbing hold of him and the sound of footsteps and shouting mixed in with the gunfire.

"Nikolas lifted his gun from his wife's head, and Eliana was ready to pull the trigger. Only for Nikolas to turn the gun on himself."

"Suicide," Ted said, opening his eyes in surprise.

"Yeah, he was cornered, no escape. He couldn't live with being caught. You know what prisoners would have done to him inside being a police officer, let alone the Albanians."

"Calista okay?"

"She's okay. She is devastated. Her family was ripped apart by his actions. However, I'm glad she wasn't a casualty in this."

"A life saved."

"It is."

Ted visioned the last moments of Nikolas, Calista and Eliana in the bedroom while he was unconscious on the kitchen floor; he was proud of Eliana and how she could pursue successfully and be unhurt. There were still more questions to answer.

"What about the rest of them? Kadeem?"

"Your friend Elijah and his officers and others got them as they scarpered like cats. They didn't get to the end of the street before they were stopped. They're here in Athens being processed still. Officers from Albania have come over to support; it's hectic in the main room."

Ted nodded at his approval; he was glad no one got away.

"Kadeem?"

"Sorry, yes, he is okay. We're talking with him about a deal, an exchange of information from what he knows: locations, identifications. He assisted in the crime, but we will see what we can do to help him."

"What about the port operation?"

"Yes, the girls are safe, and half of the men died in the shootout."

"Where did you get them?"

"The port exit road. Something spooked, and the task force moved in."

Ted glanced at the frontman, once accused and smiled. Ted swallowed his dry throat and the contents of saliva in it.

"Listen, I'm sorry," Ted stuttered.

Andries raised both hands before him, palms facing outwards, looking directly into Ted's eyes.

"Please. Don't be sorry. You are in a hospital bed. It's the least you should be worried about."

"But Andries, we thought it was you."

"You were all doing a thorough investigation, and I would have done exactly the same if it was anyone else. They were clever; Nikolas was clever. They played us all."

"What happened? When did they release you?"

"They held me and charged me after the interview. I was in discussions with my lawyer about the next steps. I had a lot of time to think of things and how I could escape this mess. Then yesterday morning, I was told I was free to go; all charges had been dropped, and that's when I heard about what happened. They asked me if I wanted time off, and I didn't; I wanted to finish the investigation."

"I'm glad you're out of that cell, Andries."

"So I am," Andries said with a smile and laugh.

"Does Rose know I'm here?"

"She knows. She is on a flight over roundabout... Now I'd say they had to delay telling her until we knew what was happening," Andries replied, looking at the room's clock.

"Thank you for letting her know."

"It was Eliana, actually."

"Eliana? Where is she?" Ted asked.

"She had to go back to Israel. Her father had a heart attack yesterday afternoon. What a couple of days for her," Andries shook his head sympathetically.

"Is he okay?"

"Eliana was here actually visiting you when she got the call from her mother. She said it seemed bad, so she rang me late last night to say she was heading to the airport and wouldn't be working today or for an extended period."

Ted looked down at the floor, saddened that he wouldn't be able to see Eliana, but she had a more important thing to worry about currently.

"Ted, you need to take some time off, too."

"I've only just arrived!"

"I know, but look at you. Mr Brave, but you need to rest."

Ted thought about the order. He remembered Simon had suggested he discuss his difficulties, and through Eliana's persuasion in the bar.

"Maybe I'll take some time off, Andries. I'll confirm with Simon and let you know."

"Don't worry. Take it. I can hold the fort for now with my officers. The protests have died down, and people seem more relaxed. It may have been proved I'm innocent, but I still feel the department will still be judging me, you know, from the visits to the club."

"Yeah, will anything come from that?"

"We will see, maybe a warning or a suspension, I don't know. But for now, I have my job while they investigate."

"Thank you, Andries."

"Don't mention it. Anyway, I've got to go."

"Sure, thanks again."

Andries reached over to a bowl of grapes sitting on the table next to Ted's, picking a few off and eating them. Andries offered Ted the bowl, but Ted refused.

"See you soon, Ted. Don't rush back," Andries said with a smile as he exited the ward door.

Ted lay back on the hospital bed and briefly closed his eyes. A buzzing noise commenced from the table beside him, where Andries had taken the grapes. He reached over to what he thought was his phone. The stretch proved painful, but he reached it through a small cry of pain shooting through his right shoulder. He clicked the screen, which illuminated the phone's home page. It was filled with texts and missed calls from his wife, parents, and colleagues. A fresh one appeared on his screen before he could manoeuvre through the first messages.

Hey, Let me know when you are awake.

Ted immediately pressed the dial option through the message screen, and the call was answered after a few rings.

"Eliana. Are you okay?"

"Hey, Ted, I'm okay. How are you?"

"I'm good; I woke up not long ago, and I'm still coming around. Andries was here when I woke, so he told me everything. He told me about your dad."

"Andries has been there all day, more times than anyone. Said he wanted to be there when you woke up—so did I, but I had to go."

"He got to see me wake up."

"It's romantic. Did he kiss you to wake you up?" She laughed.

There was an exchange of laughs before the conversation lulled.

"How is your dad?" Ted asked.

"He had a funny turn and had several small heart attacks, then a major one. I'm with him now, but he is sleeping now."

"Is your mother there?"

"She is; she hasn't left his side, just like Andries with you."

"Do you think they'll talk again?"

"We will see. But it seems we are a family again, and I'll take that."

"I hope he comes through it okay, Eliana."

The conversation gathered a pause, but Eliana filled the silence this time.

"Thank you."

"Eliana, I heard what happened from Andries after I was shot."

"Probably the best scenario."

"I agree. But you did well, Eliana. You did real good."

"Thanks, Ted."

"I'm sure we will keep in touch, right?"

"Yeah, of course."

"I may not be able to get back to Greece to work; this virus from Wuhan was pretty bad. I think Israel is going into lockdown very soon, but I know my father needs me for now."

"Just worry about your father for now, even if the world is starting to become chaotic."

"When are they releasing you?"

"I'm not too sure, but soon, I hope."

"Well, take care, Ted; speak to you soon."

"You, too, and best wishes to your father."

"Thanks, Ted. Goodbye, stranger."

Ted smiled and began to navigate the screen to check his World News App, trying to see the seriousness of the virus spreading in Asia. Ted was interrupted by an older gentleman doctor entering the room. The doctor was wearing a blue surgical mask upon entering. He closed the door behind him and returned his gaze towards Ted.

"You're awake. Excellent."

He reached over to check the IV drip to the side of his bedside without saying a word.

"When will I be able to leave?" Ted began.

"Good question, Mr Chester. I hope you are in a few more days, but we must run more checks before letting you leave. It's my understanding you are returning to the UK? Your wife is on her way, and one of the officers said you were going home, no?"

"Yeah, I hope so."

"Very well; I will get the senior doctor to come in and start the checks immediately. I may need to call the UK to ensure you have continued treatment there, too."

"Thank you, doctor."

The gentlemen picked up the file slotted in the holder at the end of the bed. He skimmed the files and made a brief note on one of the pages before closing it, placing it back in its slot, and approaching the door. Ted watched the man grab onto the door handle before looking towards Ted.

"Reading your file, Mr Chester. You are fortunate to be alive."

Ted knew if the bullet had entered him at another point, he could have been lying in a more sombre place than a hospital bed.

"I appreciate what you've done, Doctor; thank you."

"Have you ever heard of a cat with nine lives?" the doctor stared with curiosity.

"I have."

"Maybe you are like one of them. You've certainly used up one of your nine lives, Mr Chester. Be more careful in future," he said with a smile.

Ted smiled back, and the gentleman exited the room. Ted was left alone with his thoughts; he was tired, and his eyes grew heavy with the whirlwind of interaction he had partaken in. His eyes began to close, drifting into another temporary coma, but one he could wake from with his own control. He began dreaming of his only desired interaction, seeing his family. Although, as the pictures played out in his dreams, the lurking demons still haunted him. He dreamed of being at peace with them once and for all.

Chapter 40
Cheshire, England

T HE ROOM WAS OLD-FASHIONED, with wooden finishing throughout and Painswick Amber Oak that lined the floor in puzzling shapes. A large dark oak bookshelf matched a similar stain finish to a desk table and chest of drawers. The room gave the essence of a stereotypical room where one lets go of one's feelings in a safe space. The one thing that seemed out of place from the professional surroundings was a model of an R2-D2 model and X-wing Starfighter next to row of leathered bound books.

Ted's body sank into the leather chair opposite his chosen counsellor, taking care as he sat with his arm held in a cast. He'd already partaken in three previous counselling sessions. Ted knew details on present troubles would be today's topic of conversation, and he wasn't sure he was willing to open up just yet, although the friendly counsellor may be able to break the tightly slotted lock.

They'd recapped on the previous session for over twenty minutes, and Ted was already clock watching at the skeleton dial on the wall. David noticed the interference in Ted's mind, wanting to reignite the conversation.

"Anything else you want to discuss?" David probed, staring intently at Ted on the Emerald colour, singular sofa.

David kept a fair grey beard, aged in his mid-fifties, and had a short head of grey hair with thin-framed glasses. Ted returned the glance with a one-word reply.

"Don't think so."

"Nothing at all you would like to discuss today?" he continued, staring intently at Ted on the sofa.

Ted's silence in the room was prolonged. His mind was wandering from one thought to the next.

"Seeing as your not very forthcoming, maybe I could suggest something?"

Ted waved his hand to proceed.

"We haven't discussed a topic so far that I think could be important, if you don't mind? I can see your mind racing and I don't know if this is the topic you are distracted by."

Ted let out his right hand to signal for David to continue.

"Okay. I would wait for a few sessions and build up a frame of work before delving right into it. If you don't want to discuss this, just tell me. So, I want to ask: What outcome would help you with the guilt you said you felt with those two girls?"

Ted fell back in his seat and let out a deep breath. He leaned his head back, his neck puzzled into the nook at the top of the chair. He looked up at the ceiling, trying to imagine the perfect scenario.

"I'm not going to bring them back," he said with outstretched arms.

"Is that what troubles you?"

"The most, yes. Besides all the stuff from my past, the present brings out those difficulties again."

David nodded empathically, now grasping his hands together in a ball.

"Okay. But what can you impact? What would help you with your feelings?"

"It would be going back in time and saving those two girls from Timisoara."

"Okay."

"However, there has been an update," which caused Ted to sit up straight.

Although Ted was discussing a still classified case, which was within the centre of an extensive evidence-collecting process. Anything mentioned within the four walls of their sessions was between themselves and no external participants. Client and counsellor privileges. Although these privileges could be broken if the counsellor thought the client would bring harm to themselves or others, which was not the case.

"I know I said they have been investigating their disappearance since July last year. Last week, I had a call from someone at Europol."

David nodded and clasped his hands together in front of his mouth, showing signs he was intently listening.

"They received some intel from where they could be hiding," Ted continued.

David raised a hand, offering his palm towards Ted.

"Listen, you don't need to tell me the whole case. We have privileges, but there is no need for the details. However, I'm starting to see your point, so please proceed, but leave out the details."

Ted retraced his momentum and skipped the finer details.

"So, what I'm trying to say is, if there was a positive outcome from the intel they received, then I feel there would be an enormous weight inside me that would lift, you know?"

"I totally understand. However, what if they weren't the two girls from Timisoara?"

"Well, I would feel relieved, because they may have been victims of the same crime."

"But you hope that it's them?"

"I would have some form of closure, you know. I'd be able to sleep at night from the terrors. I've been taking Diazepam to help myself sleep at night since I took a break from work; the pain in this arm kept me up most nights."

Ted felt his free arm on the shoulder of his wound, pressing against it softly while performing a slow rotating motion with his shoulder to ease some of the pain.

"I didn't know you were on those."

"The doctor prescribed them to me."

"I see. You should have told me; it's part of the questionnaire before commencement."

"I'm sorry. My wife doesn't even know I'm on them."

"Okay I'll just make a note of that, but nothing more. Anything else?"

Ted looked blankly back at David without response.

"Are the night terrors a problem still?"

"Yes. But they're better with the pills."

"What if the night terrors don't stop?"

"I'll sort something out."

"Well, you can always use relaxing bedtime routines if those are a thing in your house, or keep a sleep diary..."

Ted pulled a face at the prospect of writing down his thoughts and feelings or narration from the night. Although he could see the benefit of it, someone who could track those dreams and seek a deeper meaning.

"Okay, I see you wouldn't be too interested in that. We could discuss that another time. Let's change it up."

"Sure."

"Okay, how's your relationship with Rose and the kids been since our last session?"

"The kids, okay. They don't know about the pills, the dreams, or my thoughts. Rose, it's tough. Tough on her. I'm up and using the spare room because it disturbs her."

"The terrors, the lack of sleep?"

"Yes. The pills work, then sometimes they don't. It's like coffee if I have four or five cups. It doesn't give me that buzz any more. I feel I'm immune to it."

"Suppose it depends on the coffee," David smiled.

"Very true."

Ted returned the smile and lifted his left hand to glance at the time. The session was typically fifty minutes to one hour, approaching thirty-five currently.

"Oh, I've got to call a taxi and go and pick the kids up from school."

"No problem. You mentioned leaving early; I'm happy to leave it there unless you have anything important to discuss before you go, Ted?"

Ted briefly looked down towards the wooden floor, following one of the lines zigzagging through the floor.

"No, I think that's enough for today."

"I agree. Well done."

"Thank you."

"When are you able to drive again?"

"I'm unsure, maybe another month or two."

"Thank God for health care."

"I agree," Ted said, searching his phone to order a taxi on an app.

A few seconds passed, and he navigated the screen to order a taxi from the clinic to his daughter's school. David snapped his fingers, remembering an important message that had escaped his mind.

"Sorry, Ted, I forgot to say before. This may be our last session in person. I will be offering all my clients an online service from next week. I'll let you know on what videoing platform."

"Is that because of the virus?"

"It is. The cases are growing, and I don't want to take risks. Besides, the media say there may be a lockdown at the end of the month."

"No problem, let me know."

Ted pushed his good arm into the chair to assist his rise from a seated position.

"See you next week. I hope the little one is coming along okay," David said.

"Yeah, all is going well. We have another scan tomorrow."

"A boy, is it, by the way?"

"Yes," Ted smiled widely.

"Two daughters. You must have been hoping for a boy."

"I certainly was."

Ted took a few steps across the room, heading towards the door, knowing this may be the last time he saw David in person for a while.

"Actually, I've just forgotten; I'll let you know if I can attend next week," Ted said, turning back to face David.

David twisted in his seat, resting his arms on the large armrest.

"No problem; how come?"

"I may have a trip to make."

"A mindfulness trip, I suspect?" David smiled.

"Something like that."

Ted smiled back.

"By the way. I was going to say, what was that phrase you saw in Matala? I'm thinking of using it for one of my clients, maybe using words to help him."

"The Joni Mitchell lyric?"

"No. It's something like..."

"I'm not sure I remember."

"Just remembered! *Today is life; tomorrow never comes.*"

Ted smiled and nodded, reflecting on the first time he saw the mural in Matala.

"That was it. It's a good saying."

"I think so, too," Ted said, entering the space and closing the door on the way out.

Outside, Ted climbed into the taxi waiting outside the grounds of the private clinic. The main road with a row of terrace houses was far beyond the green lawn that separated the car park. They exchanged a conversation about his injury, in which Ted explained he fell from a ladder at home to keep a low profile. The driver manoeuvred around the curved road leading to the exit, a junction linking the main road, and turned left.

Ahead, Ted spotted a cat darting across the street with pace and narrowly missed the oncoming vehicle, which swerved into the taxi's lane. The driver quickly moved back into their own lane at high speed, narrowly avoiding the front of Ted's taxi, but not before the driver had slammed the brakes. The violent movement flung Ted forward, but the seat belt kicked in, crashing him back into his seat with a jolt of pain shooting through his shoulder. The driver was gripping both hands on the wheel, now in neutral gear. Ted screwed his face tightly as the pain pulsed around the wound. He rubbed his left hand over it, pushing down slightly to relieve the ache.

"Are you okay, sir?" said the driver.

"Yeah, I'm okay."

"The bloody stupid cat ran out into the road and nearly caused a crash," the driver said, shaking his head. Out of the window, Ted noticed the brave cat had stopped and sat on the pavement, its black tail wrapped around the front of its legs, glancing at Ted with locked eyes. The cat broke its stare, turned its body, headed towards an open garden gate, and disappeared behind the hedge.

The cat vanished, and Ted noticed the taxi driver look towards the gap, shaking his head and making a tutting sound. Ted also glanced, with no sign of the cat through the gate., He sat back in his seat and closed his eyes. He remembered what the doctor had said to him in the hospital.

"Nine lives."

Chapter 41
Dubai

A SCREAM ECHOED THROUGH Sheikh Mohammed Bin Rashid Boulevard, overpowering the sounds of vehicles manoeuvring under the night sky. The engines of high-end and luxurious cars roared along the road, illuminated by palm trees wrapped with yellow lighting for display. Intertwined on the pavement stood streetlights, overwhelming the light from the trees. As she ran for her life, the request for help was ignored. She wore a red dress riding up her thigh as she powered along the surface road. Her blonde hair was trailing behind her as the breeze flowed through it. There were no longer heels on the soles of her feet, and she gripped a bloody knife in her fist. She had no real direction or destination as she powered her arms to maintain speed. Gold drop earrings were drawn from her ears, and a bloody steak knife was gripped tightly in one of her hands.

Suddenly, a screeching car bolted at high speed from the junction where her escape began. She was fearful, but the extra adrenaline continued to course through her veins when she watched the vehicle in pursuit over her shoulder. The bright headlights of the matte gold Rolls-Royce roared along the boulevard just like a lion would after a gazelle in the Sahara, primed and focused on its prey. The Rolls-Royce swerved around various vehicles driving along the boulevard. Ahead was a junction with a set of traffic lights. Still running on the road's edge, she pondered her next direction. She could see the headlights of the pursuing vehicle running through her along the tarmac below, as the engine pierced her ears as it approached. She thought her escape would be short-lived and worthless as the lights and noises closed in on her.

Faintly, she could hear a mechanical noise flooding the night sky behind her. The sound of rotating blades creating a vortex came from the buildings behind her. She continued to power down the boulevard, with the Rolls-Royce closing the gap significantly with every passing second. Suddenly, behind a grand building shone a bright light along the road, illuminating the streets like a theatre stage. The sound of its blades became deafening and submerged the sound of the accelerating pursuing car. She looked back to get a glimpse as she mounted the pavement area to avoid the incoming Rolls-Royce. Her movement offered protection with small, raised bollards separating the road and the pavement, causing the vehicle to swerve back into the road rather than mount the curb. She looked back again as her legs began to tire, making out the helicopter's exterior. Under the circumstances, she couldn't decide if it was the captor's helicopter, with the men's unlimited range of luxuries, or if it was coming to save her. The aircraft swooped low over her and turned at nearly one hundred eighty degrees, pointing behind her towards the chasing Rolls-Royce.

"Stop your vehicle now!" a noise bellowed from the helicopter megaphone speaker.

Above her, she could see the detail on the side of the blue-and-white striped helicopter. The wording on the side of the helicopter frame read *Dubai Police* with an Arabic translation above it.

Another voice came from the aircraft, but it was projected in another language she didn't understand, but similar to the tongue she had become accustomed to while captive. She moved at pace as she passed under the hovering helicopter; ahead were two heavily armoured and uniformed men who ran into her peripheral view. They appeared from the right of the traffic light junction, with one man running across one side of the road, reaching the central reservation. The Rolls-Royce was within yards of the junction, hunting down the blonde girl fleeing on the pavement, trying to block her next movements on the crossing.

One of the armed men dropped a black metal spike strip at the edge of the pavement and carried it across with him, dropping it to the ground just as the Rolls-Royce reached their position. She saw the scorch of red and blue lights on the other side of the road moving closer to her location as she felt her legs numb with tiredness. The sound of police sirens added to the cocktail of noises on the boulevard of Downtown Dubai. The helicopter swerved back on itself as the Rolls-Royce travelled beneath it, running over the spikes. The Rolls-Royce tires blew, leaving a large cloud of smoke as it lost traction with the road. The high-speed vehicle's motion began to decrease as it lost control of the road, swerving to the right and left and drifting into the central reservation's metal barrier. She witnessed the crash, and a swarm of armed officers approached the vehicle.

Her legs gave way, and she collapsed to the floor. The vehicles' sirens and the rotating blades above her flooded her mind. She felt exhausted in her seated position but still gripped the knife tightly; her hand was white and achy.

"Is it Amanda?" a voice said within the cascade of noises.

She lifted her head. Looking down on her position was the portrait of a man. She couldn't see his identity because of the blinding lights from the helicopter searchlight. The silhouette moved, and the man stretched his hands as if surrendering. Adrenaline still reverberated through her veins; she continued the fight-of-flight response.

"Get away from me!" She stood up using her last energy reserves, shouting while wielding the dinner knife in full defensive mode.

The man moved one foot in front of the other slowly towards her aggressive attack position. He dropped his left hand but maintained his right hand, pointing in her direction as he cautiously approached.

"Easy. I'm Louis Dupont, an officer from a unit within Interpol specialising in human trafficking. We know who you are. You were kidnapped in Berlin last year, taken through Europe, and boarded a plane against your free will to the UAE with a woman called Toni Laurent."

Louis noticed she was distracted with her thoughts as she seemed to remember the horrors she had faced. She was illuminated by the helicopter searchlight as if she were the star in a Broadway musical. She was the starring role; they were the reason she was there. He continued communicating the information he knew about her so she would be distracted, allowing him time to move slowly and defuse the situation.

"Your father and mother, are waiting for you back home..."

Louis reached his right hand forward quickly and grabbed hold of her wrist, which held the knife. Amanda stood frozen as her grip on the blade loosened, and its metal crashed on the tarmac floor. She stared forward but saw through whatever she envisioned; she was reminiscing her troubles and treasuring the savoured moments of freedom that were to come.

"It is over," Louis said.

Louis moved his left hand to the top of her shoulder, and the same with his right hand.

"Where is Toni?" she said as her eyes pierced the officer's eyes for the first time, seeking an answer.

"Toni is safe."

"How? Where is she? How did you find me?" she asked.

Louis smiled as she searched her face for clarification that she was safe and well.

"Let's get you off this street and to safety."

"I want to know where she is!"

"There's someone who can tell you all about what happened."

"Where?"

Louis looked up at the helicopter, lifting his arms in a signal to lower the helicopter.

"Clear the road for landing," Louis radioed.

"In the helicopter?"

"No, behind you."

Louis lifted his hand, pointing towards the pavement behind Amanda, where she had collapsed. She turned tentatively, instantly confused about the man she saw standing on the pavement's edge. One of the man's arms was in a brace, holding his arm across his chest. As the helicopter lowered, the trees swayed through the power, and the motor's noise became deafening. A man walked across the tarmac towards her position with a beaming smile as he fought against the breeze. Amanda looked up at his face as he approached her space, still confused about who this man was. The man broke the silence.

"Hi, Amanda."

"Who are you?"

"That's not important right now, but no one will hurt you anymore."

The man gave a thumbs-up to Louis, who observed the conversation from a distance, speaking into his communications device.

"Victim is secure; get ready to take her away."

Amanda heard the word *victim* and turned to look back towards Louis. She was still distracted.

"Let's go."

She returned towards the mystery man, as the sensation of relief overwhelmed her, with tears filling her eyes and beginning to run down her cheeks.

"What's your name?"

He paused as he noticed her eyes search his.

"You saved me," she said with a broad smile as she began to sob. He reached out his arms to comfort her. She stepped forward and embraced the hug, somewhat safe in his arms.

"No, you've saved me."

Afterword

Today is life. Tomorrow never comes.

Acknowledgements

The author gratefully acknowledges those who helped in the editorial works of this book. John Sutton, Tim Edwards and James Johnson were vital in giving clarity and guidance on the novel's basic fundamentals, often working on the story more than once. This is a special mention to Paul Draper, who gave brilliant and detailed advice on transitioning from a hybrid publisher to a self-publishing author. This led me to work with two brilliant people from different skill sets. One is Phillip Kingsbury, who has creatively and inspiringly brought the novel title to life on the front page. Secondly, James Abbate was a vital part of the editorial process of this book, giving clear clarity on his context and suggestions for its improvements throughout the process. Anyone who helped inspire the story, allow me to use their name for characterisation, and bring them to the page is gratefully acknowledged.

The Wasps Nest

T ED CHESTER WILL RETURN when transferred to his next posting, the Southern German City of Munich. Ted is there to support the German authorities but is soon intertwined in several investigations. A string of murders and a missing child provide a vital link. The case becomes a more personal matter once he discovers someone close to him is in danger.

About the Author

Neal R. Sutton was born in Billinge, UK, and before he started writing fictional crime novels on the side, Neal received a graduate degree in Sports and Physical Education at Liverpool Hope University, whilst contributing to the International Journal of Social Sciences Studies. Graduating, he then taught primary aged children, Sport and Physical Education. He enjoys a pint of beer among friends or watching his favourite football team. He enjoys listening to a wide range of music and reading Michael Connolly. He lives in Warrington with his partner, Son and Cat, and *Nine Lives* is his second novel. His first novel, *Eye Of The Hawk,* was released in 2022.

Website: ww.nealrsutton.com
Twitter: @NealRSutton

Also By Neal R. Sutton
Eye Of The Hawk

In 'Eye Of The Hawk' by Neal R. Sutton, we experience a fast-paced pursuit across the continent as authorities race against time to bring the organised criminals to justice and save those in danger before they are lost forever.

Available on Amazon.

Printed in Great Britain
by Amazon

34946053R00225